Praise for Joan O'Neill:

'A highly entertaining read.' *Sunday World*

'Prose that is a warm as a sunset on a hot summer's day.' *Guardian*

'A fine ear for dialogue.' *Daily Express*

'A dramatic plot, very believable human characters. Their emotions and reactions are so true, irrepressible and natural.' Katie Donovan

'O'Neill has a strong sense of place and wonderful descriptive powers - so lively that one can almost smell the rashers sizzling or feel the heat of the lush Wicklow meadows.' Maureen Cairnduff in the *Irish Independent*

'Great dialogue and terrific set pieces, all the hallmarks of Joan O'Neill's writing.' Julie Parsons in the *Sunday Independent*

'A compelling sense of storytelling.' *Woman's Way*

'Joan O'Neill takes the most ordinary, everyday, trivial details of life and by ordering them in a certain way elevates them to the level of art. This is life as we know it.' Robert Dunbar. *The Gay Byrne Show*

About the author

Joan O'Neill began her writing career in 1987 with short stories and serials. Her first novel, *Daisy Chain War*, published in 1990, won the Reading Association of Ireland Special Merit Award and was short-listed for the Bisto Award. She lives in County Wicklow with her family.

JOAN O'NEILL

Concerning Kate

CORONET BOOKS

Hodder & Stoughton

Copyright © 2003 by Joan O'Neill

First published in Great Britain in 2003 by Hodder and Stoughton
A division of Hodder Headline
First published in paperback in Great Britain
in 2004 by Hodder and Stoughton
A Coronet paperback

The right of Joan O'Neill to be identified as the Author
of the Work has been asserted by her in accordance with the
Copyright, Designs and Patents Act 1988.

1 3 5 7 9 10 8 6 4 2

A CIP catalogue record for this title is
available from the British Library

ISBN 0 340 81846 8

Typeset in Plantin Light by
Palimpsest Book Production Limited,
Polmont, Stirlingshire
Printed and bound by Mackays of Chatham Ltd, Chatham, Kent

Hodder and Stoughton
A division of Hodder Headline
338 Euston Road
London NW1 3BH

For my family

I

'Look at the traffic! You should have left work earlier!' Kate Conway said to her husband, Charlie, as she moved into the passenger seat to let him take over at the wheel.

'How could I? We were busy,' Charlie answered. He removed his jacket, calling, 'Hello, Princess, you look smashing,' as he sat in the car to his daughter, Emily, in the back seat.

'Hi, Daddy!' Eight-year-old Emily's voice was high with excitement.

Kate kissed his cheek. 'What do you do in there that makes your day so frantic?' Her eyes were on the glass building that housed the bank where Charlie worked.

'Don't ask!' Charlie snapped. 'It was murder today, everyone killing everyone else. I couldn't have got out any quicker – I can't account for every minute,' he added.

Kate ruffled his hair.

'Let's go.' Emily, impatient to be off, poked her head between them.

'As soon as I can get a gap in this snarl-up,' Charlie said.

'You look tired, love,' Kate said, with concern. 'Get another job,' she suggested, keeping her voice mild.

He gave a loud laugh. 'Doing what?'

'Open that restaurant you're always talking about.'

He glanced at her. 'You're making fun of me now.'

'No, I'm not.'

'What would I finance it with?'

'Your redundancy package.'

Charlie's face contorted with disgust. 'What redundancy package? I haven't been offered one.'

'It's on the cards, though, isn't it?'

'Obviously not this round-up! Anyway, the reality is I'd probably go nuts if I had to run a restaurant. It's a pipe-dream. Banking is really all I know, and it's a well-paid job. We don't go short of anything.'

'True.'

'Daddy! Why aren't we moving?' Emily was jumping up and down.

Charlie was wearing his important face, the one that reminded Kate that he hated being questioned.

'We're off!' he said, moving out into the traffic. 'Now, let's forget about work. Sit down and put your seat-belt on, Emily.'

'I want to forget about it, darling,' Kate said. 'Why do you think I'm looking forward to the weekend so much? No telephones, nothing.'

'I have one or two important calls to make.'

'What?' Kate's voice was sharp with impatience. 'It won't be much fun if you're going to be on the telephone all the time.'

'I won't be, I promise, and you won't even notice, you'll be having such a laugh with the others.'

'Not without you I won't.'

Charlie was a workaholic, often staying late into the night. He was employed in the foreign-investment department, and travelled extensively, promoting Ireland as an international financial centre.

They were crawling along George's Quay, the traffic at

its worst, lanes of cars all around them, miles of them, speeding up, slowing down, petrol fumes polluting the air. Kate's eyes were on the new red-brick and glass buildings as they crossed Butt Bridge, and the grey dismal ones in marked contrast.

A young man squatted in a doorway, out of work, miserable, a mug in front of him. A much younger one was in a wheelchair close by, his face lopsided under his baseball cap. This was the Dublin City of the dying Celtic Tiger and Kate hated it.

'Are we nearly there?' Emily said, as they slowed at the Blackrock bottleneck.

'No, love,' Kate answered her. 'We've got a long way to go.'

'When will we get there?' Emily asked.

'This time next year, at the rate this traffic's going,' Charlie said, bad-temperedly.

'Don't say that to the child.' Kate laughed, then turned to look at Emily's anxious little face.

'We've got the party to look forward to. We're going to have a lovely time,' Charlie said, to make amends.

'There'll be nobody to play with,' Emily complained.

'Josh'll be there. He's not due back at his boarding-school until next week.'

'He's a boy. I don't like playing with silly boys.'

'But you like Josh,' Kate said.

'He's stupid,' said Emily, her thumb in her mouth.

'Josh is a nice kid, Emily. Now stop being babyish,' Charlie growled.

Kate draped her arm across Charlie's back. 'She's only a child, darling.' To Emily she said, 'There'll be plenty of fun things for you to do.'

'Goodye,' Emily said, in a burst of triumph.

'She's getting very spoilt,' Charlie said, driving faster now that they were on the dual carriageway.

'No, I'm not,' Emily contradicted, yawning. 'I'm bored.'

'Look at the countryside. It's so pretty.' Kate pointed out of the window to distract her.

Emily leaned forward, her auburn hair luminous in the evening sun, her blue eyes bright with intensity. 'Boring,' she pronounced.

'If you lie down and get some sleep, we'll be there when you wake up.' Kate ruffled her soft curls, and covered her with Charlie's jacket.

'Good idea – it's going to be a late night for her,' said Charlie.

The soft fabric soothed Emily, while the warmth and the steady motion of the car made her sleepy.

'Thank God for that,' Kate said, relieved.

Charlie nodded. 'She'll be exhausted tomorrow.'

'With a bit of luck she'll sleep late.'

Charlie brightened. 'So can we.' He gave her knee a squeeze.

It was Charlie's older brother Frank's fortieth birthday. He and his wife Colette were having a fancy-dress party to celebrate. Their parties were always a big event. Much as she loved her in-laws Kate found their enthusiasm and energy exhausting at times.

'It'll be good,' Charlie said, as if reading her thoughts.

Eventually, he turned into the drive of Bramble Hill with a squeal of tyres, then lurched to a halt in front of a rambling old farmhouse at the edge of a wood, the trees lavender shapes in the dusk. It had been in Charlie's family for generations. He and Kate loved it. Charlie's mother Rose had signed it over to Frank two years previously, on her seventieth birthday, and had moved to a cottage in the village to be nearer her friends.

Cars were parked outside. A string of coloured lights around the barn roof swayed in the wind, and cast a rosy glow over the stone-grey house and outbuilding, giving the place a romantic look. No animals were visible, except Tinker, the terrier, whose furious barking announced their arrival and woke Emily.

She sat up and rubbed her eyes.

Charlie got out and stretched, breathing in the fresh air.

'Come on, love,' Kate said, in a caressing voice, to Emily, smoothing her hair and her Sugar Plum Fairy party dress.

'Take your time.' Charlie took her hand, helped her out, then got their bags out of the boot.

'You're going to have a great time,' Kate said to her daughter as Emily took her hand and drifted along beside her, her eyes drawn to the fairy-lights, her Sugar Plum Barbie doll tucked securely under her arm.

Emily nodded, as if to reassure herself.

Colette greeted them with a flourish. A tall, striking woman with a smiling face and twinkling blue eyes, she looked amazing, dressed as an Indian squaw in fringed suede dress and high boots, her black hair held back with a band of multi-coloured feathers. 'Come in. Great to see you!' she said, her eyes widening with pleasure at the sight of them all.

'There you are.' Frank had joined her, looking handsome in an outdoors way, his cowboy hat fastened under his chin, jeans tucked into studded boots.

'Ah! You're here.' Rose launched herself forward to kiss them all, the artificial flowers in her party hat bobbing up and down as she hugged Emily to her. 'How's my little darling?' she said, leading her into the hall with its blotchy mirror.

'Fine.' Emily was too sleepy to say any more.

The bedroom, with its familiar shabbiness and shelves of books, was welcoming with flowers. Charlie and Kate changed into the Simpsons' costumes Kate had made for them. Charlie, a brown-paper bag on his head, said, 'Come on, they'll be waiting,' his voice loud with cheerfulness.

The barn had been transformed. Lights from the DJ box threw reflections on to the dark oak beams. The floor, swept clean of mud and chaff, glowed, its shiny surface pressing back the night. A long trestle table to one side was set with crockery and cutlery, crackers and party hats. Friends were talking together in groups. Some were Colette's colleagues from the local tourist board, and others were neighbours. They all had good jobs, money and strong opinions.

Johnny Cash's voice bounced out of loudspeakers with 'A Boy Named Sue'.

Seeing their amazement, Colette said, 'It's taken a week's preparation.'

'It's wonderful,' Kate said.

Frank, at his best as host, introduced them to a few people they hadn't already met. The conversation was mostly about holidays: one couple was just back from skiing in Vail, with good reports.

'Daniella's home from Baltimore,' Frank said casually. 'She's here for the weekend. Daniella! Look who's here!' he called to a blonde in a gold dress that hugged her hips and fell in flounces like a Spanish dancer's. A gold mask obscured her eyes, a shiny crown floated on her cloud of blonde curls.

'Charlie!' she gasped. She was the focus of attention

as she picked her way across the floor in strappy gold sandals, the heels too high for the uneven surface. 'It's been a long time,' she said, in a breathy Marilyn Monroe voice, removing her mask with a smile.

'Hello, Daniella,' Charlie said, caught off-balance, straightening up to confront her squarely and hide his surprise.

Kate's heart sank as she eyed the striking woman. She'd aged little since Kate had seen her last nearly ten years ago, and was still beautiful with only the faintest of crow's feet around her sexy green eyes.

'Have you come specially for the party?' Charlie asked.

'No, I happened to be home on holiday,' she drawled.

'What a fortunate coincidence,' Charlie answered awkwardly. 'You've met Kate, my wife, before. Kate, you remember Daniella, don't you?'

'Of course,' Kate said.

'Nice to see you again, Kate.' Daniella shook her hand and told her she looked exactly the same as when she'd last seen her.

'You look great too,' Kate said, jangling with nerves, wondering if this was a set-up, wishing she could be alone with Charlie to ask him if he had known she was going to be there.

Kate had nothing against Daniella except a past that she and Charlie had shared of which Kate had been no part. Now, as Charlie took in the other woman's features one by one, she worried that this fairy queen might cast a spell on him. What if he fell for her again? Kate went hot just thinking about it, then dismissed the ridiculous notion.

A small, elegant man with theatrical eyebrows and bouffant hair, wearing a gold and white Elvis Presley outfit, stood waiting to be introduced.

'This is Woody, a friend of mine,' Daniella purred.

'Howdy,' Woody said quietly.

'Is this your first visit to Ireland?' Kate asked politely.

'Yes, Daniella persuaded me to come. I've been to Europe often on business, but never to the old country,' he added.

'Are you enjoying your holiday?'

'Very much. We've been on sightseeing trips, and we've done a lot of shopping, sweaters mainly. I dread to think what the excess baggage will be when we're flying back home. Mind you, it's cold here.'

'Nothing like the sea air to blow away the cobwebs,' Frank said.

'Bit too fresh for me. Gives me a nasty tickle in my throat,' Daniella said, with a giggle.

Charlie's sister Joanne arrived with her husband Fred, both dressed as wizards. Their son Joshua was a splendid imitation of Harry Potter, with wire-framed spectacles to complete his costume.

Fred made a dive for Daniella. 'You look spectacular,' he said to her, twirling her around.

Emily asked Josh to play with her but he wasn't interested, so she wandered around on her own.

Frank served champagne, doing his best to get the party going.

'This is like the back room of a dingy pub,' Rose said. She had returned to them and was eyeing the bottles of champagne, stashed in buckets of ice, and the crates of beer.

'Have a drink, Ma, and do your best to enjoy yourself,' Frank said, handing her a glass of champagne.

'Now, don't you go getting me tiddly,' she said.

'No, Mother,' he said.

Daniella turned to Charlie and said, 'You look so well.'

In his Bart Simpson outfit, wary of being mocked, Charlie smiled nervously.

'Honestly, you really do look well,' Daniella insisted.

'Thank you.'

'It's Raining Men' blared out.

'Let's dance,' Frank said to Kate.

Fred danced with Daniella. Cinderella, in bright red, was dancing with a dazzling white spaceman, Lara Croft bopped with Bugs Bunny, Tom with Jerry, Charlie with Joanne. Then Charlie asked Daniella to dance. She held herself stiffly at first, then gradually relaxed. There was a mysterious smile on her face, as if she was aware that many men were in love with her.

'Supper is served,' Colette called.

Rose, Colette and Joanne served salmon, cold cuts and salads to them all. The long table was a pool of flickering candlelight in the darkness as they sat down. Daniella seated herself between Charlie and Kate; Woody was on Kate's left.

Frank raised his glass, looked at Daniella across the table. 'Here's to you, good to have you back,' he said, toasting her.

'Thank you.' She smiled, raised her glass and looked at Charlie. 'You never know, I may come back for good one of these days.'

'You wouldn't want to leave Baltimore,' Woody said.

'I hear it's a lovely place,' Kate said.

Woody nodded. 'It's beautiful, if small by some standards. Lots of sailing.'

'My family thinks I ought to come back here, settle down,' said Daniella.

'I'm darned if I'll live here,' said Woody, who appeared to find the idea quite repellent.

'Woody owns a couple of cocktail bars,' Daniella said.

Kate would have liked to know if he was financially better off than the man for whom Daniella had left Charlie.

'You wouldn't want to leave all that behind, would you?' Fred gave Daniella a wink.

'I'm considering it,' she said. She had cut up her food and now laid down her knife on her plate as Americans do.

'Well, perhaps I could get used to Ireland part of the time,' Woody said doubtfully. 'Wouldn't mind a place like this,' he said.

Kate looked at him. What did Daniella see in the quiet, unobtrusive man by her side? What was he to her? Did she appreciate his qualities the way he obviously admired hers? Did he mind her doing exactly what she wanted? Was she aware of his timidity? Did she support him as he did her?

'I think it's a wonderful idea,' Colette said.

There was amusement in Daniella's voice as she said, 'Tell me what you think, Charlie.'

'I wouldn't mind living in the States,' Charlie said.

Daniella glanced at him through her eyelashes.

'Yeah. I like their way of life, the freedom,' he added.

'That is so interesting,' Daniella said, her eyes sparkling.

A shiver of fear ran down Kate's spine. Alarmed, she said, 'I would never live anywhere but here.'

'I find America a menacing place,' Rose said.

Colette stared at her. 'That's a terribly rude thing to say, Mother.'

'Not when it's the truth.'

'You can't generalise like that,' Woody said.

Charlie was listening intently, saying nothing. Daniella turned to talk to Fred. As she did so the candlelight twisted her face into devious lines.

The conversation flowed, everyone talking between

mouthfuls, laughter on happy faces. Dessert was passed round.

Emily appeared at Kate's side. 'You must eat something, love,' Kate told her.

It hadn't occurred to Emily to want food. She picked up a chicken leg, and gnawed it standing up, too excited to sit down beside her mother.

Everyone was getting along marvellously, the conversation going off at angles, the wine flowing, everyone drinking for the sake of it.

Daniella said to Charlie reflectively, 'Where have the years gone? It's all a bit hazy.'

Kate said, 'We've been living happily, haven't we, darling?'

Before Charlie had a chance to reply Colette appeared with an enormous birthday cake covered with lighted candles. She brought it to the table and placed it at the centre. 'Happy birthday to you,' she said to Frank, and kissed his cheek.

Everyone sang 'Happy Birthday'.

'Come on, blow out the candles,' someone called.

Frank blew, and gave up. 'Give us a hand here, Josh, Emily,' he called, puffed.

Josh and Emily were at his side in a jiffy. They complied with fervour, their faces red, and their cheeks bulging.

The shrill of whistles rent the air, crackers were pulled. Emily tried on other people's party hats, laughing wildly.

'Would you like some of these, Emily?' Rose was holding out a bowl of crisps.

Emily shook her head, too preoccupied with the trinkets from the crackers to be bothered with them.

Kate straightened Emily's pink party hat. 'You must eat something.'

'How are you enjoying your first grown-up party, sweet-heart?' Charlie asked, and lifted Emily into his arms.

'Good.'

'Firework display,' the DJ announced, as the music stopped.

'I want to start the fireworks,' Josh said, and ran out of the barn.

Emily squirmed out of Charlie's arms.

'Don't you go near them,' Fred said. 'We can't start until everyone's finished supper.'

'You said I could,' Josh called. 'Come on,' to Emily, who was bouncing around like a rubber ball.

They were off to the beach.

'Not on your own.' Fred was running after them, almost losing his temper.

Josh slowed down, slouched forward. 'You don't have to shout. I'm not deaf you know,' he said rudely.

'Go on and sulk. What do I care?'

Frank took over, leading the children to the spot on the beach designated for the display. A firework specialist was waiting for them. 'You've got to treat them very carefully, handle each one gently,' he explained.

They all stood watching as, gingerly, he set one alight. Suddenly a shower of red sparks burst upon the magenta sky, lighting it up. They hung suspended in the air changing the atmosphere to a magical one in an instant. The sparks shuddered and shifted, then flicked out over the bay to a sigh of 'Aaah!' from the children.

A flash of emerald green sprayed the horizon, tilted and died, followed by white chains of sparks that rose and formed hard white star shapes that spelt out a shimmering 'Happy Birthday, Frank' as they danced in the wind.

'Hooray.' Emily was clapping her hands.

'Magic!' Josh shouted, jumping up and down.

The grown-ups stood in silence, and awe, gazing at the brilliant stars reflected on the black water. Slowly, with a splintering, popping sound, they extinguished themselves, and blew off out to the horizon to be swallowed up by dark sea.

'They're dangerous, if you're not careful with them,' said Woody, looking at the long, tapering lights dying into the night.

'The sky is a picture post-card,' said Rose, putting her arms around Emily to quieten her. 'Careful, darling, don't bounce around. You're getting heavy.'

Emily yawned, stretched in her arms.

'I think it's time you were in bed,' Charlie said.

'Josh isn't going to bed for ages,' she protested.

'I'll take her.' Kate lifted her into her arms.

Emily leaned against her as she took her through the dark house. From the attic bedroom Kate could hear laughter and shouting all mixed together, as the party revellers got tipsy, music starting and stopping, but Emily was too sleepy to be disturbed by it.

Returning across the yard, she could see the dancers, veiled in the dark, their colourful hats identifying them. Daniella's body swayed as she moved slowly in Charlie's arms, her dress shiny in the light. Their faces seemed to merge, as they grew fainter in the hazy dimness. A feeling of vulnerability caught in Kate's throat as she watched them drift away.

'She looks very pretty,' Joanne said wistfully to Kate. 'Do you like her dress?'

'Too glittery for me,' Kate said savagely.

Fred grabbed Kate round the waist. 'Come on,' he said dancing intricate steps as he led her forward.

Kate managed to follow him, but was dizzy when the music ended. She strained her eyes to see Daniella and Charlie, but couldn't. Suddenly they were there, a stifled giggle coming from Daniella, Charlie laughing so much that he was doubled over.

'He really is enjoying himself,' Kate said, almost tragically, to Rose.

'Yes,' said Rose, glancing at her. She took Kate to one side. 'He won't come to any harm. That was all over a long time ago.'

With a crash the music died and the dancers stopped. Guests were leaving, standing in little groups, saying goodbye. When they'd gone, Rose, Joanne and Kate gathered armfuls of dishes and loaded them on to a trolley. They cleared the trestle table, filled bin-liners with leftovers and debris. They laughed together as they worked; delighted that the party had gone so well.

Kate went to look for Charlie. He was standing in the shadows to one side of the barn talking to Daniella and Woody, who were staying over. 'Coming to bed, love?' she asked.

'Yeah.' He sighed, then went back inside to search among the beer bottles for a full one. She followed him and waited in silence, watching him. 'You didn't have to come looking for me, you know,' he said, as if Kate had ticked him off for misbehaviour. In a way she must have done so, but without realising it. She stood mute. She had so much to say, but nothing she could put into words. He gave up his search and followed her sulkily out into the yard where a sudden downpour of rain greeted them.

'Wait there.' Frank was beside Kate, slipping his arm through hers, escorting her to the house with an enormous umbrella.

'It's torrential,' Kate remarked.
'Never mind. Worse things happen at sea.'

In bed, unable to sleep, Charlie snoring gently beside her, Kate was thinking about Daniella, asking herself why, after all these years, she had had to turn up. Rose was right: it had all been over for a long time. What harm was Daniella doing by being there? None. Surely Charlie had a right to be friendly towards her. Kate decided she was being unreasonable, but still felt furious.

2

Next morning Charlie said, 'Good party,' as soon as he woke up.

'You seemed to enjoy yourself,' Kate said groggily, snuggling into him.

'Yes, I did. Didn't you?'

'It was terrific,' Kate said. 'I hope Emily's going to be all right,' she added.

'Why shouldn't she be?'

'Josh isn't very interested in her.'

'She'll be fine. Stop worrying about her.'

'Josh is mad into sports, Joanne was saying. Emily's not athletic enough for him.'

'She's well able to keep up with him, I was watching them last night. There are all sorts of things for them to do. They'll have a fantastic time if the weather picks up.' After a pause he said, 'Kate, what's really on your mind?'

Kate moved away slightly. 'Did you know that Daniella was going to be here?' It was out before she could stop herself.

'No, I certainly did not,' he said, shaking his head. 'Nothing to do with me. She and Colette have always been friendly.'

'Doesn't seem Colette's type.'

'What do you mean?'

'Too . . . sophisticated.' Too damned attractive was what

she meant.' 'What did you two talk about that was so amusing?' Her voice sounded edgy.

'Nothing much. Mainly gossip about old mutual friends.'

'Is Woody very rich?' she asked.

'Not that I've heard. Why do you ask?'

'Strange for her to be with him.'

'Why?'

'He's a nice man but I don't get the feeling there's anything romantic between them. A woman like that with so much going for her.'

Charlie hesitated. 'He's good to her, and she's enjoying herself. She's not the type to want to settle down again too quickly.' His face was averted so Kate couldn't see his expression.

'A good-time girl.'

'I wouldn't go that far. Woody is better than the other men she got mixed up with,' he said. 'They were all of a type – the phoney bastards she seemed to attract when she first went out there.' He looked out of the window and shifted position.

'Sad in a way. Seems a shame that she's missing out on a family. I know Emily wasn't planned but I wouldn't be without her for the world – or you.' She snuggled up to him again. 'Still,' she mused, 'Daniella may yet meet someone who'll sweep her off her feet.'

The remark seemed to hit home. In an instant Charlie's face was contorted with disgust. Then, brightening, he said, 'Not Woody, for sure. He's too boring.' He shrugged. 'And she gets bored quickly. She got tired of me.'

'It went on a long time,' Kate ventured.

'Perhaps too long.' Charlie got out of bed and went to the window. 'Waste of time talking about it. Look at that blue sky – not a cloud to be seen,' he said, pulling the curtains open. 'What time is it?' He squinted at his watch. 'Wow! It's late. Better get downstairs or they'll be gone fishing without me.' He launched himself towards the bedroom door, his hand to his head. 'God, I'm wrecked.'

'The fresh air will soon get rid of your hangover,' Kate said, as he headed for the bathroom and a quick shower.

'Bloody plumbing in this house,' he complained on his return. 'Takes ages to crank up a trickle of water.'

Kate was out of bed, handing him a freshly pressed T-shirt and shorts.

'You do look after me,' Charlie said.

'It's my one real talent.' She flashed him a smile as she closed a drawer.

'I don't know about that.' He smiled meaningfully. 'I'd better get off.'

'You go ahead and have a lovely day.' She gave him a kiss, then went into the bathroom and closed the door.

She dreaded the day ahead, her digestive system shaky as she thought of Daniella. Though Charlie had sworn that his relationship with her had been a bad mistake, and that the only woman he'd ever loved was Kate, she'd always been jealous of her.

When Kate walked into the kitchen in denim shorts and T-shirt the women were all seated at the rough, scrubbed-pine table having breakfast. The men had gone fishing.

'Good morning, everyone,' Kate greeted them.

'Good morning,' Colette said.

'Did you sleep well?' Daniella asked.

'Like a log,' Kate said. 'Where are the children?'

'Out on the swing,' Rose said. 'Up since the crack of dawn.'

Kate looked out of the window to see Josh on the old

tyre hanging from a sycamore tree, Emily chasing Tinker round the green lawn.

'Such a lovely garden,' Daniella said, in her silly voice, her eyes on the roses. 'And a really wonderful house. I like the primitive, rustic setting, and all these old wooden beams. So romantic,' she added, taking a forkful of scrambled eggs.

'Fiddlesticks! There's nothing romantic about living in the country. It's a lot of hard work,' Rose said, chewing her rasher with the vigour of a dog with a bone. 'Dodgy plumbing, smelly bathrooms, cow dung everywhere.'

Colette gave her mother-in-law a brief, amused glance. 'Luckily you don't have the burden of it any more,' she said, and put a piled plate of toast on the table.

Emily came running into the kitchen, Tinker after her. 'Uncle Frank took us swimming.' Her voice was a high trill.

'That was lovely.'

'Josh kept splashing me, he wouldn't stop.'

'It was only a bit of fun,' Kate said.

'The water was freezing,' Emily persisted.

'Would you like to come blackberry-picking later on?' Colette asked her. 'We've got a nice day for it.'

'Yes,' Emily said. 'Are you coming, Mummy?'

'Of course,' Kate said.

'I'd love to come too, if I may,' Daniella said.

'We can all go,' said Colette.

As soon as breakfast was over Colette took down from the pantry shelf the enamel pails kept for fruit-picking, while Kate filled bottles with tap water.

Colette cut a swathe through the tall grass with a stick, making a path for the rest of them. Josh, behind her, beat back the overgrown bushes with a hockey stick. One by one they went through the high, thick field, ducking beneath splintery branches, Kate holding Emily's hand. Their destination was a tumbledown gable wall at the end of the lower field where luscious blackberries cascaded from the bushes. Josh and Emily reached up to pick the dark purple fruit, shiny in the sun.

'You'll be careful, won't you? Those brambles are very scratchy,' Kate warned.

They took no notice of her, picked furiously, stopping occasionally to eat the softest fruit, velvet to the touch, squashy between their fingers, warm and sweet to taste. The enamel pails filled up quickly as they worked their way along the bushes, wading through the high grass, the sun beating down on them, the fields around them baking.

Daniella, bent over her task with wisps of blonde hair escaping from her red gypsy scarf, stopped suddenly. 'It's too hot,' she complained, wiping her brow.

'Let's have a break,' Colette suggested.

Emily dropped her pail and collapsed into a heap on the grass, juice oozing from her fingers, a black circle round her mouth.

Josh burst out laughing. 'Look at Black Lips,' he called.

'Black Lips yourself.' Emily pointed at him.

Giddy and helpless with laughter they rolled around in the grass.

The grown-ups sat under the shade of an apple tree, drinking the water Colette had brought.

'Nice to see them getting on so well,' Joanne said.

'Fingers crossed it'll stay that way,' said Kate.

'I was hoping to have a kid with Buck.' Daniella sighed, her eyes on them. 'Just didn't work out that way. All I've got is this to show for five years of marriage.' She held out a blackberry-stained hand with an enormous diamond weighing it down.

'Do you regret marrying him?' Rose asked.

Daniella shook her head. 'Honest, I thought I was doing the right thing, but being married to him altered everything.' She snorted derisively. 'You couldn't even call it a marriage in the end. When he first came along, good-looking, glamorous, confident, he swept me off my feet, made me feel like a million dollars. I was taken to this party and that party, because he was in with the in-crowd. I soon found out that it was all an act. He was so superficial. Once we were married Buck changed.'

'In what way?' Rose said.

Adjusting her scarf Daniella said, 'He left me stranded. We went sailing at weekends, of course, which was bracing but not exciting. He was forever going off on business trips, and when he was home he was always tired, which made him dull and gloomy. I got bitter – and disappointed because I thought I was worth a bit more than that, I guess.'

Daniella looked pretty. Everything about her was pretty as she went on to describe her apartment in a wide, tree-lined street, an American twist in each sentence.

'Oh, I was dumped, and no mistake. Shut up in a huge apartment like a prisoner, not knowing my way round Baltimore. I soon got fed up with my own company,' she drawled.

'Didn't you work?' Joanne asked.

'Not at first. Buck figured I had enough to do to look after him. He said I didn't need to. He was rich.' She bowed her head. 'Of course, I had no money of my own, and when I think back to his grudging, parsimonious ways I'm overcome with sadness for those wasted years.'

'More fool you to have put up with it for so long,' Colette said. 'I think he should have been horse-whipped for the way he treated you.'

'If it wasn't for Woody I don't know where I'd have ended up.'

'Where did you two meet?' Joanne asked.

'On a brief visit to Long Island, Buck's family home. Woody was there to do some business with Buck. He saw how unhappy I was, gave me his business card, said to get in touch if ever I decided to escape.' She looked at the other three women in turn. 'America's not the place to be broke in, you know,' she said defensively.

'All I can say is that I hope you'll be happier in the future,' Colette said.

'Perhaps you'll marry Woody?' Rose asked pointedly.

Daniella sipped her water thoughtfully. 'I don't think so.'

'He seems a good catch,' Rose persisted.

'I'm cherishing my freedom right now,' Daniella said.

Colette stood up. 'Back to work.'

Later, on their own, Kate and Joanne had a good gossip about the party.

'Charlie was all over her,' Kate said, depressed.

'He was courteous, that's all, really. It was Fred, who was all over her,' Joanne said. 'But, then, he always did fancy her.'

'When I looked at them dancing last night I suddenly imagined them in bed together.'

'I know what you mean, Daniella does seem to drape herself over the man she's dancing with. Let's face it, she's a handful. I don't know how Woody puts up with her. Colette shouldn't have invited her. She knows Daniella's trouble around men.'

'What happened to Buck?'

'God knows. She hit him hard in the pocket when she took herself off. That's all I know.'

'No wonder she's so stylish.'

Kate felt she'd graduated in the subject of Daniella Dagget. She was like someone caught in battle without armour. If she had been going to confront her it would have been better to do so on neutral ground – and far easier if Charlie wasn't around. What would she say? 'Keep away from my husband'? That sounded childish when Daniella had only danced with him. Ah, well, soon she'd be returning to America, and that would be the end of her.

That evening was spent in the garden over a barbecue. It was a relaxed affair, Charlie and Frank cooking the mackerel they'd caught, Fred serving the women, the children squabbling over whose turn it was to have the swing. Josh kept winning the toss, and Emily burst into tears of frustration. She called to Kate that she hated Josh. 'He's a bully,' she cried.

Kate went to console her, and to inject a sense of fair play into Josh's game. Returning across the lawn she saw Charlie take Daniella's arm and walk her down the shadowy path among the trees. Kate followed, stood for a moment in the silence, listening unashamedly.

'That's not true,' Daniella was saying, looking directly at him. 'I missed you when you stopped phoning. I wondered what had happened to you.'

'Surely Colette told you how I was getting on.'

'It wasn't the same,' Kate heard Daniella say, her voice slippery as silk.

'Wasn't it?'

Kate could see Charlie's face as he spoke. He was

looking at Daniella, his eyes wary of being mocked. 'I didn't know what you were doing or thinking,' he said.

'Neither did I. I just knew I'd had enough of Ireland and its relics, and I don't mean the statues.'

'Thanks a bunch.' Charlie laughed.

'If only I'd stayed,' Daniella said, in a charged tone.

Kate couldn't hear what he said next but she heard Daniella say, 'Listen, Charlie, I told you at the time I had a job in Baltimore that I wanted more than anything.'

'And you had a man you wanted more than me,' he said. He looked towards Woody, who was leaning against the garden fence opening a can of beer. 'Where does he come into the picture?'

'He's the first person who's treated me properly since Buck.'

'If he's not that important, why are you mixed up with him?' Charlie asked.

'He's been a good friend, Charlie . . .' The rest of the sentence was lost.

'Coming back to the barbecue?' Kate called, sounding like a child faking an excuse to interrupt the adults.

'Sure am.' Daniella joined Kate.

When Daniella and Woody left, Kate said goodbye with relief. Daniella told Kate what a real pleasure it had been to see her again. She was an unhappy woman, Daniella, and Kate hadn't even been friendly to her. As if to compensate for this she went to humour Charlie, who had returned to the kitchen and was pouring himself a cup of coffee, quietened by Daniella's departure.

3

One late October evening, a month after the party, Kate was ironing and Charlie was working late. Kate liked ironing when the house was quiet, and Emily was in bed, running the hot iron slowly and evenly over Charlie's handmade shirts, smoothing out the confusions of her day with the creases. She loved the clean fresh smell of the ironed clothes as she folded them into neat piles.

Humming, she went upstairs, opened Charlie's chest of drawers to put away his clothes, and there, under the new shirts still in their Cellophane, was a jewellery box loosened from its gift wrapper. She opened it. A pair of heavy gold cufflinks lay snugly in a bed of cream velvet, 'Cartier' written in gold beneath them. The gift card read, 'To Charlie, Thank you for a magical time, All my love, Daniella.'

The ground appeared to shift beneath Kate's feet, the walls swung, the pattern on the curtains danced before her eyes. She blinked, and sat on the edge of the bed. She didn't know what to do. She hadn't heard mention of Daniella either from him or anyone else since the party and she'd forgotten about her. They must have been a present Daniella had given him years ago that he'd come upon recently. Why had she never seen them before? He'd kept them hidden so as not to remind her of his past with Daniella. That was it. Charlie loved her. She knew that.

He was a good husband, and a caring father to Emily. So, why was she worried? If only her sister Lucinda weren't in Tunisia she could talk to her.

She heard the front door open, then Charlie's rapid step in the hall. She shrank from confronting him, scared of the hurt the cufflinks might cause. She stood up and went slowly downstairs.

Charlie stood in the darkening hall yanking off his jacket, his complexion ruddy in the twilight. 'Hi,' he said, giving her a peck on the cheek, loosening his tie. 'How are you?'

'Fine.'

'What have you been doing?'

'Ironing. All put away.'

Charlie hated untidiness.

'Emily all right?'

'She wanted to wait up for you, but with school tomorrow . . . How was your day?'

'Usual.' He took off his spectacles, rubbed his eyes. 'God, I'm tired!' he said, with an energy that belied his words.

'Have you had something to eat?'

He nodded. 'Canteen.'

Her desperate need to say something about the cufflinks was growing. 'Charlie, I need to talk to you.'

'Not now,' he said, picking up his post.

'It's important.'

'There's nothing so important it can't wait.' He yawned.

He went into the kitchen and got out the bottle of vodka, the tonic from the fridge, a lemon from the fruit bowl. 'Want a drink?' he asked.

'No thanks. It's about Daniella,' she said.

He swung round. 'What about her?'

Kate faced him at point-blank range. 'I know you've

been seeing her!' she blurted out, in a high, tearful voice. She expected him to come to her, take her in his arms and say that such an idea was out of the question, but he looked straight at her, his eyes full of fury. For a second she thought he was going to strike her.

He poured himself a stiff vodka and tonic, lifted the glass to his lips and took a swallow.

Kate backtracked. 'I shouldn't have said that. I'd just like you to explain to me when and why she gave you gold cufflinks and a note with "all my love" written on it,' she said.

'They were a thank-you present.'

'What favour did you do for her?'

'Sorted out a loan on her property. Do you need an analysis of everything?'

'No analyst would ever get within a mile of you,' she shot back.

'Your prejudice against Daniella might be symptomatic.'

'Of what?'

He didn't answer. He was stalling.

'It's true!' she gasped. 'You *have* been seeing her.'

In the silence that followed Kate stood tense with anxiety that she might be wrong or, worse, that she was right. She took the opportunity to have a good look at him. His face seemed suddenly to collapse. Her heart hammered when she recognised guilt written all over it, inseparable from the shame and confusion that followed.

'Yes, it's true. We bumped into each other recently,' he said, squaring his shoulders in a pathetic attempt at defiance. 'I was planning to tell you.'

'When was this?' Kate said loudly.

'Ssh! Emily will hear you!' He went into the living room.

'I hope I've got this wrong, but did you . . . were you . . . actually seeing her?'

The look of uncertainty he gave her was of someone with something to hide. Dumbfounded, Kate returned his gaze, noting his self-consciousness.

He walked stiffly to the window. 'I was going to tell you.' He spoke with his back to her.

She looked at him aghast, the unspeakable catastrophe pushing between them, wrenching them apart. Since she'd known him she'd never held him to account, had always trusted him. But now her lovely reliable Charlie was gone, and in his place stood a stranger, a sneaky, conniving cheat.

'Why? Why did you do it?' Her outburst was like a bullet.

He ran a hand across his brow. 'I don't know. It just happened. She was here, and I was—'

'Horny, weak?'

'I never meant it to happen, Kate.' He was shaking his head.

'No, you just couldn't keep your hands to yourself, could you?' she shouted, anger erupting, sick at the thought of his hands all over Daniella's body, hands that belonged to *her*.

'It hasn't been going on for long. Only very recently . . .' He stumbled over the words.

The idea made Kate laugh. 'As if you'd tell me the truth!'

'It *is* the truth.'

'And that makes it OK?'

He had no prepared answers. Eventually he said, 'You and I haven't been happy lately.'

'What do you mean?'

He groped for the right words. 'Things between us have been strained.'

'What are you trying to do – make out it's my fault?'

'No.'

Charlie launched into a monologue about their squabbling turning into animosity. He put it down to pressure of work on his part, and fatigue on hers. True, he complained regularly about her preoccupation with Emily and the house, but Kate had never taken any notice of him.

'So, what are you implying? That this is all my doing? That I pushed you into her arms?'

'No – but you've been preoccupied lately, too tired, too busy. One excuse after another.'

'Preoccupied looking after our home and daughter. I'm the one who has to do everything because you're always at work, and take no interest in our home life.' She turned away from him. 'Now I know why.' Furious, she thought of the lists of things to do she'd made in bed, in her old T-shirt, her hair often still wet, hanging limply, while he'd moved into the second stages of snoring. She could see that he found admitting his adultery almost impossible, but she was outraged that he could blame her. It was unforgivable.

'My God, you make me sick.' She burst into tears.

'I'm trying to be honest with you and you're not making it easy.'

'Go on, then, I'm waiting.'

'Don't make such a big deal of this. It was nothing more than . . . a fling.'

'So, you decided to have a little fling with Daniella.' She could hardly bring herself to say the name. 'To celebrate the end of her marriage, was it?'

He hung his head. 'It wasn't like that. I met up with her at an office bash after Frank's party and . . .'

'What happened?' Kate crossed her arms, confrontational.

'We'd had a bit too much to drink, and we kissed, for old times' sake.'

'Old times' sake! I see.'

'We got a bit carried away. I realise now it was madness, insanity, and no big deal . . .'

'Strange, you never mentioned it to me.'

Charlie shrugged. 'I didn't see the point.' He came to her, his hand out in a conciliatory gesture. 'I don't know what came over me. I'm sorry I hurt you.' His voice trailed off, weak from making so many excuses. 'It was over with Daniella long before you and I started going out together. This shouldn't have happened.'

'That's what I had thought.' Kate eyed him glacially.

'She's no threat to you.'

'That's supposed to comfort me, is it?' Kate spat, itching to slap his face, or worse.

'No, of course not. I was merely trying to explain.' His tone was hurried, and embarrassed.

'Well, you haven't explained enough. I want to hear all about it. Go on, tell me!' she yelled.

'Kate, stop! Please! I couldn't help it.'

'So, that alluring long-legged bimbo sidled up to you, pursed her big lips at you, pushed her silicone chest into your face—'

'For Christ's sake, stop.'

Kate lost all control, and sobbed inconsolably. 'How long has it being going on?' she asked, through heart-wrenching sobs, looking at him with trepidation, fearful that his answer would devastate her even further.

Perspiration beaded his brow. 'I told you, it hasn't been "going on", as you put it. We just slept together.'

'More than once?'

'Yes.'

'How many times?'

'I don't know.'

'Oh, my God!' Kate flinched and covered her face with her hands.

'I told you, it meant nothing.'

'That's what they all say.' Overcome by a flood of tears she collapsed on to the couch. 'Well, I hope you're happy now that you've ruined everything.'

'Please – you're making things worse—'

'How could I make things any worse than they already are?'

Charlie stood sheepishly, listening to her sobs, at a loss for what to say or do next. He looked at the ground. 'Honestly, Kate, I'd forgotten all about her until she turned up at the party.'

'But she wouldn't let you forget, would she? I can tell that from the interest she takes in your appearance. Monogrammed gold cufflinks for organising a loan – what next? A gold-plated dick to remind you of how splendidly you're endowed in that department when you do her the next favour?'

She said that to embarrass him. It did.

'Do you love her?' There was desperation in her voice as she asked the question.

'Don't be ridiculous.'

'You didn't answer my question.'

'For God's sake, Kate!'

'Answer me!' she screamed.

'Calm down, this isn't getting us anywhere,' he said.

Kate took a deep breath. 'I'd like you to leave this house.'

'What?'

'I'm asking you nicely because I don't want to wake Emily.'

Charlie's eyes widened in panic. 'Don't be so bloody stupid. We can talk this through. There's too much at stake here.'

'You should have thought of that before you leaped into bed with *her*.'

'Ah, come on, Kate, I told you it meant nothing.'

'But you slept with her,' Kate protested, her voice loud and shaky, 'and that's the ultimate crime, as far as I'm concerned. And if it meant nothing why did you keep doing it?'

Charlie had no answer.

'I want you to leave. That's my final decision.'

White-faced, Charlie flung upstairs, threw his holdall on to the bed. Kate followed. Lips compressed to stop herself crying, she watched him pack. A natty dresser, he chose his coral and blue shirts, with matching ties from his vast collection. 'It wasn't serious,' he said again, as if to reinforce his argument.

'Give me a break!' Kate's face was distorted with pain and anger as she threw the gold cufflinks into the case after the shirts.

Finished, Charlie went down to the basement, where he opened and shut drawers, cramming his briefcase with folders, snapping it shut. He bounced back up the stairs again. He stood stiffly in front of her. 'I wish this wasn't happening.'

'But you can't quite keep the marriage commitment?'

'Hey, it doesn't have to be like this. Surely we can talk?'

She stood with her hands clutched to her chest. 'Please go, Charlie.'

He hesitated at the hall door. 'What'll you tell Emily?'

'Bit late to be concerned about her,' Kate said.

Without a glance in her direction and with nothing left to say, he was gone. From the far side of the front door he called, 'I'll phone you,' and slammed it.

Kate opened her mouth to say something, then shut it and choked back a sob.

'Mum!' Emily was out of bed, half-way across the landing in her bare feet, pointing down at the door from the top of the stairs. 'I heard you and Daddy shouting. Did you have a row?'

'Oh, darling!' Kate ran up the stairs to her.

'Where is he?'

'He's had to go away again for a little while, but it's going to be OK, love,' she said, squeezing Emily's shoulder.

'He never said goodbye to me.'

'You were asleep.'

Emily allowed herself to be pulled gently back into her dark bedroom. She lay in bed, her fists over her eyes. 'Did you send Daddy away?' Her voice broke. 'Did he do something awful?'

'No, love, it's work,' Kate lied.

'I want him.'

'It's all right, darling,' she said, sitting down on Emily's bed, taking her into her arms. 'You'll see Daddy soon.' Her heart was breaking as she spoke. She clasped the child to her and rocked her gently, stroking her hot little face. 'Shall I read you a story?'

Emily nodded and propped herself on one elbow as Kate took *The Cat Book*, her favourite, from the bed-side locker. 'Once upon a time a hungry cat went out to look for something special to eat,' she began, in a lulling voice.

Emily sighed and lay down on her pillow. Kate continued to read in a whisper and Emily began to suck her thumb. Soon her eyes closed. Kate put down the book, ran her fingers over her daughter's silky hair, kissed her, and crept away.

She crossed the landing to her empty bedroom. As she pulled the curtains, shutting out the dark, she thought, What a nightmare! You're going along, leading an ordinary life, everything normal, then suddenly, without warning, Daniella Dagget appears in your life and ruins everything. She sat on the edge of their bed, staring ahead, eyes unfocused, her hands gripped together. Charlie was gone. Hadn't needed a second bidding either. Wasn't even too worried about what she might do. She felt bereft and deserted, hardly able to believe what had happened. As she wept silently, she lay back on the bed.

Eventually she plucked up the courage sit up and look out of the window. The empty driveway glistened in the moonlight. Frost silvered the cars lined along the road. Kate began to tremble violently. She undressed and got into bed where she indulged in the luxury of self-pity, letting the tears run down her face as she contemplated her role in the tragedy as its hard-done-by heroine. She knew it wouldn't last so she made the most of it. It sustained her until she sank into a dreamless sleep.

4

In the morning Kate woke up beside the empty space in the bed, proof that it hadn't been a dream, that Charlie was really gone. Her mind was opening and shutting like a door, letting in unwanted sounds, and there was a helpless terror in her stomach as she watched daylight filter through the curtains.

Eventually she got out of bed, and went to the window, feeling faint at the thought of the long day ahead. There wasn't a sign of life anywhere, no evidence of the previous night's shock except the empty driveway where Charlie's car should have been. Everything familiar had gone with him. This was the new Kate, alone. All she could see was a gigantic, empty world and her alone in it. She got back into bed, lay there until she heard front doors slamming shut and car engines starting up, the sounds made clearer by the frosty air. Emily's cat, Oscar, came into the room and leaped on to the bed, purring, playing with her hair. It was time to get up. With tremendous effort she showered, dressed, made her bed and, still trembling from shock, crossed the landing to Emily's room.

Subdued, still sleepy, Emily sat up, blinking. She lifted her arms for her mother to help her out of her nightdress, her small body snow white in the morning glare.

'You're really stretching,' Kate said, noting the shrunken

sleeves of Emily's white blouse. 'You'll need a new one after Christmas.'

Emily yawned. She sat in her red uniform with her legs thrown out, sighing and sniffing in silent protest as Kate made her put her socks on.

Kate made breakfast for herself and Emily, the radio barely audible in the background. Silently Emily ate her boiled egg, dipping a strip of toast into it, her fringe falling over her face. The knot in Kate's stomach prevented her from swallowing her toast, so she crumbled it for the birds.

'I think we should get a move on or you'll be late for school,' she said, after a glance at the clock.

'I don't want to go to school today,' Emily pleaded.

'Why not? You like school,' Kate said, her head hurting with the effort of keeping her emotions locked in.

'I want to stay at home.' New strength had crept into the child's voice.

'Of course you don't. You need to be at school,' Kate said, smiling sunnily.

'I don't want to go. I want to be with you.' Emily bashed her eggshell, shifting her stare from it to her mother.

Kate's heart stood still. She almost relented, but that would be wrong. 'You've got to go to school, sweetheart. You might miss something important,' she said resolutely.

As Emily got down from the table, she said, 'Who'll stay with you?'

'I'm going to work,' Kate said, with a confidence she didn't feel.

The grandmother clock in the hall whined and whirred out the half-hour.

'Come on,' she said, gently. She wiped Emily's hands

and face with a damp towel, fetched her coat, put her lunchbox into her schoolbag, then pushed her towards the door, the reins of power in her hands.

They set off down the road, both as silent as sleepwalkers in their distress. Normally Kate loved the quiet streets of the early morning, and the tumble of terraced houses that came to a sudden halt at the river. Today she was oblivious to her surroundings. Emily clasped her hand as they took a short-cut through the park, Emily's cheeks glowing with the cold as she hopped along like a sparrow. The grass in the park was still green. A man was sweeping up the leaves. Some floated in the wind and gathered in the squared flowerbeds, which had lost their colour. Behind the trees were neat houses with nice gardens, blocks of apartments hidden discreetly among them. When Kate was a child that part of the town had been much less built up.

The wind lifted their hair, and blew russet autumn leaves across their path and dust into their eyes. At the far side of the park sycamores stood like sentinels, crows circling them, their cawing subdued in the frosty haze. The salt smell of the sea made their noses twitch.

'I want to go home,' Emily said, as they emerged from the park, and turned towards school.

Kate wanted to go back too, but knew she must soldier on. This was her first day without Charlie, and surely the most difficult. It would get easier as time went on. She took a deep breath and marched on, her purposeful footsteps beating a rhythm in her determination to keep moving. The lump in her throat twisted as she held back more tears; the cold air made her breathless.

The playground was swarming with groups of children, their shrieks and laughter filling the thin air, their red uniforms bright as splashes of spilt blood under a grey sky.

Miss Stern, Emily's teacher, began marshalling them into a crocodile. With her hand held up to silence them, she marched them through the glass-panelled doors. Emily hung back, her arms at her sides, her eyes squinting into the distance as she searched for her best friend, Hannah. Suddenly a change came over her when she saw her coming towards her.

'Will you be all right now?' Kate asked.

'I'm not a baby, Mum.' She gave Kate a hurried kiss, and went off with Hannah.

When Kate had seen Emily safely inside the school she walked to the town, past the Cock and Rabbit, Charlie's local, and continued along to the Shamrock Hotel, where she worked part-time as a receptionist. Her legs felt like jelly at the thought of her long morning session of being pleasant to people. A pain in her stomach made her change her mind. She'd phone in sick.

She went back through the park, her coat collar turned up, preoccupied with thoughts of Charlie. Often, when they were newly married, they had walked through the park, Charlie with his arm round her, stopping to kiss her as they drew nearer the trees. To think that he'd been with another woman! Kate had had no idea that there had been a lack of passion in their marriage. She had had no idea that he'd been unhappy. The thought that he might have wanted her to find out made her feel sick with sorrow. Charlie was a decent man, even though he took her for granted, and was guilty of the odd burst of rage when things didn't go his way. Why had he left those cufflinks so carelessly in his drawer? She felt so alone. The vaguest sounds disturbed her – the fluttering of a bird in the hedge, the snapping of twigs. Thrushes calling from the taller trees seemed to sing, 'Sorry, so sorry.'

She pulled her jacket round her and concentrated on her breathing until she got home and let herself into the house. She was half expecting to find Charlie there, having changed his mind and returned home with a desperate urge to prove to her that Daniella would not come between them. No such luck! Cursing herself for the pathetic coward she felt herself to be, cursing him for what he'd done, she phoned work and made her excuses.

In the silent house she went from one room to another, pulling the curtains, blocking out the world as if there had been a death in the family. In Charlie's absence the house was full of him, his hacking jacket on the rack, his muddy hiking boots under the hall table waiting to be claimed for another trek in the Wicklow mountains. His favourite CDs were piled neatly next to the stereo. Now there was nothing but silence. Kate made a cup of coffee and sat in the perfect stillness of the living room listening for his phone call or his footstep, hanging her head over the sofa, clinging to it to stop herself collapsing.

She glanced at her watch from time to time and was amazed by how slowly the morning passed. Asking him to leave had been a drastic thing to do. Perhaps she'd been a bit hasty. Kate wondered where he'd stayed the night – probably somewhere anonymous like Jury's Inn. He wouldn't want his best friend Brian Savage to know he'd been thrown out for being unfaithful – or any of his friends, for that matter. How long would it be before he phoned? Maybe he wouldn't. She checked her watch. Breathing deeply and steadily she zapped out his mobile number, and waited. It was switched off. She phoned the bank.

'Hello,' a woman's voice answered, bright and optimistic.

'Charlie Conway, please.' Kate slid her fingers over the mouthpiece to disguise her voice.

'He's not in today. Can I take a message?'

'No thanks.' Kate put down the receiver, grief engulfing her. No doubt he had taken a day off work to cosset himself with endless cups of coffee and a shoulder to cry on. She thought of Daniella and her silly laugh. What if he'd gone to the States and told Daniella that he'd been thrown out of his home because of her? His selfishness, his thoughtlessness were beyond Kate's comprehension. But she knew he wouldn't have gone away without saying goodbye to Emily. She resisted the urge to dial his mobile again, feeling hurt and betrayed.

The doorbell rang. She didn't want to answer it. She wanted to be on her own. It rang again. Frowning, she stood up slowly, her head aching. Her watch told her it was one o'clock.

Her mother, moving impatiently from one foot to the other to keep warm, said, 'I phoned you at work. They said you were sick. What's wrong? I've been worried about you.' Mary Gainer marched ahead of Kate into the living room.

'I'm not sick as such,' Kate said, stalling, aware of the threat her mother's outrage posed once the whole horrible mess had been unleashed. 'It's Charlie. He's gone.'

'What do you mean "gone"?'

Kate felt hot, and her head pounded. 'He's left home,' she said, on the verge of fresh tears.

Astonished, her mother looked at her. 'What? Walked out? Just like that?' She snapped her fingers.

'No, I asked him to leave.' Kate slumped back on to the couch.

'Ah, here! Have you lost your marbles?' Mary looked at her as if she was insane. 'Why on earth would you do a thing like that?'

'He's been seeing his ex-girlfriend,' Kate said, in the hushed tone one uses when announcing a death in the family.

'I don't believe it. Charlie would never be unfaithful to you.'

'He has been.'

Incredulous, Mary put her fist to her forehead. 'Dear God! I can't believe what I'm hearing. How could this be? Why didn't you phone me? I'd have been straight over.'

No matter what had gone wrong between Charlie and Kate in the last eight years, Mary had always taken Charlie's side when Kate had needed sympathy. That was why Kate hadn't phoned her mother.

'Where's he gone?'

Kate looked at her mother with bleary eyes. 'I don't know. He could have gone to her.'

Mary's anger surfaced. 'I don't understand it. You love one another, don't you? What was the matter with you, being so hasty? You can sort this out.'

'It's not that simple.' Kate leaned back into the cushions.

'You shouldn't have asked him to leave.'

Shut up, Mum! she wanted to say, but her mother's anger had knocked the stuffing out of her. 'I don't know what to do,' she said. 'I've never felt worse than this.' She burst into tears.

Just at that minute Oscar startled her by leaping on to her lap.

'I'm sure things aren't as bad as all that,' her mother said, plumping up the cushion beside her. 'There must be some explanation.'

'Oh, he came up with some crummy excuses, but how can you excuse behaviour like that?' Kate sniffed.

Mary sat beside her. 'Calm down, and tell me exactly what happened,' she said.

'I found a jewellery box with expensive cufflinks in it among his shirts and a card from Daniella thanking him for a wonderful time. He hadn't even bothered to hide them properly. I accused him of having an affair, expecting him to deny it, of course, but he didn't.'

Mary shook her head as Kate sobbed.

'I'm so sorry. You are in a bad way,' she said. 'I hate to see you so miserable. I wish I could think of something to jolt you of it. What about a nice blueberry muffin that I brought you?'

'You've enough to do without worrying about me.' Kate hiccuped.

'I'm your mother. It's my job to make sure you're all right.'

'I haven't slept a wink. I don't know how I'm going to get through this. He said things were bad between us, that we weren't getting on well lately, but I wasn't aware of it. I must be stupid.'

'He's making excuses for himself. Listen, Kate, people mess up their relationships every day of the week, but they seem to survive. Do you have anything urgent to do today, apart from collecting Emily?'

'No.'

'Why don't you go back to bed now, and get a few hours'

sleep? I'll tidy up for you, and get Emily. If Charlie phones I'll have a word with him. I'd like to hear what he has to say on the subject.'

'No, Mum, please don't do that,' Kate begged. 'You can't interfere. It'll only make things worse.'

Miffed, Mary said, 'Then you'll have to talk to him, sort out what happens next, that kind of thing.'

The clock ticked in the silence. 'I just don't understand it,' Mary said. 'I wish Lucinda was here, she'd know what to do.'

'Have you heard from her?' Kate asked, wishing it were Lucinda and not her mother she was talking to now. She'd understand it all better than Mary did. 'Maybe this was a way of telling me that he didn't really want to be married any more. Maybe he only married me because I was pregnant,' she said.

'I never heard such a load of rubbish in all my life,' was Mary's reply. 'Now you're feeling sorry for yourself, and it won't get you anywhere.' With that, she went to get Emily from school.

Kate felt helpless as she lay on the couch, cursing herself for the snivelling coward that she was. She got up and put a Perry Como CD on the stereo to drown out the quiet, but his dulcet tones made her more distraught than ever. She wasn't sure if she could go on.

She pressed 'eject' and replaced Perry with Elvis, his haunting voice singing 'Are you Lonesome Tonight?'. Swallowing the tears, she felt herself shrink under his great, melodious voice as it teased, haunted and hollered, an anthem to the great romance of Charlie and Kate Conway. She lay back mouthing the words. A tragic victim, she sobbed heartily, as if she were taking her last breath, until she fell into an exhausted sleep.

'Did Daddy phone, Mum?' Emily asked, rushing through the door.

'Not yet,' Kate said, jumped up and squeezed Emily to her in a bear hug.

That evening, when Emily was tucked up in bed and there was still no word from Charlie, Kate opened a bottle of wine and poured herself a glass, thinking of Charlie pouring her wine, kissing her, saying, 'You'll never know how much I love you,' against her ear. She drank it, then refilled the glass, stared out blindly into the darkness.

There was no point in drowning her sorrows like this. She'd wake up with a massive hangover, and that wasn't on with a child to look after on her own. Back went the wine into the fridge. Kate slammed the door shut. It rattled infuriatingly, and the calendar pinned beside it fell to the floor. She picked it up, noticing that 17 October was ringed, a week's time. They had tickets for the opera festival in Wexford that night, and her mother was to have Emily. She thought of Charlie and herself getting dressed up to go out. She went up to bed, wallowing in the sheer pain of remembering. In the bathroom mirror there were big circles under her eyes, tear streaks down her face. She went into Emily's room. Her hair was tousled on her pillow and one arm was flung out; her teddy bear teetered on the edge of the bed. She looked vulnerable.

In bed, Kate thought that Charlie might phone soon in the hope that she would change her mind. Maybe he'd had to do what he had done to get Daniella out of his system once and for all. Maybe she'd been foolish not to listen to him. She was scared to think of what the future held – Charlie was everything to her. She hoped that, wherever he was, he was as miserable as she was.

5

Kate was working as an air hostess with Aer Lingus when she met Charlie at a party. It had been given by her younger sister, Lucinda, a photographic model who had graced all of the top magazines and mixed in the same circles as Charlie and his friends. Kate had returned from a holiday in Hong Kong to find that her father was ill. Charlie comforted her. Their next meeting was at a christening of the baby of a mutual friend, when Kate had nursed the baby to let the mother have a well-earned drink. They had talked and talked. Their third encounter was at a rendezvous in London. Charlie would meet her in the strangest places, sometimes when she was on stopovers in Washington or New York.

A handsome banker and a keen yachtsman, he had a glamorous lifestyle. He'd swept her off her feet. He introduced her to a new life: trips abroad on the beautiful yachts of rich clients and friends, summer afternoons sailing his own boat, *Miranda*, moored at Bramble Hill where they spent most weekends, afterwards making love under the stars. She remembered how proud she was when he proposed living together, half drunk on a bottle of champagne in a Paris wine bar.

Kate loved his family, and they loved her.

He took her home to introduce her to his mother. 'He's

still vulnerable,' Rose had warned. 'He was so upset when he split up with Daniella.'

His vulnerability was part of the attraction, especially in such a gorgeous man.

'Who would have thought,' Joanne had confided, 'that he could be so happy again? I'm glad he's found someone down-to-earth who'll keep his feet on the ground. You've taken him by surprise, jolted him out of himself. You're good for him.'

'He's been through the mill,' his sister-in-law Colette had said. 'You're gentle with him, a sight for sore eyes, the absolute cure-all.'

'What happened to her?'

'Dumped him for her boss in Baltimore, a rich banker. She was a gold-digger, broke his heart,' said Joanne. 'He was well rid of her,' she added, and insisted that Kate should forget about her. 'Go for it,' she'd advised.

They'd rented a flat in Ranelagh. Kate wasn't entirely happy that Charlie hadn't mentioned marriage: more than anything she wanted the full white wedding, bridesmaids, confetti, the lot. When she broached the subject he'd smile and kiss her and say, 'It might spoil everything if we rushed into it.' She'd tease him regularly about being a commitment phobic, and he would pull a face, and say, 'When the time is right we'll tie the knot.' She was prepared to wait until he was ready because she was so in love with him.

Kate continued flying until her pregnancy put a stop to it. Emily was already making her presence felt when they got married quietly on holiday in Barbados. Emily came into the world kicking and screaming, a big, bouncing baby, unreservedly taking over their lives and their hearts. Kate gave up her job to take care of her.

Charlie worked all hours to make enough money to buy a house of their own, and Emily kept Kate busy. When the baby was a year old they had bought their three bedroomed Victorian house, in need of refurbishment, close to the sea in Dun Laoghaire. With its red door, its south-facing, secluded garden of roses, clematis and apple trees, Kate loved it. When Emily started school, she had found her part-time job at the Shamrock Hotel to help pay for the house to be restored to its original glory.

'A receptionist!' her mother had said indignantly. 'In a hotel! I wouldn't have thought a job like that would be fulfilling enough for you.'

'It's handy and not too demanding,' Kate insisted.

Eventually, it stopped being a joke and became another thing they squabbled about.

As soon as Lucinda got back from Tunisia, Kate phoned and told her the whole story almost in one breath.

'Oh, Kate! I don't believe it,' her sister gasped. 'Stay right there. I'll come as soon as we've finished this shoot.'

Kate cleared the table and began to make pastry for a chicken pie for lunch, thinking of her sister. Lucinda was always coming to her rescue – that time on holiday in Spain when the waiter had tried it on, Lucinda had smashed her fist into his face, threatening to 'kill the shit'. That must have been ten years ago. When Kate told her she was pregnant, and scared to tell Charlie, Lucinda had stared at her red-ringed eyes and said, 'What are you crying for? It's brilliant news. I'll tell Charlie with you, he'll be over the moon.'

She remembered their childhood, the quarrels, tearing each other's eyes out over toys, the more serious rows when they were teenagers, fighting over clothes and makeup, then borrowing, lending, protecting each other especially where boys were concerned.

There was the time when Lucinda had stormed over to Ian Harper, Kate's first boyfriend, shouting, 'You bastard,' after Kate had caught him at the cinema with Lisa Cullen. They were always together, hiding in the garden shed in the dead of winter, shivering, smoking, having to light their cigarettes several times, splitting their sides laughing over the boys of their acquaintance. Sometimes their rows were big ones, with Lucinda storming off, not speaking to Kate for a long time. So much of their shared past merged into one big memory bank of laughter and tears.

The doorbell rang and Lucinda breezed in, five foot ten, blue-eyed, her blonde hair cut in a trendy bob falling over one eye, dressed in a black trouser suit and white shirt. With her flawless complexion, perfect jawline and gleaming white teeth, she was sickeningly beautiful.

Kate took one look at her and burst into tears.

'Oh, no!' Lucinda said, her eyes wide with sympathy, her bee-stung lips shaped into a soothing hush, and took Kate's trembling body into her arms, hugging her tightly, saying, 'There, there,' softly, words Kate barely head: she was crying too hard.

Patiently Lucinda stroked her hair and let her cry her heart out as she used to when they were kids to calm her. 'I brought you some bits and pieces,' she said, when Kate stepped back, drying her eyes with the back of her hand.

She put a large bag of groceries on the table, removed a bottle of red wine, opened it and poured two glasses, then handed one to Kate.

'So, when did all this happen?' she asked.

'Last week. It was like a scene in a film. He was packing,

leaving before I realised what was happening. I wanted to say, "Stop, don't go," but I felt paralysed. I couldn't do anything, not even when he was going out of the door, saying goodbye.'

'Why didn't you phone me on my mobile?'

'I tried. I couldn't get a line.'

'Shame about that. How did Emily take it?' Lucinda asked, flicking the crumbs from the chair before seating herself and crossing her long, shapely legs.

'She was quite upset when he left. She thinks he's away on business.'

'Children are resilient. It's you I'm anxious about.' Lucinda eyed Kate's pale face, her limp hair, her jeans and creased T-shirt.

Kate sighed. 'I'm still reeling from the shock, but the hysterics are over, and I'm not having nightmares any more.' She raised her head. 'I can't eat, can't sleep. I just feel sick all the time thinking about him with her.'

'Oh, Kate!'

'I just want this to stop, and I can't think what to say or do to make it stop. I loved him so much, Lu.'

'You still do. You're hurt, that's all.'

Kate sniffed. 'I miss him. But don't worry, I'm not about to fall apart.' Kate looked like death but she took the chicken pie out of the oven, and a salad from the fridge, and placed them on the table.

'Brave girl.' Lucinda got out knives and forks. 'Have you heard from him?'

'No, he said he'd ring, but he hasn't. Still mad as hell with me for flinging him out, I'd say.'

'Did you phone him?'

'Once, but he wasn't there, and I'm not doing it again. As if I'd go crawling to him.'

'I suppose not.' Lucinda took a mouthful of chicken pie. 'This is absolutely delicious.'

'Good.'

'What are you going to do?'

'I don't know. I'm just going from day to day as best I can for Emily's sake. I don't have a choice.'

'I can't believe it – his ex, for God's sake! How pathetic is that!' Lucinda took a sip of her wine.

'She was at Frank's fortieth birthday party – remember I told you about it?' Kate looked at her. 'He couldn't resist her. One scent of her and he was in there.' Kate clenched her fists until the knuckles went white. 'True, our lives had been a bit boring recently, but nothing to warrant being deceived like that. What happens if he goes off with her?' Kate's lip trembled again.

'If that were to happen, and it won't because you'll make sure it doesn't, he'll get enough of her lifestyle and come running to you with his tail between his legs begging you to have him back.'

'If he'd thought with his brain instead of what's between his legs it wouldn't have happened. Men!' Kate shuddered.

'Too right!' Lucinda laughed. 'But, seriously, that Daniella goes through men like wildfire. Poor Charlie will never be able to keep up with her.' Lucinda knew all about Daniella from the gossip among their mutual friends.

Kate looked away. 'Even if he came back on his hands and knees I don't think I could have him back the way I feel right now.'

Lucinda stared at her. 'Don't say that.'

'Honestly, Lu, at the moment I couldn't sleep with him – ugh! I don't know if I'll ever be able to trust him again.'

Lucinda's brow furrowed and her mouth hardened. 'He's a monster to do this to you.'

'Just as we'd got some security in our lives.' Kate's eyes glistened with fresh tears.

'And stability, with Emily and everything. It's awful what's happened. How are the finances?' Lucinda asked.

'I haven't given them much thought. We have a joint account – Charlie's salary's paid into it every month.' Kate paused. 'Oh dear. What if he stops the mortgage payments?' Her face was dead white.

'Bastard. It's a tricky situation, and it needs careful handling,' Lucinda advised.

'I don't know what's going to happen.' Kate closed her eyes and threw back her head, the effort to think too much for her. 'I'm confused, I need time.' She frowned. 'I'm in a sort of limbo and I can't stand it.'

'I understand.'

'I really don't know what's going to happen next.' Kate gazed listlessly in front of her.

'Don't make any hasty decisions. Wait and see. Meantime, let's finish our lunch, and go for a walk before you collect Emily from school. The fresh air will do us both good.' They cleared up and went out.

'I never asked how things are with you,' Kate said guiltily, as they walked along.

Lucinda smiled shyly. 'Oh, Kate, I've met the most wonderful man. His name is Diego. He's Mexican.' She went silent.

'And?' Kate prompted.

'Nothing, just that he's the most gorgeous hunk I've ever met. A six foot five Adonis.' She laughed, but as Kate looked into her face she knew that to Lucinda this guy was different from the rest.

*   *   *

'What's wrong, Mum?' Emily asked, on the way home.

'Nothing. Why?'

'You look funny.'

'Funny?'

'Sad. Is it because Daddy hasn't phoned yet?'

'Yes.'

'He will,' she said matter-of-factly. 'He promised.'

It wasn't much fun on her own. Not that Charlie was a bundle of laughs. He was serious most of the time, and particularly over the last year when he'd been withdrawn as if he was holding something back. Kate had assumed that his work had made him distant because he was away so much. It hadn't been his fault, she had reasoned. He couldn't do anything about it. She had tried to get him to share it with her, looked for opportunities to talk about it, but Charlie had refused her access to that part of his life.

Now she didn't know where she stood. She'd just have to wait to hear from him, get through it as best she could. It was difficult and lonely. Kate didn't want to be on her own. She was scared.

6

Days went by. There was still no word from Charlie. At home Kate sat on her own, thinking her heart would break from loneliness. There was no one to say good night to, no one to wake up to each morning. Kate missed the old Charlie, the way that he had been. She thought about him all the time, wondered where he was and what he was doing.

Being on her own with Emily was hard, and she hated it. So did Emily. All Kate wanted was to get her life back to how it had been before. Her mother phoned with daily news bulletins – who was ill, who won the golf competition, the staggering price of everything. Some days she came round with a bowl of chicken broth, or a casserole and aired her views on Emily's diet, and the child's lack of 'proper' meals.

'Gone to the dogs, this family,' she would say, throwing accusatory glances at pizzas in the freezer. She never meant to cause trouble but she would argue with Emily, who howled over her broth, protesting that she preferred chicken nuggets. It made Kate feel as if she were a child again too.

When Charlie still hadn't got in touch, Mary said, 'You could come and stay with me for a little while. You and Emily could have the spare room – though where all your things would fit I don't know.'

'No, thanks, Mum. I want to be on my own,' Kate said emphatically.

She was desperately trying to guard the boundaries of the tangled wilderness that was her life. Although she loved her mother she couldn't imagine living with her, even short-term. Mary didn't just clean her house, every morning she attacked it, blasting it with the vacuum cleaner, and crashing ornaments about in her paranoia over dust and its mites. Kate far preferred to be on her own, trying to come to terms with it, even if it made her miserable.

During sleepless nights she abandoned herself to self-pity. When she did sleep she dreamed that she'd lost Charlie, and would wake to realise that it was reality.

One night she was collapsed on the couch after Emily had gone to bed, half asleep, the telly on low. The phone rang and she answered it, expecting to hear his voice, which she hoped for and dreaded at the same time.

'Hello, Kate,' Charlie said, subdued.

'Charlie! Where have you been?'

'London, working. I just got back.'

'Why didn't you phone?'

'I was giving you a chance to cool down.'

'Have you any idea what you've been putting me through?'

'Kate, we need to talk,' he said, without answering her.

She stood there silent, wary.

'Kate, are you there?'

'Yes.'

'How about meeting me for lunch tomorrow?'

Tension filled the silence. Kate felt terrible to be talking to her husband as if he was a stranger. She wanted to burst out crying, say, 'Charlie this is me, Kate, your wife,' and beg him to come home right now, this min-ute.

'I'm working. I can't get into the city.'

'I could come out to Dun Laoghaire. Meet you at the Purty Kitchen – say, one o'clock?'

'OK. I'll be there.'

Kate couldn't wait to hang up and ring Lucinda. 'Charlie phoned. He wants us to meet for lunch tomorrow for a heart-to-heart.'

'Good. You have to face each other some time, but you'll need to make an effort with him, Kate,' Lucinda warned.

'I don't know if I've got enough backbone for it.' Kate's voice was full of doubt.

'You'll cope.'

Helen Horton, manager of the Shamrock Hotel, tapped the reception desk with her pointed red nails. 'So, you're back,' she said, lips pursed, scandalised by the length of Kate's absence.

'Yes.'

'I had to fill in for you myself.'

She always reminded Kate of a poodle, with her coiffed hair and snooty nose. 'I'm sorry about that. I was sick.'

'I'm sure.' Helen drummed her nails on the desk. 'Don't look at me like that,' she said, as her mobile rang. She turned away to answer it, sparing Kate a tongue-lashing. 'Now,' she said, clicking it off, 'we have a group of travel agents in for an incentive conference today. I expect you to be at your charming best – and not just for an hour but for the whole morning,' she snapped.

She clacked off on her ridiculous high heels, clicking her phone on as she went.

Charming? I'll give her charming! Kate pasted on a
sweet smile that hurt her mouth.

She concentrated on it every time she said, 'Good
morning, how can I help you?' to a guest. She was
courteous to the stream of people she encountered during
the morning, helped them with their endless enquiries and
performed all the tasks that her job demanded. She even
smiled brightly when one man from the conference came
to reception and leaned too close to her, his head tilted
awkwardly in his need for her exclusive attention. Feeling
sure he wouldn't be fobbed off with an information pack,
the glossy little brochure with all the details of the day
printed for easy reference, she kept her eyes on his drab
beige suit, her smile fixed, eyebrows raised. 'What would
you like to know?' she asked reluctantly, feeling a personal
question hovering on his coffee-stained lips.

'What do you do in your spare time?' he asked.

Please, not that old chestnut, she wanted to say, but she
remained polite: she might lose her job if she was rude to
difficult people.

She pretended to consider this, and said firmly, 'Would
you like a newspaper to read during your coffee break?'

'No thank you, Miss,' he said. 'Would you like to go
out with me this evening?'

'No, thank you, Mr Tully,' she said, reading the name-
tag on his lapel. The smile was pained now. 'I have a
husband, a daughter, a house,' she said, hoping to put
him off.

'No problem. I've got a couple of kids of my own.'

'Oh!' So he'd been down this route before.

He continued to ask questions. Before he took himself
off he gave her a tip of one euro. She looked at the coin,
the value he'd put on her time, and slipped it in the St

Anthony box at the side of the desk, releasing a long sigh of relief, surprised by her resilience. It was an endurance test, and she got through the rest of the morning by distracting herself with a plan of campaign to deal with Charlie.

Vivian, the senior receptionist, came on duty. 'How are you?' she asked.

'Much better, thanks.' Kate had explained the situation to Vivian on the phone briefly, anxious to tell her before the word spread. Vivian had been kindness itself, assuring her that she'd stand in for her, offering to call and visit her or take her to lunch. She was a good friend, but she didn't need to know the whole sorry saga.

Vivian gave her a quizzical look, waiting to hear more. When Kate said nothing she asked, 'How's Charlie? Any news?'

'Not yet. I'm meeting him for lunch.'

Vivian looked at her in wonderment, clearly, anxious to provide whatever emotional support she could. 'You'll get through it, you know, you're a good couple,' she said, making her desire for a happy ending known, and giving Kate a lift that carried her along for the rest of the morning.

'How's Emily?'

'Reasonably OK.'

A woman coming to the desk interrupted them. They exchanged glances that indicated they'd talk later. Kate talked to the woman. She knew that Vivian understood what an effort it was for her to put on this act, that she realised just how much Kate's life had been upset by Charlie's selfishness: her own husband had left her after only a few years of marriage.

As one o'clock drew nearer Kate braced herself for her meeting with Charlie. Patience and cool tolerance would have to be exercised. There would be no crying and definitely no pleading. It was imperative that she looked smart so that he would see she wasn't falling apart. Most importantly, she must grab his attention as soon as she walked into the restaurant and keep it throughout the meal.

If she did want him back, and she was still too hurt to know, she'd have to be clever rather than insistent. But she wouldn't trivialise his affair by avoiding the subject. They would have to talk about it before they could get on with their lives.

At ten minutes to one she checked herself in the mirror in the ladies'. In her black trouser suit she told herself that she was more sophisticated and elegant now that her bones weren't so well covered: her new slimness was an advantage even she couldn't deny. She refreshed her makeup, applying lots of mascara to accentuate her big brown eyes, and concealer to the circles beneath them. She still had on the gold chain Charlie had given her for her birthday around her neck, she noticed, as she brushed her mane of red hair. She gave her face a final check in the mirror, and saw that it was as pale as a frightened child's, but her eyes were bright when she went to battle with her man – or for him, whichever the case might be.

Before she left she had a stiff vodka and tonic to overcome her anxiety. She took deep breaths to steady herself as she walked along. When she reached the Purty Kitchen she felt ready to sort things out.

In fact, she felt grand.

7

Breathless, Kate arrived at the Purty Kitchen at five minutes past one.

Charlie appeared from nowhere. 'Kate!' he said softly.

She stopped for a second and held his gaze, nervousness sending shivers down her spine. Oh, God! This was insane: her own husband was stepping towards her like a stranger. People passing them glanced in their direction, knowing something was wrong between them.

'This is awkward,' he said. 'There's no use pretending otherwise.'

She nodded, her eyes sliding past him, determined not to make it easy for him. She led the way into the restaurant, found a free table.

'What'll you have? The fish here is always fresh,' he said, when they were seated. He handed her the menu.

'I'm not very hungry.'

'You've got to have something.'

'OK, I'll have the tuna bake.'

'I'll have the steak sandwich.'

As soon as they had ordered Charlie met her eyes, his own veiled and narrowed. 'I was worried about you.' He looked as if he was already considering how she might behave.

'Then why didn't you get in touch sooner? I didn't know where you were.'

'As I said, I wanted to give you time to cool down.'

Charlie straightened his tie. 'I do understand why you did what you did, Kate,' he said, placating.

'That's a start. I wish I understood why you did what you did.'

'I feel terrible about it.'

'I feel terrible too, alone with Emily.'

'How is she?'

'She keeps asking for you all the time.'

'It wasn't my idea to move out,' Charlie said, his voice raised.

'You gave me no choice.'

'Perhaps not,' he conceded.

There was an awkward silence.

Kate took a deep breath. 'I just don't understand how we got to this stage. I mean, before Frank's party we were a happy little family. You never said there was anything wrong.' She started crying, despite her resolution not to.

Charlie chewed his lips, his eyes downcast. 'Where to start?' He addressed the table.

'At the beginning. Start with Daniella Dagget,' she shot at him, breaking her rule about keeping calm.

He looked at her with the eyes of a small child who has misbehaved. 'Don't raise your voice, Kate,' he said, glancing round the restaurant

'Is she still in Ireland?' Kate persisted. She was pushing against the boundaries, all the time telling herself she had a right to know. Wasn't it because of Daniella that they were sitting together in this restaurant, with its new wooden floors and shiny surfaces, like two strangers, each of them now leading separate lives?

'No. She's back in the States.'

'What did you do with Woody?'

'What do you mean?'

'While you were shagging Daniella.'

'Kate!' He broke off, evidently afraid of being overheard. 'Ssh.'

'That's what you were doing, wasn't it? Let's call a spade a spade – or a slut a slut in this case.'

Red-faced, Charlie raised his hands helplessly. 'Kate! Don't do this. Listen, I think we should try to take a step back from our emotions and talk rationally about this.'

'Forget my emotions? How in God's name do I do that?' Kate closed her eyes, then heard his voice saying her name. She opened them again. 'Listen, Charlie, just give me straight answers. That's the only reason I'm here. To sort this out.'

'I'll try to answer all your questions if you try to keep calm. This is a public place.'

Their meal arrived. Charlie began to eat.

Kate eyed him, waiting to hear what he was going to say next.

'What I did was dreadful, there's no excuse for my behaviour.'

'Now we're getting somewhere.' She sat back.

'I behaved disgracefully, I realise that, and I'm taking my punishment for it – but can't we just try to put all this behind us? Get over it? Look, I don't expect you to understand, but I do think the fact that I'm trying to apologise might soften your heart at least enough for us to be able to hold a conversation.'

'So, you think an apology gets you off the hook?'

'No, but it's a start.'

'You put me through hell, Charlie.' Kate cut into her tuna.

'I know, and I'm sorry.' Charlie looked up at the ceiling. Kate desperately wanted to say, 'Let's go home, and make love' – that had always sorted out the worst rows in the past – but she couldn't get the words out.

Charlie reached out a hand to her.

Kate ignored it. 'I don't know. The humiliation I've suffered. Your ex, of all women!'

Charlie threw up his hands in protest. 'Kate! Stop it.'

'I thought what we had would last.'

'If you love me you'd be able to get over this.'

'Everyone thought I was so lucky when I met you,' Kate said sadly.

'I thought *I* was lucky.'

'Is there anything else I should know about? Have you been seeing Daniella secretly all along?'

Charlie looked away.

'Charlie?' Kate's voice trembled.

'Yes – I mean . . . well, it was nothing. She was at the Christmas party, can't even remember much about it.'

Kate's stomach hit the floor. 'You were with her *last* Christmas Eve?'

Charlie blushed.

Kate was speechless, recalling that evening, the joyful task of decorating the Christmas tree with Emily. They had unwrapped each delicate ornament from its tissue paper and carefully positioned it on the tree, Emily overwrought with anticipation. She'd fallen asleep on the couch waiting up for Charlie. His noisy entrance in the early hours had woken her.

'And all that time you were with her!' Kate felt sick.

'Go on, rant at me if you want to. I deserve it.'

Quietly she said, 'I thought you'd outgrown falling in love with unsuitable women.'

Charlie shifted uneasily in his seat.

'It's all to do with the fact that she makes you feel good,

makes you feel young.' Without taking a breath Kate continued, 'If you think I'm going to try to compete with that tart you're wrong.' She frowned – she'd be bound to lose any contest between them anyway.

'Don't call her that, you don't even know her. God, Kate, you're making this so difficult.'

'Don't pull that face. I'm the victim here, not you.'

There was sadness in Charlie's sigh as he put down his knife and fork. 'You're a terrific person, Kate, and I've been thinking about us. I realise how important home and stability is to me. I only want you and Emily, and more kids, a boy next, maybe.' He smoothed down his tie. 'I'm looking forward to that.' He looked at her hopefully, perhaps for some indication that he had made a breakthrough. Fiercely he said, 'I never meant any of it to continue. It was Daniella who got in touch with me. She kept—'

Kate waved her knife at him. 'You're shifting the blame again, Charlie.'

'No, no.' He cringed.

Kate took a handkerchief from her handbag, blew her nose, and said, shakily, 'I was the stupid, trusting wife. I bet she's having a good laugh at my expense right this minute. If you could have seen me after you left! Getting through that first day, then the second. I fell apart, pacing up and down, all hours of the day and night.'

'And I was having a ball? You didn't care about me, and if I had a place to stay,' Charlie said angrily.

'I'm getting out of here. This conversation is going nowhere.'

'What about your lunch?' Charlie got to his feet, helped her as she tottered to hers.

'Stuff the lunch! I don't want it.' She dropped her napkin.

'Where are you going?' Anger seeped into Charlie's voice.

'Home.'

In the street he stood before her, his body taut. 'Aren't you going to give me another chance?' His eyes flickered while he waited for an answer.

'Can you give me a guarantee that you won't ever set eyes on her again?' She was afraid to move, afraid to breathe.

Charlie's eyes eluded hers; his body shrank away from her. He said, his voice barely above a whisper, 'I work for the same bank, she's friends with my family, I may not be able to avoid bumping into her.'

'Who's to say you won't shag her again?'

Charlie punched the air in a hopeless gesture. 'I told you . . . For Christ's sake, Kate, give me a break.'

'Why should I?'

A wall of silence went up while she waited for his answer.

'What can I do to persuade you to let me come home?' Charlie said.

She looked at him. His deception had made him undesirable in her eyes. 'I don't know if I want you back.' Her head was thumping and she had barely got the words out.

Charlie didn't move, just waited until what she'd said had sunk in. When it had, an amazed expression came over his face. 'We can't leave it like that.' He put his hand on her arm. 'Couldn't you be a little reasonable here? I'm fed up living from day to day in crummy hotels. If you loved me this wouldn't get in the way.'

'I'm going.' She turned and walked away, her legs weak, each step taking her away from the safety of him. She pressed on, knowing he was watching her.

At the church he caught up with her. 'Kate, don't go.' He was almost crying. 'I wish it hadn't happened.' He hit his forehead with his fist in frustration.

'So do I.'

She kept walking, hoping to restore her equilibrium with the distance she was putting between them. What the hell did he mean? That he couldn't help it?

'Kate!' He ran after her.

She stood waiting, arms akimbo, in the middle of the busy street.

'We'll go on a second honeymoon. That should sort us out.'

He tried to take her in his arms but she struggled free. 'Let me go,' she cried.

'For God's sake, control yourself, Kate,' he said, seeing the long scratch from her fingernail that blossomed on his hand. 'You may not believe this but I still love you.'

'Then why did you have to go and spoil everything?' Kate's shriek whiplashed his face. His blue eyes were even bluer now with shock.

'Right! If that's your attitude I *will* get lost, but you'll pay for this. I'll provide for Emily, but I'm not paying the mortgage while I'm forced to live in hotels or rented accommodation. Do you understand? Can you hear me?'

He backed away, the wind lifting his hair as he went. Her eyes followed his retreating figure as he leaned into the wind. As she stumbled up the street she struggled for control. Her eyes misted as she walked along, gazing at nothing. Horns honked at her impatiently as she strode across the street oblivious to the red light at the pedestrian lights. She jumped back, stubbed her toe on the kerb. Bastard! How dare he do this to her? She wiped her hand across her eyes.

The lights changed. Marching on, she felt ridiculous, diminished, less of a woman. What a fool she'd been to trust him. Would he do it again? If she wasn't sure of him how could she ever have him back?

She'd spent all those years with him, made love to him at every opportunity. She remembered at the beginning how thrilled with her he'd been, his protectiveness making him strong in her eyes. They'd shared good times, had seen each other through bad patches, but it was different now. Their special love and the sweet intimacy they'd shared had been smashed to pieces. The world had got hold of him and changed him. So had Daniella.

This time there would be no reconciliation, no hot kisses on her tear-streaked face, no breathless apologies and ripping off of each other's clothes to expend their passion. It was over. She was back to square one. Wasn't that better than being married to a man who didn't love her? To have it end in this terrible way was more than Kate could bear, but there was no way she would let anyone walk all over her. The last hour they'd been together had opened her eyes to so many things. First, that she could live without him – the main one.

What was she going to do for the rest of her life? Live like a nun? Oh, no! Start all over again with someone new? No, she couldn't think of that. She braced herself for the grief that lay ahead. She felt as lost as a small child separated from its mother in a supermarket, terrified to face the rest of her life alone. She wouldn't think about it, not yet. She had to collect Emily from school, get some shopping on the way. Salad for dinner – no, the weather was too cold. Chicken and chips, Emily's favourite. Get home before the rain.

8

'He apologised?' Lucinda asked.

'Yes. He feels guilty, and is trying to clear his conscience,' Kate explained.

'And you accepted?'

'No, I didn't.' Kate picked up a towel and dried her hands.

'Oh, Kate!' Lucinda put her arms round her sister. 'You really are in trouble if you're not going to accept his apology.'

'I know, but so much has happened so quickly that it's unreal, difficult to know what to do.'

'I'm sure it's going to be OK,' Lucinda said. 'You two will have to sit down and talk properly, not just over lunch in a restaurant.'

'It's so painful, raking through it all.'

'I know, but you can't accept the situation as it is. You'll have to have him back eventually.'

Kate looked at the tiled floor, not so sure about that.

'Time is a great healer,' Mary said, when she called round. She repeated it several times in an effort to console her crumbling daughter.

It would take more than the time she'd left to her, Kate explained, wishing her mother would take herself and her platitudes off, and let her get on with her grieving. Then she was sorry for having such an unkind thought.

Mary continued to come and go, taken for granted rather than appreciated. Kate wanted to phone Charlie. Several times she went as far as picking up the phone, dialling the first and second digits, rehearsing the words she'd say to him, then replacing it, knowing that she hadn't got over what he'd done. His dalliance with Daniella, if that was all it was, had put an impossible barrier between them, and if loving him meant that she had to suppress her bitterness, forgive him, she just couldn't do it, no matter what.

Sadly, she wasn't the only victim. Emily was suffering too, missing him desperately. Emily looked forward to his calls, giving him all her news, until one Saturday he didn't ring when he'd promised he would. She waited and waited, restless and impatient. Finally she fell asleep, her Sugar Plum Barbie on her damp pillow next to the telephone.

Emily was lost, disoriented, suffering the degree of fear and loneliness that one feels when a parent dies. She watched avidly everything that was going on, listened to every conversation, tried to piece it all together, confused by Kate's lame explanations. Kate should have known how difficult it would be to explain it all to Emily. One evening she followed the little girl up to her bedroom. 'Are you OK?' she asked.

Emily nodded, calm now as she concentrated on the Nutcracker Prince and Sugar Plum Fairy, disinclined to talk. She was struggling to be brave but her bafflement and her inability to express her feelings about the situation swamped her small features, which were already blurred with sleep. She was too sad and tired to make a fuss, but the longing in her eyes for answers gave lie to the pretence that she didn't need to know something terrible was going on. Oscar, curled up at the foot of her bed, purred contentedly.

There was nothing for it but to tell her the truth as simply as possible, and soon. Perhaps that would relieve the pressure. Now, watching her daughter, Kate couldn't bear the child's grief – her heart was broken.

Some days were worse than others, but the biggest problem was having time to think. Trying to fight off her misery she cleaned the house, dusted and polished every surface, getting right into all the nooks and crannies. She couldn't stop. She would rush home from work and set to in an effort to rid herself of the anger, anxiety and heartbreak. She springcleaned Emily's room, tidied away her clothes, put all her toys in a box, except for the Barbie clutter. In her own room, she dusted the chest of drawers that housed Charlie's clothes and his computer, wondering why he hadn't bothered to take it. She rearranged his brushes and toiletries on the dressing-table, and put his mountaineering books back where they belonged, cursing him for keeping his brains in his trousers.

One day, as Mary arrived she was setting the table for dinner.

'You'll wear yourself out,' her mother said.

'Keeps me occupied. Anyway, the house needed a good clean-out.' Kate was distracted, in a hurry to get on with something else. She didn't want to sit and talk to Mary, knowing the conversation would inevitably lead to Charlie.

'There are other things you could do with your time.'

'Such as?'

'Get into shape with that mountain bike of yours. You never know whom you might meet in the park. Take Emily on hers. And there's the books I brought you from the library to read, and the shopping trip Lucinda wants to take you on.'

'I don't want to go shopping with Lucinda.'

Neither did she want to spend her days waiting for a phone call from Charlie that wouldn't change anything. However, she took Emily for a walk on the beach after chicken nuggets and chips at McDonald's in the hope that it might distract them both. The sea was grey, the east wind merciless. Kate walked along, thinking of the beach at Bramble Hill, and Charlie seducing her there one glorious summer's day. Within minutes of her having changed into her bikini she'd caught his dark, speculative glance. Eyes hungry with desire, he had warned her that he had to have her there and then. Her 'Don't even think about it in broad daylight' did nothing to quench his ardour. Her decorum had disappeared when he took her out to sea in his boat and made passionate love to her under the setting sun.

From that moment on she was enslaved, so madly in love that she couldn't hide it. Filled with a passion that was unleashed by his merest gesture, touch or glance, she made herself available to him whenever he wanted her. She refused to meet her friends in case he called, cancelled dates to play tennis or go drinking with them. She adored him and told him so repeatedly, eager for him to say he loved her in return. He never did.

She slimmed down, wore sexy clothes, worried that she wasn't glamorous enough for him and his friends. Once he forgot their date, leaving her to stand out-side a theatre in the rain for over an hour. Eventually, soaked to the skin, she went home to bed and cried herself to sleep. He apologised, sent flowers, brought her chocolates. For a while afterwards his behaviour was perfect, but he did it again, leaving her waiting for him at a friend's party. Scared that Charlie's interest was waning, she was only too happy to let him off with a feeble excuse.

The shock of her pregnancy shook them both. Charlie accepted it, and changed: he became more caring, and careful of the way he treated her. Yet Kate often wondered what the outcome of their romance would have been if it hadn't been for Emily.

'Mummy, my hat!' Emily cried out, wrenching Kate back to the present.

The wind had whipped it off her head. Kate tore after it as it was carried dangerously towards the sea. Emily pranced up and down, excited and worried, while Kate splashed into the foam to retrieve it. Then, her wet jeans dragging her down, she returned to Emily with the sodden lump of wool.

They headed home, hand in hand, huddled together, Emily attempting to cheer Kate up with her chatter. 'When will we see Daddy?' she asked suddenly.

'Soon.' Kate's answer died in the wind. 'I'm sorry about Daddy not being at home with us. I really am,' she said, as they walked up the road.

'Did you have a fight with him?' Emily demanded as she looked up at her mother.

'Sort of, yes, in a way, but I don't want you to worry. It will be OK.'

'What about?'

'I can't say, Emily. That's between Daddy and me.'

'Was it my fault?'

'No, sweetheart, of course not.'

'I want him,' Emily said.

'He'll phone us.'

Kate was appalled to think that Emily might blame

herself in any way. She redoubled her efforts to reassure the child. 'It's to do with Daddy and me, nothing at all to do with you. You are a good girl, and we love you very much.'

'I know that, but what 'xactly is it that you and Daddy are fighting about?' Emily asked.

Although Kate had been waiting for this question she hadn't prepared an answer. 'It's not the way you and Hannah fight, and then make up. It's more complicated than that,' she said.

'He did something bad, didn't he?'

Emily had grasped something was terribly wrong and this was festering in her, despite Kate's denials. Kate knew she was going to have to tell her the truth sooner rather than later. 'Yes, he did,' she said, with a wave of relief. 'But it'll be fine.'

Emily shifted her shoulders, a gesture that indicated to Kate that she was not satisfied with this information. 'Julie's mum and dad are getting sep'rated. Are you and Daddy getting sep'rated?'

Kate was shocked that Emily knew about such things. 'Oh, no, nothing like that. We've got some problems to sort out when Daddy comes back, that's all. You see, we needed a bit of time apart to think about things.'

'How long?' Emily asked.

'A little while,' Kate said.

'When 'xactly is Daddy coming home?'

'I'm not sure, but he'll phone us tomorrow or the day after.'

Emily shrugged and stuck her thumb into her mouth. Kate wanted to take it out but stopped herself. She watched Emily slouching along, her coat collar pulled up around her earnest little face.

'Listen, why don't you invite Hannah to supper this evening?' she said, in an effort to distract her.

'Miss Stern's taking down names for ballet classes. Can I do it?'

'You'd love that,' Kate said, wondering how she'd pay for the lessons.

Emily nodded, giving her a smile.

Kate wondered why Emily wasn't inviting Hannah to their house these days: she used to be with them so much. It must be that the emptiness in the house, the unspoken sadness, worried her. Kate wanted to promise Emily that in no time at all they'd be together again under one roof, but she couldn't because she didn't want to lie to her. The tragedy was that Emily was too young to understand an explanation like 'Your father was a selfish man who forgot about us and thought only of himself and his pleasure. I can't let him come back home because I hate him so much for what he did to us.' She was too young for mother-and-daughter chats like that. She missed her father too much to feel comfortable about anything Kate said to her: he was the one who'd always been protective of her, who had stood between her and Kate when Kate was cross with her. Emily was too young to understand what had happened. And it wasn't fair to her: Charlie had done what he did without any thought for her. It was one thing for him to ruin Kate's world, but quite another to ruin Emily's.

'Daddy and I love you very much,' she said again, to reassure her. The words were inadequate, she realised.

They walked home quickly. Kate resolved to talk to a professional about the situation. She needed help. When they got in there was a message on the answering-machine from her mother. She couldn't bring herself to lift the phone – her mother had done so much for her but she didn't want to talk to her just now.

Instead she ran a hot bath for Emily, and put all their wet clothes into the wash, where she found Charlie's dirty tracksuit under a pile of curtains. The sight of it reminded her of Charlie jogging in the park alongside her. She pictured him, face glowing, long, muscular legs moving rhythmically, and felt the heartbreak afresh.

'I'm going to bed,' Emily said, Oscar in her arms, her thumb in her mouth.

'You haven't had your supper yet, darling.'

'I'm not hungry.'

'But it's too early for bed.'

'I'm tired.' She went quickly up the stairs and closed her door behind her. Kate stood there, hands clenched, not knowing what to do.

Barbara Butler, Kate's neighbour, called round. She was married to Maurice, an accountant who worked in the city. 'Are you all right, Kate? You look very pale.'

'I'm fine,' Kate said.

'I won't delay you.' Barbara always prefaced her chats with those famous last words. 'I just called to tell you that we're having a few friends in tomorrow night to meet Jack Marsden, a friend of Maurice's. He's been working abroad and has come back to live here. He's staying with us until he finds somewhere. We'd like you to come.'

'Thank you,' Kate said, trying to act normally.

With her beautiful home, wealthy husband and her daughter Hannah, Emily's friend, Barbara was the envy of the neighbourhood. People gravitated towards her because she was a born organiser and gave lavish parties.

'It's nothing special, just a little get-together to introduce him to our friends, and make him feel at home.'

'Where's he from originally?'

'County Meath, but he's been in the States for a long time. He's a freelance photographer. A very good one.'

'Oh!'

'Charlie away?' Barbara asked, looking beyond Kate suspiciously, an innocent smile on her glossy lips.

So the rumour machine had started already. Barbara probably knew exactly how long he had been gone.

'Business?'

'Yes,' Kate said abruptly.

'Anyway, see you for the party,' Barbara said.

'It's very kind of you to invite me,' Kate said, unable to think of an excuse to get out of it. 'I don't know if I can make it.'

'Problems?' Barbara hovered, eyebrows arched expectantly, hoping for details. Her instinct for trouble was uncanny.

'I kicked Charlie out.' Kate's voice wavered.

'No! What happened?'

'Another woman,' Kate said bluntly.

'Oh, Kate! I'm so sorry. Is there anything I can do?' Barbara put her arms round her, and ushered her into the kitchen where she put the kettle on.

Kate shook her head. 'Nothing. I don't know what to do myself.'

'Are you going to have him back?' Barbara asked.

'I really don't know.'

Barbara couldn't have missed the foreboding in Kate's voice. With an arm round her shoulders, she said, 'Who knows what might happen? You may get back together.'

'We'll just have to wait and see,' Kate said, noncommittal. Then she said, 'I can't plan my life around Charlie at the moment especially if we're not going to stay together.' She thought suddenly that they'd never again share Sunday mornings together, lying in bed, newspapers littered about them, Emily happily watching cartoons downstairs. Nor would they have suppers. Charlie would not doze by the fire or plan his next hike with his friends in some far-off mountains, Kate wishing she could go too, longing for the excitement but knowing she wouldn't leave Emily with her mother to attempt anything so dangerous. The three of them would no longer walk in the park, Emily hopping and jumping, rain threatening in the dark hour before her bedtime.

'How will you manage financially if Charlie doesn't come back?'

'I don't know. He says he won't continue paying the mortgage if I persist with this.'

'You could always take in a lodger,' said the practical Barbara. The garden flat had been done up. It had a separate entrance which would make it ideal for letting.

'Charlie hasn't moved out permanently. All his stuff's still there.'

'Just while you're deciding what to do. It would ease your cash-flow problems, give you some independence,' Barbara persisted.

A lodger would indeed give her some disposable income, Kate thought. She could manage – her clothes were adequate, and Emily had plenty to keep her going too. She could economise, too, cut her own hair and Emily's, use the sample shampoos and body lotions from the hotel. It would be a step on the road to independence. 'Even if I was interested I wouldn't know where to look for a lodger,' she said.

'It so happens that Jack's looking for a place. Just temporarily. You make sure to come on Saturday night and meet him. It'll do you good to get out,' she said meaningfully. 'Now I must dash, I've things to do, but don't let me down. Informal, eight o'clock.'

With a toss of her bubbly blonde curls she was sashaying down the drive, hips swaying, before Kate had had a chance to say another word.

9

On Friday evening, while Emily was swimming, Kate went down to the basement to try to make it look inviting on the off-chance that she decided to let it. Charlie had accumulated so much stuff, she thought, as she cleared out old letters, bills, photographs and theatre programmes. She had to force herself to put his books and files into more bags along with souvenirs they'd collected on their travels. She staggered with them to the shed and dumped them there for Charlie to collect at a later date.

She relined the drawers, and found one of the sweaters he used at the gym. It smelt of his sweat and aftershave. She wept into it, grief overwhelming her. She couldn't go on alone, she just couldn't! How dare he put her in this position? She pulled herself together, then cleaned the tiny kitchen, and the bathroom with the newly installed power-shower for use after training sessions. She dragged the rowing-machine and exercise bike into a corner, pulled posters of semi-nude women off the walls, vacuumed and dusted, and put a bowl of freshly cut flowers on Charlie's desk. Then, feeling dirty, she went upstairs and had a shower. Hungry for the first time since Charlie left she made herself a chicken sandwich.

That night Lucinda called to find her sitting beside a fire full of charred papers. 'What are you doing?'

'Having a bonfire,' Kate said dully. 'Charlie was a great

one for writing love letters when he was in the States before we got married. I kept them all. Now I don't need them any more. I've been rereading them, and they mean nothing to me.'

She laid more letters on the fire, and bedded them down with the poker. The draught from the chimney made them flutter in a thin, blue flame, and ashes floated upwards.

'I wish there was a more pleasant way of parting,' she said, more to herself than to her sister.

'Are you sure you want to get rid of them? You might regret it,' Lucinda said. The photographs recorded some of the most important events that had happened in their lives.

'It's cathartic, this slow burning,' she answered, staring at Charlie's smiling face as it crinkled and shrank.

'Won't he want some of these?' Lucinda picked up some important-looking documents.

'I've no idea.'

'He may need them.' Lucinda put aside a couple of pages with columns of figures on them.

'Tough,' Kate said, and snatched them back. She glanced at them, then threw them ruthlessly on to the fire. 'I think I'm doing the right thing,' she said. 'The fact of the matter is that I've been dumped. Used, abused, left on the scrap-heap.'

'For God's sake, listen to you! You're pathetic! You'd think it was the end of the world.'

Kate didn't answer. She was trying to compose herself. She might have known Lucinda wouldn't understand.

She said eventually, 'It is, as far as I'm concerned. Maybe I'm weak and selfish, with no moral fibre, but for once I feel entitled to wallow. I'm sorry, I know that's not what you want to hear but it's the truth. What do you expect me to do? Jump for joy?'

Lucinda rolled her eyes. 'I sympathise, Kate, really I do, but you'll alienate us all with that attitude.'

'You're right. I've pined long enough.'

Kate got up to wash her hands, annoyed that Lucinda disapproved of her destroying Charlie's possessions.

It was a difficult evening, with Kate drinking red wine rapidly, and pushing her vegetarian lasagne around her plate long after Lucinda had finished. She opened another bottle of wine as soon as the first was finished.

'You're drinking that stuff like water. I wish you could stop thinking that your life is over,' Lucinda said.

'What do you expect? It's the way I'm going to feel for a long time to come, now that I've decided not to have Charlie back.'

'I know. I should be more understanding. I'm sorry.'

'I don't expect you to understand.'

'At least you still have your home,' Lucinda consoled her.

'For the present.'

'How are you going to manage?'

'Charlie has said he will support Emily, and he paid the mortgage up to the end of the month. Barbara knows someone who might be interested in renting the basement.'

'A lodger?'

'Yes. I wish I could manage on my own, not have to take a penny from Charlie, but I can't with what I earn. I'm not sure if I want to share my home with anyone.' Kate's lips tightened.

'You don't want a lodger, but you find living alone intolerable.'

'And scary. I sleep with a hammer under the bed.'

'Think of the bright side. You can do something for yourself,' Lucinda said. 'Do something you've always wanted to do.'

'Like what?'

'Go to college.'

'That would cost too much. Anyway, what I've always wanted to do was marry Charlie and live together for the rest of our lives, but I can't tolerate his behaviour.' She bowed her head sadly.

'There may be an alternative.'

'Such as? I don't feel as adventurous as I used to. In fact, I'm quite scared of life.'

'Kate, you've lost your nerve, gone in on yourself.'

'I'm worn out with grief.'

'Understandable, but not good.'

'I can't help it.'

'For Emily's sake, you'll have to start taking an interest in things soon, in other people. You're a beautiful person with a great personality, and you'll have a life again, I promise.'

Kate arched her brows. It was hard to take an interest in people when all she wanted was understanding, sympathy, advice and money – not necessarily in that order.

'Why don't you let Mum take care of Emily, let the house and go bungee-jumping in Australia or white water-rafting on the Zambezi, or deep-sea diving somewhere? That's what I'd do.'

'I can imagine. How's your love life?'

Lucinda shrugged. 'Complicated.'

'Diego not matching up?'

'There's a bit of a crisis. He's big into yachts, and some

new venture of his seems to be taking up a lot of his time.
Or someone new.'

'Someone more important than you?'

'Any time I see him he's flanked by suits and rushing off
to a club-house or some rich person's pool for a meeting
with sharks.'

'Could be genuine.'

'Could be.' She looked out of the window, sad and
doubtful.

Kate's neighbours were an assortment of professionals
with highly paid jobs. The wives were always busy,
working part-time, caring for the kids. One, a nurse,
was involved in the local family-planning clinic; one was
a marriage-guidance counsellor. Another was a member
of Greenpeace and spent her free time fighting pol-
lution. Among them Kate felt inadequate, as if she'd
lost her place in the world. Maybe she should get a
full-time job. Doing what, though? She couldn't go
back to being an air hostess because of Emily. Anyway, Aer Lingus were letting a lot of the older staff
members go.

They greeted her warmly.

'Where's Charlie?' Sarah Leonard, another neighbour,
asked.

'He's . . . em . . . away,' Kate said.

Barbara's husband, Maurice, squeezed past, bumping
into the inquisitive Sarah, jolting her drink, almost spilling it. 'Sorry!' he said to her, grabbed Kate's arm and
pinned her to him protectively. 'You all right, Kate?
Drink?'

'Yes, please, a drink would be nice.' Kate smiled.

'It's terrific of you to come in the circumstances,' he

said, his voice low – and maddening – with a mixture of familiarity and servility. 'I heard the news.'

'Yes, well . . .' Kate lowered her eyes.

'Maurice!' Barbara called.

'Excuse me.'

Gemma Gleeson, another well-meaning neighbour, came over to her, 'I'm sorry to hear that you and Charlie have broken up,' she said.

'Oh, it's not so bad,' Kate gabbled, blushing. 'I'm coping.'

As she glanced from one to another she realised that they'd all heard, and felt like a rabbit caught in the headlights of an oncoming truck, not knowing what was coming next. 'There's a positive side to being single,' she said, more to the room than to Gemma, but as they looked at her expectantly she couldn't think of one.

All eyes were on her, the women's full of surprise and sympathy, the men waiting to hear what she was going to say. All Kate wanted to do was run out of Barbara and Maurice's house, with its minimal furnishings, discreet lighting, canapés, dips and booze, but her path was blocked by the circle of eyes as they stood in awe of her. Well, what could she say? 'Charlie's fine, don't believe those rumours you've heard about him going off with his ex. It's all lies'?

'Johnny and I have been together for ever, haven't we, darling?' Gemma cooed, at her big, fat husband.

He gave his wife a tight smile, and slunk to a corner of the sofa with a plate of smoked-salmon savouries and his pint, too lazy to join in with the party never mind leave home.

Kate felt bereaved, a burden to these neighbours and friends, who didn't know what to say or how to behave.

She realised that Charlie's departure couldn't be ignored, but she would have preferred to stay off the subject.

She looked away distractedly, and caught the eye of Tim, her work colleague from the Shamrock Hotel, who lived in the basement of next door but one. A part-time barman, he pulled the perfect pint, which kept the punters coming back regularly. By day he was a struggling writer. Decked out in tight flowery trousers and a sweatshirt that proclaimed 'MEN ARE FOR CHRISTMAS NOT FOR LIFE', he came to her rescue, tripping jauntily over to her with a plate of mince-pies and slipped an arm round her. 'Don't take any notice,' he murmured. 'Playing off-side, was he?'

'Yes.'

He whistled through his teeth. 'Isn't life a bitch?' he said, fluttering his eyelids, but she could see that he was genuinely sorry.

'The one he did it with is, for sure,' she muttered.

'Here, have a mince-pie. They're fully baked, not like that certifiable husband of yours, leaving a gorgeous, desirable woman like you.'

'He didn't leave. I threw him out, and now I'm taking the consequences.'

'I suppose it has to be got over,' he said thoughtfully.

She nodded.

'Let's skip the party. Come down the pub for a pint,' he suggested.

'I'd like nothing more—'

Barbara was beside her, a tall, dark man at her heels.

'Kate, may I introduce you to Jack Marsden? Jack, meet Kate.'

'How do you do?' Jack said formally, examining her. When he shook her hand his grip was strong. She straightened, holding her ground. 'I hear you're a photographer,' she said, observing his thin, handsome face, his black hair, perfect teeth. Mid-thirties, perhaps?

He tilted his head sideways and smiled at her, a smile that reached his beautiful turquoise eyes, as deep as the deepest sea, so deep you'd never get to the bottom of them. He returned her gaze with a clear, dissecting stare.

'Are you enjoying being back?' she asked.

'So far so good,' he said.

Someone caught his attention and Kate moved back, let her hair fall forward so he wouldn't notice her eyes lingering on him. His hand was steady as he lifted his drink to his lips, clearly at ease. She wondered what he was making of all this middle-class respectability.

'Barbara tells me you've got a basement to let?' he said, and looked intently at her.

She took a deep breath. Steady, she told herself. Don't rush in to anything here. 'I'm not sure if I . . .'

He raised his eyebrows. 'You weren't planning on having a male lodger?' He grinned.

'No, no, it's just that I haven't fully made up my mind about letting it at all.' She'd messed up. He wasn't going to be put off easily.

'Let me know when you've come to a decision. I might be interested – if you don't take too long, that is.' He was letting her know the score.

Barbara pushed between them, disappointed that she'd missed the best part of their exchange. 'OK?' she asked.

With a casual, lopsided grin he said, 'Women!' and followed Barbara, broad shoulders raised as he eased his way to the women at the far end of the room. Kate couldn't help staring after him.

'He thinks he can walk into this neighbourhood and

throw his weight around,' Tim said to Kate, his eyes following him too.

'Exactly what I was thinking. And now I have to go – Mum's babysitting. She doesn't like to be up too late.'

'I'll see you home.'

'No, honestly. I'll be all right. Excuse me,' she said, as she made her way through the elbows and slipped out.

10

Two days later the doorbell rang. Kate switched off the vacuum cleaner to answer it.

Jack Marsden stood there, a haversack slung over his shoulder.

Kate froze, hand arrested on the doorknob. 'Hello,' she said. 'Can I help you?' A draught caught her hair as she stepped forward.

Casual as a cowboy, hands stuffed into the pockets of his jeans, his body curved towards her, he stepped in uninvited. 'Here I am,' he said.

Taken aback, Kate said, 'I wasn't expecting you.'

Unabashed, he moved further into the hall and dumped the haversack on the floor. 'Barbara said it was all right for me to move in,' he said, and deflected any attempt she might have made at refusal with, 'That's OK, isn't it?' He said it in the tone of a robber who'd broken in and was holding her at gunpoint.

'She did, did she?' She pushed her hair out of her eyes distractedly. Her mind raced. What was Barbara doing? Jack Marsden was here with his luggage and she knew next to nothing about him. He could be a mass murderer for all she was aware. Barbara should have kept her nose out, and he should have had the decency to view the basement and discuss it with her properly. Annoyed, she said, 'You haven't even seen it.'

'I'll see it now. It's only until I get a place of my own.'

Kate stood motionless, unsure what to do next. He beckoned towards the stairs. 'After you.'

She hesitated.

'Well, aren't you going to let me see it?' he asked.

She opened her mouth to say no but said, 'Yes, of course,' instead.

She caught a glimpse of herself as she passed the hall mirror: hair dishevelled, baggy tracksuit – she looked more like the cleaning lady than the newly single sexy neighbour. She went down the flight of narrow stairs, Jack at her heels like a terrier.

When they reached the basement, he mooched around, opened one of the desk drawers then eyed the empty wardrobe, the bare hangers, with satisfaction, and checked the chest of drawers. Kate stood to one side, arms folded, trying to see it through the eyes of this stranger.

He rifled through the kitchen cupboards, peeped into the tiny fridge.

'It's probably not big enough for your needs. There's no oven, just the hob, and the bathroom is tiny,' she said. 'We had it redecorated, and . . .' she hesitated '. . . my husband used it as an office – and a gym, of course,' she added.

'So I see,' he said, his eyes on the exercise bike and rowing-machine in the corner.

Kate felt that he could at least have found something to approve of.

He went and examined the bathroom. 'It's adequate for my needs,' he said pleasantly.

Kate stood arms folded, stubborn. 'I'm afraid you're putting me on the spot here. I really need to think about it before I make a decision,' she said, her reluctance to have him making her sound brusque.

'If you want to forget the whole idea, fine by me. You obviously don't want a lodger.'

'It's not that.' She back-pedalled. 'It's all a bit sudden, and I don't know you – don't know anything about you.'

'I thought Barbara would have told you all about me,' he said, in surprise.

'She didn't say much at all.'

He looked at her levelly. 'What do you want to know? Ask me anything you like.'

She felt uncomfortable as she tried to frame a question, not knowing where to begin. 'How old are you?' sounded stupid and condescending.

'You're putting me on trial here. You probably don't want me around the place,' he said, turning from her.

She put her hand to her forehead. 'Look, I'm sorry if I've offended you, I didn't mean to be rude. It's just that I hadn't thought of letting it to a man. Shouldn't I ask for a reference or something?'

'Barbara's known me for donkey's years, she'll give me a good reference if you're worried. Now, I'll leave you to make up your mind. Here's my card with my mobile number on it. I'll be at the photographic lab for the rest of the day if you'd like to give me a ring.' In the hall he picked up his haversack. 'If you decide not to have me as a tenant there's no sweat. I'm sure there are plenty of other places.' He glanced around regretfully. 'It's just that this would be perfect for a couple of months.'

A couple of months' rent would give her time to sort herself out. She looked at him uncertainly. 'If you want it for such a short time we could give it a try, I suppose.'

'I'd like that very much.' He smiled.

'Then you can have it for two months.'

'You're sure it's all right?'

'Yes.' She smiled. 'I don't know what else to say.'

He took a wad of notes from his pocket and handed it to her, his expression blank as his hand touched hers. 'A month in advance, OK?'

Kate counted it. 'That's far too much.'

Seeing the uncertainty on her face he said, 'I'd hate you to think I was taking advantage of you.' There was a hint of amusement in his eyes as she stuffed the notes into the pocket of her jeans, too embarrassed to count them in front of him. Cheek!

He beamed at her, and she couldn't help smiling back, although she was wary – and who could blame her? Gorgeous as he was – and he was pretty gorgeous – he had a nerve.

'I'll be back tomorrow evening about teatime,' he said.

'Right. See you then.'

'It's a date.'

A date with him was unthinkable! A shiver of fear ran down her spine.

'Relax,' he said, reading her thoughts. 'You never know, we might even get on.'

His last words made Kate hasten to the front door. Contriving to conceal her embarrassment, she said, 'If you'll excuse me, I have to collect my daughter from school.'

'Sure,' he said, picked up his haversack from the hall floor and took the steps two at a time.

Kate shut the door rapidly and glanced at his retreating figure, distorted through the stained-glass panel. Her arms ached. Her whole body ached. What was she doing? What kind of person let her husband's space in his absence, at the behest of a neighbour who thought she was an eejit for letting him go in the first place? How dared Barbara push her into this? Kate considered phoning to ask her what she thought she was doing sneaking Jack Marsden into her house without a by-your-leave, but decided to wait until she'd calmed down. Barbara had meant well.

She set off for the school thinking of her new lodger. The wad of notes, still in the pocket of her jeans, made her feel satisfied that she'd done the right thing. But as she waited for Emily at the school gates nagging doubts took hold of her.

Why was tension mounting at the thought of Jack sharing her house? Why hadn't she told him a straight no in the first place? Because she couldn't afford to turn him down. And she couldn't change her mind now, even if she wanted to. She was cornered and she knew it. The need for money was paramount. Now there would be less financial pressure.

11

That evening Barbara called round.

'Thanks for letting Jack descend on me without warning,' Kate said.

'He was packed, ready to move in, said you'd agree to it once you realised what a good proposition it was.'

'So he was propositioning me!'

Barbara laughed. 'He's obviously paying you a decent rent.'

'He's a bully.'

'No way! He's as gentle as a lamb!' Barbara said. 'It's so important for him to have a fresh start, with no reminders.'

'Of what?'

'He had a bad experience in the States. Of course, he knew in his heart she wasn't the right woman for him, but break-ups are always unpleasant. It was his decision to take your garden flat,' she said, changing the subject quickly. 'I didn't interfere.'

'Not half!' Kate protested.

'Stop whingeing, Kate.' Barbara gave a theatrical sigh of impatience. 'Jack hasn't been convicted of any crime. You're a big girl now, well able to cope with him.' She hadn't meant to sound so sharp and apologised when she saw that Kate was hurt.

'As long as he doesn't expect any more than there is,' Kate said pointedly.

'I've known him a long time and he's the salt of the earth. You won't regret your decision.' Then, happy that she had reassured her friend, she took herself off.

'Where did he come from?' Mary asked, looking down into the basement window the day after Jack moved in.

'Didn't I tell you? He's my new lodger.' Kate had purposely kept this piece of news from her mother. Then, seeing the consternation on her mother's face, she added, 'Only for a couple of months.'

'But who is he?'

'A friend of Barbara and Maurice.'

'Why isn't he staying with them?'

'They haven't got a room they can spare.'

'What does he do for a living?'

Questions, questions.

'He's a photographer, freelance. He'll get an apartment-cum-studio as soon as he can find a suitable one.'

'He's going to be untidy about the place.'

'No, he won't.'

'Mind he doesn't take over,' she warned.

'He's restricted to the basement – or garden flat as Barbara insists on calling it – so I won't have to deal with him much.' Mary looked doubtful, so Kate added, 'Look, Mum, I'll cope,' to banish the fear her mother's words had evoked, but she spoke with more confidence than she felt.

Her mother leaned back in her chair. 'Won't he get on your nerves?'

'No, he'll be working most of the time.'

'Where does he go when he's not working?'

'I don't know. I didn't ask.'

Mary looked towards the door to the basement. 'He'll get on your nerves,' she warned, wagging a finger.

Kate had had enough. 'Mum, let's drop the subject.'

But Kate did mind when Jack positioned Charlie's desk at the window, and seemed to be there permanently. He would be there in the mornings, cleaning his cameras, or sorting out papers, when she passed with Emily on their way to school. He would catch her eye, and wave. She would stare at him crossly, but he would only smile back. He'd be there, looking out, when she came home.

What was he playing at, gazing out at her every time she passed like she was some sort of entertainment? Did he get off on watching her coming and going? Another thing that annoyed her was the scruffy, leather-clad courier who arrived at regular intervals with packages for him, and lounged around, sitting on the garden wall, smoking and chatting to him, sometimes even eating his lunch.

Why couldn't she be indifferent to Jack, wave back to him, shrug him off? Because she felt hemmed in by his constant watching from his window and she was fed up with it. He was invading her privacy in his quiet, insidious way. She wasn't having that: she was perfectly capable of taking care of herself. She would have to ask him to stop watching her every move.

One morning on her return from school, she went down the few steps to the basement.

Jack came to the door. He was wearing a creased T-shirt and boxer shorts. Leaning on the door jamb, he said, 'Hi there. This is a pleasant surprise. Would you like a coffee?'

She leaned towards him, and her hair fell forward. 'I'd like you to move yourself away from the window,' she said.

He shot her a look of surprise. 'Why?'

'I don't want your surveillance every time I come and go.'

Jack seemed startled, then roared with laughter. *'What?'*

'If your plan is to be in my line of vision you can forget it.'

Jack gaped at her. 'What are you on about?'

This was awful, but Kate was determined not to back down. 'You're watching my every move and I don't like it.'

Jack winced, but before he could say anything she went on: 'I'm not a child. I don't need minding. In case you don't realise it.'

He recoiled in horror. Evidently he hadn't anticipated a confrontation like this. 'I sit at the window to work, read the newspaper and stuff, just getting on with my normal day.'

'You're seriously invading my space with your nosiness.'

'I wasn't aware that I was snooping,' he said.

'You're a peeping Tom.'

'At that remark Jack lost his temper. He brandished his fist in the air, as if he was about to hit her. 'Don't flatter yourself! Who do you think you are? Jennifer Lopez?'

'And your bikers and their litter.' Kate felt great elation to hit back at him.

He stood drumming his fingers on the door. Then he said, 'Bollocks!' and laughed.

Kate tried to keep cool. She stared back at him, wanting to tell him to leave, but thinking of the rent money. 'Better move away from the window all the same if you don't want to be thrown out on your ear,' she said.

'Are you trying to stop me working? Without that window space the place is claustrophobic – I'm squashed to death.'

She folded her arms. 'You knew that when you took it.'

'I need all the space I can get,' he persisted.

'You don't need to prop up the window.'

'Fuck off,' he said, and slammed the door in her face.

Back in her living room, head throbbing, Kate closed her eyes. The best policy was to avoid him. She'd give it another week, and if that didn't work she'd ask him to leave.

The phone rang. It was Mary. 'How are you getting on with your lodger, what's-his-name?'

'I'm going to ask him to leave.'

'What? You can't do that. You need the money. You're depriving Emily, taking the food out of her mouth.'

'For Christ's sake, Mum, Emily's fine, and you were against him the other day.'

'Then I got to thinking, Where would she be without his rent to help? And don't swear at me.' Mary ranted on about how little hassle Kate was prepared to take to keep her home.

Kate bit her tongue. She loved her mother, and she needed her: she was crucial in her plan to keep Charlie at bay. Eventually she got away from her. Shakily, she went to get Emily from school. Jack would probably leave now that she'd forced the issue of his spying on her. Did she really care? No, she wasn't cut out to be a landlady and his leaving would relieve the tension.

That evening, just as Jack was crossing the road, slipping off to the pub, Lucinda called to see her.

'There he goes,' Kate said.

Lucinda leaned towards the window to get her first glimpse of him. 'He's tasty,' she said, with the wicked smile she reserved for men she fancied.

'Yes.' Kate surprised herself by admitting it.

'What does Barbara think of him?'

'You know Barbara. She fancies the pants off any good-looking male.'

'Oh!' Lucinda looked disappointed.

'Don't worry. She's happy with Maurice.'

'Why should it worry me?' Lucinda was standing at the window a mirror in her hand, piling on the mascara and lip-gloss. 'I just wonder if he's as good as he looks?' She turned to look at Kate meaningfully.

'How would I know? Why don't you go after him and find out for yourself.'

'Funny you should say that . . .' Lucinda's voice trailed away. After a pause she said, 'I'd like to see some of his photographs while he's out. Can I have a look?'

'There aren't many lying about, and I haven't got a spare key to his flat,' Kate lied.

'Is he quiet?' Lucinda asked.

'Moves around stealthy as a cat, you'd hardly know he was there.'

'What happens if he doesn't like it here? Photographers can be the fastest quitters in the world, you know.'

'That's up to him. For the present he's someone I have to put up with.'

'Don't be like that. You might get to like him.'

On her way home from work next day Kate went to the video shop, got out *Bridget Jones's Diary*, and was looking forward to a quiet night in. When she reached home she noticed that Jack's curtains were drawn.

The doorbell rang sharply just as Hugh Grant discovered Bridget's big knickers. Who could it be? She wasn't expecting anyone.

It rang again, persistent.

Kate heard Emily get out of bed and run downstairs.

'Is your mummy there?' Jack said, through the letterbox.

She ran down the hall. 'It's the basement man!' she said.

Kate could see his face outlined in the stained-glass of the door. She opened it a few inches. 'What can I do for you?'

Wearing an old fleece, stamping his feet, blowing into his hands, he asked if he could come in for a minute or was she going to let him freeze to death on the doorstep?

Kate didn't move.

'I'm going down to the pub. Like to come for a quick one?'

'I don't accept drinks from strange men.' Kate moved back to shut the door.

Jack put his hand on the frame to prevent her shutting it in his face.

'You're not allowed in,' Emily cried gleefully, from behind Kate's elbow.

He grinned. 'Emily can come too. It's early enough.' He made it sound as natural as a family outing.

'She's tired.'

'No, I'm not,' Emily contradicted her, staring at Jack. 'I'd like to come to the pub too.'

'We're not going,' Kate said crossly.

'Ah, please, Mum!'

'Now look what you've started,' she accused Jack.

Jack shifted uncomfortably from one foot to the other. 'I have a problem with this "peeping Tom" accusation. Couldn't we discuss it over a bite to eat? I haven't eaten all day.'

'There's nothing to discuss.'

'I think there is, and you look as if you could do with

a square meal,' he said, appraising her from top to toe, manoeuvring himself closer.

Cheek! 'I'm not exactly fading away.'

Emily stuck out her tongue at him.

'Emily! That's rude,' Kate admonished her.

'You could do with a little cheering up, then?'

'So I'm bad-tempered as well as anorexic?'

'I didn't say that. What I said was that we could discuss it. Get your mother over to babysit. Put on your lipstick and I'll pick you up at nine.'

Bully! But something about the way he flashed his turquoise blue eyes at her as he issued his instructions made her agree.

'OK.'

Emily clapped her hands. 'Can I watch *Bridget Jones* with Granny?'

'No!' Kate had given in on too many counts already. 'You can watch *Step Club Juniors* until Granny gets here.'

Emily scooted off to the living room, scattering toys on the way. Jack smiled at both of them and went back down to the basement, whistling.

Kate phoned Mary, who agreed on condition that she was home by half past eleven at the latest. Then she went to have a shower and put on her makeup. She had barely enough time to change into her jeans and her black top, before he was ringing the bell. She might have known he wouldn't take long. Let him wait. Emily would entertain him while she did her hair. She checked and rechecked her face in the mirror to make sure she was looking good, determined to show herself as a woman who could stand on her own two feet.

They went to the Indian restaurant on the corner.

'What'll it be?' Jack asked, handing her the menu.

'Hot prawn curry, please.'

'And what'll you have to drink?'

'White wine.'

The restaurant was busy. Some of her neighbours were among the locals sitting at the tables. Kate felt everyone's eyes on her as they called greetings to her, surprise on their faces as they waited to see how she was getting on with Jack. Why was she wasting her time sitting here being stared at? She'd squandered the best years of her life with Charlie, and she hadn't got any more time to squander. She was thirty-one, getting older by the minute.

Kate watched him give the order with confidence. Scrubbed up, wearing a turquoise shirt that perfectly matched his eyes, he was better-looking than ever. He had it and he knew it. Who would have thought he'd set such store by his clothes?

What was the story with him anyway? Who had broken his heart in America? There was no evidence of a woman friend at the moment, and he didn't look like a confirmed bachelor. The waiter came with the Chardonnay Jack had ordered, and poured it.

'Cheers!' Jack raised his glass, his eyes half closed as he looked at Kate, seeming pleased that he'd charmed her off her pedestal and persuaded her to come out with him.

'Cheers!' Kate raised her glass, sipped her wine.

'You like keeping me on tenterhooks, don't you?'

'What do you mean?'

'I knew you'd come out with me, and I knew you'd rent me the flat.'

'Oh, you did, did you?'

He nodded. 'So, I moved away from the window. Now, what's the score? Still think I'm in the wrong?'

Calmer now, Kate said, 'You probably didn't realise that you were watching me like a hawk.'

'I'm not the only one. You're worth looking at.' Jack's eyes were on her admiringly. 'And, by the way, you look very fetching in that top, probably even more so out of it.'

Her stomach tightened with embarrassment. He was too personal. She hardly knew him. She blushed. 'Excuse me?'

'I'm paying you a compliment.' Jack grinned. 'Anyone with half an eye in their head can see how attractive you are.'

He looked around the restaurant. Sure enough, a few men had their eyes on Kate.

She said abruptly, 'I'm a private person. I don't like being on display, and also I think that we should establish some ground rules so we know where we stand with each other.'

'I see.' Jack was giving her his full attention.

'People usually do when they share a house, don't they?'

'We're not exactly sharing, are we? Not that I'd have any objection.' He grinned again – wickedly.

'Jack! This is important.'

'I know – you want to instruct me on bin day and keeping the place clean, I suppose. I don't mind cleaning. I'm not big on tidying up. But I don't want to cause trouble by breaking any more rules.' His eyes twinkled as he said, 'So, what about having people stop over? Have you any objection to that?'

'Your flat's not big enough for visitors.' Then the full implication of his question hit her. 'Like a girlfriend?' Her voice was steely.

'No one in particular.'

Kate was taken aback. She couldn't believe it. He'd only just broken up with someone, according to Barbara. 'You're not intending to bring a string of women to the flat, are you?'

'No, of course not. The difficulty is if you want me to let you know in advance . . .' He raised his eyebrows. 'That could be a bit awkward . . . especially if I don't know myself. As I said, I don't want to break any rules.'

Kate wasn't sure if he was teasing her. She wasn't enjoying this line of conversation. God! How had she got herself into this mess? she wondered, raking her hair back.

'I'd keep them out of your way, of course. Kate, stop looking at me as if I'm some kind of pervert. I'm one hundred per cent heterosexual, if that's what's worrying you. Hand on my heart.'

'I believe you.' She supposed she should be grateful for something.

Jack straightened. 'Is there anything else?'

'No, it's just that I lead a quiet life, and I want to keep it that way,' she said.

He eyed her. 'You've really gone into yourself, haven't you?'

'No, I'm . . .' she was going to say 'upset', but changed it to '. . . adjusting to not being part of a marriage any more.'

'Since your husband left?'

She fiddled with her glass. 'Yes, but we won't go into that. Barbara must have told you what happened.' Not that it was any of his business.

'I didn't listen. I prefer not to clutter my mind with Barbara's trivia.'

Kate gave him a look to see if he was serious.

'It's not trivial.'

'I didn't mean it like that.' Jack poured more wine. 'It must be hard for you on your own with Emily.' He sounded sympathetic.

'I have my family,' Kate said, determined not to let him pity her. 'My mother is very supportive. I'm lucky to have her. Mind you, she's also very dramatic, so I try not to share too much with her.'

'Do you have brothers and sisters?'

'I have a sister, Lucinda. She's a successful model, travels a lot. She's a good pal too, but she gets on with her life, and good luck to her.'

'I've seen her.'

'She's just back from a shoot in Tunisia.'

'The way I see it is this,' Jack said. 'We're both mature adults and, although far removed from each other in disposition and personality, there's no reason why we shouldn't get on. I mean, there are some pluses in having a man about the place, aren't there?'

'I'll try to think of one.' It was Kate's turn to tease.

Their meal arrived. They ate with enthusiasm, both hungry. The curry was just the way Kate liked it. She took a gulp of wine to cool her throat, then checked the bottle. Better slow down. It wouldn't do to get half-cut. She felt awkward. It was like being on a date that she couldn't handle. She was finding it difficult to think what to say next and the restaurant was stuffy.

She looked at Jack. He was having no such problems, eating with gusto, enjoying himself. Or seemed to be. As far as he was concerned, she thought, the evening was going well and there was no reason why that shouldn't continue.

'Delicious,' Jack said, looking up from his plate.

Kate cleared her throat. 'Yes,' she agreed.

They exchanged a glance.

What did it matter if he wasn't her type? She probably wouldn't see much of him, now that she'd cautioned him to keep his distance, Anyway, he'd probably move out as soon as he found somewhere more suitable, which wouldn't take too long.

As soon as they'd finished the meal Kate looked at her watch. 'I'd better get back. Mum will be wanting to get home.'

At the house, Jack said, 'Coming in for a coffee?'

'No, thanks. I'd better go on up.'

'I have vodka, beer?'

She shook her head. 'I've got to let Mum go. Thanks for the meal. I enjoyed it.' Suddenly she realised that she had actually enjoyed the entire evening.

She was going up the steps when he said, 'We'll do it again some time.'

'Yeah, why not? That would be nice.'

'Meanwhile I'll try to keep out of your way.' He was teasing her again.

'I'd appreciate that.'

She walked into the hall. 'Did you enjoy yourself?' Mary asked, her coat on.

'Yes, it was a nice meal.'

'You'd want to watch out for him,' her mother said, looking down over the railings. 'He's good-looking. He's trying to get on the right side of you.'

'Mum! You were spying on me.' Kate laughed.

'Only while I was waiting to go.'

Kate went to her lonely bed. There she lay, lost, wondering what would happen to her and Emily if she were to stay on her own. She could always move to a smaller, more manageable house. She'd probably have to sooner or later anyway. But where would she find a house she loved as much as this one? This was the house of their dreams, near the shops, close to Emily's school and beside the sea. Kate wouldn't give it up easily, not if she could find a way to hold on to it.

Jack was part of the solution. Jack! There was something about him that made her uneasy . . . His self-assurance, arrogance, perhaps that's what it was, and the fact that he wasn't her type. She doubted she knew what her type was any more, and imagined that if she did eventually go looking for a man she'd want someone she could rely on not to do the dirty on her. She knew she had faults and failings, she could be a real pain in the ass sometimes, but surely someone out there would appreciate what she had to give. Someone who'd feel concern for her, take her into consideration. As she fell asleep Kate thought that such a man probably didn't exist.

12

When she returned from work the next day Colette's car was in the driveway, but there was no sign of her anywhere. Puzzled, Kate put her key into the lock just as Colette came up the basement steps, Jack following her.

'Hello,' Kate said, in surprise.

'There you are.' She beamed and kissed Kate's cheek. 'Your lovely lodger has been entertaining me. I've seen some of his marvellous photographs. Thank you so much, Jack.'

'You're welcome. You'll be all right now that Kate's back,' Jack said, with a smile.

'Yes, thank you, nice to meet you, Jack.'

With a wave at Kate he disappeared back down the steps.

'Such a nice man,' Colette said. 'Strange to think of him as your lodger.'

'Yes, isn't it?'

Colette was looking pale, and thinner than when Kate had last seen her at the party. There were shadows under her eyes as if she hadn't slept. As Kate led her into the kitchen, she asked if Kate had been all right since they'd last spoken on the phone.

'It's been a nightmare,' Kate admitted, sitting down.

'I can imagine,' Colette agreed.

'But I'm bearing up,' Kate assured her, as her sister-in-law peered closely at her. 'Would you like coffee, or something stronger?'

'Coffee would be fine.'

'Have you seen Charlie?' Kate asked.

'Yes, we had a row over his behaviour. I was so upset, and when we didn't hear from you this last while I thought I'd better come and see you.'

'You knew he was seeing Daniella before I found out, didn't you?' Kate sounded antagonistic but needed to know the score from Colette's point of view.

'Yes,' Colette said sheepishly.

'Why didn't you tell me?'

The look Colette gave her was a distinctly guilty one. 'I didn't know what to do. I didn't want to upset you. I thought it would blow over.'

'Why did you invite her to your party in the first place? It was such a stupid thing to do, knowing what she was like.' It took a lot for her to say that, but it appeared that hearing it took more out of Colette.

She looked as if she'd been hit as she said, 'I know Daniella likes a challenge, and she can be crafty, but I didn't realise she had such a mean streak in her. It never dawned on me that she would cause all this fuss.'

'Fuss? You call the end of my marriage a fuss?' Kate looked at her.

'I didn't mean it like that. Kate, if I had thought for one minute that this would happen—' Colette stopped. 'Look, I wouldn't have wanted you to get hurt for the world.' She made a face that said she was fed up with having to take the blame for it all, and no matter what she said it would be the wrong thing.

Kate didn't mean to be hurtful to Colette either – they'd

always got on well – but this business had put them in a difficult position. It was a no-win situation for both of them.

'Kate, I'm sorry this happened, especially in my home,' Colette said. 'It never occurred to me that Charlie would do a thing like that virtually in front of us all. What he was thinking of I'll never know.'

'Neither will I,' Kate said.

'As far as I was concerned, you and Charlie were happily married. If I'd thought that there was any likelihood of him and Daniella – well . . . you know that, of course, I wouldn't have invited her.'

'I know that. I'm sorry, I shouldn't blame you.'

Colette sighed. 'That's the problem with me, always seeing the good side in everyone. I'll never learn.'

'There's not much good in Daniella,' Kate said.

'What did she think she was doing?' Colette said. 'She's too forward for her own good.'

'I suppose he never really got over her,' Kate mumbled.

'Nonsense! He had too much to drink. That's the only thing I can think of. It seems that he'd been going through a bad patch at work, and she was . . .' she hesitated '. . . consoling him.'

'Did he tell you that?'

'Yes.' Colette's eyes shifted. 'I think he felt he was stuck in a rut, trapped in his job. He was hoping to get out and do something different. The bank is a dead-end job. Not that I'm making excuses for what he did but he'd been unhappy for a long time.'

'Yes, but it's a job, isn't it? One that affords us a good life-style.'

'Yes, but think about it, Kate – same routine, day in day

out. He could do it with his eyes closed. He wanted a bit of a change.'

'Well, he got that, didn't he?' Kate said sarcastically.

'It's landed him in all sorts of trouble too, even at work.'

'And where does it leave me? He was my whole life. I gave up everything just to be his wife. I ran circles round him trying to please him, always looking after him, at his beck and call.'

'I know you did.'

'I think he got bored with me. Well, if he thinks I'm going to beg him to come back he can think again. I'm going to prove to him that I can manage without him.'

'Of course you can,' Colette said, humouring her. 'You've proved that with your gorgeous lodger downstairs. Another man about the place won't suit Charlie at all. He'll be so jealous because you're a very attractive woman, Kate, and that's the way to have him. Shock tactics, it's the only thing.'

'I don't know. I never wanted this,' Kate said, overwrought. 'I'll have to get a full-time job. I won't be able to manage otherwise.'

'What about Emily? Who'll look after her?'

'Barbara takes her to ballet and swimming with Hannah two afternoons a week, and Mum will always help out. She loves taking care of Emily.'

'Well, make sure you don't overdo things,' Colette persisted.

'I'd prefer to be at work. I hate hanging around here on my own,' Kate said.

'Frank and I could help you out financially if you're really stuck.'

Kate blushed.

'For the time being', Colette added. 'It's the least we can do.'

'No, thanks,' Kate said. 'I want to prove to Charlie that I can make it without him. I'll get a real kick out of that.'

'As long as Emily doesn't suffer any more than she is already.'

'She'll be OK.'

'I sincerely hope so. You ring me if there's anything I can do to help. Meantime, will you and Emily come down for the weekend? Rose is dying to see you both.'

'That would be lovely.' But Kate bit her lip, dreading the thought of visiting Bramble Hill with the memory of Daniella and Charlie together there still fresh in her mind.

13

Several days after Christmas Kate was clearing up after supper when the doorbell rang.

Jack stood there with his camera case slung over his shoulder and his tripod under his arm. 'Hello!' she said, and let him step inside. 'I didn't expect to see you.'

'Hi! I wonder if I could photograph the sunset through the trees from the back garden? It's perfect just now. Brilliant for my present project.'

'Which is?' she asked, straight out.

'A commission on Irish landscapes for *National Geographic*.'

She was about to say no, it wasn't convenient, when a sudden impulse overtook her. 'Why not?'

'Thanks. It won't take long,' he said.

In the back garden they stood together observing the play of light on the few remaining leaves, then he made his way off down the garden to where the trees hemmed in the park and cast deep shadows on the grass. Oscar followed him, picking his way gingerly through the thick grass, his tail floating.

As Jack was heading back down to the basement Kate intercepted him. 'Come in and say hello to Emily,' Kate said.

'I'll just dump these downstairs first, if that's OK.'

Minutes later he returned to the warm, cheerful house

where the smell of cooking was all-pervasive. Emily was sprawled on the living-room couch watching television. 'Hello, Emily,' he said, and sat down next to her.

'Hi,' she said, acknowledging his presence, but her eyes never left the screen.

'Would you like to stay and have some dinner with us?' Kate asked him.

'I'd love to,' he said.

'Turn off the telly, love,' she said to Emily. 'Dinner's ready.'

Jack got to his feet and followed her into the kitchen.

Kate laid the table, putting out knives and forks, and the napkins that were kept for visitors.

'Smells good,' Jack said, going to the sink to wash his hands.

Kate removed the casserole from the oven, set it on the table as he sat down, and put a bowl of green salad beside it. Emily hung back watching Jack as he lifted the lid, letting out the delicious aroma of chicken.

'Emily, come and sit down,' Kate said.

Emily was reluctant to take her place, suddenly shy with Jack's presence at the dinner table. To fill the awkward space Kate quizzed him about his landscape photography.

'It's a personal thing since childhood. My grandfather lived in Donegal. He was a wildlife photographer for the *National Geographic*. He took me on several of his assignments throughout the changing seasons – autumn's my favourite. Of course, I love photographing snow, especially in sunshine. Having said that, I'll photograph anything.

'I bet you like the snow too,' he said to Emily, now seated at the table, her elbows on it as she studied him.

'Yes,' she said.

'Making snowmen, sliding down the hill on your toboggan.'

'I don't have a toboggan.' Emily bit into a chip slowly, not saying another word slopping her milk on the table.

Jack told her to call him Jack, in an attempt to win her confidence, but she was having none of it. She barely nodded, and pushed food into her mouth so she wouldn't have to answer him. Did she have to behave like a baby? Kate wondered. She tried to compensate for the lack of conversation by offering Jack some more chicken, which he accepted with alacrity.

It was taking Emily ages to eat her dinner.

'Emily, aren't you hungry?' Kate asked.

'No.'

'Are you going to help me clear up?' Kate enquired, when they'd all finished.

Emily didn't answer.

'Of course,' Jack said, and neatly piled up the dirty dishes.

Kate stacked the dishwasher, and he moved back to the table, but Kate could feel him keeping an eye on her as she made the coffee.

'Do you get fed up being by yourself all the time?' he asked her, as soon as Emily had disappeared back to the television.

'I have plenty to do,' she said. 'And what are your hobbies?'

'I love jazz. There's a jazz club I hang out in . . .'

Emily was back, tweaking Kate's skirt. 'I don't want him here,' she whispered.

'Ssh.' Kate tried to appear indifferent.

'I want him to go,' Emily said, with renewed strength.

'Now, Emily, be kind,' Kate said, worried about Jack's discomfort, and Emily's attitude.

'I don't like him,' she said, in a confidential whisper, then returned to the television.

Jack stood up. 'I'd better leave you two in peace.'

'That's a joke,' Kate said.

'Thanks for the meal. It was delicious,' he said politely.

'You're welcome,' Kate said, awkwardly.

He was gone, swinging away in that long stride of his, taking the basement steps two at a time.

'That was very rude, Emily,' Kate said, as soon as they were alone again.

'But I don't like him,' Emily insisted.

'You don't know him yet. You'll get to like him – he's a nice man,' Kate argued, thinking that it was good for Emily to get to know people.

'He's not my daddy. Send him away.'

'I certainly will not.' Then, more patiently, Kate said, 'I'm not trying to replace your daddy with Jack, Emily.'

'I hate him,' Emily burst out, and raised the television volume louder.

'Go to bed at once.'

The child ran from the room in torrents of tears.

Kate shuddered. Her worst fears had been realised. Everything was happening too fast for Emily to take in. First Charlie going off suddenly, then this stranger appearing from nowhere. It wasn't fair to confuse and upset her like that. Maybe she should get rid of Jack, take in a student from UCD instead. A nice girl Emily would like who could babysit to give Kate an occasional break.

After a few minutes Emily came back downstairs and went to her mother. Kate lifted her in her arms and took her to the couch. She sank her head onto Kate's shoulder and began to suck her thumb. 'When will Daddy come back, Mum?' she asked, in a sad little voice.

'Soon,' Kate said. It would be dreadful deprivation for the child to be left without her father because of her parents' selfishness.

'When?' Emily persisted.

'I'll ask him as soon as he phones,' Kate promised. 'Would you like some jelly and ice-cream?'

'OK.' Emily went to the table and sat swinging her legs, waiting.

She ate her jelly and ice-cream quickly, then went to bed. Kate settled down to watch television, but her mind was on how she could solve her problems with Charlie. She could phone him and shout at him for what he'd done to them, but what good would that do? He'd only shout back. He'd become difficult, and secretive, doing exactly what he wanted to do, entertaining no arguments about it. As long as she continued to refuse to have him back he would continue to be difficult to deal with.

The phone rang, making her jump.

'Any word?' Mary asked, no need for her to refer to Charlie by name.

'No, he's still away.'

'I worry about you and Emily alone. Have you got the central heating on? It's so cold.'

'Yes, we're fine, Mum.'

'I'm sure he'll soon be back, and you'll have a good talk,' Mary said consolingly. 'Meantime, get yourself a nice cup of hot chocolate, soothes the nerves and it'll help you sleep.'

'Yes,' Kate said pleasantly, to avoid an argument about the dietary drawbacks of chocolate late at night.

As soon as she put the receiver down, the phone rang again. It was Charlie this time.

'Nice of you to call,' Kate said sarcastically.

'I'm phoning now, aren't I? I was up to my eyes.'

There was an ominous silence while Kate tried to keep calm as her anger rose. She wanted to shout, 'Fuck off,' into the mouthpiece but for Emily's sake she kept quiet.

'Is that Daddy?' Emily was coming downstairs.

'Yes.'

Emily held out her hand for the receiver. 'Daddy, when are you coming home?' she asked. Then, after a pause, she said, 'Come for dinner tomorrow, Daddy. Jack did and I didn't want him here.' She turned to Kate. 'Daddy's coming for dinner,' she said, with a big smile.

'Is that OK with you?' Charlie asked, as soon as Emily let Kate speak to him again.

Kate took a deep breath. 'Yes, you can come.' She wanted to say, 'You're not staying,' but decided to be civil for Emily's sake. 'I've got to get Emily off to bed. See you tomorrow night.' She put the phone down.

'I'm going to look pretty,' Emily said, and insisted on choosing the clothes she would wear before she agreed to get back into bed.

14

Next morning Emily was up and dressed and in the kitchen first, chattering about the evening ahead as she ate her cereal. After school she decided to make a pastry man for Charlie with the left over pastry from an apple tart Kate was making for dessert. First she cut him out, then she put currant eyes in him, and currant buttons down his front, busily patting him into shape, thoroughly occupied with what she was doing. Kate enjoyed her company in the kitchen, as Emily concentrated on her task and bits of pastry were strewn across the table.

'Daddy'll love this,' Kate said, placing the pastry man in the oven to bake. She glanced at the clock.

Emily's eyes followed hers. 'He'll be here soon, Mum,' she said, and put her arms round Kate.

'We'd better tidy ourselves up.'

'Good,' Emily said. 'Can I wear my new pink cropped top Granny bought me?'

'No.'

'Mum, *pleeeease*!'

Kate was adamant. 'Granny shouldn't have bought it. You're too young for it.'

'Can I wear it for my birthday, then?'

'We'll see.'

*   *   *

In her bedroom Kate looked into the mirror. Her hair, which had grown luxuriantly in the past, was limp and lifeless, her face was pale, her cheeks hollow, and there was tension around her eyes that hadn't been there before. She showered, then blow-dried her hair gazing out of her bedroom window at the view she loved so much: the sea, inky blue and calm, the lights of the promenade reflected in it. She'd have to bring up the subject of money, and this would cause a row. To give herself courage she put on lots of makeup.

Downstairs she helped herself to a stiff vodka and tonic, anxious about the evening ahead. She heard the sound of tyres, the slam of the car door, and Emily charged off to greet her father.

Charlie was on the dot. 'Hello, sweetheart,' Kate heard him say to Emily, his voice buoyant.

Emily was full of excitement, hugging him, hopping around, fidgeting with his tie.

'Hello, Kate.' His voice was more subdued as he peered at her.

'Hello, Charlie.'

'How are you?'

'Fine,' Kate said stiffly.

'Daddy, you never said goodbye to me when you left,' Emily interrupted.

Charlie looked confused.

'You were asleep, love,' Kate reminded her gently.

'That's right. And I had to leave in a hurry,' he said, staring accusingly at Kate.

He lifted Emily up and balanced her on his shoulders as he took her into the living room, where she wriggled all over him as soon as he sprawled himself on the couch. Kate glimpsed her contentment, then scanned Charlie's face to try to gauge how he was. As far as she could see he was much the same. His hair was cut shorter, its red-gold sheen gone. Soon it would begin to turn grey. His eyes were puffy, probably tired from travelling. He was certainly thinner – his beer belly gone.

When Emily had finally calmed down they returned to the kitchen. 'How have you been?' he asked. The question was posed pleasantly, but he moved about restlessly.

'OK,' Kate lied. She moved back and forth busily, trying to fake an air of complacency.

'I'm impressed that you've managed so well.'

'Not that well, Charlie. I'm not in the mood for flattery.'

'We'll talk later.'

'Dinner should be ready any minute,' Kate said. Self-consciously she bustled about checking the oven needlessly, shifting plates, her heart hammering.

Kate served from the counter while Charlie got Emily to sit down in her place. Twitchy and dishevelled, he seemed preoccupied as he uncorked the wine he'd brought and put it on the table, then fetched the glasses, his contribution to the meal.

Kate sat opposite him, dreading having to get through the meal with him. In the silence while they ate she wondered what to talk to him about. She used to ask him about work and his friends.

'How's work?'

'Same as usual,' he said, giving her no encouragement to ask more.

He didn't say where he was staying, and she certainly wasn't going to ask. Emily was the only subject they could address without risking a row.

'Emily's getting on well at school.'

'You always fit in well at school, don't you?' he said.

Emily nodded, hunched over her meal, taking tiny

mouthfuls to make it last. 'I'm going to be a photographer like Jack,' she said, trying hard to keep things going, diverting him with her own brand of entertainment so that he wouldn't feel like a visitor.

Charlie frowned. 'Who is this Jack you keep on about?'

'The man who lives in the basement,' Emily explained.

'What?'

'He's the new lodger,' Kate said.

'Lodger?' Charlie looked puzzled.

'I've let the basement,' Kate said, with authority.

'You did what?' Charlie exploded.

'I had to do something.'

Charlie's anger boiled over. 'But all my stuff's there.'

'I moved it into the shed. You can have it any time that's convenient for you.'

Emily, lips pursed, watched them, a silent referee.

'We'll talk about it later,' Kate said, taking a sip of wine in an effort to hold her tongue. To say much more about Jack now might arouse Charlie's temper and wreck the fragile peace between them.

Emily sat there, smiling at them.

Kate knew that Charlie loved his child, and wouldn't want a row in front of her, so they had to rely on Emily's chatter to get them through the rest of the meal. Finally, Emily left the table and began drawing, by which time the wine had eased their awkwardness.

Looking directly across the table at Kate, Charlie said, 'You're not eating much.'

'I'm not hungry.'

'Are you lonely?'

She looked up, surprised. 'No,' she lied.

'You've got the lodger, of course. I suppose he's company for you,' was his barbed comment.

'I don't see much of him.'

'Nice man, is he?'

'No,' Emily called.

Kate's stomach clenched. She bit her lip to stop herself chastising Emily – couldn't chastise her, anyway, for saying what she felt. She wasn't going to make excuses for Jack either. Why should she? There was nothing to hide.

'What's the score with you and him?'

'No score. He's a friend of Barbara,' she said, defensive and embarrassed all at once, and furious with herself for rising to it.

There was no need for this: it wasn't as if she was involved with Jack. How corny would that be?

'Photographer?'

'Yes.'

'Hardly your type, I would have thought.'

'He's trustworthy,' she said.

'Can't see what he could offer a woman like you.' Charlie was trying to catch her out, she knew.

'Rent, which helps with the mortgage so I don't have to rely on you.' She took pleasure in that remark.

'I hope you're happy with the arrangement,' he sneered.

She kept her eyes down, cross with him for pursuing this line within Emily's earshot. Her hands tightened on her knife and fork as she tried to think of something benign to say.

'How's Lucinda?' he asked.

He was desperate to turn the conversation in a non-controversial direction, Kate thought. 'She's fine, drops in often,' she said. Her sister was much more dependable than he had turned out to be.

'How's your mother?'

'Not too pleased with you.'

'I can guess.'

'I made dessert,' she said, changing the subject.

'What kind?'

'Apple tart.'

'I shouldn't,' he said.

Starving to look good for his fancy woman. Daniella came back into Kate's mind, not that she'd been far from it. He was cutting calories, probably going to a gym too. She could have done without a reminder of Daniella. Cross, she called to Emily to get her gingerbread man.

'I made him specially for you,' Emily said proudly, as she put it in front of him.

Charlie bit off its head. 'Nice,' he said, and gave some to his daughter.

'OK,' Kate said.

Charlie took the plates to the counter, then wandered into the living room while Kate made coffee. He sat down, picked up a cushion and tossed it to one side. Emily picked it up, hugged it to her.

As soon as he had finished his coffee Charlie looked at his watch. 'Do you mind if I skip off now?' he asked.

'No.' Kate rose.

'Daddy, don't go,' Emily whined. 'You can stay here.'

'I can't, honey. Your mummy won't let me,' he said, kissing the top of her head and hugging her.

She didn't want to be hugged, didn't want him to leave. 'Will I see you again soon?'

'Before you know it,' he said, and gave her a piggyback up the stairs to bed.

Coming back to the living room he sat down and took a long gulp of wine, looking around at the rack of CDs, the books, the heap of toys in the corner. He picked a CD, snapped it into the machine, and sat for a while tapping his fingers to the music.

'What are we going to do?' he asked.

Kate felt a wave of sadness. 'I don't know.'

'You're a master at dodging the issue.'

'I'm not dodging anything. Do you expect me to ignore what happened?'

'Basically, yes.'

'How can I when what you did made me so unhappy?'

'You think I'm happy?'

'Tough if you're not. It's your own fault. Do you think we can lapse back into our former lives?' she asked, holding his gaze.

'No.' Charlie's eyes were evasive, but his jaw was set. Then he said, his voice heavy with guilt and despair, 'I hate living like this, Kate, staying in hotels, rows, missing you and Emily. I want to be with you. Emily needs me – you can see that for yourself.'

All his hopes were pinned on this. It left Kate balancing on a tightrope between a new start for Emily's sake and her own desires. 'I know she does,' she said finally.

'What's the problem, then?'

'I'm afraid something terrible will happen again, that you'll fail me just when I begin to trust you, and it would be worse a second time.' Her voice was taut.

Unable to look her in the eye, he glanced at the floor, self-conscious. 'You're making excuses, assuming, generalising,' he said.

'You can't offer me the security we had or anything much at all, in fact.'

Charlie laughed cynically. 'Not a very enticing prospect, then, am I?' he said, self-deprecatingly.

'No.'

He stood up, bumped against the armchair. 'If that's the way you feel I'd better go, but I warn you, Kate, you're doing more damage this way.'

Kate could feel his warm wine-smelling breath on her face as he struggled to control his temper.

'I don't want to become a shadowy figure, at the periphery of Emily's world, and that's what'll happen if you continue to refuse to have me back.' He was slurring his words.

'It won't. I'll make sure of that.'

He caught her by the shoulders, shoved her against the wall. 'When will you start trusting me again?' There was a catch in his voice.

'Charlie, you're hurting me.' She slid away from his grasp, rubbing her arms.

'When?' he insisted.

'Give me time.'

'That's all you ever say, "Give me time." How long do you want?'

'As long as it takes.'

'As long as you leave me out in the cold you won't get a penny from me. I'm not paying the mortgage if I have to pay hotel bills as well.'

'Get out.'

'I'm going,' he said, exasperated, making for the door.

'I'll call you a taxi.'

'I'm perfectly capable of driving.'

'You're over the limit – you don't want to lose your licence.' Kate went to the phone.

Charlie snatched it out of her hand. 'I'll do it.'

While they waited for the taxi to arrive Kate returned to the kitchen to tidy up, her head swimming. The house was quiet with only the creak of Charlie's footsteps as he paced up and down, and his heavy, impatient breathing. Kate hoped the taxi would arrive quickly: she was not sure how long he'd last before he exploded.

As soon as he heard it he loped to the front door. She followed him. 'I hope it goes well with your lodger,' he shouted, and was gone into the pitch-black night, slamming the door behind him, all hopes of a new beginning vanishing with him.

A gust of cold wind swept through the house.

He wasn't really interested in what the lodger meant to Kate. He was furious with her for having the audacity to keep him out of his own home, for leaving him to flounder in the big, wide world. Charlie had a knack for self-forgiveness. He didn't feel the need for prolonged guilt. Kate's blood pounded in her ears.

Emily was awake when Kate looked in on her. 'Has Daddy gone?' she asked.

'Yes, love.'

'I love Daddy,' was Emily's simple reply. 'Do you love him, Mum?' she asked, suddenly looking into Kate's eyes, her own vivid with candid enquiry.

The question took Kate by surprise. 'Yes, of course I do, sweetheart.'

'Not as much as you did before.' Emily looked at her mother sideways, her eyes challenging, evidently knowing that there was something much deeper and more painful to it than that.

Kate's heart fell with a thud into her stomach. She felt the walls close in on her, squeezing the breath out of her. She grabbed the bedhead to steady herself as she faced her daughter. The light had gone out of Emily's eyes. Kate bent down and pressed the anxious face to her.

This was serious. The child was in a state of acute

sorrow: Charlie's departure had left her in a whirl of mixed-up images and confusion. His continued absence had unhinged her. He was an incalculable loss. Kate could see now that both of them had neglected their child with their selfishness, and now Emily badly needed reassurance. She would have given anything, at that moment, to be able to soothe away Emily's fears so that she could survive this. But she didn't want to resort to lies. If she said, 'Don't worry, Daddy will be home in a day or two, everything will be fine,' with no evidence to support this claim, she might do the child more harm than good because it might be very different from the truth.

Kate had no idea what the truth might be, but leaving her child suspended in ignorance, with incomplete answers and no comprehension of what was going on, seemed cruel. 'I'll talk to Daddy,' she said, stumbling over the words, stroking Emily's auburn hair, trying to allay her fears. 'See what's to be done.'

'Then what will happen?' Emily asked distrustfully, her jaw jutting as she tried to puzzle things out for herself.

'We'll sort something out,' Kate said brightly, knowing that there was no guarantee of anything. She was ashamed of her inadequate answer, but she had to try to regulate Emily's world, not make things worse by projecting her own fears on to the child.

Emily bit hard on her lower lip to staunch the tears that were filling her eyes. 'I'll be very good,' she said.

'Oh, sweetheart, this isn't your fault.' Kate held her tightly. None of this had anything to do with the beautiful child who thought that being good and obedient would repair the damage between her parents. Kate knew that she would look back on this exchange many times during her life, and remember her daughter's challenging eyes.

Should she let Charlie come home? If she gave in, he'd have to sleep in the spare room because she wasn't ready to share their marriage bed again. There had been a time when she couldn't sleep without him, couldn't get comfortable until he was snugly tucked in beside her. Now the very thought of him lying next to her made her feel sick. Her loathing of what he'd done ran deep.

What would be the point of having him back under those conditions? Yet, if she kept refusing what would the next step be? Deep down she felt that their journey together through life was coming to a conclusion.

With a sickening sense of failure she went to bed, visualising herself as the single mother to an only child for the rest of her life – attending parent meetings, school plays on her own. What would Charlie do? Move into an apartment? Perhaps he'd go off to live happily ever after with Daniella – although he'd strenuously denied any chance of that happening and blamed Kate for prolonging the sorry mess. As she tried to sleep she was unable to erase from her mind the look in Emily's eyes when Charlie left. No one gets through a situation like this unaffected. Resentment welled up in Kate. She was furious with Charlie for his betrayal, tired of trying to withhold her feelings for Emily's sake, and his unfairness in blaming her for keeping him away filled her with rage. All she hoped was that Emily wouldn't be too badly affected.

15

The next morning, at eleven o'clock, Jack strolled into the Shamrock Hotel.

'Hello,' Kate said, surprised to see him. 'Not working today?'

'No.' Jack smiled. 'Thought I'd give myself a bit of time off.'

'Such idleness,' she teased.

'Now that I'm here I might as well have a drink in comfort. Will you join me?'

Kate looked at her watch. 'It's my break. I'll have a cup of coffee with you.'

'Hello,' Helen Horton said, arriving on the scene.

'This is Jack, my new lodger.' Kate introduced them.

'I see!' Helen pursed her lips as if she were scandalised, but took his hand.

'We're going to the bar.'

'Would you like to join us?' Jack asked Helen.

'No, thanks, I'm on duty,' she said, tapping her red nails while she observed him.

'I'll be back in ten minutes,' Kate told her, then led Jack to the bar.

'What'll it be?' Tim asked.

'A coffee and a pint of Guinness for Jack here, Tim.'

'Right.' Tim turned away while he filled the glass.

Jack said, 'Cheers!' and took a gulp. 'That's good.' He

relaxed in the warmth, quite at home in his surroundings, not appearing to notice Kate's curiosity.

'So, what did you really come here for?' she asked.

'To see if you were all right?'

'I'm fine. Why shouldn't I be?'

'You had company last night.'

'Charlie. Did we disturb you?'

'Not at all. I heard raised voices, saw the car. I was anxious about you, that's all.'

'There's no need. I'm OK.'

'Good.' Jack finished his drink, slipped his change into his pocket and, with a quick goodbye, sauntered casually out of the hotel. He quickened his pace and the park enclosed him. Kate, watching his retreating figure, wondered what he thought of it all.

When she returned home Jack's jeep was gone. She made herself a cup of tea, picked up the newspaper and scanned it, then went straight to 'Situations Vacant' and studied the columns. She could find only one job she was interested in: catering manager for an executive boardroom, but she wasn't qualified for it. She'd lost her way, didn't know which turning to take, and it was all Charlie's fault. The doorbell rang.

'How ya,' Pete, the postman, said. 'This is for your man downstairs. Wouldn't fit in his letterbox. Will you give it to him?' He looked at her apologetically as he handed her a large brown envelope.

'I'll make sure he gets it,' Kate said.

She heard Jack returning and decided to take his post down to him. He was putting his key into the lock, lifting up the rest of his mail as he went in, when Kate appeared at his door.

'Hello,' he said, smiling, welcoming her like a long-lost friend. 'Come in.'

Kate followed him inside.

'Junk most of it,' he said, putting the letters down on his cluttered desk.

'Sorry to intrude,' she began.

'No intrusion.'

'The postman gave me this for you.'

'Thanks.' He took the envelope, examined it and threw it on to the desk.

Kate held her breath.

'I was out all day yesterday so the place is a tip – you'll have to excuse it. I don't notice it unless someone calls. I'm quite detached from it,' he said, frankly.

'That's OK.' Why was she nervous? In her own house, for God's sake. 'You've fixed it up nicely.' She glanced around.

'Thanks.' He had prints pinned to a huge noticeboard on one wall. There were books on shelves, stacked in corners, on the table, everywhere but in an ordered way. A Turkish rug was in the centre of the floor, a table with a lamp making it quite cosy.

'Would you like a cup of coffee? Decaff.' Jack indicated the couch, removing newspapers from it as he did so.

His cosy domesticity put her at ease. 'That would be lovely, thanks.'

While Jack made the coffee Kate looked at the photographs on every available wall space, announcing his talent and his durability. There were world political figures, Bill Clinton with Ariel Sharon, Tony Blair shaking hands with Bertie Ahern. Further along the wall Oriental women looked out with soulful eyes, protective of their children as they held out their bowls waiting to be fed, many with a beaten look on their faces. There were also photographs of women showing the full gamut of emotional expression – anger, hatred, harmony, desire. Some photographs were of men, their faces twisted in pain, or grimacing in anger, eyes strained, mouths grim. Kate looked intently at them all.

'That was a recent assignment,' Jack said, his eyes following hers. 'I found the subjects on my travels. They were too interesting to turn down. Get them before their emotions are completely obliterated, was what I thought. Women in the developing world willing to let people see their struggle with family, children, money, a lot of them upset by their partner's drinking or abandonment. The lack of jobs gives their menfolk a lack of responsibility.' Jack was fired up.

'You can see the women's resentment and disappointment. There are no false images here,' Kate said, impressed. 'You don't mind the hardship in these places?'

Jack shook his head. 'On the contrary, I quite like it. It's often hard to find what I really want to photograph in affluent societies,' he said. 'I also take photographs of interesting Irish people too. These Dublin women, for instance.' There were worn-out inner-city women, alongside itinerants with gold hoop earrings, and rich women, students, executives and factory workers. 'And if nobody wants to buy the photographs, tough!' Jack added. 'Though usually they do.'

She noticed that the fine lines around his eyes deepened when he smiled.

A half-finished sketch of a woman with a beautiful face, her eyes covered with a hand, lay on the desk. It had been painstakingly done, like a drawing in some art book. There was another complicated portrait of the same woman, semi-nude this time, her hand touching her flowing hair, her anatomy in perfect detail from her ribs to her thigh-bone, the rest covered in fig leaves.

Kate wondered who the model was, but didn't ask. Similar sketches were scattered around, making the place look like a small studio.

'My etchings.' Jack grinned self-consciously.

'Excellent!' Kate said. 'I didn't know you were an artist too.'

'It's just a hobby. I enjoy drawing.' He handed her a mug of coffee, stood over her, and rested his hand on the back of the couch.

Kate looked up at him, and could see that he, too, felt the awkwardness of not knowing someone well. He was looking at his own work with that critical, not-sure-of-himself expression.

'You're interested in women,' she said. It was an obvious statement.

Jack grinned. 'Aren't all men?'

Kate laughed. 'Stupid thing to say.'

'I would like to be really good at art. You like art?'

'Yes, not that I know much about it.' Kate felt edgy, not knowing what to say next.

'And how have you been keeping?' he asked.

'Well, thank you. By the way, I must apologise for Emily's unfriendliness. She's not normally like that – she was tired.'

'I understand. She's protective of her dad, missing him too, I'm sure.'

'Yes.'

'Everything OK?' Jack asked.

'Thanks.'

'Sorry, don't mean to pry. You don't have to talk about it if you don't want to.'

'Not at the moment, if you don't mind.'

'What have you been doing with yourself? Anything exciting?'

'Looking for a full-time job. I thought I might find something easily, but . . .' She took a deep breath. 'There's nothing suitable.'

'Don't be discouraged.'

'Easier said than done.'

'I'm going to take photographs tomorrow. It's your day off, so why don't you come with me?'

'I'd have to be back for Emily,' she said, a note of doubt in her voice.

'Of course I'll have you back on time for her, but it'll do you good to get away for a few hours. We'll go straight there, and back,' Jack said persuasively. Suddenly she felt scared. Going for a landlady–tenant meal with him was one thing but this idea had all the connotations of a date. She knew Jack only slightly, and having been married as long as she had, any suggestion of spending time with a man who was virtually a stranger to her seemed wrong, like being unfaithful.

'Go on, say you'll come.'

'I'll make a picnic, if you like.'

'That would be lovely. Don't go to too much trouble, will you?'

Kate was nervous as she packed chicken salad, a wedge of Brie, rolls, wine and a flask of coffee into the wicker hamper Charlie had won in a golf tournament, then added two wineglasses and paper napkins, salt and pepper. She was looking forward to the next day.

16

They drove in Jack's jeep to Glendalough, and climbed up the side of the woods above the Upper Lake, stopping to look down at the water below them, which shimmered in the winter sunshine, and the ruin of the old church amid the green trees, and grey rocks. 'St Kevin's Bed is further up there.' Jack pointed to the jutting rock above them. 'Do you think you can make it?'

She glanced up, measuring the distance. 'Of course.'

They climbed on up the hill, Jack leading the way, Kate following in his footsteps, picking her way over roots and loose stones, not once looking down but keeping her eyes on the sheer path. Jack stopped every so often to gauge the difficult ascent. 'Are you sure you want to go on?' he asked, anxious that the terrain was getting too steep for her, unsure of her climbing capabilities.

'Yes,' she said, with exaggerated confidence. 'I've never been up this far. I'd love to see St Kevin's Bed.'

After a few minutes' climb Jack stopped. 'We can turn back any time you like,' he said, taking stock of the terrain again, 'just let me know.'

'Keep going,' Kate assured him, out of breath from scrambling up the slope but energised by the exercise.

St Kevin's Bed was a flat boulder in a small, natural enclosure of dark, pitted stones surrounded by sheer rock face. They sat on a sheltered slab gasping for breath, taking it all in.

'I don't know how St Kevin managed to sleep there,' Kate said, when she had recovered, looking at the rough stone.

'He was too busy doing penance to bother with mundane things like sleep,' Jack said.

She laughed.

'Worth the effort,' Jack said, his eyes on the landscape, his hand on her arm. 'I'm glad we persevered, aren't you?' he asked, his breath warm on her face as he turned to her, skin glowing.

'Yes.' Every fibre of Kate's being was charged by his touch, and her heart was still fluttering in her ribcage from the exertion.

The tower, pale in the weak sunshine that flickered through the trees, and surrounded by the ruins of the old church, was to their left. Jack snapped away to capture its evanescence. 'Impressive at close quarters,' he said. 'More so than I expected.'

'You've never seen it before?'

'Only in photographs. It's magnificent.'

Kate had to agree wholeheartedly.

Jack continued to click away, a pulse beating in his temple as he concentrated. He finished, put his camera back into its case and slung it over his shoulder.

A mist was rolling in over the lake, veiling the far slopes. 'I think we should go down,' he said, as it crept towards them.

The descent was steeper and further than they thought, loose stones on the narrow path making their progress slow and difficult. Kate followed Jack. Tentatively she moved only a few inches at a time, concentrating on her balance, her eyes averted from the panorama below her. Every step took them deeper into the mist.

She slipped.

He caught her, his hands grasping her waist. 'All right?'

'Fine,' she said, embarrassed.

He held her hand for the final lap. Her fingers dug into his flesh as, carefully, she planted one foot in front of the other, feeling her way.

'Great!' he said, when they were finally down. 'Now the tower.'

As they came to it Jack stood still to take a photograph, trying to measure its height against the sky.

Inside, the circle of sky above them threw down enough light for them to see their surroundings. Weeds abounded through the slits of windows and crevices in the stone. A bird fluttered somewhere in the dim recess.

'I can't imagine anyone living here,' Kate said, shivering with the cold.

'It was a watchtower for the old monks, most likely,' Jack said. 'Come on, time for lunch, I think.'

'Good,' Kate said, with relief.

The picnic lunch was welcome. They sat on a bench near a wooden paling, watching some boys play football. Kate handed Jack his food and he lifted out the bottle of wine, then filled her glass. 'Good wine,' he said, approvingly.

Kate shared out the cake she'd brought. Jack took the smaller portion and ate it silently as he watched the football.

The woodsmoke and farm smells, of animals and straw, on the breeze brought the sweet fresh smell of clean country air. It was quiet except for the hammering of builders reroofing a house across the field, music filtering from their stereo. The church clock struck the hour broad-casting midday. The wine relaxed them. 'This is good,' he said. 'I like picnics.'

It *was* a good picnic and, so far, a beautiful winter day, though rainclouds on the horizon looked threatening.

They were enjoying the easy friendship that was grow-ing between them as they talked. Kate asked Jack about the scenery on Cape Cod where he'd lived for several years. His voice had some American nuances, she noticed, as he described the wide, shady, tree-lined streets, spacious white houses, and trim lawns, boyish in his enthusiasm for the magnificent blossoms, and the wildlife there. 'I prefer living in Ireland,' he said. 'I'd love to buy a house somewhere around here.'

'We used to come here when we started dating, Lucinda and me,' Kate told him. 'The things we used to get up to.' She laughed. 'That was before Charlie came on the scene. One of our first dates was over there by the lake. I remember a whole gang of us coming here one time. We fancied ourselves as climbers and went up to the top of that hill. We brought Charlie here too. He was game for anything – and you know something? I thought he was great. I knew he was on the rebound, and was desperately trying to make a new life for himself. Colette, his sister-in-law, told me.'

'Do you wish he was home?'

'I don't know – I don't know what I want. All I know is that I don't want to spend the rest of my life feeling like this.'

'Trust me, you won't.'

Kate looked at him. 'The voice of experience?'

'You could say that.'

'It used to be so much better, you know, with Charlie.

I remember right back to those awful discos we used to go to. Charlie was good fun, always showing off, doing tricky steps, twirling around until he was dizzy. He was carefree so naturally I thought he'd got over . . .' She had been going to say Daniella's name but thought better of it. After a pause Kate said, 'Did Barbara suggest bringing me here?'

'In a way. I mentioned that I was going to take some photographs and she said a day out would give your spirits a lift.'

'I thought she had something to do with it. She thinks I need "taking out of myself", as she calls it.' She took a sip of her wine.

'And has our climb lifted your spirits?'

'Yes,' she said, surprising herself. 'It has a little. If only it were less complicated.'

'Would you like to tell me about it? Or don't you trust me with your secrets?'

The way he looked at her made her feel as if he could read her thoughts. 'It's not much of a secret by now.'

'I haven't heard your version of it.' He leaned forward, his eyes pinning her down. 'If it would make you feel better to talk about it I'd be happy to listen.'

'I'm not sure I can put it into words.' Kate swallowed.

'Try.'

'I haven't got to grips with everything that's happened. Sometimes I can't believe I'm on my own. I'm watching telly and I take it for granted that Charlie's sitting there, in his chair. I almost see the shape of him out of the corner of my eye. Can you imagine it? How sad am I?'

'It's only natural. You were together a long time.'

'I hate the way I feel, thinking my life's over because of Charlie. What's wrong with me?'

17

That night it snowed. In the morning the ground stretched out white and endless. Everywhere was quiet, the traffic muffled. Kate and Emily padded through the silent, ghostly park, with the snow swirling about them. Emily, scarved and mittened, stopped to make snowballs with Kate urging her to hurry or she'd be late for school. The child took her time, anxious that the snow would melt while she was in her classroom and she would miss it.

'It'll still be there when you get out,' Kate said, pulling her along impatiently, anxious to get to work, but Emily was indifferent to her pleas, and more argumentative than usual.

Later that day Jack, Kate and Emily, togged out in windbreakers and wellington boots, ignored the cold and went to the park to build a snowman. They worked quickly, piling the snow high, shaping the body first, then the head. They put in stones for eyes, and a carrot for his nose, their hands freezing in their wet gloves. Jack put an old hat on the snowman's head to complete him.

Emily pranced around, puffing and panting, her boots making deep imprints in the snow. Jack hurled snowballs at schoolboys, who flung them back, their voices high with excitement. Cold, and breathless, they went into Mao's, a cozy little place on the sea-front, yearning for something to warm them up. Blowing on their hands, stamping their

'Absolutely nothing.'

She looked at him. 'I don't trust people any more.'

'With good reason.'

'I now realise that Charlie never really wanted to be married,' she said, and went on recklessly about how he'd left the country when she'd kicked him out, making things worse for Emily.

Jack was watching her as she spoke. 'I'm sure there are plenty of other men who would gladly date you.'

'I don't want an emotional commitment – no commitment of any kind ever again. All it causes is misery and heartache.'

'Give yourself time, and you'll think differently,' Jack said easily.

She didn't tell him how hard it was to go back to her dismal, lonely house, how difficult it was to convince herself that she had made the right move, and that she had the most intense pangs of loneliness that frightened her. It would have been a relief to talk even more frankly than she had, a step forward in their friendship, but Kate wanted Jack to think that she was succeeding in making a life for herself, that she had lots of support in doing so.

On the way home Jack was quiet, almost distant. Kate kept her eyes on the scenery, regretting her disclosure, feeling disloyal. It had embarrassed Jack. Now, put off, he'd probably keep his distance, and that would be that.

feet, they joined the queue. Jack ordered cocoa and a doughnut for Emily, coffee for Kate and himself. They chatted above the hiss of the espresso machine. Emily ate her doughnut hungrily then licked her fingers, staring out at a fresh fall of snowflakes. 'I liked that,' she said.

'So did I,' Jack said. 'Let's hope the snow lasts a few days so we can do it again.'

Next morning the sun shone early, melting the snow. Patches of green appeared in the marbled ground. Their snowman was tilted to one side, its hat askew. 'He'll be gone when I get home,' Emily said, with sad resignation.

Back from work that day, Kate was hanging out the washing when she heard the doorbell. She hung the last sheet on the line and made her way down the garden path just as it sounded again. 'Coming,' she called.

A tall, attractive girl with long glossy black hair and perfect makeup stood there. 'I'm looking for Jack Marsden,' she said.

'He lives in the garden flat.' Kate pointed downwards.

'He said to meet him here, but he doesn't appear to be at home.'

'Perhaps he forgot. You know what men are like.'

'Hardly. We are going to an important lecture at UCD, he wouldn't forget that.'

'Would you like to come in and wait?'

'Thanks.'

Kate stepped back. The girl walked past her down the hall.

'Living room's on the left,' Kate said, following her.

In the living room she turned to Kate. 'By the way, I'm Chloë.' She gave a wide smile, showing whiter than white teeth.

'Coffee while you're waiting?'

'No thanks, I never touch the stuff. I'll have a glass of water, if that's not too much trouble.'

'None at all, I won't be a sec.'

Kate went into the kitchen. How inconsiderate of Jack to leave the girl for her to entertain when she wanted to put her feet up before Emily got home.

'Thanks.' Chloë raised her arm to take the glass from Kate. Her denim jacket parted revealingly to show off her big bust.

'How long have you known Jack?' Kate asked, to fill the awkward silence.

'Since he took over our photography class. I'm studying for a degree in it,' she said proudly. 'Jack's so talented and enthusiastic he makes me want to push myself as hard as I can.' She gave an ecstatic smile.

'Really?'

They both heard the sound of his jeep at the same time. Chloë jumped up. 'Here he is now,' she said, going to the door to meet him.

Jack was lifting out a heavy cardboard box from the back of his jeep. As he was carrying it down to his flat he caught sight of them standing together. He stepped back, astonished, almost dropping his load. 'Hello, Chloë, Kate.'

'I was waiting for you,' Chloë said sweetly.

'Just give me one sec.' He let himself into his flat and came bounding up the steps a minute later, hunky, dishevelled and flustered.

'Sorry, I got delayed.'

'That's all right.' Chloë gazed up at him adoringly. 'Kate's been entertaining me.'

'Good. Thanks, Kate.' He faltered, at a loss for what to say next.

'Don't mention it.'

'Well, let's go,' Chloë said.

'Yeah, 'bye, Kate.'

'It was nice to meet you,' Chloë called over her shoulder.

They had gone down to the basement, laughing together. A short while later they strolled out, Jack looking like Russell Crowe in *A Beautiful Mind*, carrying his briefcase, a camera slung over his shoulder. Chloë minced along beside him, so young, so eager, politely opening the gate for him. They got into his jeep chatting, enthusiastic about the evening ahead. Kate watched them drive off. Her thoughts drifted, conjuring up images of them dining alone later. Jack was good company, but surely Chloë was too young for him. Maybe they were just friends. She thought of the long evening stretching ahead, and felt a stab of envy.

That evening Jack phoned. 'Thanks for being so nice to Chloë,' he said. 'I'm having a few friends in for drinks Saturday night. Is that all right with you?'

'Of course it is.'

'Would you like to come?'

'You don't have to invite me.'

'I'd like you to come. Then the noise won't bother you.'

It would be rude to refuse, Kate thought.

On Saturday evening she dropped Emily at Mary's house, dreading the evening ahead. She'd showered, and got out her best dress, plain and elegant; she'd bought it in Paris the previous year. She wondered what Jack would make of it. Would he even notice it?

Jack looked most attractive, in an open-necked white shirt, when he opened the door. 'Come and meet my friends,' he said, smiling broadly, standing back to let her step inside. He followed her, saying, 'Let me introduce you to everyone.'

Heads turned.

'Meet my landlady, Kate,' he said.

'You wouldn't like to share her, would you?' someone said.

'Not on your life,' Jack said, making a joke of it.

Everyone laughed.

Chloë, in see-through top, miniskirt and high heels, sidled up to her. 'Hi, Kate, love your dress,' she said, above the sound of laughter and clinking bottles.

'Hi, Chloë. Thanks.'

Jack handed her a glass of wine, and introduced her to his friend Paul Byrne, a tall, blond man who eyed her critically. 'I can see why Jack is so keen on living here,' he said.

They were all laughing, looking at Kate who blushed.

'You're not the archetypal landlady,' Paul said, defusing the situation, and making Kate laugh.

'What is the archetypal landlady?' she asked.

'Someone strict and unsexy, who talks about the politics of housework and chores all the time. You're none of those things. I'd know that just by looking at you,' he said.

'We've had our chore-rule chat and, believe me, there's plenty of housework on my agenda. Are you a photographer too?' she asked, for something to say.

'No, I'm a teacher,' he said, 'in an inner-city school. I teach ten-year-olds.' He went on to talk about his job.

'Sounds really interesting.'

'As far as I'm concerned it's the best job in the world. The kids are terrific. And what do you do?'

'I work part-time as hotel receptionist, and take care of my eight-year-old daughter.'

'You're married?' Paul asked, looking at her ringless finger.

'Yes, but for how much longer I don't know.'

'I see. Lots of people divorce, these days. No harm in it if you're not getting along,' Paul said.

More people arrived, calling greetings across the room to each other. Kate didn't know anybody, apart from Chloë, and Jack took her by the arm, introduced her to the new arrivals and their wives, going to great lengths to make her feel comfortable. Chloë passed around dips and bites. She was all over Jack, while he kept the drink flowing, making sure everyone was having a good time.

They were all talking about holidays. Kate envied them. She would love to be able to laugh and chat easily.

'How about you, Kate, where would you like to go?' Paul asked, to include her in the conversation.

'Disneyland, if I could afford it. My daughter Emily is dying to go.'

Barbara and Maurice arrived. 'Enjoying yourself?' Barbara asked.

'Yes,' Kate lied.

'How are you getting on with Jack?' She eyed the stick-thin girls surrounding him.

'Very well. It's working out fine,' Kate said.

'I wish he'd get himself a real woman,' Barbara said.

'What do you mean, a real woman?'

'Someone his own age for a start. Look at that young girl flirting with him. She's so obvious and there's nothing admirable about it. She's only a child.'

'He's enjoying it.'

'That's all right when you're starting out, but he's

knocking on a bit now. Could do with a good woman to settle him down. Someone bright and smart, like you, Kate, who would appreciate his talent and encourage it.'

Blushing, Kate laughed. She retreated with Paul to a corner and talked about the photographs on the wall. At the end of the night Paul invited her out to dinner. She refused as graciously as she could.

'How did you get on with Paul?' Jack asked her, when everyone had gone home and she was on her way upstairs. 'I thought you'd be well suited. He's not interested in a serious relationship either.'

Kate froze. 'Were you trying to fix me up?'

Jack looked alarmed. 'Was I wrong?'

Kate raised her chin defiantly. 'Yes.'

'Sorry, I didn't mean to embarrass you – that's the last thing I wanted to do.'

'I was more scared than embarrassed.'

'Of what?'

'I don't know. Meeting people, I suppose.'

'You had no need to be. You were the most attractive woman there,' Jack said.

'Thanks, but that doesn't make me feel any better.'

'You've got to help yourself, Kate. Go out and about, live a little.'

'I'm trying by being here,' she protested defensively. 'But look at me, I'm lost,' she added. In a trembling voice she said, 'I'd better go.'

'What's the hurry? Tell me about it.'

She looked away in panic, thinking of the sudden changes in her life – the struggle to get up in the morning, the rush to school, walking across the park to avoid people on the streets, the same with shopping, and the drag of going to work.

Fearing that he might see her misery, she lifted her chin and glanced at him. 'It's a long way from the life I had. I don't feel safe any more,' she said, unaware that her face revealed the panic, the emptiness, the confusion. 'Life's intolerable.'

'Safety is an illusion. It can easily be broken. You can never really be safe unless you believe in yourself, and that the world is a good place with good people in it.'

'What if people let you down, and you find out things you never believed were possible?'

'You still have to give it a go. Who else will help you if you don't help yourself?

'Easier said than done. My life's destroyed,' she said, picturing herself as an old woman in dressing-gown and slippers, squinting at her book through thick glasses, or lying in a solitary bed, her hair thin and white, medicine bottles everywhere.

'Of course it isn't. Let their comments run off you like water off a duck's back.' He clicked his tongue. 'Be rude, if you have to. The only important thing is survival. Get out there and find someone, perhaps the right one this time.'

'You make it sound simple – but the reality is so different. It would be like finding a needle in a haystack. Maybe I'll never be able to live with a man again. Maybe I'll pine for the rest of my life, never be able to find my way. When I think of all those wasted years . . .'

Suddenly, it all seemed too much for her and she went to stand by the window silently, her hands shaking. Jack was beside her. His fingers closed over hers. 'Come and have another drink,' he coaxed her.

He handed her a glass of wine.

She sat down. He pulled his chair closer to hers.

'You'll find yourself. You'll learn to cope,' he said.

'I suppose so,' she said, and forced herself to return his gaze.

'Being single isn't the end of the world.'

'It makes me feel unreal.'

'Take baby steps – and take Emily out. The child needs to get out more. I'll come with you, if you like. It'll make Charlie jealous.'

Kate smiled. 'And there was me thinking you were all into yourself.'

He laughed. 'Well, what do you say?'

'Yes, that would be nice, but I don't think anything would make Charlie jealous at this stage. Besides, I've been messed up and the truth is things are difficult for me. I'm not prepared to let any man invade my space at the moment, as you've probably gathered.'

She hated the thought of dating, meeting people, the tedium of making conversation, carousing, the need to gear yourself up to meet new people, to talk, to act a part to impress. But the worst thing she could do was settle permanently into the role of wronged woman.

'You'll get through this, you know.'

'I'm sure I shall.' She stood up.

Jack got up too and came close to her. She could feel his breath on the back of her neck. 'If you'd like to come out to the pub with me any time – just to get out, no strings attached – feel free,' he said.

She turned to face him. 'Thanks, I will.'

He smiled at her, and she smiled back. 'I'd better be going, it's very late.'

On a sudden impulse Jack bent his head and kissed her lips, taking her by surprise. Flustered, she pulled away, wanting to be gone.

He caught her arm. His face was flushed as he said, 'I'm

sorry, I shouldn't have done that. I ought to have known better.'

He looked so worried that she said, 'It was only a kiss, nothing to worry about.'

She couldn't see his expression in the dim light as she left.

18

The following day Charlie called round late. 'We need to talk,' he said, brushing past her into the hall as soon as she had opened the door.

'What is it this time? Another big discussion about us and where we're going?' Kate asked.

'No.' Charlie took a deep breath. 'I came to tell you that I'm going away.'

'Where?'

'New York.'

'New York!'

Kate had got it into her head that some distance between them would teach Charlie a lesson, prove that their marriage was either worth fighting for or not. But Charlie had to go one better, didn't he?

'Before you jump to conclusions I've been asked to go there with a team of experts from the bank.'

Kate was torn between relief – she wouldn't have to make a decision about having him back – and fear that he would be gone for good. 'Oh!'

'It would be a longish stint, that's the difficulty.' He was standing in front of her, his eyes burning holes in her.

'How long?' she asked, in trepidation.

'A few months, longer, maybe.'

'Longer! I wasn't prepared for this.' She stumbled over

the words that stuck in her throat as she tried not to let him see her devastation.

'Neither was I.'

Liar! He'd organised it. There must be more to it than he was telling her. A partial view of the situation was all she was getting, and she was obliged to accept it, though she suspected he had a deeper and more hurtful reason for leaving the country than the one he was giving her.

'It hasn't obviously taken much persuasion.'

Charlie groaned. 'I've worked in New York before, and I've always told you I'd like to go back there. Now seems a good opportunity, the way things are between us.'

'You'll be able to spend unlimited time doing what you like, seeing whom you like.'

'I'm going away because I can't bear hanging around here waiting to find out if you're ever going to have me back or not, and what your real feelings towards me are.'

To be fair he *had* liked New York, and *had* said often that he'd like to go back, but this time it was different. 'It's just that it seems to be coming out of the blue. Like your adultery,' Kate said.

Charlie laughed bitterly. 'You can't resist having a cheap shot at me at every opportunity, can you?'

'You're the one who couldn't resist Miss Fancy Pants, and now look where we are.'

'This has nothing to do with her.'

'And I'm still hurt. What do you expect?'

Charlie sighed. 'Yes, well, it's hard for me to accept everything on your terms. I kept hoping that you'd change your mind, but I can't go on living like that, wanting things to be the way they were. You won't let me back and I'm doing something about it.'

'Running away.'

Clenching his fists to control his temper Charlie said, 'I'll take Emily out for the day on Saturday, break it to her gently, if that's OK with you.'

Kate's eyes were blurred, but she tried to keep calm. 'I'll have her ready,' she said.

Off Charlie went, back to planning his new life.

For a long time after he'd gone Kate felt redundant and stupid, trying to puzzle it all out for herself. How had they come to this? She'd held on to Charlie all these years for support, and now that there was nothing to hold on to she was losing her balance. She wasn't herself – she wasn't anything, and no amount of complicated explanations from Charlie as to why he behaved as he had would change that.

She phoned Lucinda, and asked her to come over as soon as possible.

An hour later Lucinda gasped when Kate filled her in on the latest news. 'How did you get to this stage so quickly?' she asked, pulling back the curtains to let in the afternoon light.

'I've been asking myself the same question,' Kate said. 'I didn't think he'd act like this.'

'You imagined he'd keep begging until he'd finally worn you down?'

'Something like that.'

'You'd better talk to someone, both of you, get a good counsellor.'

'Pointless. Charlie's made up his mind.'

Lucinda put her hand on Kate's arm and smiled at her. 'No, he hasn't. He's testing you to see how long you can hold out.'

'Didn't sound like that to me.'

'You and Emily mean a lot to him, Kate.'

'Yeah! If that's the case then why is he going so far away?'

'To force your hand – maybe frighten you into having him back.'

'He can't do that,' Kate said impatiently.

'That's exactly what he's trying to do, though. He's taking off so that he doesn't have to make any big decisions, putting everything on hold.' Lucinda gestured helplessly. 'You can't just accept this. You've got to confront him about finance – the mortgage and household expenses, sort all that stuff out before he goes.'

Kate shrugged. 'I can't.'

'What are you going to do, then?'

'I'll pay the bills until the money in our account runs out. I'll continue as before. Emily and I will be fine.'

'I'd like to believe that. Would you like me to have a word with him?'

'God, no.'

'Why not? We get on OK on the surface.'

Kate didn't think it was the right moment to tell Lucinda that Charlie considered her a blonde bimbo with a chequered love-life, and certainly not someone whose opinion counted for anything. Instead she said, 'He wouldn't listen to you.'

'And I thought I was the one in this family with the chaotic love-life,' Lucinda quipped. Back from modelling next spring's fashions in Bermuda, and a split with her wealthy boyfriend Diego because their relationship wasn't going in the direction Lucinda would like it to go, she was frustrated. Not that she had been sure where exactly she had wanted it to go.

'If I had a euro for every time you said that . . .' Kate said – Lucinda's love-life was as rocky as the Rocky Mountains.

'It's lonely on your own,' Lucinda said, serious this time. 'And with a child to bring up it'll be hell.'

'You're telling me! I'm getting a taste of loneliness.'

'There's still a chance that you might sort things out, I'm sure of it.'

'Maybe he's got other plans.'

'Daniella?'

Kate nodded. 'Her. Or someone else.'

'What will you do?'

Kate shook her head sadly. 'I'm too shut down to make any decisions about anything. I can only just get through the day.' Kate covered her face with her hands. 'I just wish things were the same as they used to be. I want Charlie, but the way he was before Daniella came on the scene. I want me to be the same as I was then.'

'That's not possible, but Charlie might never stray again, Kate. I mean, how do you know unless you give him a chance to prove it? And if you don't you might regret it.'

'If I do I might regret it even more. That's the trouble. I don't know what to do. Charlie's changed, Lu. He's bad-tempered and impatient all the time now.'

'Surely that's because he was forced to move out.'

'Well, I need time and he's in such a mad rush to go off just like that.'

'As I've said, he's punishing you, Kate. What have you told Emily?'

'She knows we had a fight, not much else.'

'She hasn't been given any consideration in all of this, if you don't mind me saying so.'

When Lucinda left Kate burst into tears. The bastard! The complete bastard! she thought, as she cried her heart out. She wiped her eyes. There was no food in the house. She'd have to go to the shops.

On Saturday when Charlie came to take Emily out he

was his old self, bubbling with enthusiasm, kissing her spontaneously. He and Kate didn't hold a conversation. Emily was happy to see him; she didn't notice. They went off together giggling. When they returned Emily was full of the rides she'd been on in the funfair, and keeping the budgie he'd bought her out of Oscar's reach. While she was feeding it, he packed the last of his belongings into the big suitcase he and Kate had bought for their honeymoon.

As he left he passed Kate in the hall, his body eluding hers in his hurry to speed up his goodbyes with Emily. Before he got into the car he gave Emily one last hug, then clasped Kate to him briefly, making a dutiful effort while Emily still clutched his hand. He was there, present, but he was already on the plane, taking off, and Kate knew it. He was doing what he wanted.

He drove off, waving as he rounded the corner. Emily stood on the footpath, tears running down her cheeks, waving frantically until he was out of sight, her body stiff with grief.

They went back inside. As soon as Kate had shut the door behind them she panicked, looking for a solution to the gaping hole his departure had left and finding only the budgie in its cage with which to distract Emily. Charlie had told his daughter that he'd probably see her soon, that he'd be renting an apartment in New York and she would have a holiday with him in the summer. What he didn't tell her was that he'd be at work all day, and that she could not be there by herself, among strangers. Even if he got a babysitter, she'd still be a stranger. It was unlikely, too, that he would come back soon, regardless of what he had said to Emily. Not for a long time, anyway.

Charlie wouldn't be around to hear Emily scream for him in the middle of the night, or watch her crying for him,

Kate thought. He was slipping away from his responsibilities. The life he'd been living with them wasn't the life he wanted obviously. He'd let fun triumph over parenthood.

Emily loved him, and he loved her. So how could he go off and leave her like that? Because having his own child, helping to take care of her, had never been enough for him. In any case, he hadn't wanted Kate to get pregnant.

Had Emily understood the real situation, the agony of losing him and the pain of missing him still to come, she wouldn't have been playing happily ten minutes after he had left. Emily hadn't been enough for him, but neither had Kate. If she'd agreed to have him back would he have been content to have her as his jailer? No. It had had to end, but did it have to end this way? What choice had he now but to seek a new life with a new woman? Or an old flame.

All the things that she'd taken for granted, all the things they'd discussed, which had seemed important at the time, no longer mattered to Charlie. Kate was seeing the structure of her life collapse like a pack of cards. It reminded her of when her father had died suddenly, after only a brief illness. Her mother's grief had been terrifying to watch, and after the initial shock she'd put up a protective barrier refusing to talk about him.

It was amazing, looking back, that the golden days were gone. Living alone, without the security of family life, was no way for a woman to rear a child. Perhaps this was the price she had to pay for all the years when she'd been so happy. Kate would have to go on for Emily's sake, if not her own. And she needed a contingency plan. What it would be she had no idea.

When the alarm went off an Monday morning she turned over. She dreaded having to face the day. She got out of bed reluctantly and went to wake her daughter.

Emily's eyelids wavered. She sat up suddenly. 'Daddy's gone to America?' was the first thing she said, her voice full of resentment.

'Yes.'

'But he'll be back to visit us,' Emily said.

'Yes,' Kate agreed, acting as if she believed it for Emily's sake.

'He said he'd phone me.'

'He'll phone as soon as he can.'

Emily crawled out of bed, pushed Kate away as she tried to help her put on her uniform, protesting that she could do it herself.

Kate went to make breakfast. 'I don't want cornflakes.' Emily pushed away the bowl. 'They're disgusting.'

'Since when?'

'Since always. I hate them. I want Coco Pops.'

'There are no Coco Pops. Eat what you're given,' Kate said.

Moaning, stirring the milk into the cornflakes with her spoon, spilling them on to the table, Emily ate a few spoonfuls, grimacing with each one to make her point.

Kate kept her mouth shut for the sake of peace and quiet and drank her tea in the sunlight that poured in through the kitchen window.

In silence Emily put on her shoes, and ducked away from Kate when she tried to comb her tangled hair. She refused point-blank to let her mother straighten her tie.

They set off for school, both bereft as they walked through the deserted park.

That evening Colette phoned, distraught that Charlie had gone to the States and inviting Emily to stay. Kate said she would bring her down.

19

Frank greeted them warmly and took Emily off to see the new foal.

Kate and Colette went into the living room for privacy: although Rose was in the house she wasn't being included in this chat. It wasn't fair to upset her, especially when she was so furious with Charlie and finding it so hard to believe what he'd done. Colette was furious with Charlie too.

'So now he's off to New York. God knows what's going to happen next,' Colette said. 'What does he think he's playing at?'

'I don't know.'

'Is he still seeing Daniella?' Colette asked.

The question quivered in the air between them.

'He said not but I don't really know. He's become bitter and secretive. I thought you might know something.'

Colette shook her head. 'Charlie hasn't mentioned Daniella to either Frank or me. We just don't understand it.'

Kate sighed. She'd have to stop giving Colette a hard time or she wouldn't be welcome any more. She'd hate that, for Emily's sake more than her own, and she could do without any more trouble.

'What'll you do next?' Colette asked.

'I've no idea,' Kate said, gazing into the fire, watching the flicker of the red and gold flames. That was what she loved about Bramble Hill, the warmth and comfort. But today she wasn't enjoying herself. She couldn't get out of her head the sight of Charlie and Daniella going into the woods together.

'Will you be able to get over this, Kate, and take him back?' Colette's voice was almost pleading. She didn't know that what Kate and Charlie once had between them was being wiped out with their continued arguments.

Kate, chin jutted out, said, 'I'm trying to forgive him and come to terms with what happened but it's very difficult.'

'I can imagine,' Colette said.

The fire spat and crackled; the smell of burning applewood was all-pervasive.

Kate went on, 'Charlie isn't the man I thought he was, Colette. He's living a lie. Everything he said was a lie. I've no respect for him any more and I don't know what to do.'

Colette save her a gentle, beaten look. 'I know he was unfaithful, Kate, but you've got eight years of marriage and a child to consider, not to mention friends, commitments, responsibilities.'

Kate hadn't the strength to resist, but she was too stubborn to surrender. 'I know Charlie apologised, but it's not enough. He can't give me any guarantees. He could be still doing it for all I know.'

Colette said, 'He's guilty and repentant and he wants to come home. You can hardly ditch him for one indiscretion. The important thing is what's going to happen in the future. You have to think of Emily too.' She took Kate's hand.

'I know.' Kate nodded. 'I never dreamed I'd ever think of packing in my marriage, but if Charlie isn't prepared never to see Daniella again it seems I haven't got much choice.'

'We'll support you, whatever you decide.'

'Tea,' Rose announced, carrying in a silver tray with her best willow-pattern cups and saucers set on a lace cloth, with home-made fruit cake and chocolate biscuits beside them. 'Try this cake, it's a traditional recipe.'

Much as Kate loved her mother-in-law this was not the right time.

'Thanks, Rose,' Colette said. 'Will you put it down here?'

'You all right, Kate?'

'I'm fine.'

'Frank's going to give Emily riding lessons on Trixie. She's very docile. Perfect for a first lesson.'

'She's mad keen to learn,' Kate said.

'She seems fine. Is she?'

'She's OK – doing well, in fact. Keeps me busy.'

'Kids are always on the go. Where they get the energy from I don't know,' Colette said, pouring the tea.

Rose had changed since she'd heard of Charlie's affair with Daniella. Always a curious woman, with opinions of her own, she insisted on taking a lively part in the conversation, asking Kate what was happening. 'But when is he coming home?' she insisted, still under the illusion that he would recover from whatever foolhardiness had overtaken him, and would become the Charlie he had been before.

'I'm not sure about that,' Kate said truthfully.

'I'm sorry about what happened, Kate,' Rose said. 'I can't believe he cheated on you. That Daniella should be shot. Just because she was invited to the party didn't mean that she could come in and do what she liked.' She spoke with venom. She, too, was angry with Colette for inviting the woman, and made it clear without putting it into words. Colette was paying for it, but not nearly as much as she would have to if Charlie didn't return home. Rose was worried about her youngest son – her favourite son, if the truth be told.

Kate's brow creased as she leaned forward and picked up her cup. Her hand shook as she lifted it to her lips. She was in a state, hardly capable of drinking her tea. It was going cold anyway.

Two red spots appeared on Rose's cheeks as she glanced at the photograph on the sideboard of Charlie and Kate on their wedding day. 'He's a negligent father, that's what he is, and I'm ashamed of him,' she said, angry, wary, then looked back pityingly at Kate. 'How could he leave poor little Emily? She's so like him. Every time she looks at me with those eyes I see Charlie.'

There was a scuffle at the door. It was Emily back. She flopped on to Kate's knee. 'The foal's beautiful, Mum, he's four days old,' she said, delighted to know something Kate didn't. 'I was allowed to pat him. I'm hungry,' she said, eyeing the chocolate biscuits and bouncing down from Kate's knee.

Rose held out the plate to her.

'Look at your hands,' Kate said. 'Go and wash them first.'

'Come on, I'll get you some orange juice,' Rose said, 'and another pot of tea.'

'No, thanks, Rose,' Kate said, and stood up. 'I'd better be going.'

'But you're staying for dinner! Wicklow lamb, your favourite,' Colette protested.

'And bread-and-butter pudding,' Rose said.

'Stay, Mum,' Emily said.

Over dinner Rose was quiet, as if she were waiting for Charlie to appear in the doorway so they could all get back to the way they had been, and her little world would be as it was before all this had happened. Frank was tender and patient, glanced in her direction, smiling to encourage her. Colette was desperately trying to act normally. Kate felt that they wanted to keep her in the family circle, pretend that nothing had changed, while she, aching with pain, was acutely conscious that everything had changed. Looking around her, she could see the sadness in their eyes. Charlie's transgression had made all the difference.

Before Kate left Rose said to her, with hope in her voice, 'I hope you'll forgive him for this, and be able to sort out your differences, get back together, for Emily's sake if nothing else.'

'We'll see,' Kate said, but her eyes said that it was never going to be.

'Are you sure you won't stay?' Colette asked.

'No, thanks. Honestly, I've got a hundred and one things to do.'

Colette and Kate walked out to the car, Emily swinging between them. Colette gave her a hug. 'Keep your heart up.'

'I'll phone you later, see how you're getting on,' Kate said to Emily, and kissed her.

'Don't worry about her, she'll have a great time.'

'I know she will, and thank you.' She hated the thought of leaving her daughter behind, even for such a short time.

20

Kate was huddled on the couch watching television when someone knocked persistently at the front door.

It was Jack, with a sullen Oscar in his arms. 'Hello there, did I disturb you? I could see the flicker of the TV from the garden but no lights on, so I phoned to see if you were all right, then came to investigate.'

'Sorry, I didn't hear the phone,' Kate said. 'I must have dozed off. Come in. Oh, poor Oscar, I forgot all about your supper.' She took the cat from him, and explained that Emily was with Charlie's family.

Oscar sprang out of her arms and headed straight for his bowl. Kate and Jack followed him into the warm, neat kitchen, where Kate opened a tin and fed the cat.

'Colette invited us for the weekend,' Kate went on. 'They've got a farm – cows, sheep and a couple of horses. Great for Emily, but I couldn't cope. She'll be back tomorrow. I suppose I should be glad to have the place to myself, but I miss her. It's so empty without her.'

'It certainly is,' Jack said.

On impulse Kate asked, 'Would you like some supper? I hate eating alone.'

'What an excellent idea. I'll get a bottle of wine.'

A little later as she made a spicy chicken and tomato sauce, and boiled pasta, Jack offered to set the table. 'No, we'll eat in the living room as there's only the two of us.'

He got out the glasses, and poured the wine. Kate made a salad, with black olives, chunks of tomato and feta cheese. She served two steaming plates, and took them to the coffee table in the living room. On television George Bush was proclaiming to the world his stance on terrorism.

'I don't like him,' Jack said, and forgot all about the US President as he began to chat about photographs he'd taken in a gay bar over the weekend for a magazine. He expanded on bits of gossip he'd heard about some minor celebrity who frequented it. He was keeping the conversation going to compensate for Emily's absence, and Kate nodded reflectively, contributing little.

'I'll make coffee,' she said, when they'd finished.

'Things aren't OK down on the farm, are they?' Jack asked, when Kate returned.

'Frank and Colette were lovely to me, but their guilt and heartbreak over what happened was upsetting. Colette was trying to get me to have Charlie back. His mother, Rose, is furious with him but she thinks I'm crazy to let it go this far. She probably blames me for his defection to New York because I haven't taken him back, though she didn't say as much.'

'That kind of pressure can't be helpful.'

'I wanted to reassure them that it would be all right, that Charlie could come back and we'd survive, but the truth is that our marriage has really broken down, and we can't seem to get back on track. Everything's gone wrong. It isn't the way we planned our lives.'

'His stint in America might be good for both of you. See how you get on without one another.'

'I didn't want him to go. I wanted to say, "Yes, it'll be all right, you can come back," when he asked me, partly because I'm terrified of being without him – but I'm even more terrified of having him back in case he's unfaithful again.'

'You're managing on your own, aren't you?'

She shook her head. 'I'm managing, but that's all. I'm not getting on with anything. It isn't easy. I don't know how we're going to get over it. If we split up his family will be very upset, and think badly of me for being so selfish. They'll see me as a hard-hearted, unforgiving bitch, the ultimate breaker of the marriage vows. They'll forget that Charlie instigated it all, and that will make things even more difficult for Emily.' Kate didn't know why she was pouring her heart out to Jack about her marital difficulties. It wasn't as if he could provide any answers.

'You shouldn't care too much about his family. Think of your own survival. You've got to put yourself and Emily first.'

'I know, but it's not easy to forget about them.'

'Charlie seems to have managed it.'

'Yeah, living like a single man in New York. It must be paradise for him.' She drank some coffee. 'It's his singleness that's getting to me, has been all along. In a peculiar way he's always stayed separate.'

'You could do with a night out to cheer you up. I'll babysit if you want to go out with the girls.'

'That's sweet of you, Jack, but not at the moment. Maybe later on.'

'Whenever you feel you'd like to. Don't leave it on the long finger to get going again. You don't want to go round moping, doing nothing about it – don't give Charlie the satisfaction. And you don't want Emily to see you upset all the time. That'd be bad for her.'

Kate leaned forward. 'Give me time.'

As soon as Jack had left, Kate phoned Bramble Hill to say goodnight to Emily, but she was already in bed, asleep. Colette sounded cheerful. 'Don't worry about her,' she said. 'She's loving every minute of her stay.'

During the night the phone rang, waking Kate out of a deep sleep. It was Charlie to say he was settling in. 'Good,' Kate said, genuinely relieved. 'Where are you now?'

'At the hotel. It's near the office, quite handy,' he said. 'How's Emily?'

'She's staying at Bramble Hill, having a great time by all accounts.'

'Oh! That's good. I'll phone her there.'

There was no mention of transferring money into their account and she didn't ask.

'How is he?' Mary asked, the next day when she called in.

'He seems fine.' Kate didn't tell her mother that she was obsessed with suspicions of Charlie's ongoing infidelity. This she confided to Lucinda, back from Milan where she'd been taking part in a big catwalk show for Gucci. She was used to working with the best models in the business. Although she complained about the rigours of a top model's life, she was still star-struck by some of her assignments.

'He probably has Daniella in New York with him.'

Lucinda tilted her head to one side. 'Hardly. Do you know what, Kate? You need to do something to stop you fantasising about him.'

'What?'

'Well, look at you. You're in a rut, slopping around wearing the same old tracksuit day in day out. You've let yourself go. You've made no effort with your appearance since all this happened.'

Kate, embarrassed, fiddled with the coffee percolator. It hissed and spluttered.

'What do you suggest I do?'

'You need cheering up. What about some retail therapy? A new rig-out? Let me take you in hand.'

Kate shut her eyes tight. 'I have no money.'

'My treat.'

'But I'm not going anywhere special.'

'Since when was that a prerequisite for buying a dress? And I'll wangle an extra invitation to Bono's party next week.'

'Oh, no, I couldn't face that.'

Lucinda argued. Kate capitulated, and let herself be dragged into the city centre. Grafton Street, with its impeccable shops and minimal window displays, was Kate's favourite. Silk blouses and neat stacks of cashmere sweaters adorned the exclusive shelves. Dresses by Roberto Cavalli, Missoni and Christian Dior, all Lucinda's favourite designers, hung side by side on racks. Delicate jewellery was displayed magnificently.

Kate longed to buy the beautiful clothes but she didn't have that kind of cash, or places to go to be seen in them.

'Do you have anything in her size?' Lucinda enquired of the shop assistant in the Powerscourt Design centre, and pointed at a rail of chiffon designer dresses.

The shop assistant scrutinised Kate: she wouldn't be as easy to cater for as her sister – she knew Lucinda and her highly developed taste. She produced a double silk chiffon print dress in brilliant fuchsia and orange, embroidered at the waistband, which was totally unsuitable, then a cream jersey Christian Dior number that would have looked perfect on Lucinda's sinuous, ephemeral frame, but did nothing for Kate. The bright lights highlighted every flaw.

In another shop Kate closed her eyes and squeezed herself into a size eight sea-green chiffon cocktail dress with a plunging neckline and a slit to her thigh. 'It's not me!' she protested.

Then Lucinda pushed her to try on a tiny black *diamanté*-encrusted number obviously designed to fit a flea. The sales assistant encouraged, anxious to satisfy the requirements of one of the hottest models around.

'I can't do this, Lu,' Kate moaned, cringing with humiliation.

The eagle-eyed sales assistant saw her distress and helped her out of it.

Kate returned to the changing cubicle, dressed quickly and marched outside. As they trawled one shop after another Kate became demoralised. The woman she'd been before Charlie's fling would have been thrilled to spend time with Lucinda: she would have enjoyed herself no matter what. She'd been a different person then, worried about no more than where she and Charlie might holiday, or the latest film or play they might go to see. Now all she wanted was to go home.

'I'll have to have a makeover,' she said, giving up her search.

Thus began the health regime *à la* Lucinda.

First came the session with Lucinda's health and beauty therapist, Sonia, who took Kate into a tiny cubicle, smothered her in fluffy white towels and started with a facial to 'keep your face from fallin' in'.

'Your skin's shockin' dry.' This tersely delivered information was followed by a haughty lecture on clogged pores as Sonia diligently administered her facial potions and peptides, massaging Kate's face with her spectacular nails to 'reignite your exhausted complexion'.

Lips compressed, she buzzed a tiny machine over Kate's face and lectured her on the importance of buying the right products, all of which could be supplied by Sonia, and having regular treatments.

'This cream I'm using stops wrinkles short-term. You need to use it regularly,' she said, squirting more on to Kate's face.

'I think I'll go for Botox injections next time,' Kate said. 'Save the hassle. They're on sale over the counter now, I hear.'

'They're a lot of bollocks,' Sonia said, her lips barely moving. 'And painful.'

Next came the eyebrow shape – Sonia swiped the tweezers to and fro – then the eyelash tinting, which stung like mad.

Kate's mobile rang. The perfect excuse to get Sonia to stop. She raised herself up. Sonia pushed her back down. 'Let them wait. You're entitled to a little uninterrupted pamperin',' she said, and put the phone out of Kate's reach. She proceeded to paint Kate's upper lip with hot wax, then took it off with an excruciatingly painful yank.

'What the—' Kate gasped, through gritted teeth, raising herself up again to protest, eyes watering, lip burning.

'You wanted to get rid of your moustache, didn't ya?'

Kate gazed at the swollen red lumps over her eyes and the red, blistered patch above her upper lip. She resembled a singed chicken.

'You'll look lovely when the blotches wear off,' Sonia assured her.

'Really?' Kate said doubtfully, exhausted by the whole

procedure. She left, mortified at the thought of bumping into some acquaintance.

'That was sheer torture,' she said to Lucinda, who examined her defoliated face.

'It'll be well worth the effort,' her sister said dismissively. 'You can't afford to neglect yourself. Not in this day and age where looks count for everything.'

Kate followed her out into the busy, rain-sodden street, feeling so violently wretched that she wanted to throw up.

Lucinda's car squelched along and crunched to a halt outside Milano's, her favourite restaurant of the moment. The window table had been reserved for her. Kate seated herself, letting her breath out slowly in an effort to relax, her eyes on the luscious pizzas on the counter.

'I'm hungry after all that,' she said, reading down the menu.

'Green salad and mineral water,' Lucinda ordered, and refused point-blank to let Kate have pizza.

On Kate's next day off Lucinda took her to Sheer Park, her gym. All the Geri Halliwells at the aerobics class lifted their arms in unison, straining their Lycra gym gear to the strains of 'It's Raining Men'. Kate was exhausted after five minutes. 'I can't do this,' she whined.

Lucinda cleared her throat. 'You haven't got it yet, have you? You have to plunge straight in.'

'But—'

Lucinda held up her hand. 'Look, Kate, I'm not trying to put you down. It might seem like that but I'm pushing you forward, pointing you in the right direction. I've masterminded this plan for you. It's for your own good.'

'Oh, God, Lu, is it really necessary?' Kate asked, picking up a cushion and sitting on it.

'Trust me, at the end of the day you'll thank me for it. If it wasn't I wouldn't be here, now, would I? I've got other things to do.'

'Absolutely. So have I,' Kate said, making for the door.

'Look, let's be honest here,' Lucinda remonstrated. 'We both know that Daniella is a joke. Everybody says it, but what she's done to your marriage is no joke. When are the consequences of what's she's done going to sink in? She stole your husband, Kate.'

'You don't have to remind me.'

'Now you've got to steal him back.'

'I don't know if I'm that desperate,' Kate said.

Lucinda laid her finger on her lips. 'Don't say that because you don't mean it. Look at it this way, you've got a fight on your hands, and it's with her. Now, trust me, and try the exercise bike.'

She walked past Kate, leading the way to the machines.

Kate's eyes were on the 'at-your-own-risk' signs pasted on to them.

Lucinda adjusted the bike. 'Hop on.'

'All right, but not too far,' she said.

Lucinda forced her to pedal endlessly, enough to get her all the way down the Liffey as far as Butt Bridge if she were on a proper bike. After five minutes she slid to the floor, wheezing, her bum lacerated by the sheer steel saddle.

'Another five minutes,' Lucinda said.

'I can't. I'm knackered,' Kate panted, frantic.

'You'll be glad you perserved when Charlie's begging to come back.'

Kate wasn't convinced. 'I'll die if I don't stop,' she moaned, examining her chafed thighs. She went to the changing room, showered, took her clothes out of the locker and dressed. She'd her hair blow-dried, and her makeup on before Lucinda returned.

'I don't think I'll bother coming back here. It's a health hazard,' she said.

'But we've only begun.'

'I'll walk more. I prefer walking.'

Lucinda glanced at Kate's reflection in the mirror. 'It's not enough.'

Lucinda picked up a hair-dryer and continued to study her sister's reflection in the mirror. 'Why are you so negative, Kate? It's just a matter of a few simple exercises that's all.'

'Simple!' Kate walked past her to the bench to put on her socks and shoes. 'It's a complete battle, start to finish.' She took her bag and started for the door. 'I'll wait for you outside.'

As she waited she wondered if Charlie was worth this extra pain. Hadn't he made her suffer enough? What did she need to impress him for with permanently arched eyebrows and a swollen upper lip? And would he even notice? Hardly, unless he held a magnifying glass up to it for close inspection, which was highly unlikely.

21

When Kate got to work next morning she didn't go straight to Reception, but walked across the car park to the side entrance of the bar. Tim was stacking glasses in the dishwasher. 'Kate!' he said. 'What's up?'

'I need a coffee to revive me before Helen gets in.'

She drooped on to the barstool, exhausted, unable to sit comfortably.

Tim walked around the bar to her, took her hands, looked at her. 'What's this all about?'

'I went to the gym with Lucinda.'

Tim laughed. 'What did you do that for?'

'I only agreed to go to it on condition that it didn't involve anything too strenuous. When we got there she nearly killed me. Look at me closely, Tim. I think I'm going to die. This is the result of Lucinda's efforts to change me into a lusted-after superbabe like herself,' she said.

'But why? You're lovely as you are.'

'According to her, I've got a weight problem, a self-confidence problem, and I'm clinically depressed. She thinks a breakdown is imminent if I don't pull my socks up. And these are diversionary tactics she's devised to prevent it.' Although Kate spoke lightly, she was voicing a lurking fear that Lucinda might be right. 'I haven't got what it takes to fight back,' she added.

'You mustn't take her diagnosis seriously. She's not a doctor.'

'Maybe I need therapy.'

'Don't automatically assume that, but it is important to analyse what's causing the pain. A lot of it may be from your relationship ending rather than the loss of the relationship itself. I'll get your coffee,' he said, going back behind the bar.

'Listen, Kate, you're attractive, funny and clever,' he said. 'The fact that you're a bit down at the moment isn't your fault. It's Charlie's. You want to ditch that no-good husband of yours and move on,' he advised, and passed her a cup. 'Live a little.'

'Emily would be short of a father.'

'No, she won't. She'll probably see more of him.'

'Anyway, I think he's left me, slipped away in the hope that I wouldn't notice.'

Tim flung back his head and laughed. 'No such luck! That pathetic slob'll be back before you know it,' he said. 'Have you talked to him recently?'

'He phoned.'

'What did he say?'

'Very little, just that he's settling in. He's being cagey.'

'Nothing about Daniella?'

Kate shook her head.

'I don't get it,' Tim said. 'Doing the dirty on a lovely woman like you.'

'I don't exist for him any more. He's not interested in me. I'm too dull compared with Daniella.'

'I don't believe that. He's shallow and self-absorbed and doesn't appreciate a good woman.'

'I'm dying for some chocolate,' she said, accepting the bar Tim had put in front of her. 'I must be addicted. I've been having withdrawal symptoms, since Lucinda put me on her awful diet,' she said, and rolled her eyes.

'Who needs men when you've got chocolate?' Tim said encouragingly. 'Listen, Kate, you're a beautiful woman. Right now you're suffering from social isolation and straitened financial circumstances, but you've got to attack the problem head-on. If there's anything you want to do, do it now, while you can. See this break-up as an opportunity, a catalyst to look at yourself and change for the better. Otherwise you'll grow bitter and pissed-off with the world.'

'You're probably right. How do you know so much about heartbreak?'

'Been through it. I took my own broken heart to a therapist, a new-age crystal-gazer recommended by a friend. It's a way of getting over a relationship, I suppose, but not as good as throwing yourself wholeheartedly into the social scene. I partied for Ireland, anything to block out the pain, and three months later I found myself able to say his name again without bursting into tears. I'll be thirty next month, and I'm hoping to quit this job soon and become a full-time writer. I've sold a couple of stories recently, and it's getting easier.'

'That's brilliant.'

Bursting with his future hopes and dreams, Tim talked eagerly about them as he leaned over the bar, arms crossed.

'Perhaps it's time for an alternative strategy, but I don't relish the thought of partying for Ireland. Besides, it isn't possible with Emily to look after.'

'I'll babysit for you any time, you know that.'

'Thanks, Tim, I appreciate it.'

'Don't forget, you're not alone. There are plenty of people in your predicament. Who knows? You might meet someone nice – plenty of fish in the sea.'

'So they say.'

'Look, do anything that moves you forward, now that the initial shock is over. Who needs him anyway? Why don't you come out with the lads and me tomorrow night?'

'Where to?'

'The Cock and Rabbit. We'll get very drunk and talk a lot of bullshit.'

Kate laughed. 'Great! I'll look forward to it.'

She went to Reception feeling a curious sense of elation, as if a burden had been lifted from her and life might get better after all. Maybe there was something in this simple self-help that Tim was advocating. Maybe time *did* heal, as her mother had said.

True to his word Tim babysat when Kate went out with Vivian and the other girls from the hotel during the following weeks. He showed Emily how to make cut-out dolls with paper and paste, leaving snippings and bits of cotton wool, for hair, all over the place.

Emily was getting to know Jack better too, and to like him. She missed adult company in the house, so on Friday evenings Kate would invite him to a supper of fish and chips. Emily loved it when Jack sketched cats for her, which he did regularly – big ones, little ones, fat ones, skinny ones. She considered Jack 'very good' at drawing. She couldn't think why he didn't spend all his time drawing cats.

After Emily had gone to bed Kate and Jack would chat, sharing the day's trivialities. Jack's reputation as a photographer was spreading and he was very busy. 'There's never enough time to photograph what I really want to catch,' he complained, rubbing his eyes. 'There's so much human life going on that needs recording – the crowds on the pavements, the train travelling along the track, people wooing each other.'

*   *   *

Kate's finances were reaching crisis point: Charlie hadn't lodged any money in their account. Mary said, 'I don't know what you're going to do if you don't tackle him about it.'

'I've used up our savings, but it's the future I'm worried about. I've had a lot of expense. I suppose I could let the spare room if I get desperate.'

'You don't know what riff-raff you'll be subjecting Emily to.'

'I don't want to move,' Kate said. 'I love this house. I'd miss it terribly, and the garden.'

'You'd be better off in a small apartment for just yourself and Emily.'

'Did you say apartment?' Kate asked, shocked.

'I'm only trying to help. You'll get into debt if you stay here. Then you'll be even more depressed.'

They were quarrelling again, and Kate didn't want that. 'I'm sorry, Mum, I didn't mean to snap at you,' she said.

But Kate was broke. Her clothes were few, and she hadn't been to the hairdresser for ages. She used no makeup, apart from a touch of moisturiser. She got extra hours at the hotel doing relief work as housekeeper. Her duties consisted of making sure that all the rooms were properly cleaned, checking the linen, opening windows. If there was a conference on at weekends, she worked overtime. The extra money she made was put aside to pay the mortgage. But with all her economies and effort Kate seemed to have less and less. Her food stocks had depleted, and producing well-balanced, interesting meals was now a conjuring trick. The splurges on ice-cream, biscuits and chocolate could never have been managed without Mary and Lucinda's generosity.

'Would you like to come to the pub tomorrow night?'

Jack asked casually, one Friday over supper. 'It would do you good to get out.'

'OK. I'll ask Mum to babysit.'

'It's only a drink with Jack,' she said to Mary.

'You be careful,' her mother warned. 'That Jack might have interesting possibilities for some lucky woman, but not you. You're still a married woman.'

'As if I could forget,' Kate said.

Mary arrived early. She amused Emily while Kate showered. Even though they were only going to the pub it felt to Kate like dating, and it was hard. She wore a black top and her jeans again. Emily was excited, watching her putting on her makeup, desperate to try out the gold tubes. She pinched one when Kate wasn't looking and smeared on some lipstick. Then she dabbed powder over her face and sprayed on some perfume.

The pub was packed with couples drinking and eating. Jack ordered from Terry, the owner. Kate was edgy, knowing how her presence with him might look to an outsider.

Jack took the drinks to the nearest table.

'So, what have you been doing?' Kate asked. 'I haven't seen you around.'

'I was in Mayo photographing Ashford Castle for an advertisement. How have you been?'

'Emily was playing up. She was in a bit of a state after school but I couldn't get out of her what was wrong.'

'Poor kid!'

'Shouldn't be talking about her, sorry.' Kate could never put Emily out of her mind the way Jack could his job. Although he lived for it, and it made him the man he was, he didn't feel the need to talk about it all the time.

'No problem. You know I have a soft spot for Emily.'

'Yes.'

'So, what else did you do on your day off?'

'Nothing exciting. Went to the travel agent's, got some holiday brochures.'

'Where are you thinking of going?'

'Disneyland.'

'That's OK. I can afford that.'

Kate shook her head, laughing. 'You're not invited.'

'I'm not?' Jack looked up in mock surprise.

She studied her fingernails. She mustn't get too serious with him. 'I'm joking,' she said. 'You know I can't afford a holiday. I got the brochure to please Emily. Charlie might take her some time, you never know.'

On the way home they walked along the sea-front. A thick mist was coming in from the sea. Kate inhaled the chill air, glad of it after the stuffiness of the smoky pub.

'Are you hungry?' Jack asked, as they passed the chipper.

'Yes, I am now.'

Jack bought fish and chips, which they ate in the living room while he talked about his family. He told her about his older brother Al, who'd inherited the farm, and his wife Maeve, their two boys, who were cornered at every hand's turn to help out. Then there was his wild sister Theresa, who'd entered a convent the previous year to everyone's astonishment.

'Would you like to live on the farm again?'

'Never,' he said. 'I love my life as it is. I don't mind giving Al a dig out sometimes when they're really busy, but that's it.'

Kate watched him eating his chips, blowing on them, enjoying them. He loved his food. When he finished he leaned back and crossed his arms. 'How about you? What would you like to do if you had the choice?'

Kate looked at him quickly and smiled. 'I'd like to backpack through Cambodia and Vietnam, see places I've always wanted to see, live rough for a while. Take one day at a time, not knowing where it might lead me.' She laughed at the idea of it.

'It's nice to see you laugh,' Jack said. 'I don't know what's wrong with that husband of yours, going off like that. Doesn't know the treasure he's got at home.'

'Barbara told me you had a girlfriend in the States.'

'Yes, that's true.'

'What happened to her?'

Jack shrugged. 'It didn't work out. We wanted different things.'

'I'm sorry.'

'Don't be. I'm not. I wasn't ready to settle down. Besides, I wanted to come back here. She was tired of moving from place to place and she wasn't interested in living in Ireland. Who could blame her? She's American.'

'Understandable.'

'You know something?'

'What?'

'I'm glad we met.'

Kate blushed. 'Really?'

'Yes, really. I like living here. I know I have to get a place of my own but I'll hate leaving.'

Her heart leaped. 'Thank you. I'll miss you when you've gone.'

He looked at her, surprised. 'I thought you'd be glad to see the back of me.'

'On the contrary, I'll probably let the flat again. I don't like being by myself.'

'You won't be on your own long, Kate, not a woman like you.' He stood up. 'I should get going,' he said, as he put the plates into the dishwasher.

Their shoulders were touching and she glanced up at him, to see his expression change as he faced her.

'Kate, did I tell you how lovely you look tonight?' He reached out his hand, took hers and encircled her in his arms. His weight against her, his warmth seeping into her were intoxicating. He pulled her closer to him. Her head was spinning. For a second she closed her eyes.

He kissed her gently on the lips.

When she didn't withdraw he kissed her again.

'We shouldn't . . .' she began.

'Don't say anything,' he whispered.

'Jack!'

'No talking, there's nothing to discuss,' he said, pulling her closer, kissing her again, whispering into her ear, 'just relax.'

She felt her shoulders relax, she was breathing more freely, fuzzy with the rumblings of desire. His lips were soft against hers, gently persuasive as he pushed his tongue into her mouth. She surrendered to him. She hadn't been kissed like that since . . . *ever*.

They were melting together, breathing unevenly. They stopped, tried to gauge each other's reaction. Kate could see the naked lust in his eyes beneath their dark lashes.

She turned away from him, but he brought her face back with a touch of his forefinger. He was kissing her again, urgent this time, his tongue tasting, exploring, driving them both mad with desire. She closed her eyes against this blazing passion and threw herself into his arms. The wonderful smell of his skin, cool mint and cologne, was thrilling. She was in danger of falling for this, letting Jack have his way.

Their wanting one another took them over, making them forget themselves and everything else. For once Kate couldn't care less what was going to happen. Then his hand was under her top. How had he managed that? So smooth and swiftly too.

She put her hand on his chest, moved back, studying his face.

He looked at her. 'I want you.'

Her eyes widened. They were alone, no one need ever know. 'Kate?' He was stroking her hair, waiting.

'I . . .' She was scared. She didn't want to be intimate with any man, but she knew she was going to find it hard to say no. It would be far easier to say yes.

There was Emily asleep upstairs to consider, and there was her marriage. Though the vows she'd made to Charlie seemed a lifetime ago, they were still important to her.

'I've wanted to make love to you all night,' Jack said, kissing her again

She could feel his breath on her skin. It would be so easy to let him. There was nothing she wanted more.

The phone rang, bringing them to their senses. Kate didn't want to pull away.

'I'll have to answer it. It might be important.'

It rang and rang.

'Hello! Charlie!' she gasped, smoothing her hair with her hands, pulling down her top as if he could see her.

'Kate, hi, did I wake you?'

'No, I was just . . . going to bed.'

'I was anxious about Emily. She was upset the last time I talked to her. Is she all right?'

'Yes, she's fast asleep. It's one o'clock in the morning here.'

'Sorry to wake you. I'll phone tomorrow.'

'Fine, I'll tell her.'

When she put down the phone, Jack said, 'I'd better be going.'

'You don't have to leave because Charlie phoned.'

Jack wavered. For a second Kate thought he might stay.

'Doesn't seem such a good idea now, does it?' he said formally.

The spell was broken. It was no use: he was uncomfortable with the situation, anxious to get away.

Kate felt foolish. She didn't want him to leave.

'I'll see you.' He was gone, running down the steps as if he couldn't get away fast enough.

Damn Charlie, Kate swore. What next? she wondered. Jack wouldn't be back for more, that was certain. Served her right for getting involved with him in the first place. She'd nearly lost control with all the kissing. She'd better get to bed – work tomorrow, she thought. It was all her fault. She shouldn't have dropped her guard. Just because Jack was strong and comforting it didn't mean he wouldn't let her down in the end.

'Just as we were beginning to get it together,' she told Lucinda, next time she saw her. 'But I know it was wrong with Emily upstairs and everything.'

'Stop blaming yourself. He's a sexy devil,' Lucinda said. 'If you were going to have an affair he's perfectly eligible; single, free, sexy, full of *joie de vivre*. But is that what you want?'

'No, it isn't,' Kate said emphatically. 'Maybe it's just as well Charlie interrupted us. I haven't decided what I want yet. It's too soon.'

22

Jack hadn't popped in for ages and Kate was concerned. Why was he so evasive? Perhaps he, too, had been affected by the kisses they'd shared and realised it had been a mistake. Lately when the doorbell rang she had checked through the spy-hole to see who it was. She watched Jack come and go and wondered how he was getting on.

Eventually, one miserable wet afternoon, he appeared. She checked herself in the mirror before she answered the door.

'I know you're in there,' he shouted, through the letterbox.

'Hi,' she said.

'Are you going to leave me here freezing my nuts off? Aren't you going to invite me in?' he said, with his beautiful, brief smile.

She stood aside.

'Seems like we've been avoiding one another.' He was smiling. 'And it's silly.'

'Seems so.'

'Kate, I didn't mean to upset you. I'm a clumsy bastard.'

'And I can be a bit hard at times,' she admitted.

When she didn't say any more he said, 'If you don't want me around I won't make a nuisance of myself. I'll go.'

'I didn't say that.'

'I was worried about upsetting you like that. Things got a bit out of hand. I didn't mean them to.'

She looked at him.

'I wondered how you were. I couldn't get you out of my mind. You've got to me, Kate, you really have.'

She searched his face. He seemed sincere.

'It's bloody silly don't you think? avoiding each other just because we . . . just because—' He stopped. 'This isn't easy. The trouble is, I'm finding it very difficult to keep away from you, you know? It's not an easy situation to be in.'

'I know,' she watched him, 'but we can't go on pretending that the other one doesn't exist, living in the same house.'

He moved closer to her, and she thought he was going to touch her but he rubbed his chin reflectively. 'I had time to think,' he said.

'And . . .' she prompted.

'I thought about you as a person, what you're like and everything, and decided that I like you. I like talking to you. Damn it, Kate, I'm not just another bloke,' he said. 'I'll be honest with you. I really fancy you, and I just want to know if I stand a chance.'

Kate couldn't believe her ears. She was not sure she could handle all this honesty.

'I was going to phone you, but I wasn't sure if you'd speak to me. I couldn't get that night out of my mind.'

She moved away, ran a hand through her hair. She'd missed him too. You don't have to be in love to miss someone, she reasoned. Having a friend was allowed. But did she want more?

'Tell me to leave and I'll pack up and go now, if that's what you want.'

How could she? That was the last thing she wanted him to do. He didn't want to go either.

'If it's awkward for you I'd rather leave,' he added.

'No, don't do that, Jack. I missed you too.'

Jack held her gaze. His smile deepened the dimples in his cheeks, and transformed his face, making him boyish.

'I don't know if it's worth the hassle, that's the only thing,' she said.

'You're worth a lot to me. That's why I'm here.' His eyes crinkled. 'Look, come down tonight. I'll cook us a meal.'

Without hesitation Kate said she would.

She needed to keep her wits about her, though. She didn't know what Jack was about. He might be wasting her time. On the other hand, she might be wasting his.

When he opened the door he grinned, showing immaculate teeth. 'You made it,' he said, and took the bottle of wine she handed him.

The flat was tidy, and smelt of furniture polish mingled with cooking aromas – definitely garlic in there somewhere. The coffee table, set for two, was flanked on either side by an armchair. A new set of photographs was pinned to the wall, landscapes this time. There was one of the trees in the park, the sun setting behind them, another of Kate smiling into the distance – Oscar, on the wall beside her, looked as though he was about to leap at something. 'I didn't know you took these.'

Jack opened the wine, poured it into two enormous glasses and handed her one.

She sat in an armchair, and he took the one opposite.

'So, how have you been?' he asked, awkwardly.

'Fine.' She clasped her hands together in an effort not to let him see the nervous state she was in.

'What have you been up to?' Something was burning. 'Excuse me.' He went into the kitchen. Kate could hear him moving around busily.

Finally he returned with two steaming plates. 'Dinner is served. Chicken casserole.'

'I didn't know you were such a good cook,' Kate said.

'This is standby from my student days,' he said.

Kate tasted it. 'Delicious,' she pronounced.

After fruit salad Kate asked if she could look through his albums. He spread them out on the floor where they sat, then turned page after page of photographs that told his life story. One was of his mother, a beautiful, broad-shouldered smiling woman. Another was of a much older woman, his aunt, painting at her easel. There were photographs of him as a child with his family.

'Like another drink?' he asked, his tone seductive, eyes soft as a summer's night sky.

'Yes, please,' Kate said, and gave him a sexy smile.

'I'm just glad we sorted things out,' he said. 'You're an important part of my life, these days.'

'Even with all the complications?'

'What complications?'

'Me being married. You must resent Charlie.'

He looked at her speculatively. 'I can tolerate him from afar.'

'Me too.'

They both laughed.

Jack said, 'I don't think anything about your relationship with Charlie, Kate. In fact, it's hard for me to imagine it because you've been on your own since I met you.'

'I can understand that, but the fact remains that I'm married, and I've got baggage. Emily, for instance.'

'Emily's not baggage.'

'Oh, yes, she is.'

'Well, hand baggage, maybe, but I like her. I won't be making demands on you, like forcing you to get a divorce or anything. And that's enough of the serious stuff. Why don't we forget everything and enjoy ourselves? More wine?'

'I've had too much already.'

'So what? You're not driving. You can do what you like. It's good to let yourself go occasionally – you don't often get the opportunity.' Jack made it seem like the right thing to do as he filled her glass. He gazed into her eyes, and smiled at her as he pressed 'play' on the stereo. Jeff Buckley sang 'Lover, You Should Have Come Over'.

'Let's not think about anything tonight, except us.' He ran his hand along her leg, touched her neck, his eyes still on her. The wine and their close proximity made her tingle with desire. He reached out and touched her face. Pressed closer. She ran a finger down his cheek. What would Charlie say if he could see her like this? Forget Charlie. She didn't want to think about him. She felt relaxed, in control. She moved closer to him. He stretched out, making himself more comfortable, slid his arms round her, pressed his body to hers. Kate snuggled up to him. They were locked in each other's arms. For the moment all that mattered was that they were together, enjoying each other, like Jack had said, forgetting everything and everyone but themselves.

He kissed her deeply, a divine, passionate kiss that seemed to go on and on. With his lips against her ear he said, 'Come to bed?'

Silence. Kate was thrown.

He pressed his face into her shoulder, waiting for her answer.

Unsteadily, she got to her feet. He pulled himself up, leaned forward and touched her cheek. She swayed slightly. 'Just give me a minute,' she said, and went to the loo.

When she'd flushed it she gazed into the mirror as she washed her hands. She ran her finger over her lips, bruised from his kisses. Suddenly, she realised that she was going to have to get undressed in front of him and panicked. She would have to take off all her clothes and reveal the faint stretch marks at the tops of her thighs, the roll of flab around her tummy. She hadn't been intimate with a man other than Charlie for such a long time. She wished they were in her place. It would be much more comfortable in her bedroom, rather than this squashed space. Stop being so negative, Kate Conway, she told herself. She took a deep breath, and went back to Jack, who was sitting at the side of his bed waiting for her.

He took her face in his hands, kissed her eyelids, her lips. 'Are you OK?' he asked.

'Fine.' She hesitated. 'Can I have another glass of wine?' Shit, she was letting him know she was nervous.

'Of course.' He got to his feet.

When he returned he said, 'All that matters is us here together now.'

She sipped her drink slowly and put the glass on the floor.

They were on his bed, Jack kissing her lips, her neck, moving down to her throat. At the same time his fingers were undoing the zip of her jeans slowly, his thumbs touching her bare skin. She closed her eyes tightly to concentrate. Something moved deep inside her as he ran his fingers over her stomach, and slipped his hand downwards.

She wanted him.

What the heck? Who could tell what the future for them might be, or if there would be one? Reaching up she pulled him closer and struggled out of her jeans. Quick as a flash he removed her top. Next stage would be nakedness. Jack pulled off his sweater, and removed his jeans. Kate held her breath to stop herself panicking.

Could she do it? She'd thought she'd be all right, thought she'd be in control. But now it was as though she'd been thrown into the deep end of a swimming-pool, and was thrashing around, drowning. She sat up. Did she have the nerve to go through with this? It wasn't a simple matter of just wanting Jack. There was the gap that Charlie's departure had left, which couldn't be filled. He wasn't disposable, after all. How much of her past was she prepared to throw away for a quick roll in the sack? There were many unanswered questions about Jack too. Briefly she closed her eyes to stop the blood rushing to her head.

'Is it really that bad?' He was leaning forward, a puzzled smile on his face.

He was breathing rapidly. Was it nervousness or excitement, or both? A fine, broad, muscular chest he had too. He was a handsome devil, no doubt about it. If only she could just look at him and not have to do anything.

'What's the matter, Kate?' he asked gently.

'I just . . .' She stopped.

'Are you nervous?'

'Yes.'

'So am I, if that's any consolation,' he said, and laughed.

'Not as nervous as me.'

'Believe me, I am,' he said, and put his arm round her. She watched him watching her.

'It's okay,' he said. 'You've nothing to worry about.

We'll take it slowly.' He held her for a long time. 'Tell me what you're thinking. What's going on in that complicated mind of yours?' he asked.

'I feel bad. I don't know what we're getting into,' she said. 'I don't know if it's worth the risk.'

How could she tell him that she was too scared to do it? That it had been a long time since she'd . . .

'There's no risk. You don't think I'm stupid enough not to have protection.'

'It's not that. It's just that I can't . . .' she blurted out, getting off the bed, pulling on her top.

Jack was beside her. 'Kate! Wait! There's no pressure on you to do anything you don't want to.' His eyes were on hers, understanding.

Acutely embarrassed, she rubbed the back of her neck. 'I'm sorry, Jack.'

'Don't be, it's OK. I like you too much to want you to do anything that would make you feel uncomfortable, or that you'd regret.'

Kate reached out and stroked his face. 'Thanks for that. I like you too Jack.'

He pressed his cheek to hers. She felt like a spectator observing the drama of someone else's life.

'We can put it on hold for the time being. It's your decision and I'll go along with it. Inconsiderate of me to rush things.'

'It's not your fault.'

He kissed her cheek. 'Another time, perhaps?'

'Fair enough.'

Despite his reassurance Kate felt foolish.

Jack hesitated for a moment, then got to his feet awkwardly. From his shuttered expression it was impossible to know what he was thinking as he struggled into his jeans.

Kate dressed, said, 'good night,' and ran up the steps.

In her own bedroom, she stood looking out at the night sky studded with stars then drew the curtains. Her head was muddled with unanswered questions about Jack and her. Put to the test, she'd discovered that she wasn't ready for a relationship with him – or with anyone for that matter. He'd been a real gentleman. Yes, Jack was a gentleman, a 'diamond geezer', as Lucinda would call him, and she'd well and truly messed things up with him.

23

The next day, at work, Vivian couldn't believe her ears when Kate told her what had happened. 'You what?'

Kate repeated, in an undertone, 'I chickened out at the last minute.'

'Was he really that bad?' Vivian snickered.

'It's not funny, Viv!' she was mortified just thinking about it.

'I know, and I'm sorry.'

'It wasn't Jack's fault, it was mine. At the last minute I couldn't do it – and I mean at the very last minute.'

'But why, if you were all het-up and ready for action?'

'I was too nervous. I panicked.'

'Were you expecting not to be?'

'No.' Kate laughed shakily. 'I wasn't expecting anything. We both got a bit tiddly and suddenly it seemed like a good idea – until we got started.'

'How did Jack take it?'

'He was great, said it didn't matter, but I felt bad.'

'Wow! He didn't think you were teasing him or leading him on?'

'If he did he didn't say so. He was wonderful about it. Blamed himself for being too eager.'

Vivian shook her head as if in disbelief. She started to say something and stopped, reflected for a moment. 'He's not gay, is he?'

'Certainly not.'

'Then he's one in a million.'

'I know that. How will I ever face him again?'

'He'll be fine about it. He obviously fancies you like mad and is prepared to give you time.'

'Is this the way it's always going to be for me?' Kate asked her. 'Backing off at the last minute? Do you think my sex-life is over for good?'

'No, of course it isn't,' Vivian assured her. 'You need time to get over Charlie, that's all.'

The phone rang. Vivian answered it. 'Yes, she's here,' she said, mouthing Jack's name to Kate as she held the receiver out to her.

Kate motioned it away with her hands; she couldn't talk to him now. She stared at the ceiling while Vivian said, 'She's with someone at the moment. Can I get her to call you back?' She waited, felt a rush of relief as Vivian hung up. 'He said he'd phone you at home. You'll have to talk to him sooner or later you know,' Vivian warned.

Kate agreed: she had another few hours to get a grip of herself.

Helen Horton appeared from nowhere. 'You forgot to lock the linen cupboard yesterday evening,' she said, wagging a forefinger at Kate.

'Sorry,' Kate said.

'Make sure you lock it in future. Can you stay until four o'clock today? Sally can't come in until then.'

Kate nodded. 'I'll phone my mum and ask her to pick up Emily, but I must be home by quarter past.'

'Fine. I'll relieve you myself if I have to,' Helen said, and went off rattling her bunch of keys.

*   *   *

Kate did some shopping on the way home. The phone was ringing as she got in.

'Oh, hello, Jack,' she said. 'Thanks for calling back.'

'Are you all right?' he asked, apprehensive.

'Yes, I'm fine, thanks,' she said, and apologised again for the previous night's débâcle.

'Maybe we should get together soon, just to talk, get back on track. What do you think?' he suggested casually.

'Yes, of course.'

'I have to go to Cork for a couple of days unfortunately, so I'll give you a shout when I'm home.'

'Great.'

She went to the kitchen, made herself a cup of tea, sat down in the living room and threw off her shoes as Emily and Mary arrived.

'I'm starving. Anything to eat?' Emily said, going to the fridge with a look of expectation. 'Oh, good,' she said, and took out strawberry yoghurt, her favourite.

'So, how was school?' Kate asked and hugged her.

'All right. There's a new girl in our class. She's from Mozambique. Macoumi is her name.'

'Really!'

'She can't speak properly.'

'She probably doesn't know much English.'

Emily nodded. 'I like her, though. She has shiny hair and lovely coloured bobbles. Can she come for tea some evening soon, Mum?'

'Yes,' Kate said. 'That would be lovely. One day next week?'

'I'll ask her.'

'There you are,' her mother said, catching her arm as soon as she came in late from work the following evening.

'You've got a visitor,' she whispered, her eyes indicating the living room, then swooped forward leading the way triumphantly.

At the door Kate stopped in her tracks and blinked. 'Charlie!'

He stood up. 'Hello, Kate,' he said solemnly. 'Sorry to surprise you like this.'

'Wh-what are you doing here? I thought you were in New York.' Kate stuttered.

'I came back early. I wanted to talk to you.'

'You could have phoned,' Kate said. 'Is something wrong?'

'No! Well, nothing serious,' Charlie forced himself to smile, but kept his eyes downcast.

Kate clutched her hands nervously while she waited to hear what he had to say.

'The phone's no good. I wanted to talk to you face to face. So I flew home.'

Kate took a deep breath, raised her chin defensively. 'Mum, can you give us a few minutes alone please?'

'Certainly. I'll go and make the tea.'

'Not for me, thanks,' Charlie said.

'What do you want to talk about?' Kate asked.

Charlie's eyes were full of sadness and regret. 'It's so difficult, living this way. You and Emily here, me over there.'

'I know.'

'Do you?'

'Yes, of course I do, but Emily and I are all right, we're managing.'

'Well, I'm not. I can't stand it, Kate. I've missed you and Emily too much to stay away any longer. I had to come back. We've got to sort this out, once and for all. I know what I did was terrible, but I bitterly regret it.' There was desperation in his eyes now.

'I don't know what I'm supposed to say to you, Charlie.'

He took a step towards her, contrite. 'I know I'm asking a lot but, please, Kate, I'll do anything I can to make it right between us. Just tell me what it will take to convince you that I love you, and I'll do it. I can't bear to be without you.'

Speechless, Kate stared at him. He'd made it clear in the past that he wanted to come back but never before had he pleaded like this. She looked at him blankly. 'What's the point of all of this when you can't guarantee that you won't see Daniella again?'

Charlie shook his head. 'I can guarantee it, and I do. I promise I'll never see Daniella again.'

Kate couldn't believe her ears. 'But why now and not before?'

'Because I realise what a mistake I made. Daniella is nothing to me, compared to my family.' Frantically, he ran his fingers through his hair. 'Kate, when are you going to realise that you're everything to me? You and Emily are my whole world.'

'Then why did you have to go and smash it up? With her!' Kate shouted.

His eyes burned with shame as he said, 'Because I couldn't resist her.'

Kate stared at him. 'What is it about her that she has such power over you?'

'Had, past tense.'

'She must have been great in bed.'

Charlie flinched at her directness. He gazed at the floor as she persisted, 'She was obviously better than me.'

He didn't answer.

'Well, was she?'

'No, it wasn't that. It was the way it ended the first time. When she finished with me she gave no reason. Just said it was over and walked off. She refused to discuss it. Laughed at me when I asked her to meet me to talk about it. She thought I was pathetic when I couldn't accept that it was over. Then, all those years later when she turned up at the office Christmas party, all over me, I was . . . overwhelmed, I suppose. Stupid, I know, and childish. But I didn't arrange to see her again, Kate, I promise you. Nobody was more surprised than I was to see her at Frank's birthday party.'

'I remember,' Kate said, trying to keep the pain out of her voice. 'She wiggled her bum at you, and you went running just because you'd never got her out of your system. Broke up a home and a family just for a shag. All that sneaking off and for what? To inflict humiliation on me.'

'I know, and I'm paying for it now.'

'I presume you saw her when you were in New York.'

He nodded. 'She happened to be there, yes.'

'What a coincidence,' Kate sneered.

Charlie's eyes shifted away. 'We had dinner and . . .'

Kate put her hands over her ears. 'I don't want to know,' she said.

'You asked and, besides, if you remember I only went there because you refused to have me back.' He was losing his composure

'So, I threw you into her arms again?'

'No, no – listen, Kate, I'll do everything I can to make it up to you.'

Kate squared her shoulders, and looked into his face. 'It was nothing short of cruel what you did, Charlie, making a public spectacle of yourself and our marriage, making Emily and me suffer like that, the agony you put us through.' Kate was unstoppable. 'Do you realise the grief you caused, especially when it became public knowledge? You betrayed me, you dumped me for your ex.'

'No, I didn't.'

'You did, whether you meant to or not. That's what all the lies, and deceit amounted to. Too bad you got found out.'

'Kate!' Charlie cried. 'Stop, please.'

But Kate couldn't stop. 'So now the guilt is too much for you, and New York doesn't work out, you miss us, you realise that what you had at home was better than all the running around with Daniella.' Kate was unsparing.

'Kate! Listen!'

'You come back just as I'm beginning to get my life back together, begging for a new start, promising the sun, moon and stars, after ruining us. You ruined us, Charlie. Do you understand that? You ruined us, and who's to say you won't do it again? I'm not having it – I'm just not having it.'

She burst into floods of tears, slumped on to a chair and covered her face with her hands, her whole body shaking with sobs.

Charlie was beside her, his arm round her shoulders. She shook it off, stood up and moved away from him. Charlie had no choice but to let her cry. When she'd calmed down a little he took a tentative step towards her. 'I don't blame you, Kate. You've every right to be furious with me.'

'I know,' Kate sobbed.

'But I'm no good without you. I've proved it. You've got to believe me.' His voice sounded desperate. 'I'm begging your forgiveness, I want to stop all this and come home. We're a family, we have a lot to lose if we let it go.'

Kate's rage surfaced again. 'Do you think I haven't thought about that? I've thought of nothing else, every minute and hour of the day since you left,' she said furiously. 'You're the one who took it all for granted.' She sobbed uncontrollably again.

'I know.' He put his arms around her now, holding her shuddering body.

Her strength deserted her. She collapsed against him. He moved with her to the couch, sat her down, held her and stroked her hair. Slowly, her anger evaporated.

She longed for things to be as they'd been before she discovered his unfaithfulness. She began to think of the future, and the possibility of being a family again. For Emily's sake, even more than her own, she would have to consider it. Emily was still suffering, missing Charlie terribly. What if they could put their marriage to rights and give themselves a future together? If Charlie was back there would be no more emptiness in their lives, no more trying to explain his continued absence to Emily. He would be home for good, and he'd have learned from his mistakes. The more Kate thought about it, the more she was tempted to agree.

'I'll never hurt you again, Kate, never put you through this. It'll never happen again.'

'And Daniella?'

'What about her?'

'What if she turns up again?'

'She won't.'

'What makes you so sure?'

'I told you I'd never see her again. I've promised. Apart from anything else she's too much for me. I could never keep up with her lifestyle, going here, there and yonder – cruises in the Caribbean, weekends in Bermuda, mixing with the rich and famous, name-dropping all over the place.'

Kate hadn't thought of that.

'It was awful waiting here for you, your mother fussing around me. Was she covering up the fact that your lodger was looking for you to go out for a drink with him?'

'Jack's not here. Anyway, he's a good friend, that's all,' Kate snapped. 'He's been very kind to me. He knew what I was going through. You didn't expect me to go into hibernation, did you?'

Charlie looked remorseful. 'No, I suppose not.' Then, cheering up, he said, 'I'll spend the rest of my life making up to you for what happened, if you'll give me a chance. We'll start over, help each other work at it together. What do you say?'

Would she be able to start again, or would she bring up Daniella's name every time he failed her in some small way, or came home late too many nights on the trot? Would it be better to say, 'Sorry, Charlie, I'd rather go it alone, I've got used to my own ways, I'm managing perfectly fine without you'? Was she managing fine on her own? Yes, amazingly, she was. It was difficult, and she was working harder than she'd ever worked before, but she was doing OK, paying her bills. And what of Jack? She liked him, enjoyed his company. All that would have to stop. He would have to go. Was it worth losing him – and the independence she'd acquired? She would have to think carefully about it.

'Could you find it in your heart to love me again, Kate?'

Kate said, 'I never stopped.' The words were out before she realised it was true. She did love him. She'd loved him from the moment they first met. He'd been the only one for her, even though she'd known that he was nursing a broken heart. She'd been prepared to take that risk.

'We could have a great life together, go places with Emily, do the things we've always planned and dreamed of.' His voice softened as he said, 'We owe it to Emily to try to make a go of it. We have so much to make up to her for.'

Kate's mind was racing. Charlie was right. Emily needed him – she longed for him to come back. This was his chance to repair the damage.

'What do you say?'

Kate could feel his heart pounding as he waited for her reply.

'Maybe we could give it a go,' she said, after a long pause.

'Oh, Kate!' Charlie took her in his arms, and held her tight. As his tears flowed he made no attempt to stop them. They hugged one another, clung together like two people drowning, kissed with the desperation of people possessed with the purpose of putting things right between them.

'Let's go to bed,' Charlie whispered, his hot breath on her face, longing for her in his eyes. His arm was across her shoulders tightening its grip, steering her up the stairs, brushing away any obstacle she might put in his way. Charlie drew the curtains. She didn't think about anything except the two of them. The outside world didn't matter. This was the moment, they were together, and everything was settled. They made love with renewed passion, taking one another greedily.

Afterwards they lay entwined, Charlie breathing peacefully, Kate by his side, unwelcome thoughts of Daniella intruding once more.

'Daniella knows you're never going to see her again, doesn't she?'

Charlie shifted uncomfortably. 'Yes, I told her.'

'How did she take it?'

He hesitated.

'Was she upset?'

'Yes, very. She did everything to try to hold on to me, but when she grasped that I was having second thoughts, and missing you and Emily so much she gave up.' He sat up. 'She'll get over it. Daniella always bounces back. It's over, Kate. She's knows that.'

'And she's accepted it fully.'

'More or less.'

'She'd better keep away this time. I mean it, Charlie.'

He took Kate in his arms. 'She will.'

'Yeah! She'll find another mug pretty quick. They're like moths to the flame where she's concerned.' Kate looked up at his handsome face, shadowed in the moonlight. She couldn't believe that she was lying in his arms. She thought of Jack and wondered how she'd break the news to him that he had to leave. There had never been anything permanent about their arrangement, but Kate couldn't help wondering how he'd take it. She had an uneasy feeling that he would be far from happy. Still, she had her husband, and Emily had her father again. That was all that mattered. Wasn't it?'

Suddenly she thought of the shock Emily would get when she woke up in the morning to find Charlie there. 'Maybe you'd better not stay tonight,' she said. 'The shock might be too much for Emily.' And Jack, if he comes back early from Cork, she thought. 'I'd rather tell her gently, then have you come home properly so she'll understand.'

'You're right. I'll stay at Bramble Hill, come back tomorrow.'

He promised to phone her first thing in the morning, and left her to ponder what had just happened. She'd taken back her husband without too much of a struggle or even much discussion in the end, and why not? She had been alone long enough, and it was terrifying. The thought of bringing up Emily on her own had frightened her, but the thought of a future alone was even worse. It would be a relief to have Charlie home.

24

Emily came home from school and saw Charlie sitting at the kitchen table. 'Daddy!' she cried, incredulous. 'You're back!'

'Hello, sweetheart.'

As he opened his arms she flung herself into them. He lifted her into the air and twirled her round. She squealed with delight. As soon as he put her down she said, 'You're staying this time, Daddy, aren't you?'

'Yes.'

'Yippee!' she shrieked.

Kate watched her little face, red with happiness and excitement, as she jumped around. She went to Charlie, clung to him, asked him endless questions, and told him all her news. It was like it had been before he left. Kate hoped they were doing the right thing. One thing was certain, Charlie could never leave again. Emily could never be put through all that pain again. But, it wouldn't happen. Her daddy was home where he belonged and he was glad to be there. Now all they had to do was pick up the pieces of their shattered lives and start afresh. This time it had to work.

Over dinner Emily chattered away, telling Charlie about Hannah's new rollerblades, and the computer game her granny had bought her. 'It's called "Cool Look – Barbie Fashion Designer".' She paused only to take a mouthful

of food, or a drink of milk. Charlie's smile stretched from
ear to ear as he listened to her. 'Can I have rollerblades
for my birthday, Daddy?'

'I thought you wanted a pony.'

'Yes, I want a pony too.'

'It's working out fine with Emily,' he said, as he helped
Kate clear up.

'She's thrilled to have you home,' Kate agreed. She
looked up and caught the delight in his eyes.

'And are you thrilled too?' he asked tentatively.

Now Kate saw apprehension. 'Of course.' She gave him
a hug to reassure him.

He held her close. 'Thanks for giving me another
chance.'

'I'm glad I did.'

Kate was happy that they were all together again. When
Charlie had unpacked it was as if he'd never been away.
He and Kate made love again that night. This time Kate
managed not to think about Daniella. At six o'clock the
next morning Emily bounced into their bed, and snuggled
up to Charlie. He tussled with her and teased her as Kate
tried to get her ready for school. 'She'll be late,' Kate
complained.

Emily, overexcited, said, 'I don't care.'

Charlie offered to drive her to school.

'That's a bad habit I don't want to let her get into.'

'Just this once won't do any harm,' Charlie said. Then
he remarked, 'I see your lodger is back. You can give him
notice tomorrow.'

Kate said, 'Right, I will,' and suddenly dreaded the
prospect. She wanted to speak to Jack. He would have
noticed Charlie's car outside and he'd want to know what

was happening. How he would take the news was her main worry.

As soon as she'd waved Charlie and Emily off she clattered down the steps to the basement and rang Jack's bell. It was a beautiful morning, with the sun shining, and the birds singing. Jack flung open the door. He looked terrific in a dark blue sweater. 'Top of the mornin' to you, Kate,' he said, in a fake lilting brogue, giving her a huge grin.

'Hi, Jack.' Kate shifted uncomfortably.

'Coffee?'

'No, thanks, I can't stay.' She hovered on the doorstep.

'Yes?' He moved closer to her.

His aftershave smelt of lime and mandarins; its fragrance evoked memories of his kiss.

'There's something I've got to tell you.'

He looked at her.

'Charlie came back.'

Jack let out a deep breath. 'I thought I saw his car, but I don't get it. I thought he'd gone to New York.'

Kate nodded. 'He had.'

'So, why is he here out of the blue? Is something wrong?'

Kate took a deep breath. 'Because he missed us so much.'

'So he's moved back in?'

'Yes.' Stuck for words, she looked away.

'He feels guilty and he's come back to clear his conscience?' he demanded bitterly.

'No! It's not like that.'

'So, what is it like? Now he's seen that you and Emily are OK, will he bugger off again? Is that it?'

'No, of course he won't. He's back for good.'

The colour in Jack's face drained. 'Yeah! Until the Daniella woman turns up,' he said, his eyes steely.

Kate brushed the hair out of her eyes. 'She won't. He gave me his word.'

'Oh, well, then, that's fine.' Jack's voice was loaded with sarcasm. 'Just like that? No questions asked?'

'Of course there were questions. Lots of them. But we sorted it out.'

Stunned, Jack said, 'Well, you seem to have got all the right answers.'

'Most of them.'

'Why didn't you tell me sooner?'

'I didn't know. It wasn't planned. I came down to tell you straight away because I know it will affect you.'

'Oh!'

Her heart sank as she looked at his lean face, taut with confusion. 'Jack, I have to make the effort for Emily's sake as much as mine. She's thrilled he's home. It was very difficult for her with me trying to manage on my own.'

'I thought you were doing very well.'

They stared at each other.

'I don't want to be alone,' Kate explained. 'We're a family, after all.'

'Yes, of course. I should say I'm pleased, if it's what you want, but I can't. It would be a lie.'

'Oh, Jack, I'm sorry. I'd no idea this was going to happen. I never thought Charlie would even want to come back. But he's here now and that's that.' Kate stopped, unsure how to put into words that Jack would have to leave. 'I hope you'll understand.'

'Yes.' Head bowed, Jack nodded.

Kate was grateful that she hadn't let things between them get out of hand. She knew with certainty that if they had slept together she would have found it impossible to accept Charlie back into her life. Besides, Charlie probably wouldn't have wanted her, because despite his despicable behaviour with Daniella he was narrow-minded enough not to tolerate his wife doing similar.

'I suppose you'll want me to leave. You'll be needing your space,' Jack said.

'I know it's upsetting, asking you to go at such short notice, and I'm really sorry.' The truth was that Kate was sad and confused: she didn't want him to go.

Jack shrugged. 'I'll be out of here before Charlie gets back this evening. You've enough to worry about without having to add me to the list.'

'It doesn't have to be that quick.'

'I'd prefer it that way.'

'Where will you go?' she asked anxiously.

'I'll find somewhere. Let that be the least of your problems. I'll slip away unnoticed.' Suddenly he seemed strong, confident, glad to go.

'Will you keep in touch?'

'I think it's better if I don't,' Jack said, glancing at his watch, moving imperceptibly away from her as if to say, 'Your time is up.' 'I'd better get packing.'

'I'm really sorry, Jack.'

'It's OK, can't be helped,' he said briskly, attempting a smile.

Kate was filled with the desire to say, 'I'll miss you,' but stopped herself in time. Instead she said, 'Well, good luck,' faltering on the step, apologising again for the short notice.

'Thanks.'

They stared at each other.

'Goodbye,' she said.

'Goodbye,' Kate.' He looked past her, as if she'd already gone.

She turned away, a lump in her throat, already feeling the loss of him keenly as she mounted the steps.

With Charlie's return her emotions were all over the place. As the days went by she found that at one minute she was up in the air, delighted with life, at the next down, worrying about the future. She couldn't help thinking of Daniella and wondering what had really gone on between them, if she was truly out of Charlie's life. The main thing was that she had her husband home, and happy to be there. Jack's departure was the sad consequence of it.

Slowly, life returned to normal, Charlie going to work early each morning, making sure to be home in time for supper as often as he could to be with Emily and help her with her homework. Although Emily was ecstatic to have him back she was apprehensive every time he came home even a little late. She would ask him over and over again if he was home for good, and he would reassure her with a big smile that he was never going to leave her, ever, his eyes full of regret for the pain he'd caused her.

One evening Emily was out of drawing paper. 'Let's go down to the basement, see if Jack's left some of his,' Kate said. She hadn't been down there since Jack left. She hadn't had time, and also she hadn't wanted to be reminded of him. It was too much like his private space still. She held Emily's hand as they went downstairs.

The place looked abandoned, with only the landscape photographs still on the wall, and a few books and CDs in a box. Jack obviously hadn't time to remove them in his haste to get away.

Emily, fascinated by the photographs, said, 'I haven't been down here since it was Daddy's office.'

'Here's some drawing paper,' Kate said, finding a sketchpad underneath a pile of papers. 'It's good quality. I hope you won't waste it.'

'I won't. I want to paint a beautiful picture and send it to him.'

Kate sat down in one of the armchairs while Emily mooched around. She missed Jack. She had no idea where he'd gone, and Barbara hadn't volunteered any information about him either. He'd probably told her not to because he'd wanted to get completely out of their lives, which was exactly what he'd done.

It was the casual friendship they'd developed since he'd become her lodger that Kate missed most. He had always been ready for a chat. His willingness to listen, coupled with his close proximity, had made him invaluable during the lonely times. From the time they'd met he'd been on her side, and he'd given her good advice too.

Her heart ached as she thought of his smile, his deep belly-laugh at something Emily had said. She recalled the meal he'd cooked for her, almost letting it burn in his attempt to make her welcome. She felt herself blush as she thought of his kisses, and the mess she'd made of their potential night of passion. Even then she must still have been harbouring a hope of saving her marriage.

Charlie's return had blown their friendship sky high. She would probably never see him again, she thought, so the best thing to do was forget him, and get on with her life. Still, she couldn't help wishing she could talk over her present predicament with him. Tell him about the doubts she'd been having since Charlie's return, and the fairy-tale ending that hadn't yet materialised but that she was still hoping for.

25

Kate was in Reception, going through her bookings for the forthcoming week, when she glanced out of the window and saw Daniella getting out of a red sports car. 'It's her,' she hissed to Vivian.

'Who?'

'Daniella. That blonde in the car park.'

Vivian's eyes followed her gaze to the glamorous woman locking her car door. 'What's she doing here?'

'I've no idea. Charlie said nothing about her coming back. Oh, my God, she's coming in. What'll I do? Cover for me for a few minutes, will you, Viv? I'll be in the loo.'

'Go and talk to her.'

'I've nothing to say to her.'

'Say anything. Find out what she's up to.'

'Why?'

'Listen, Kate, she's the woman who wrecked your life, who took your husband thousands of miles away from you. Don't tell me all hell isn't going to break loose when Charlie finds out she's back. You need to find out what's *really* going on.'

'Oh, my God . . .' Kate felt her face go scarlet. 'Here she is.'

'I'll leave you to it,' Vivian said, moving discreetly to the far side of the desk.

'No, don't go,' Kate hissed.

'Good morning, madam, can I help you?' Vivian asked, as Kate shrank back.

Daniella smiled at her. 'I'd like to book a double room.'

'Certainly. How many nights?'

'Two, please.'

Vivian took down her details.

It took a minute for Daniella to recognise Kate. Then her jaw sagged. 'I didn't know you worked here.'

'I've had this job quite a long time,' Kate said.

'Charlie never said—' Daniella broke off, blushing, her eyes dropping away from Kate's steady gaze.

'He probably didn't mention me much at all,' Kate said sarcastically.

Daniella shot her an anxious look, and Vivian moved away.

They continued to study each other.

'How could you do what you did?' Kate said quietly.

Daniella trained her eyes on Kate. 'I assume this is to do with Charlie,' she said.

'I don't know of anything else we could possibly have in common.'

Daniella looked down her nose. 'If we're going to hold a conversation we'd better go somewhere less public.'

'It's up to you,' Kate said.

Daniella turned and left. Kate followed her.

Outside, they sized each other up.

Daniella said, 'You're wondering why I'm here.'

Kate folded her arms. 'In Dun Laoghaire, of all places.'

'There's nothing romantic about my visit, I can assure you, if that's what you're thinking. My mother is in St Michael's nursing home, convalescing from a severe stroke. I'm here to spend some time with her.' She opened her bag, rummaged for a cigarette.

'I want a guarantee from you that you'll keep away from Charlie, and leave us alone.'

'That might be difficult.' Daniella lit up, blew smoke into Kate's eyes. 'Charlie's family and mine are neighbours. We've known each other most of our lives. It's inevitable that we'll bump into one another from time to time.'

Kate caught her breath. 'I want you to keep away from him. He's promised me he's finished with you.'

Daniella gripped the handle of her car door. 'Well, then, you've got nothing to worry about. Isn't that all you need to hear?' She scrutinised Kate. 'What other reassurance do you want? Or don't you believe him?'

'Of course I believe him. I just want to hear it from you,' Kate said defensively.

Daniella smiled wickedly. 'What does it matter who finished with whom as long as you've got him back with you? Surely you don't need to hear my version of it, do you?'

Suddenly Kate felt insecure. 'I think I do. There are so many unanswered questions.'

'Perhaps it's best that way. You may not like my side of the story.'

'I want to know the truth.'

'You still don't trust him?'

'I want to know how long your affair has been going on. Did it really only start at Frank's birthday party, or had it been going on since the previous Christmas?'

With a shrug Daniella said, 'What does it matter now?'

'It matters to me.'

Daniella's green eyes were mocking as she said, 'Our affair lasted five years.'

'Five years!' Kate couldn't believe her ears.

Daniella nodded. 'You did insist that I tell you.'

'But that's not possible.' Kate's voice was shrill. 'Charlie hadn't seen you for years until that Christmas party . . .' Her voice died away.

'Well of course he would say that. He wouldn't want you to know that we'd met up every time he came over to the States.'

Kate's mind raced. That hadn't been very often.

'Not to mention all the times I nipped back here.'

Kate couldn't take in what Daniella was saying. Heart pounding, she whispered, 'But Emily would only have been three years old.'

'I know.'

The ground rocked beneath Kate's feet. She couldn't get her breath. Charlie had deceived her all those years and she never knew.

'Are you okay?' Daniella sounded worried.

'It's not true.' Kate was shaking her head frantically in denial.

Daniella shrugged. 'It is. I didn't want to tell you. You forced it out of me.'

'But why?' Kate asked. She felt sick now.

Daniella sighed. 'Charlie wouldn't leave me alone. Kept in contact with me all the time, even when I didn't want to hear from him.'

'That can't be true. Didn't you get married during that time, to . . . Buck?'

Daniella giggled. 'You don't think that put Charlie off? As a matter of fact that's when I really appreciated having him in my life. But, then, when you found out last summer, and threw him out, things got messy. You see, when I got transferred to New York he, too, got a transfer. He wanted to move in with me permanently, said you wouldn't have him back because of me, and that his marriage was over. Of course, I had no intention of living with him, ever. That wasn't part of my plan. He was a good friend, and a great support when my marriage went bad, but I never wanted anything permanent. I tried to send him back to you but he got even more forceful with me.'

'I don't believe you,' Kate said.

'It's the truth. Charlie became a nuisance because by then there was someone else in my life, someone very important I was hoping to get more involved with. Eventually I chucked Charlie out, end of story. Don't get me wrong, we had a great time and everything but, let's face it, Charlie was hardly the catch of the century. I needed someone who could take proper care of me. I mean financially, and he had more financial commitments than he could handle.'

Horrified, Kate gazed at her, hardly able to believe what she was hearing. 'After destroying his marriage you didn't even want him?'

'Oh, I did, but only as a friend, not to share my life. It was unthinkable, impossible. Honey, I was doing him the best favour ever. He already had a family and he was missing Emily so much. I knew he'd regret it if his marriage ended. I persuaded him to go back to you both.' She seemed pleased with herself.

Kate propped herself against Daniella's car to stop herself fainting.

'Look, we were childhood sweethearts, and that's where it should have ended, in our childhood,' Daniella said. 'But Charlie, bless him, would never let go. I got resentful in the end.'

'Why do I still not believe you?'

'Because you don't want to,' Daniella said patiently.

'But, hey, suit yourself. I've had no contact with him since I got here, and if I do come across him I'll keep my distance. You know, since he went back to you the feeling of freedom is marvellous. I feel reborn.' She chuckled.

'I'm delighted to hear it,' Kate said.

'Now, I really must go. Mum's expecting me, and she gets fretful if I turn up late.'

Daniella got into her car and fastened the seat-belt. 'I never took Charlie as seriously as he took me. We were never meant to be, I told him that. Stubborn as a mule, he wouldn't listen. Liked to think he could wear me down. At least now I've proved he can't, if that's any consolation.'

'No, it isn't,' Kate whispered. 'But I do know that Charlie's stubborn.'

'Oh, by the way, please cancel that room I booked,' Daniella called back, as she drove off. 'I won't be staying in this hotel.'

Grief-stricken and bewildered, Kate staggered back to Reception.

'Kate!' Vivian, seeing the state she was in, led her to the ladies' and sat her down near a window. 'What happened? What did that tart say to upset you like this?'

Kate took a deep breath. 'She said that she threw *him* out, sent the lying, cheating bastard back to me.'

'You mean he didn't really want to come home, he was lying all the time?'

Kate grimaced. 'Only came back because she didn't want him, and he'd nowhere else to go.' She looked up at Vivian. 'Their affair lasted five years. *Five bloody years, Vivian!*' Kate was shouting.

'Is that what she told you?' Vivian said, astounded.

Choked up, Kate nodded violently.

'And you believed her?'

'Yes,' Kate gasped, through sobs.

'Ssh . . .' Vivian said. 'You're upset.'

'I feel sick.'

Vivian threw open a window, helped Kate put her head out of it. 'Breathe in and out slowly,' she said.

'I'd no idea . . . none at all.'

'Kate, listen, for all you know Daniella could have been lying. This might be some kind of paranoid plot to get Charlie back. You know what they say about a woman scorned.'

Kate thought for a moment. 'No, I don't think she's making it up. She sounded too genuine, and convincing.'

'Then if she didn't want him why did she have an affair with him for all those years?'

'It was a game to her. Once he was safely married she thought she'd have a bit of fun with him occasionally. It never occurred to her he'd want her permanently, and be prepared to leave me to get her. That's when it all went wrong, and I got him back.' Kate gripped the window-frame for support.

Amazed, Vivian said, 'What a bitch she is. I feel sorry for any man who has the misfortune to cross her path.'

Kate straightened up and, with a shaky grin, said, 'Not half as sorry as you will for Charlie when I've finished with him.'

'What are you going to do?' Vivian asked, alarmed.

'I don't know. First, I'm going home. After that . . . well, we'll see.'

Vivian followed her out to the foyer. 'Kate, will you be all right?'

'I'll be fine.'

'Don't do anything rash, will you?' Vivian cautioned.

But it was too late. Kate was already out of earshot.

26

Kate soldiered on until four o'clock. Mary collected Emily from school. Kate walked home slowly, her mind in turmoil as she tried to come to terms with Daniella's version of events. Five years! Not the quick fling Charlie had described, but a long, drawn-out affair. Five years of being together, dinner parties with friends, and sex. To cap it all, Daniella had ended it. Not the other way round, as Charlie had said. This couldn't be happening. One minute her world was stable, Charlie back in his place as head of the family, Emily happy, everything going nicely, at the next it was collapsing around her again.

Kate's mind raced back to that time. She tried to think rationally. Charlie had been an attentive husband and a caring father, but mostly at weekends because he had to work such long hours during the week. Their conversations took place late at night, or in the early hours, both too tired for anything more than quick exchanges. So how had he had time for Daniella with such a demanding job and a family to look after? But Daniella had been telling the truth, Kate felt sure of it. Daniella, with her beautiful, sexy body, knew all the tricks required to get a man, and how to keep a man like Charlie running after her. All she had to do was crook her finger and he would fabricate an excuse to go to her. When he was at home with Kate and Emily he was probably biding his time until he could be with Daniella.

Why hadn't she suspected it? Because he was far too clever for her, phoning home regularly whenever he was away. Kate had a contact number for him at all times, through his office and later his mobile. She had talked for ages on the phone to him, telling him about Emily's morning at nursery school, if the washing-machine had broken down. Oh, God! He had probably been in bed with Daniella during those pathetic calls to his hotel in New York when Emily had measles. She blushed with shame just thinking about how stupid she'd been. Emily had been running a fever and Kate had panicked, had pleaded with him to come home telling him that she couldn't manage without him. Thinking about it made her blush even more with mortification.

So, he'd crept back home to good old Kate as soon as Daniella had tossed him back on the scrap-heap. He'd seized his chance when he saw how upset Emily was. Oh! The shame of it! What a fool she'd been. She glanced down at the empty basement as she went up her steps, wishing Jack was there to lend a shoulder to cry on. As she put her key into the lock and went into the empty house she burst into tears. She'd have to confront Charlie as soon as possible, but she'd have to be careful too, curb her tongue, not make too much of a scene in front of Emily. The last thing she wanted to see was Emily upset again.

By the time Charlie came home from the office, tired and dishevelled, Emily was in bed. 'God! What a day,' he said. 'Honestly it's been one crisis after another. I don't know how that new manager, Hopkirk, keeps his job. Blathering, overweight upstart. I'd forgotten how bad things could get in that stuffy hole.'

Kate gritted her teeth. 'Would you rather go back to New York?' she asked mildly.

'Of course not. I'd rather be home here with you and Emily, even if it does mean working with a crowd of assholes in a poky hole of an office.' He got himself a drink, then went to her, put his arm around her shoulders. 'You seem a bit frayed this evening, would you like a drink?'

'No, thanks. Charlie, why didn't you tell me that Daniella was home?'

He turned to her, his face pale. He was breathing hard. 'Kate, you may not believe this but her coming back here has nothing to do with me,' he said harshly. 'How did you know she was back?'

'She came into the hotel this morning to book a room to be near her sick mother. She seemed to have no idea that I worked there, or so she said.'

'The reason I didn't mention it was that I didn't want to worry you, didn't want you to think I was still seeing her. I gave you my word and I've no intention of going back on it. Please believe me.' He went into the living room and dropped on to the couch.

'I do believe you.'

'You do?' He looked at her suspiciously.

'Yes.'

As relief flooded through him he perked up. 'Honestly, Kate, if I never see Daniella again it won't bother me.' He took a sip of his drink, switched on the television.

Trembling, Kate took the remote control out of his hand and switched it off.

'What are you doing?'

She faced him. 'I know you won't be seeing her again.'

'Well, that's good. It's gratifying to know that you trust me at last. Something's got through to you. Now, will you please let me put the telly on?'

'Daniella got through to me. She told me the whole story.'

Charlie blanched. 'What d'you mean?'

'She told me the bits you omitted to tell me, like the fact that your affair lasted five years. Five years, Charlie!' she shouted. 'Tell me that's not the truth if you can.'

Startled he jumped to his feet. 'I only saw her on and off during those years, not all the time, Kate.'

Kate's horrified expression made him plead, 'I didn't tell you because I didn't want to make things worse for you.' He put his hand to his head.

'For me!'

'Oh, God, Kate! I was trying to spare you by keeping back the details.'

Kate's jaw clenched. 'You were trying to spare your own hide. Just as you spared me from the fact that she finished with you when you started pestering her to let you live with her in New York, the reason why you went there in the first place.'

Charlie hit his hand against his forehead. 'Kate, it wasn't like that. She's lying. I missed you, I wanted to come home.'

'Only after she threw you out.'

Charlie studied the floor. As Kate looked at him she knew instinctively that Daniella had been telling the truth.

'I went through hell with that bloody woman, and her neurotic behaviour,' he said.

'No, it was I who went through hell with you. So did Emily.'

'I'll make it up to you, Kate, both of you, honestly I will. Please believe me, and give me that chance. What Daniella told you is her slant on it.' His eyes were brimming with tears.

'You had your chance, and you couldn't even tell me the truth.'

'I didn't want to hurt you any more than I'd done already,' he pleaded.

She swung round and said, in a low voice, 'You weren't thinking of me. Charlie, I don't know what you expected from me, but I do know that I was never enough for you, you always wanted her. If you'd got her in the first place I wouldn't have featured in your life at all.'

Charlie shook his head. 'That's not true.'

Kate didn't give him a chance to say any more. 'When I think back I was pathetic the way I went for you with a sledgehammer, determined to get you, knowing about her but believing I could make you forget her.'

'That wasn't the case . . . It wasn't like that . . .'

'It's my own fault,' she went on desperately. 'It was all my own fault.'

'Kate!' Charlie went to her. 'There was nothing wrong with you, nothing wrong with the way we lived together. It was just—'

She pushed him away. 'We were all wrong together. Oh, I thought I was happy with everything the way it was but now, knowing what I do, I feel stupid.'

'It wasn't your fault, it was me, wanting something more, feeling something was missing. I was foolish because you're the one I loved all along. I found that out the hard way. I still love you, Kate, please believe me.' He tried to put his arms round her.

'Get away from me.' She shook him off. Wretched, she began to weep. Charlie didn't know what to do or where to look. Then she wiped her eyes and raised her head proudly. 'I can't take any more of your lies and betrayal. I don't want you in my life. Not now, or ever.'

Stunned, Charlie shifted away from her. 'You don't mean that.'

'I never meant anything as much. You can go and live with your girlfriend, if she'll have you, fly off into the sunset with her for all I care. Now, get out of this house. The sight of you makes me sick.'

'Kate, you're being ridiculous.'

'Am I? Well, if that's the case I'm sorry. I just can't handle us together any more.' Suddenly Kate knew that it was true. She didn't want him there. She couldn't face any more of his deceit, couldn't take any more of the lies he dished out to her. She'd had it with him.

'But what about Emily? I just can't disappear on her again.'

'Leave Emily to me. I'll look after her.'

'You can't do this, Kate.'

'Watch me.'

Charlie sank on to the couch, his hands over his face, the tips of his fingers touching. He began to sob unrestrainedly, the tears flowing down his cheeks until his whole body seemed submerged by them. Kate stood there and let him. It was like looking at a stranger. Seeing this grown man, her own husband, reduced to such childish behaviour left her untouched. It was his own fault, all his doing, and now he was looking for her pity. What a dickhead, she thought, and the full force of her rage swelled inside her. Wasn't he only getting what he deserved?

Finally he looked up at her. 'Won't you reconsider?' he asked.

'I'll go and pack you a bag so that you won't disturb Emily.'

This triggered a fresh bout of crying. As she left the

room she said, quizzically, 'You do realise, Charlie, that this is all your own doing?'

A haze of sadness hung in the air between them.

'Yes,' he said finally.

Kate went upstairs, checked that Emily's bedroom door was firmly closed, then went into their bedroom and packed a few essentials for him; toothbrush, pyjamas, change of underwear, socks and a clean shirt.

When she returned downstairs Charlie was gone.

Her legs turned to jelly. Maybe it was her fault too. She'd been so happy and content, rearing Emily, keeping her house clean and cooking their meals, that she hadn't noticed Charlie's misery. She'd enjoyed working part-time too. It had all been enough for her. Why hadn't it been enough for him? Why, oh, why hadn't she sensed he wanted more? Why hadn't he talked to her about his unhappiness? Then they might have been able to do something about it. The questions kept coming into her head, but she could find no answers. She sank down further into the couch, and realised that she was back to square one, on her own again.

She picked up the phone and rang Lucinda, who answered on the first ring. She told her sister the whole story, amazed at her own calmness. 'I must have been stupid, and pathetic,' she finished.

'Ssh,' Lucinda said. 'You don't have to beat yourself up over it, Kate, recriminations are the last thing you need. Charlie treated you like shit. It was pathetic the way he bullied you, using Emily to fight his way back in, knowing you were desperate about her unhappiness. I could see exactly what he was up to.'

'Why didn't you say something?'

Lucinda sighed. 'How could I? You might have seen it

as interfering and Charlie certainly would have. You know he doesn't appreciate any intrusion into your life at the best of times – and, besides, this was something you had to find out for yourself.'

'Well, I did.'

'If you want me to come round I will.'

'No, I'm all right.' Kate was surprised to find that she was. 'I'll go to bed. I'm tired. Telling Emily that her daddy's gone again will be the hardest part. I dread it.'

'I can imagine. Listen, I'll meet you for lunch tomorrow, if you like. We can talk it over.'

'Are you sure?'

'Yes, I've nothing important on – I was going to phone you anyway. I'm dying for a chat.'

'Great. See you then.'

Kate looked in on Emily on her way to bed. She was fast asleep, one arm flung out, her hair fanning the pillow. The latest Harry Potter book, which Charlie had bought for her, lay on the bed beside her. Kate wondered how she was going to explain her father's absence. A pain stabbed her chest at the thought of poor Emily having to go through all the heartache of Charlie leaving home again, yet Kate knew that she could do nothing to spare her that. She would never put up with Charlie again. He could do what he liked, beg, plead, use Emily as an excuse, but she'd never let him back again. She was finished with him for good.

Next morning Kate woke with a start. She'd forgotten to set the alarm and it was almost eight o'clock. Her heart skipped a beat as she remembered the disastrous events of the previous evening. She jumped out of bed, showered, dressed and went to call Emily. 'Wake up, sweetheart,' she said, shaking her gently. 'Come on, you'll be late if you don't get up.'

Emily got out of bed and rubbed her eyes as she trudged to the loo. 'Has Daddy gone to work?' she asked sleepily, when eventually she made it to the kitchen.

'Ages ago,' Kate said hastily. There was no time to explain now. She prepared breakfast and Emily's lunch.

Emily dawdled over her cereal still half asleep.

'Emi, come on, hurry up,' Kate said, and ran upstairs to fetch her daughter's swimsuit and a towel from the hot press, put it into her sports bag, then raced back to ransack the child's chest-of-drawers for her swimming-cap. Why Emily didn't keep it in her sports bag Kate had no idea.

Emily protested that it wasn't her fault they were late.

'I know, sweetheart. I just don't want you to get into trouble with Miss Stern.' Kate put her lunchbox and a milk shake into her schoolbag.

'Who cares about Miss Stern?' Emily said sulkily. 'I don't.'

It was so difficult, Kate reflected on the way to school, to keep up with the routine of school, friends, ballet and swimming lessons. On her own again it would be harder. She would be gone all day most days from Emily, and would miss so much of her daughter's childhood. She used to love taking her to the swimming-pool, the sight of her waiting on the edge for instruction from Miss Rafter, the coach, shivering with cold and excitement. 'What do you do at Hannah's house?' she asked.

'Watch telly, play computer games.'

'You don't go outside if it's nice?'

Emily shook her head. 'We watch videos. Hannah's got *Stuart Little Part 2* and *Spy Kids Part 2*.'

Emily was watching far too much television, Kate

thought. She'd seen every video suitable for her age several times, and was up to date on all the cartoons. She would have liked to talk to Barbara about it, but she couldn't. To interfere might upset the arrangement they had. Emily was safe with Barbara and it was so reassuring to have her as backup. She'd hold her tongue for the time being.

27

At Reception Vivian stood with both elbows on the high desk and her chin cupped in her hands. 'You'll get through this, you know.'

Kate's throat tightened. People were coming and going. One man sat reading the sports section of the newspaper, glancing up every time the swing doors opened. Two women leaned against the soft cushions on the couch chatting together, waiting for a taxi. A bearded man and a smiling woman arrived with their luggage. Kate greeted them with a cheery 'Good morning.'

The man leaned forward inquisitively, the woman stood silent as they were checked in. Kate handed them their room key and wished them a pleasant stay. Luckily it was a busy morning and she kept going. Her desire to keep things running smoothly made the time go by quickly. She'd found in the past that ensuring the comfort of other people's lives helped her escape her own troubles.

Lucinda arrived at one o'clock sharp. She looked more stunning than ever in a pink top and tight leopardskin pants tucked into beige boots. Her silky blonde hair swayed as she walked, accentuating the tan that had recently been refreshed in Tobago.

As soon as they were seated in Mao's and had given their order, Lucinda said, 'I'm amazed – you're not having a hissy fit or anything.'

'I'm determined not to,' Kate said. 'It's not worth upsetting myself over him.'

'That's the spirit.' Lucinda was delighted. Leaning forward she said, 'I know it's hard, Kate, but it's lucky you found out. If you'd carried on with Charlie, God knows where you might have ended up. You were trying to do what was best for everyone and you probably didn't even notice that he was manipulating you all the time.'

Kate nodded. 'I haven't told Emily yet.'

'Where did you say Charlie was?'

'The usual, that he'd had to rush off to a conference. I'll have to tell her the truth soon.'

'She'll be fine,' Lucinda reassured her. 'It's you I'm worried about.'

Kate sighed. 'I'm better than I was the last time. In fact, I'm quite good.'

'You're marvellous, Kate,' Lucinda said. 'You're the one who's got to keep everything going.' For a moment she was reflective. 'You spend every waking minute trying to earn enough to pay the bills. This time you'll have to make him pay up. God, what a shit he turned out to be in the end.' In a low, husky voice, she said, 'Bloody men, they're all the same.'

Kate nodded not wanting to talk about it any more. 'Tell me about Tobago. Was it wonderful?'

'Absolutely magnificent. Not that I saw much of it, only the hotel swimming-pool and the night-clubs. And the men! Oh, my God, they were gorgeous.'

'Anyone in particular?' Kate was expecting news of Diego.

'I fancied all of them.'

'You're a bad girl, Lu, I thought you only had eyes for the one and only.'

'Yes, I have. But there's no harm in looking.'

'Haven't you been missing Diego like mad?'

'Of course I have, but I'm not going to admit that to him now that we're back together.'

That afternoon Kate went to school to collect Emily. As soon as the bell rang the children flooded out. Kate watched her daughter cross the playground in a group of noisy little girls, all chattering together, her schoolbag dangling and a painting in her hand. When she looked up and saw Kate she shouted 'Mum,' joyfully, and ran across to her. 'I thought you were working.'

'I got off early,' Kate said, and kissed her.

'Look what I did.' Emily held out the painting: it was of a smiling brown man and woman holding hands with a child, an enormous yellow sun hanging over them, blue sea in the background. 'It's me and you and Daddy on holiday.'

'That's beautiful, Emi,' Kate said, impressed and sad at the same time. She took her hand and steered her out of the gates, anxious to get away. Emily was in no hurry, proud to let her friends see that her mummy was there. Later that evening she was so engrossed in *Sabrina, the Teenage Witch* that Kate hadn't the heart to give her the bad news.

The next evening, Emily was invited to tea at Hannah's after school. Kate ate her quickly prepared supper, of pasta smothered in tomato and basil sauce, in the living room, flicking through the television channels. That was one advantage of being on her own: she could watch telly and eat at the same time. Not that there was anything worth watching. She looked at her empty plate. She'd have to keep up her exercise or she'd put on weight again and be in trouble with Lucinda.

If only the doorbell would ring, she thought, and some-one would call unexpectedly – like Jack used to or like when she was a child. Her aunt Florrie, her mother's sister, would arrive out of the blue in a taxi, having travelled up from Cork for a 'visit'. She would be laden with presents for everyone: yards of the best material from her shop for Mary to make summer dresses for them all, a blouse for Mary, a fine wool jumper for Kate's father. There would be home-baked fruit cake in a tin, country butter and fresh eggs. Oh, God! She'd have to tell Mary about Charlie. Now was a good time to do it, with Emily out of the way. She picked up the phone and put it down again: it was only fair to tell her such bad news to her face. She turned off the television, tidied the kitchen, changed into her tracksuit and went out.

Her mother was sitting at her old sewing-machine, making a dress for Emily's performance in *The Nutcracker*, the end-of-term ballet in aid of Ethiopia. The fine pink tulle and netting were spread out before her.

'It's a bit late in the evening to be doing that, Mum, isn't it?' Kate asked. 'You'll ruin your eyes.'

'I want to get it finished,' Mary said, carrying on deter-minedly.

It was typical of her, putting Emily's needs first when she should have been relaxing with her feet up. 'There's plenty of time.'

'I know, but I promised Emily I'd have it ready for her to try on tomorrow. Anyway, what brings you round at this hour?'

Kate told her.

Mary put down her sewing. In a choked voice she said, 'I never heard of such a carry-on.' Then she burst out furiously, 'How could he do it?'

'I don't know.'

'I can't even imagine it. All those years when I honestly thought he was genuine, and all that time . . .' She took a deep breath, shaking her head in disbelief. 'How wrong I was. What a way to treat my daughter! How dare he?' Her voice was full of vehemence.

'Maybe some of it was my fault,' Kate said.

'Ah, here! You're talking rubbish now.'

'Well, it could have been.'

'How do you make that out?'

'I didn't pay him enough attention. I remember him complaining about it soon after Emily was born, but I didn't listen.'

Their eyes met. Mary looked hard at Kate, her cheeks red, her mouth compressed into a hard line. 'How could you?' she asked. 'One baby was enough for you to cope with.'

'There must have been something I did wrong.'

Mary laughed mirthlessly. 'There doesn't have to be. He's a man, isn't he?' She continued with her sewing. The whir-whir of the wheel, and the thump-thump of the treadle as her feet powered the machine, in a frenzy of quick jerky movements that gave vent to her anger, reminded Kate of her childhood.

'I know what I'd like to do to him,' Mary said, through clenched teeth, as she grabbed her scissors and snipped off the thread. 'And to think of poor little Emily, an innocent child in all of this.' She crashed her foot down again. 'Hasn't that poor child been through enough? What did you tell her?'

'Nothing yet.'

'That's shocking!'

Frightened by her mother's anger Kate said, 'It'll be fine, Mum, honestly. The worst is over.'

'You make sure it is,' Mary warned. 'For both your sakes, get what you can out of him. Hang on to everything. Don't be foolish this time. Don't let him get away with anything. He'll ruin your life if you let him.'

'I won't, I promise you.'

Calmer now Mary sewed pink fine-woven satin ribbon into the gathers of the bodice that fell into folds from the yoke. 'Take him to the cleaners. That'll make your pain easier to bear, and buy you more time with Emily. That child needs you now more than ever.'

To keep her mother quiet Kate promised she would.

'Will you be home this evening, Mum, or will I be going to Granny's?' Emily asked, a few days later on their way to school.

'Granny's picking you up, but I'll be home by seven.'

'But, Mum, you said you'd be early today.' Emily sniffed.

'There's been a change of roster.'

'No!' Emily moaned.

'I have to work, love, you know that! If I don't work we don't eat!' Kate shouted. Instantly she regretted her outburst. 'Sorry, Emi,' she said, the guilt in her heart for not having told Emily the truth driving straight through her.

At the school gate she hugged her. 'Off you go, sweetheart. Enjoy your day, see you this evening.' She let her go waving happily, though she felt far from it.

Why had she been so short with her? It wasn't Emily's fault she had to work – and she wouldn't be home early any day in the near future. She felt guilty about that: she'd miss dinner with Emily almost every evening for at least the next week and would only have an hour with her before her bedtime when she would be too exhausted to hold a proper conversation with her.

Kate felt tired thinking about it. She was tired of responsibility, and of feeling miserable and rejected. Yes, Charlie had rejected her. That's what it had amounted to, and just when she'd fooled herself into believing that life was good again. It was all too much to bear. This was something that other people went through, not her. She felt bad for Emily too. Emily – her beautiful little daughter with her light auburn hair, who was a good, clever child, doing no harm to anyone – deserved more than she could possibly give her.

Kate didn't want to be an anxious mum, tough on a daughter who only wanted to spend more time with her. Emily was getting a raw deal. With Charlie's absence, and Kate's lack of time, the quality of her life would deteriorate.

She recalled the look in Emily's eyes as she had stood at the school gates and vowed to make it up to her. After all, the break-up of her marriage wasn't the worst thing that could happen: that had been going on slowly over a period of time. The biggest mistake Kate had made was to let it drag on in the hope of saving it. The worst scenario for Kate would be if anything were to happen to Emily.

28

Colette was waiting for Kate outside the house. 'Kate, we've got to talk,' she said, following her up the steps. 'It's about Charlie.'

'I thought so. Where is he?' Kate asked.

'At Bramble Hill, just for the present.'

'And he sent you to plead with me to take him back.'

'No – well, not exactly.'

'Forget it,' Kate said, before Colette had a chance to draw breath.

'Kate, this is not like you. Charlie's desperate!' Colette cried.

Kate swung round. 'I don't care how desperate he is, I've finished with him.'

'You can't do this to him – throw him out whenever you feel like it.'

'Is that what he told you? That I threw him out on a whim?'

'Of course not, but I presume you had another silly argument and that he's waiting for you to calm down. He learned a sorry lesson the last time, you know.'

'You would have thought so, after all that happened. You wouldn't think it could get any worse.'

Colette frowned as she looked into Kate's eyes. 'I know he's not seeing Daniella still. That's all finished.'

Kate met her gaze. 'It's what he did in the past.'

A puzzled look passed over Colette's features.

'Do you know how long his affair with Daniella went on? Five years.'

'*What?*' Colette gasped.

'Every opportunity he got he was with her – when he went over there or when she came here.'

'Oh, my God!' Colette said. 'It's unbelievable. Are you sure?'

'I got it straight from the horse's mouth,' Kate confirmed.

There was a pause before Colette said, 'Daniella might have been lying. I've known her most of my life and she always exaggerated everything. I'd check it out, if I were you.'

'Charlie confirmed it when I confronted him.'

'But how did he manage to keep it a secret?'

'Very well. There were no clues, he was too smart for that,' Kate said angrily. 'There was me bringing up Emily, totally ignorant of what was going on.' She laughed at her own stupidity.

'But this is outrageous.'

'You're telling me! How he faced me day after day with that on his conscience, I don't know, but he did.'

Colette sat down suddenly.

'Would you forgive him if he were your husband? Would you?' Kate persisted.

Dumbfounded, Colette shook her head. The line of defence she'd prepared for Charlie was smashed to smithereens.

'Of course you wouldn't.' Wound-up, Kate continued, 'I found it hard to forgive a fling but when I found out that it had gone on for all that time I just couldn't cope. Did you know that if Daniella had agreed to settle down with him he'd never have come back, and to hell with Emily and me?'

Colette looked at her incredulously, horror stamped across her brow. 'He was always restless, always looking for something more in the last few years,' she said. 'I thought it was blind ambition.'

'Obviously leading a double life was getting to him.'

'But why did he do it? He was happy with you,' Colette said.

'Was he?' Kate was pacing up and down. 'That's what he let me believe, but I was never enough for him. I shouldn't have married him.' She put her palm to her forehead. 'I proposed to him. I pushed it.' Kate hadn't meant to say that, but it had slipped out.

Colette shook her head. It was all she had the energy to do.

'I've never admitted that to another soul, but it's true.'

'Who proposed to whom doesn't make a jot of difference,' Colette said.

'What do you mean?'

'Charlie is his own man. Nobody pushes him. If he hadn't loved you he wouldn't have agreed to it, and he did love you, Kate. I know because I asked him at the time.'

'You did?'

'We talked about it just before the wedding. He was really happy about it.'

'I don't believe you.'

'I swear to God.' Colette crossed her heart.

Thank you for saying that, Colette, but if he'd been that happy he wouldn't have got back with Daniella. I didn't give him the buzz she did.'

Defeated, Colette said, 'I suppose not.'

'My big problem now is Emily. What am I going to say

to her this time? How do you tell a child that the father she adores is a lowlife, cheating rat?'

'Ah, no, don't do that, Kate. It'd be insane to tell her the details. Don't disillusion her. She's too young, it would destroy her,' Colette advised.

Kate put her face into her hands. 'I can't stand it,' she said. 'I can't fucking stand it. I don't know what to do.'

Colette was by her side, massaging her shoulders. 'Do nothing for the moment. Not while you're depressed like this. This whole thing has taken its toll on you. Bide your time until you've calmed down. Tell Emily Charlie's away on business.'

'That's what I told her this morning but I can't fob her off for ever.'

'You don't know how it'll pan out. You might relent—'

'No!' Kate screeched. 'Not this time. It's well and truly over. I won't have him under my roof ever again!'

'I hate to stand by and watch you both fall apart,' Colette said sadly.

'Charlie'll pick himself up pretty quick.'

Colette collected her handbag. 'Are you sure there's nothing I can do?'

'I've given up. I don't love him the way I did.'

'What will you do?'

'I'll carry on the same as before. What choice do I have?'

'What will I tell him?' Colette asked.

'Tell him that the next time I talk to him will be through my solicitor.'

'You really mean that?'

'I do.'

Colette was shocked. 'Please consider this, Kate. Don't do anything in haste. You might regret it. Wait until you've calmed down and you're more rational.' She gestured helplessly at the room. 'You'd miss all this if it were taken from you. It's your home, Kate,' she pointed out, as if Kate didn't already know that. 'You've had a lot of setbacks,' she commiserated, 'but this is your marriage we're talking about. You can't just cast it aside.'

'Charlie did it, not me.'

Emily was perched on the couch.

'Time for bed,' Kate said, switching off the television.

The phone rang. Emily ran to it. 'It's Daddy,' she cried. 'Daddy, when are you coming home?'

In that beat of silence Kate felt her heart flip.

'Oh! I'll get Mum.' She came back into the room, pale and shaken. 'He wants to speak to you.'

Heart sinking, Kate went into the hall. 'I can't go on like this, telling lies to the child,' Charlie said. 'You haven't told her, have you?' He was raising his voice.

'No, and I feel really bad about that.'

'You'd better do it unless . . . you've changed your mind.'

'No, Charlie, I'm sticking to my guns.'

The phone went dead. Kate came back into the room.

Emily looked at her, wide-eyed. 'Daddy's not coming home, is he?'

Kate put her arms round her. 'Not for a while, sweetheart. We've problems to sort out.'

Emily sucked in her breath. 'You're getting sep'rated, aren't you?'

'Eh . . .'

'I knew it,' Emily said, with a sigh of inevitability. 'You told me a lie. You said you weren't when I asked you.' She burst into tears.

'We weren't then.'

Emily rounded on her. 'But he said he'd never leave again!' she cried, tears running down her cheeks.

'I know he did, Emi love,' Kate said, holding her stiff little body, stroking her hair, 'and he meant it at the time. But Daddy and I aren't getting on. I know it's hurting you, and I'm sorry about that. We tried, we really did. It just didn't work out. Sometimes things happen that can't be helped.'

Emily shuddered, and Kate dried her eyes with a tissue. 'You're cross with him again, aren't you?' She bit her lower lip.

'It's not as simple as that, Emily,' Kate said, her insides twisting in agony. 'Daddy loves you and he always will no matter what happens between us.' Having to explain things to Emily without being able to tell her the truth was the hardest thing of all.

'Will I see him soon?' Emily asked, after a while.

'Of course you will. He's staying at Bramble Hill while he's looking for a place, somewhere close by so that you can see a lot of each other.' Kate tightened her arms around the child. 'It'll be all right. Daddy will take you out for whole days, sometimes weekends.'

'Where?'

'Anywhere you want to go.'

Emily perked up. 'Will he take me to Disneyland?'

'Maybe in the summer holidays.'

She took Emily up to bed, tucked her in and read her a chapter of her book. Then she saw that her eyes were closed. As she turned off the light Emily's eyes snapped open. 'What are we going to do, Mum? We're all alone now.'

'Of course we're not. You'll see Daddy all the time, and we've got Granny and Lucinda and—'

'But they don't live here. It's only us; even Jack's gone. It'll be lonely,' she said, rotating her Sugar Plum Barbie ballerina round and round on the little stand.

'We'll get by, we have lots of friends,' Kate said, trying to inject some enthusiasm into her voice.

'I'll help you,' Emily said. She stroked Oscar, who'd hopped up onto her bed. 'I'll feed Oscar myself.' Her attempt at being grown-up made it all the more painful.

Later Kate got undressed mechanically, and took a shower to steady her nerves. In the bathroom mirror her face was gaunt, her eyes hollow. In bed she stretched out and closed her eyes. Her marriage to Charles Stuart Conway, which she'd expected to last a lifetime, was finally over. While he was preparing for a new life she had been left to put hers and Emily's back together. Charlie would argue that it didn't have to be that way, but she knew that it did.

In the not too distant future she wouldn't be married any more. She'd be a single mother, no one's wife. A feeling of strangeness washed over her at the thought of it.

She'd have to get used to living alone again. There would be no Charlie coming in from work each evening, Emily greeting him with her usual whoop of delight, chattering away to him while Kate served dinner.

She found it hard to accept that she was finally a woman on her own. This was her new life. She'd have the freedom to do whatever she wanted.

Before she went to sleep she checked Emily once more, worried about her. She was sleeping soundly, her face flushed, her head thrown back as if she hadn't got a care in the world, her arm around Barbie. Kate straightened her duvet, and kissed her.

*   *   *

The next afternoon Kate took a half-day and delivered Emily and Hannah to the swimming-pool because Barbara wasn't well. As she watched the children rushing headlong into the pool, all shrieking as they hit the water she was surprised to see that Emily looked as happy and normal as all the other kids.

Later, when Emily was in bed, Kate didn't feel like being alone. She thought of phoning Jack to invite him out for a drink, get Mary to babysit, but his mobile was switched off. She considered leaving a message but couldn't think how to word it.

29

The following Sunday, as arranged, Charlie called to take Emily out for the day. He stood on the doorstep, a woebegone look on his face. 'Is she ready?' he asked Kate.

'Almost. She'll be down in a minute. Do you want to come in?'

'No!'

'Look, this is as hard for me as it is for you,' Kate said.

'I hope you don't expect me to feel sorry for you,' Charlie snapped. 'Look at you, monopolising our home and our child. Who do you think you are?'

'I am not monopolising anything,' Kate hissed under her breath.

'Oh, no? You should see yourself!' He stepped back. 'Hands on your hips, calling the shots like a fishwife, making sure I pay for all my mistakes, no matter what I do to try to make it up with you.' His face contorted with anger.

She glared at him.

'Have you given my situation any consideration? Have you thought how upset I've been?'

'No,' Kate said, and glanced over her shoulder to see if Emily was within earshot.

'I would have done anything to keep us together. You wouldn't let me.'

Emily dashed downstairs. 'Here I am, Daddy.' She ran out to meet him.

'Please,' Kate said, in a low voice, 'not in front of her.'

Charlie clenched his fists by his sides. 'Hello, Princess,' he said, and mustered a smile as he hugged her.

Emily ran back to Kate, gave her a peck on the cheek. 'Will you be all right?' she asked.

'Of course I will. I'll be at work. 'Bye, love, enjoy yourself,' Kate said.

They went off, Emily skipping to the car.

'Have a lovely time,' Kate called.

Emily waved and blew her a kiss as they drove off.

Kate shut the door, went back to the kitchen and collapsed into the nearest chair. Although their exchange on the doorstep had been brief, it had left her in a bad state. But she didn't regret her actions. Their exchange had reinforced her resolve to keep Charlie out of her life. She didn't want him any more. Thinking about it made her notice how much she'd changed since the first time she'd forced him to go. Gone was the dutiful wife whose world had centred on his wishes. In her place was a woman who was determined to make a go of it, and not spend time fretting about her weak, foolish husband.

Certain that she had done the right thing, she felt stronger than she had for a long time. And she'd more purpose than she'd ever had before. That thought gave her great satisfaction. Strange to think that only recently she had been doing everything she could to save her marriage, and all the time there was nothing to save. She got to her feet and went to work gladly, knowing she would get paid double time as it was Sunday.

That afternoon she told Tim all about it, concluding, 'I'm not having him back, ever.'

Tim gave her a hug. 'Good for you. He thought he'd creep back when all the fuss had died down, like he did before, get you at a vulnerable moment, tell you all that old codswallop again.'

'He says I'm monopolising everything.'

'Dead right too, if you are. It was pathetic, you putting up with him all these years, like some downtrodden waif. Now he can't bully you into taking him back. The fact that he can't keep you trapped in the little-wife role, day in day out, must be killing him, the gobshite.'

Kate laughed.

'I should think he's in shock with you wearing the trousers. You've learned a lot from his mistakes.'

'I certainly have.'

'Isn't that terrific all the same? Let's drink to it. It's four o'clock, a decent time to start getting drunk,' he said brightly.

'Yes, let's do that.' Kate giggled like a naughty school-girl.

Tim poured her a large vodka and tonic, and a pint of Guinness for himself. 'Here's to new beginnings, and getting rid of the gobshites of this world.'

They toasted each other.

'I really don't like Charlie any more,' Kate said.

'Great.'

'In fact I hate him,' Kate said, filled with resentment at having been cheated.

'That's fantastic!' Tim applauded. 'I'll drink to that. It's going to be all right, you know. There are plenty more gobshites out there, thousands of them. You just have to wait. The good times are coming.'

'I thought you were being positive about this.'

'I'm only coddin',' he said, with a goofy grin. 'You'll

meet someone nice some day. Meanwhile let's get drunk while you're waiting.'

'No, I have to be sober for Emily.'

Emily returned from Bramble Hill in high spirits. 'Daddy says he'll buy me a pony of my own for Christmas,' she told Kate excitedly. 'Uncle Frank will find one for me.'

When she was tucked up in bed she said, 'I asked Daddy if he was ever coming back to live with us.'

'And?' Kate asked, playing for time.

He said he's going to buy a house in a sunny place and that I can come and live with him instead. Do you think it will be in America, Mum, near Disneyland?'

Kate's heart skipped a beat. 'I don't know, darling, we'll have to wait and see.' Later on Lucinda phoned. 'I'm having a party at the weekend. You'll come, won't you?'

Kate hesitated. 'I don't think so. I'm not in the party mood.'

'It would do you good to get out.'

Kate tried to think of another excuse. 'Your friends are all . . .' She stopped, not wanting to appear rude. 'Too sophisticated for me,' she finished.

'Don't be daft!' laughed Lucinda. 'Pop over, even if you only stay for an hour. You must have cabin fever holed up in that house night after night.'

'Right, I'll come,' Kate agreed, to shut her up.

Lucinda sounded happier than she'd been for a long time as she talked about the party and who would be there. Not that she was saying much about any of the current men in her life. Since Diego's reappearance in her life they hadn't really had a proper chat about her love-life.

Now that she'd agreed to go to the party she wouldn't

let Lucinda down. She'd have her hair done, go the whole hog and get a manicure, perhaps even an eyelash tint if she could pluck up the courage to face Sonia.

Early on her day off she took the Dart to Westland Row, and headed straight for the dreaded Sonia, who screwed up her bland, glossy face, then clacked a sigh of despair when she examined Kate's eyebrows. 'You haven't been keepin' up,' she said, as she tottered around on her high heels, preparing her instruments like a surgeon about to perform open-heart surgery. 'They're nearly down to your chin.'

Gross exaggeration, Kate thought, and said, 'Family crisis.'

'No excuse.' She began plucking furiously, clicking her tongue in disapproval as she did so. When she had finished she switched to Kate's nails. 'There's no hope for these,' she said, sawing away with an enormous emery board. 'I'll have to give you the acrylics.' She advised Kate to visit her fortnightly, if there was to be any salvation of her appearance.

'I haven't got time,' Kate protested.

'You'll get no thanks for lettin' yourself go,' Sonia warned impatiently.

When Kate checked her appearance in the mirror she couldn't believe the change. 'I can't believe I'm wearing makeup,' she said, and picked up the tube of foundation that had made her skin dewy and left it unmarked by lines or wrinkles. Her lips were coated with clear gloss. Her eyebrows were perfectly arched, and emphasised by a pastel eye-shadow. She looked clean, healthy and sexy, a woman in control of her life, if slightly genetically modified, but not in the least neurotic like she really was. Her acrylic nails dug into everything she touched as she paid the bill.

Next stop was Giorgio, Lucinda's gorgeous Italian hairdresser in Sussex Street.

'Kate, how nice to see you,' Giorgio gushed, as he came to meet her, his newly shaved head shining in the sunlight. 'And how is Lucinda?'

'Fine, thanks, she sends her love,' Kate lied.

'Ah, two sisters so very different,' he said. 'You have difficult hair.' He eyed Kate's springy red mass sadly, probably wishing it was Lucinda's golden tresses. 'And what style would you like?' he enquired, twiddling the hairs of his goatee thoughtfully.

'I was hoping you could suggest something,' Kate said, knowing he'd do exactly as he pleased regardless of what she said.

He lifted up her hair, let it fall back in disgust. 'These spleet ends have to go. You have a good jawline, so a choppy look would be just the theeng, and some highlights. I make you look like Lulu. Yes?' he asked.

'Great,' Kate said, thinking how wonderful Lulu's hairstyle was. She'd read in a magazine that Lulu attributed her youthful appearance to her good hairdresser, and plenty of sex. Kate would have to settle for the hairstyle and hope for the best with the rest.

He whipped his scissors out of the pouch slung over his shoulder, like a gun from its holster, and aimed them at her hair. Long swathes fell to the floor, and Giorgio cut deeper into it. Just as she feared that he wouldn't stop until she was bald he put his scissors back, produced a razor and ran it down the ends. Then he wrapped sections in coloured tinfoil, and left her to read magazines. Half an hour later he shampooed, blow-dried, sprayed and waxed, fanning out the jagged ends fastidiously. Then held up a mirror. 'A big improvement?' he said.

Kate hardly recognised herself as she gazed at the streaky bob, cut to hover manageably just below her jaw.

'Nice 'n' sharp,' he said, admiring his own handiwork.

Sharp enough to cut his throat on if he bent down, Kate thought uncharitably. But she had to admit that the result was amazing. Her short hair raised her jawline, emphasised her bone structure and widened her eyes. She looked ten years younger. But would she be able to manage this high-maintenance style? She doubted it.

'You use this tube of wax on the ends like I did,' he said, beaming as he handed her the product from a shelf.

She handed over her Visa card, light-headed from the shock of the bill and the new style. She glided out, and went straight to Karen Millen to buy a sexy dress to go with her new sexy look.

With renewed confidence she said to the sales assistant, 'I was here recently with my sister Lucinda.'

The sales girl peered at her. 'Oh, yes, I remember you. Kept up the exercise regime, I see,' she said admiringly, as she looked Kate up and down.

'No . . . well . . . yes, I suppose I did in a way. Lucinda's having a party. I need something very smart.'

The girl went to the rail and picked out a short halter-neck lacy black dress. 'It came in this morning. I'm sure it would look great on you.'

'It's gorgeous, but tiny,' Kate said.

'It's not as small as it looks, and because it's cut on the bias it's very flattering. Why don't you try it on?'

Kate made a beeline for the changing room with the dress tucked under her arm.

When she reappeared the girl said, 'It looks fabulous.'

Kate twirled around, gazing critically into the mirror. It was the first time she'd ever seen a resemblance between herself and Lucinda. 'It's gorgeous,' she said, 'but is it not a bit young for me?'

'Of course not.' The sales assistant smiled. 'It's perfect.'

'Are you sure?'

'It wouldn't be in my interest to lie to you,' the sales assistant demurred.

'I'll take it,' Kate said, and, shuddering at the price, produced her Visa card again.

She made a dash for the Dart to be home on time for Emily.

30

Kate put on the black feather-light bra and matching thong
Lucinda had brought her back from Paris, then slipped her
new black dress over her head. It slid down her body light
as a sigh. In the mirror it looked even skimpier than it had
in the shop. She had already applied her new St Tropez
fake tan and now did her makeup. Lastly, she tackled her
hair, trying to blow it dry into the jagged style Giorgio had
created, waxing the ends when she had finished. The result
was a longish fringe that zigzagged across her face, and
floppy ends. She brushed and pulled to get the 'sharp look'
Giorgio had achieved with a flick of his wrist. She gave up
when the taxi she'd booked arrived.

She hovered on the steps outside Lucinda's apartment,
too terrified of her sister's scary friends to go in. Lucinda,
ravishing in a revealing red chiffon dress, her hair loose and
flowing, her feet almost bare in gold thong sandals to match
her tanned legs, sailed out to greet her. 'Kate! Look at you!'
she said in amazement. 'You look fabulous.'

There was a hush as the guests turned to stare, all
beautiful women in the style of Lucinda, the men foppish
but sophisticated.

'Everyone, this is my sister, Kate!' Lucinda introduced
her proudly. 'Isn't she stunning?'

There was a chorus of 'Hi, Kate!'

The place was crowded with barely enough standing

room. Kate eyed the glamorous women, the sexy men, the bottles of booze, and wondered what she was doing there. She felt fearful, a failure with a broken marriage and no hope for the future.

Then Jack waltzed in from the kitchen, casually dressed in jeans and a white jumper. The moment he spotted her his face changed. 'Hi, Kate!' he said, flashing her a smile.

'Jack! What are you doing here?'

'Enjoying the party,' he said, eyes twinkling. 'So, what do you think of this lot, then?'

'A bit frightening.'

'Could be good,' he said.

'I didn't know you were coming.'

'I moved into an apartment two doors down the hall. Small world, isn't it?'

'Small city,' she said, wondering why Lucinda hadn't mentioned this to her.

'You look great. Had your hair cut.'

'Yes.'

'Suits you.'

'Thank you.'

'How are you?' His eyes scanned her face.

'I'm fine.'

'And Emily?'

'She's well, thanks.'

'Things must be working out well between you and Charlie. I've never seen you look so good.'

'Well, no, actually. We've parted again.'

'Really!' Jack's eyes widened.

'I'm afraid so.'

'Did it again, did he?'

'No,' Kate said. 'I found out just how long he'd been with Daniella. It goes right back to when Emily was only three.'

'Oh!'

'When I realised the extent of his deceit I just couldn't take it. My love for him didn't stretch that far.'

'I can understand that,' Jack agreed. 'I thought you were mad to have him back in the first place.'

'I know you did, but I felt I had to give him another chance. As it turned out you were right.'

What Kate didn't tell Jack was how much she'd found herself thinking of him since he'd left.

More people arrived, beautiful glossy women, and tall, toned, polished men. The party got noisier, everyone talking at once, Lucinda regaling them with tales of her recent adventures with Diego in the Dominican Republic on his schooner.

'You've fallen on your feet!' someone said enviously.

'And on her back, lucky bitch,' said one of the male models jealously.

Kate tried not to be envious of Lucinda's happiness, but she couldn't help feeling on the wrong side of the track.

Lucinda took Jack away to introduce him to people, and Kate had another glass of wine to get her through the next hour. She chatted about holidays to Tanya, a friend of Lucinda, while observing Jack out of the corner of her eye. He was roaring with laughter at something Lucinda had said. Kate watched him and marvelled at how unfazed he seemed to be by her, and how well he mingled with her friends. He caught Kate's eye and raised his glass to her. She raised hers, and held his gaze longer than she should have. So what! He looked very handsome in his party gear and she'd fancied him madly when he was living in her basement but had been too consumed with guilt about her marriage to do anything about it. Now things were different, Charlie was gone so there was nothing stopping her making a play for him. He was exactly what she needed after all the heartache. She could finally be her natural self. She might even let him know how she felt because she knew he fancied her too. He was leaving now, saying goodbye to everyone, edging over to her on his way out.

'I'm slipping away, early start in the morning. Belfast bound,' he said.

'Oh!' She had been thinking she couldn't stand another minute of the rowdiness, and wanted to leave too.

'Do you want a lift home?' he asked. 'I'm going to Dun Laoghaire, staying with the guy who's coming on the shoot with me tomorrow.'

'Could I?'

'Sure!'

In the car he said, 'What a night!'

'You enjoyed yourself,' Kate remarked.

'It was good fun. Lucinda knows how to give a party and, boy, do they know how to drink, that crowd.'

'Lucinda's had plenty of practice. Parties are her thing. It's amazing how different we are.'

'Chalk and cheese.'

'We always were. I'm quite shy, really, and Lucinda doesn't know the meaning of the word. She thinks I should start dating again. She's going to try and fix me up with her friend Kyle.'

'I see.'

'I don't feel comfortable around men at the moment. I don't mean you, Jack. I feel okay with you.'

'I should hope so.'

'From the time you moved in I felt as though we were friends.'

'We are.'

The rest of the journey was spent in companionable silence.

'Here you are, safe and sound,' Jack said, pulling up outside her house.

'Would you like to come in for a coffee or a nightcap?'

Jack kept the engine running. 'No, thanks, it's very late.'

'Just a quick one.'

He shook his head emphatically. 'Thanks all the same but I'd better keep going. Tomorrow is a really big day for me, and I'll need my wits about me.'

Kate opened the passenger door. 'Maybe some other time,' she said brightly.

'Yeah, great.'

'Would you like to come to supper one evening next week? Emily would love to see you. She misses you.'

'Sure,' he said. 'I'd love to see her too. I'll phone you. Give my love to Emily,' he said, revving the engine, anxious to be off.

'Thanks for the lift.' Kate leaned over, and gave him a peck on the cheek. His skin was soft and deliciously smooth.

'You're welcome. Oh, and by the way, you ought to give the dating a chance.'

'Yes, you're right, maybe I will,' she said, with a forced smile, and got out of the car, feeling herself blush with mortification.

As soon as she had shut the car door he was roaring off down the road. Kate stood on the path looking after him. He must have read the come-on signals and known she was making a pass at him. He didn't want to know. She'd made a complete fool of herself. She thought of the last time they had been together, how much he'd wanted her. He was playing hard to get, paying her back for her rejection. She mounted the steps.

The next evening she called over to see Barbara on a
pretext about Emily's schedule.

'How did it go?' Barbara asked.

'Very well,' Kate said.

'Good, I'm glad. It's about time you got a life.'

'Jack was there,' Kate said. 'I didn't know that he and
Lucinda were neighbours.'

'Yes, great, isn't it?'

Kate wasn't so sure about that and didn't know why
she had told Barbara this. She didn't want her to know,
or anyone else for that matter – but she found that she
needed to say his name, and talk about him.

'You fancy him!' Barbara said, in surprise. 'You never
said anything when he was living with you.'

Kate lowered her voice. 'Yes, I know. I couldn't let
myself think of him in that way with Charlie still in my
life, but I've fancied him for a long time. I just hope I
haven't left it too late.'

'I think you might have. Did you know that he and
Lucinda are sort of seeing each other?'

Aghast, Kate said, 'Are you sure?'

'Oh, I'm sorry, you didn't know, did you?'

'No.' Kate felt uncomfortable.

Choosing her words carefully, Barbara said, 'They've
been out a few times recently, what with being neighbours
and everything.' Her eyes on Kate were sharp as she said,
'As a matter of fact Lucinda has invited him to Marbella
for a week's holiday. I'm surprised she didn't mention it.'

'She never said a word to me,' Kate mused. 'I know
one of her friends has a villa there, and is letting her use
it.' She was wishing now that she'd kept her mouth shut
about Jack, and Barbara was giving her more information
than she wanted to hear.

'You've had such a rough time, and been so preoccupied with your own troubles, she probably didn't want to shove her happiness down your throat. Ask her. I don't think it's a secret.'

Later that evening when Kate mentioned it to Mary she confirmed what Barbara had said. 'She seems to like him.'

'But what about Diego?' Kate asked. 'She was really keen on him.'

'He's been giving her the run-around. The last time they met he had to rush off somewhere at the last minute. She was devastated. He's too elusive for her liking. What with his jet-setting friends and his business interests she doesn't seem able to pin him down.'

'She gives up too easily.'

'If you ask me he's a bit of a playboy,' Mary said thoughtfully, 'Jack is more her type. He's stable, just what she needs. They'll probably settle down together.'

'Settle down!' Kate was appalled.

'Well, yes, in time. He'd be perfect for her,' she said. 'He'd stop her running around with playboys.'

'To be honest, Jack's no match for Lucinda, Mum. She'd be too strong a personality for him.'

'Don't be ridiculous. Of course he's well able for her. He's very good with her.'

'He's not ready for a big relationship. In fact, I know he has no intention of settling down for a long time. He told me so.'

Mary's face glazed over. 'Leave it to Lucinda. She'll change his mind for him. By all accounts he really likes her.'

'He never mentioned her to me.'

'They're probably keeping it quiet. Lucinda's not saying much but I can tell that this is the first time she's ever fancied a normal Catholic Irishman, someone from her own background, and there's nothing I'd like more than to see her settled before I pass on.'

'You're being dramatic! You've no notion of dying for at least thirty years.'

'Time's creeping on, and Lucinda won't always be young enough to gad around the world.'

'She still wants to enjoy herself,' Kate protested.

'Let's face it, Kate, the men she attracts are not the marrying kind. They just want a good time. Now, to my mind, Jack's the one that fits the bill. He's a lot more mature than any one else she's come across so far, probably more than any she's likely to encounter in the future. To tell you the truth, I'm impressed with him.'

'I can tell.'

'According to her friends, Lucinda's making a big impression on him too.'

'I'm bound to hear all about it from Jack when I see him,' Kate said. 'I've invited him to dinner next week.'

'You shouldn't have done that.' Mary pursed her lips.

'Why not?'

'I wouldn't encourage him if I were you.'

'But why not? He's a friend.'

'I know, but it's not fair to Lucinda for you to have him round now that you're on your own again.'

'That's ridiculous.'

'She really likes him, and this is her big chance,' Mary persisted.

'That's your side of it, but if she fancies him that much why didn't she tell me?'

'Because you've got enough to think about with your own problems. Seeing other people happy can be quite upsetting at a time like this.'

'I'm going to ask her straight out.'

'Careful – you don't want to rock the boat,' Mary cautioned. 'It's Lucinda's future we're talking about here. I wasn't reckoning on you spoiling it all for her.'

'How could I do that?'

Mary's eyes narrowed. 'Inviting him to your place with you on your own is playing on his vulnerability. The poor man won't know whether he's coming or going.'

'Mum! You're jumping to conclusions,' Kate protested.

'All I'm saying is that if you come between them I'll never forgive you.'

Shocked, Kate caught her breath. 'Fine,' she said. 'I'll cancel him.'

When Mary had left, Kate shut the door and leaned against it, the shock of what her mother had said seeping through her. In the kitchen she gazed out of the window, seeing nothing, chest heaving, her mind going over and over her mother's words. Lucinda and Jack! And Mary's attitude towards them! Kate couldn't take it all in. Surely Lucinda would have said something. And what had happened between her and Diego? Had she given him his marching orders just because she couldn't pin him down as Mary indicated? Kate hadn't seen much of Lucinda recently, but they'd talked on the phone. Lucinda hadn't mentioned any problems with Diego, and even if he was a little elusive surely she'd persevere a bit longer – she'd seemed so crazy about him.

Mystified, Kate recalled Lucinda and Jack laughing together at the party. He had seemed so at home with her friends. He was probably half living in her apartment already. God! What a fool she was. No wonder he'd been so reluctant when she'd virtually thrown herself at him in his car. She'd probably embarrassed the hell out of him.

Why shouldn't Jack fancy Lucinda? He was free to do exactly as he wished. So was Lucinda, as Mary had so rightly pointed out. Kate thought of her sister's looks: she couldn't hold a candle to her. Lucinda had everything going for her – and not just her beauty: she had a terrific personality, bucketloads of charm and charisma. She usually got what she wanted. Jack had better watch out, because if she'd set her heart on him he didn't stand a chance. If only she'd known, she wouldn't have made such an eejit of herself, chasing him like that.

All of a sudden she felt weary with life. The demands being made on her now that she was alone again were relentless. It was get up, take Emily to school, go to work, come home, cook dinner and do the housework. It was such an effort pushing forward from morning until night. Is that the way it was always going to be?

A wave of hopelessness washed over her. Every time she tried to build up her life, something or someone dashed it to the ground. No matter how hard she tried nothing was going right for her. It was just one humiliation after another – and now Jack was forbidden to her just when she could have done with a friend. And Lucinda was so busy that she didn't have any time to spare for her. It was all a nightmare, and Kate was feeling sorry for herself.

Take Lucinda, for instance. The baby of the family, she'd always been her mother's favourite. All her life Mary had spoilt her, giving in to her every whim no matter how outlandish, because she was so pretty and sweet and irresistible. Kate had been the solid, sensible one. Lucinda had become a star in the modelling firmament, with the world at her feet, while Kate hadn't even got a career to fall back on. Well, she'd cope on her own, and she'd show them all that she didn't need a man to survive.

31

She phoned Jack.

'Telepathy! I was just about to ring you,' Jack said pleasantly. 'How are you?'

'Fine. Jack, do you mind if we cancel next week?'

'Not at all. Has something come up?'

'No. Well, sort of.'

'What's going on?'

Kate hadn't thought to make up an excuse. 'I . . . Emily's going to a sleep-over, and there wouldn't be any point if she's not going to be here.'

'Oh! I suppose not.'

Silence.

'Would you like to come to the cinema instead?' Jack asked, taking her by surprise. 'Shouldn't be a problem if Emily's out for the night.'

'I don't—'

'We could go to see *About a Boy*. I've been dying to see it for ages, just never had the time, and you've read the book, haven't you?'

'Yes, it was very good.'

'Well, then, can't I tempt you?'

'I don't feel like going out these days.' Kate felt like a damp squib.

'It's no fun being stuck in all on your own.'

'That's true.'

'I'll call for you at half past seven on Friday, all right?'

The phone went dead before she had a chance to argue.

As the days went by Kate looked forward to Friday with a gathering sense of dread, partly because of the embarrassment of the night of the party, but mostly because of Mary's warning to her to keep her distance from him. It was stupid. Why shouldn't she stay friends with him regardless of her narrow-minded mother? She wouldn't feel so bad if she could stay in and watch telly with him, where nobody would see them together. Getting dressed up and going out was like a date.

She compromised by wearing an inexpensive pink floral patterned skirt and matching top she'd bought in the sales to cheer herself up.

As soon as Jack saw her she said, 'You look terrific.'

'Thank you.'

He left his car outside her house and they walked to the cinema through the park, where he stopped to admire the new swings and slides in the children's play area. It was like old times, only not quite. Kate wasn't at ease, and Jack didn't appear to be in a good mood, although he tried to hide it. She was tempted to ask him what was wrong, but the closed-off expression on his face made her decide not to.

The cinema was full, and Jack began to relax. They laughed a lot, and when they emerged from the cinema, Jack was still grinning as he recounted the funny bits of the film.

'It's too early to go home. Would you like to go for a coffee?' he asked.

They went to the sea-front, and sat at a pavement table

outside Mao's. It was a glorious summer evening. As they each sipped a double espresso they watched the sun sink slowly behind crimson-tipped clouds. People strolled by, some with children as if it were the middle of the day. Kate wondered why Jack had gone quiet, and whether she should mention Lucinda or wait until he broached the subject.

Finally, when nothing was forthcoming, she said, 'What's on your mind, Jack?'

He looked up at her. '*National Geographic* are not renewing my contract.'

'*What?*'

'They've taken on a new foreign photographer. He's to do the trip across America that I was hoping to do in the autumn.'

'But why?'

'This guy specialises in these goofy photographs and they seem to be going for this type of picture.' Jack looked stricken. 'I was so sure of it. I bought the apartment on the strength of it.'

'How can they do that to you?'

'Oh, they can. It's their privilege.'

'It seems so unfair.'

'When was life ever fair?'

'Don't I know it.'

'The real problem is the new apartment. I'll have to sell it if I don't get more work soon. It's as simple as that.'

'What will you do?'

Jack raked his hair out of his eyes. 'I'll have to get another job, not easy in my specialist field.'

It was on the tip of Kate's tongue to offer him the basement if he had to sell his apartment, but she dared not. 'Have you got anything in mind?'

'Oh, you know, I'll do whatever I can get for the time being – weddings, launches. Lucinda has said she can get me work with her agency.'

'That's a lucrative market.'

'I know. Not my thing, though.' He stared ahead, thoughtful for a moment. 'I'll possibly have to go back to the States.'

'No!' Kate gaped at him in horror, her stomach twisting at the thought. 'You can't do that.'

Jack laughed. 'Why not? I've done it before.'

Embarrassed by her outburst she stammered, 'It's a drastic course of action.'

'But possibly the only one.' Jack's voice was full of resignation.

She kept her eyes on the HSS ferry as it sailed out between the outstretched arms of the piers, its white hull golden in the sunset. She didn't want Jack to see her heartbreak.

'What about you?' he said. 'You've got something on your mind too. I can tell.'

Kate shut her eyes for a second. When she opened them she'd recovered her composure. 'I'm fine,' she said, feigning a smile.

'I know you better than that.' He was looking at her, his head almost imperceptibly inclined. After a brief silence he said, 'Tell me, what is it?'

She raised her chin defiantly. 'Honestly. There isn't a problem.'

'Yeah,' he said softly. 'And I'm a Dutchman.' He looked at her. 'So why don't you want to tell me, then?'

She gulped. 'I think we'd better make tracks, it's getting late,' she said, drained her coffee cup, and got to her feet.

Slowly they made their way home. This time Jack was glad to come in for a drink – he needed the company, Kate guessed. He sat in the living room sipping his wine as if time stretched on for ever.

There was a ring on the doorbell.

'Who could it be at this hour?' Kate said, puzzled.

Her stomach heaved when she saw Charlie on the doorstep. 'I've come to take Emily to Bramble Hill,' he said.

'At this time?'

'I got delayed at a meeting – I left you a message. Didn't you get it? I said I was taking her to look at some ponies. It's the only chance I've got between now and her birthday.'

Oh, no. Kate groaned inwardly and said aloud, 'I didn't think to check the machine when I came in, and Emily's at a sleep-over.'

'So, I've come all this way for nothing,' he said, and pushed past her. His eyes widened at the sight of Jack, who was now standing in the living room, half a head taller than Charlie, and tatty in his washed-out sweater and jeans.

'You've met Jack, my ex-lodger.' Kate glanced nervously from one to the other.

'Briefly.' Charlie snorted and stared at him sourly.

Their eyes locked.

'Hello,' Jack said.

In the silence that followed Jack scratched his head. He looked at a loss, as if he wanted to be anywhere but there.

Charlie continued to stare at him, as if he were expecting some kind of explanation for his presence. Finally he said, 'Having a cosy night in?'

Kate gave a dismissive shrug. 'No, it's nothing like that. We were just having a chat.'

'And a drink,' Charlie said, his eyes on the wine bottle.

'Would you like one?' Kate asked.

'No, thanks, I'd better get off.' Brusquely, he stepped back. 'Wouldn't want to cramp your style,' he threw at Jack, as he left.

Kate followed him, hastening him on his way.

'I'll call for Emily tomorrow morning,' he said.

'OK.'

'This time have her ready and waiting.'

He stormed down the steps, banged the door of his car, and tore off in a temper.

When she returned Jack was downing the dregs of his wine. He glanced at Kate to make sure she was all right.

'Sorry about that,' she said. 'He's the last person I expected. What must he think?'

'Who cares what he thinks? It won't do him any harm to see you with another man. With a bit of luck he might realise that you're not his property any more, brainless jerk that he is.'

'Knowing him, he'll think I'm an unfit mother.'

'Not at all. On the contrary, he might stop taking you for granted.'

Kate saw Jack off and went to bed, wishing he was back downstairs. Having him there had made her feel safe. She'd loved their casual evenings together, when they had watched television late into the night. Through their cosy chats they had got to know each other well. Kate knew, for instance, that he liked a particular blend of expensive Italian coffee that was difficult to get, that ice-cold beer was a favourite drink, and that he preferred soccer to rugby.

In his time in the basement he had become a good friend to her and Emily. He'd enjoyed teaching Emily to sketch. Emily had warmed to him, too, often telling him things about school that she didn't tell Kate. But now all that seemed to have changed, the boundaries were more defined, and Kate knew that it would be to her detriment to push at them. As she put out the lights, she felt like an abandoned child.

32

The following Sunday evening Charlie brought Emily home late. She was fast asleep so he carried her up to bed.

'Could I have a word with you?' Kate said bravely to him, as he was leaving.

'Yes?' He hovered in the hall.

'I think we should separate for good.'

She was shaking as she said it, suddenly terrified of the significance of her statement: she would be losing him altogether. Also, she was scared of losing Emily to him for long stretches as the years went by but in her heart of hearts she knew it had to be done: she couldn't go on living like this.

'What?' Charlie said, white with shock.

'It seems the next logical step,' Kate said. Kate knew little about the legalities involved in separation, which frightened her. Their rows, misunderstandings, whatever had gone before, were nothing compared with her ignorance of these matters.

'But that's not what I want,' Charlie said stubbornly.

As he spoke a red splotch appeared on each cheek, a sign Kate recognised: he was close to losing his temper. She forced herself to remain calm in an effort to regulate the situation.

'Well, I do,' she said, her pain deepening as she regarded his horror.

Furious, Charlie said, 'Emily will suffer most – you know that, don't you? She'll be devastated, or don't you care about her feelings?'

Kate knew this assault was a ploy to get her to change her mind. 'I don't expect her to sail through it, but I'll look after her. Make it as easy as possible for her.'

Charlie eyed her carefully. 'And if that's what you want you'll have to leave here. The house will be sold, not that that will be a problem. Houses like this are like gold. People are desperate for them.'

He was teasing her, talking off the top of his head. It meant nothing. He was only voicing another crazy scheme to get her to have him back.

'I'm not ready for this. You're not selling my home,' Kate told him.

'You can't have it both ways. If we're to live apart permanently I'll have to have somewhere of my own. This house will fetch enough to buy a small apartment for each of us. Even you must see that.'

It was Kate's turn to be horror-struck.

'It shouldn't come as any great surprise to you,' Charlie went on. 'If you're not prepared to have me back then that's the end of it. There are two bedroomed townhouses being built at the far end. They're quite cheap. You can buy one of those.'

'That's insane! Emily's school is beside us here, Mum's not far and the shops are down the road.'

'I don't care. It's the only thing to do if we both want to have a reasonably good lifestyle without having to scrape. I'll set the wheels in motion, give it to Slater's auctioneers. Sam Slater will phone you to make an appointment to value it.'

The ground opened up beneath her. She felt suspended

in a space of incomprehension, a dark place beneath waiting to swallow her up. To engage in this ludicrous conversation was to make it real. Charlie was being whimsical, probably out of desperation, fear or confusion. He couldn't really mean this.

'You can't do that!'

'You think I'm doing this to get back at you, Kate? Well, I'm not. It's in our best interest.'

'You mean it's in *your* best interest,' Kate shouted, as she followed him to the door.

He whipped round, red-faced with temper. 'You see yourself as the innocent, wronged bystander in all of this, don't you? Well, let me tell you you're nothing of the sort.'

'What do you mean by that?'

'You've had that lodger of yours cosily shacked up here virtually since I left, and he was only too happy to worm his way in as soon as my back was turned.'

'I did nothing of the sort. I let the basement to him in desperation. You didn't give me a penny piece after you left, and this has nothing to do with Jack. He's well and truly gone.'

'Not very far. Wasn't he here with you the other evening? It was quite obvious to me what was going on. It's most likely been going on since the beginning.' Charlie was shouting, trying to frighten her.

'What are you talking about?'

'I saw the way you were looking at each other. You could hardly wait to get him upstairs!'

Anger flared in Kate. 'You're disgusting, Charlie Conway. You make me sick.'

'Really? Well, you make *me* sick too. I don't think you're a fit mother for Emily. If we're going to separate I think she should live with me.'

Kate lost her temper. 'I've put up with enough from you!' she shouted. 'So much that I can't take any more!'

'I'll talk to you when you're able to talk sense, then.'

'Get out!' Kate shrieked, and yanked open the front door. Charlie almost ran down the steps.

The resounding bang of the front door woke Emily, who shot out of bed like a bullet and hurtled down the stairs. 'Was that Daddy shouting?'

'Yes. He's gone now, love. Come back to bed.'

Standing before Kate, hands on hips, confrontational, Emily said, 'Why was he upset?'

'Just a silly argument,' Kate said.

She pointed a finger accusingly at her mother. 'He wanted to come home and you sent him away again! Didn't you?' she cried.

'No, Emily, I didn't. He was going back to Bramble Hill.'

'I want my daddy here with me,' Emily wailed.

Kate helped her back to bed, and stayed with her until she was asleep. She was learning to accept the unravelling of their lives, but she was more afraid of its manifestations than she had known.

On her way to bed Kate went into Emily's room. She was fast asleep, cuddled into the hard, plastic Nutcracker Prince and the Sugar Plum Fairy, who seemed welded together these days, Kate noticed. The poor kid didn't understand why Charlie had had to move out again, although she'd taken it better than Kate had expected – perhaps because she didn't believe he was gone for good. How could Kate possibly tell her that their lovely home was to be sold? Moving house might destroy her little world. She couldn't, any more than she could tell her what a bastard her daddy was.

*   *   *

'I don't know why you're so surprised,' Mary said, the following day. 'Charlie's been intent on getting rid of this house for a long time now.'

'I thought he'd change his mind, knowing it's so handy for Emily and school.'

'When are you going to cop on to the fact that he's never going to consider either you or Emily when his own comfort is at risk, the selfish pig?'

The next time Charlie phoned Emily answered. 'Hi, Daddy,' she called loudly, into the receiver. After a pause she said, 'I just want to live with you both.' Another pause, while she listened to Charlie. Then she said, 'I want to come and see your new apartment as soon as you get it.' Silence. 'OK, Daddy, hold on a sec, I'll get Mum. Mu-um!'

Charlie's voice was brisk and businesslike as he said, 'I've given the house to Slater's to sell.'

'So soon?'

'No time like the present.'

Kate couldn't bring herself to retaliate, with the tension between them so explosive and Emily in the living room.

The next day when she got home from work, the words 'For Sale' were emblazoned on a sign inside the gate. That afternoon Mr Slater phoned to ask if he could bring a client, a Mr Jeremy Peterson, to view the house the following morning at eleven o'clock. It was Kate's day off. She had no choice but to agree.

Next morning she'd just finished making the beds when there was a knock on the door. A tall, attractive middle-aged man, with a shock of silver-white hair, stood there. 'I'm Jeremy Peterson. I hope I'm not too late. Got held up in the traffic.'

'How do you do?' Kate said, shaking hands with him. 'Won't you come in? Where's Mr Slater?'

'He got held up so I said I'd pop along ahead of him. I have to get back to London this evening. Sorry if I'm a nuisance.'

'Not at all,' Kate said politely.

'What a lovely house.' They went into the living room and gazed around. 'Splendid-sized room – and these long windows, I love them. But you're much further out of the city than I'd planned.'

'We have the Dart line. It's very fast and frequent.'

'I suppose that would make a difference.'

Kate took him upstairs.

'So this is the master bedroom. Very nice.'

'Yes, and here's the guest bedroom.'

'That's a good size too.'

'And this is my daughter's room.'

He went to the window and looked out. 'Nice garden, such lovely trees. So quiet, and peaceful.'

Kate led the way downstairs to the basement.

'My word, you've got plenty of extra space here. My wife could have her grand piano here, play it all day without disturbing the neighbours.'

Kate's heart flipped over at the thought of a strange woman occupying her home.

On his way out Mr Peterson said, 'I'm enchanted.'

'Thank you,' she said.

'I'll talk to Mr Slater. He'll contact you.'

'OK,' Kate said, hoping he'd change his mind.

'And thank you for showing me round.'

Mr Slater phoned later. 'Sorry I couldn't make it.'

'I don't appreciate having to show strangers around my home,' Kate said.

'It won't happen again, I assure you, Mrs Conway. I like to have a hands-on approach with my clients, for your sake as well as theirs, so we can get the best possible results.'

'I'd prefer it that way too,' Kate agreed.

'As it turns out, this buyer is serious. He's taken a real liking to your house and is ready to make an offer. Everything is in place, finance, mortgage, so the money's not a problem. He's gilt-edged.'

'But I can't sell it yet. I've nowhere to move to.'

'I'll find you something suitable. Now, this is a good time to get a house of quality at a good price in Dun Laoghaire. You'll have no trouble. As for our client, his company is moving him to a city branch. I had to persuade him, of course, that everything he wants is right here.'

'Oh!'

'Mr Peterson would like to see the house again with his wife. There are a few things he wants to iron out. Can I bring him round tomorrow morning? I have a key.'

Kate agreed, rang off and sat down, glad to be on her own. The house was empty and silent. She thought of her situation. Time had lessened the pain, but the wound hadn't healed. On a practical level she was worse off now because she didn't even have a lodger. The house was too big for Emily and her. She was tired of trying to survive from day to day, all her earnings poured into a house she was going to lose anyway. On the other hand, as long she had it she knew she could get an income from it. Why not move into the basement, and let upstairs? That way she'd have a place to live, albeit cramped, and a good income without having to move. Jack had managed there.

The rent money would pay the mortgage, and with her job she'd manage the rest of the bills. Yes, she'd try to keep the house. It was their home, Emily's and hers, and she wasn't going to make it easy for Charlie by letting him sell it just because he wanted to get rid of his responsibilities. She'd find a way.

A full-time job was something she could manage without. She'd keep in touch with her friends, make new ones. She was scared, terrified of losing her status, and felt ashamed of her cowardice.

She relayed the latest news to Tim over coffee. 'I keep waiting for the day when I can truthfully say that I've finally let go of Charlie Conway. Maybe I should let him sell the house.'

'Won't make a blind bit of difference. That day will never come as long as you've got Emily to share. He's an essential part of her life, as are you.'

'It's all so painful. I can't be with him, and I can't seem to get away from him either.'

'That's the way it is and you might as well accept it,' said the ever-practical Tim.

'I'll keep that in mind,' Kate said.

'Forget about him tomorrow night and come to the dogs with me and the lads.'

Kate laughed. 'I've gone to the dogs already,' she said, but she agreed to go. Shelbourne Park would be a diversion. If nothing else, she could have a flutter and a few drinks – she might even win a bit of money.

33

When Lucinda arrived Kate was making a vegetarian lasagne for dinner. 'Hello!' she yelled, through the keyhole. 'Anybody home?'

'Hi! When did you get back?' Kate asked, as she opened the door.

'Yesterday. Didn't have to work today. Here, I brought you some good Spanish wine.' She put the bottle in the middle of the kitchen table.

'Lovely, thanks.'

'I've got news,' she said, her eyes wide and bright, her cheeks flushed. 'You'll never guess.'

Kate bit her lip. Oh, my God! Lucinda was going to tell her about Jack and she didn't want to hear it. 'I think I already know.'

'You know! But how?'

'Mum let the cat out of the bag, sorry.'

'But I haven't told her yet.'

'Well, you must have said something. She knows all about it.' Kate rushed on: 'I had no idea. I didn't even know you were seeing Jack. You could have said something, Lu – I am your sister and it was so strange to hear it from Mum, like it was a secret.'

'Sorry, I didn't think it was all that important,' Lucinda said. 'What did Mum say?'

'That you were keen on him, and that Jack was deadly serious about you too.'

'Jack and me!' Lucinda said incredulously. 'What an idea!'

Kate swallowed. 'You must have said something to her about fancying him. You could have said it to me, especially as he was my friend originally.'

'Kate!' Lucinda laughed. 'Stop talking, listen for a minute.'

Kate gazed at her.

'God, Mum doesn't half exaggerate!' She perched herself on a stool. 'There's nothing going on between Jack and me.'

'What?'

'I got friendly with him when he moved into his apartment. We used to bump into each other in the bar on the corner. I wasn't doing anything much at the time, and he was at a loose end too, so we went out together a few times. It was no big deal.'

'You went on holiday together to Marbella, didn't you?'

'There was a group of us. It was Mum's idea to invite him because I told her he was lonely, so just to please her I did. Well, not entirely. He's good fun, and he was trying to settle into his new apartment, and I felt sorry for him.'

'Didn't he try it on when he was there?'

'Not once. He was an absolute gentleman, as Mum would say.'

'How did she get it so wrong?'

Lucinda laughed at her sister's bewilderment. 'You know Mum. Wishful thinking on her part. It was more a case of Mum fancying him for me rather than me fancying him. He's so nice and kind but I'm not in love with him – or he with me, for that matter. Don't say anything to Mum though. She didn't mean any harm by trying to fix him up with me.'

Kate bit her lip. 'That's the trouble with her. She never does mean any harm. She just can't help interfering.'

Lucinda took her arm. 'Kate, I know you like Jack.'

Kate changed the subject. 'What's your news?' she had remembered that Lucinda had come to tell her something and they'd got sidetracked.

'It's about Diego.' Lucinda beamed as she spoke his name. 'We're all sorted.'

'What? I thought you two had finished.'

'Not exactly. Oh, we had a few problems but he arrived in Bangkok out of the blue last week when I was there, wined and dined me, took me to an open-air concert and told me how much he'd missed me. Then he flew off early the next morning. God, Kate, I was exhausted. We were awake all night,' she confided, in a hushed tone although they were on their own.

Kate laughed at her exuberance.

'And, Kate, you'll never guess!'

'He didn't pop the question?'

'He did!'

'Oh, my God!'

'I said yes.' Lucinda was ecstatic, as she held out her left hand for Kate to see the ring she'd been hiding behind her back. A diamond the size of a walnut caught a ray of sunshine from the kitchen window and flashed all the colours of the rainbow.

'Wow!' Kate gasped. 'It must have cost a fortune. Did he sell one of his yachts to buy it for you?'

Lucinda giggled. 'He's absolutely loaded, coining it with his luxury cruises.'

'But are you in love with him?' Kate asked anxiously.

'I'm totally besotted.' Lucinda pushed back a wisp of hair; her diamond sparkled dazzlingly.

'This calls for a celebration,' Kate said, and opened the bottle of wine. 'Here's to your and Diego's happiness together. What a surprise!'

They touched glasses. Lucinda went on eulogising about how gorgeous he was.

'Are you having a party to celebrate?'

'In a couple of weeks' time, as soon as Diego can get here. We'll have a big do. You'll have to get all glammed up again for it, Kate. Buy another new dress, get your hair and nails done again. I want you looking gorgeous,' she said, eyeing Kate appraisingly.

'I won't let you down,' Kate promised.

'You're going to love Diego. I'll invite Jack too. He likes Diego.'

Two weeks later Mary and Kate were waiting at Mary's house to welcome Diego, who was being met at the airport by Lucinda.

'I'm so nervous,' Mary said, patting her new perm. 'Trust Lucinda to get involved with a rich tycoon, totally out of our league. What'll I say to him?'

'Be yourself and you'll be fine,' Kate advised.

They came through the front door, laughing loudly. Kate heard a man's voice say something and the two laughed again.

'Hi, everyone,' Lucinda called gleefully. She bounced in, wearing a skirt no bigger than a curtain pelmet, a dark, handsome man bringing up the rear. Kate couldn't believe her eyes. This man was seriously beautiful. He was tall and slim, with smooth dark hair, a strong, angular face the colour of cinnamon, heavy-lidded eyes and a sensuous mouth.

Lucinda introduced him to Mary first.

Mary was instantly bowled over – Kate could tell by the worshipful look on her face, as if he were royalty – and straightened up to her full height. 'Diego,' she said, and held out her hand. 'I'm so glad to meet you.'

Diego brought it to his lips. 'It's a real pleasure to meet you too,' he said musically.

Eventually he turned his attention to Kate. 'You must be Kate?'

Kate held out her hand. 'How do you do?'

'I'm delighted to meet you too,' he said, looking into her eyes.

His were irresistible dark pools of charm and intelligence. Kate could see how Lucinda would fancy him above all the other men she'd met. She blushed, not sure what to say. What had Lucinda told her about him? That he was from a first generation Mexican-American family who had sacrificed their language and culture to move to New York and live in a slum when he was only nine. It seemed incredible. He looked as if he'd been born with a silver spoon in his mouth.

Emily, who had been waiting patiently, was suddenly shy when Diego said, 'And this is Emily?'

'Yes.' The child caught her breath, awestruck.

'Make yourself completely at home,' Mary begged him.

Diego didn't need a second bidding. As Lucinda settled down into a big bucket chair with a glass of wine and Mary busied herself with cooking the meal, Diego insisted on helping, stirring the sauce for the steak, mixing the dressing for the artichoke salad, tasting it to see if it was right.

'Well trained,' Mary said appreciatively.

'I like to act busy,' Diego laughed. 'Always did help my mom at home.'

Kate set the table, and Lucinda stirred herself to light the candles.

'It's such a relief that you're not vegetarian,' Mary told him.

'I'd live on steak if I could,' Diego said. 'Yes, medium rare, that's perfect for me, thanks.'

Mary served the meal, her desire to please Diego taking precedence over everything else. He carried the steaming plates to the table, serving Lucinda first. Throughout the meal he was most attentive to her. Kate had never seen such tenderness in a man's eyes before. But he was seriously beautiful and he knew it. Would Lucinda match up to him?

Once Mary had seated herself at the head of the table, in her role as matriarch, she began to ask him questions about his background.

He was from a large, boisterous family, and had run away to sea when he was seventeen, he told her. He'd subsequently put himself through night school and business college.

What had taken him to the South of France, Mary asked. He leaned across the dining-table in an intimate way to explain to her about his luxury yacht-rental business, which he ran from his villa in Nice. It was boom time at the moment, he told them, so good that he'd recently expanded to Marbella.

'How did you get into it?' Mary quizzed him, like a judge, barely pausing between each question, zealous in her cross-examination to compensate for being the only parent.

Abashed he said, 'I fell into it, literally.'

Lucinda laughed.

'It's true,' Diego said. 'A friend had a couple of small yachts, ran into financial difficulties, asked me to help out with a loan. When I realised its potential I got immersed in it. It sort of took over from my other interests. Now everything's neatly wrapped up, and it's making tidy bundles of money. I can relax more, concentrate on the cruises and leave the boring bits to my reliable staff.'

Diego told all this while eating heartily. He assured Mary that he never intended to see another poor day. His career was first and foremost to him, he said, and he would continue to further it with deals far and wide.

'You might even start up here, with the new marina opened up and all the facilities.' Mary encouraged him.

'It'd be a sure bet if you could guarantee me the sunshine,' Diego said, smiling.

'That's the trouble, we can't,' Kate said. She glanced at Lucinda, who was nodding in agreement.

Mary sat back, apparently satisfied that this man would be able to give Lucinda the sort of life she deserved.

Emily suddenly found her voice. 'I like your shiny eyes and your shiny hair.'

'Emily!' Kate cautioned her.

'Why, thank you.' Diego laughed delightedly.

What an elegant man he was: wise, sharp, and respectful too, with an open expression that conveyed he was happy to be grilled by his future mother-in-law. Kate breathed a grateful sigh. He was turning out to be perfectly suitable. Kate could tell by Mary's expression that, as far as she was concerned, everything was on course for a wonderful life for her Lucinda.

How long would he be staying, she enquired. Only a

few days, he told her. He was leaving for the States next Monday.

'And tell me about you, Kate,' he said charmingly. 'Are you getting your life back together?'

'Doing my best.' Kate had no inclination to discuss it.

'She has a good job at the hotel,' Mary said.

'It's a bit boring. I'd like to do something more with my life,' Kate admitted.

'What's stopping you?' Diego asked. 'You could go to college when you get sorted out, get a qualification that'd guarantee you a better job.'

'It seems an impossible idea at the moment.' Kate was thinking of her finances.

'It's not as if you live in the desert or anything,' Diego said. 'Surely there are colleges locally.'

'Yes, there are.' The notion was appealing.

To her great relief the telephone rang. Lucinda answered it. It was for Diego.

When he left to answer it Lucinda looked from her mother to her sister. 'What do you think of him?' she asked.

'He's absolutely charming, delightful,' Mary enthused.

'Gorgeous,' Kate added.

'I told you so.'

After the meal, Kate went home with Emily. Lucinda and Diego went to meet Jack. Diego and he had struck up a friendship in Marbella, and seemed to get on well.

As time went by, Mary became more and more obsequious towards Diego bowing and scraping to him all the time. It was getting on Lucinda's nerves, so she was relieved when he left for New York. Before he departed he invited them all to a party in Nice for the official launch of Euphoria, his new luxury cruise company; he would pay all their expenses.

Lucinda, exhausted, feverish, deprived of sleep by all the clubbing they had done, was touchy and easily hurt. She confided to Kate that she was already having doubts that marriage to Diego would work. 'It will be his second and he's wary, although he tries to hide it.' He was encumbered with an ex-wife, a tiny woman who couldn't cope with anything. She relied on him too much, was always ringing him up no matter what part of the globe he was in, making demands on him. Lucinda was far from happy about it.

'That explains why he got nervous when it came to a full-blown commitment. It's his past – he spent a long time trying to get out of a loveless marriage and still feels guilty about it,' Kate said.

'Precisely.'

'Lu, you're crazy to have doubts at this stage. Just get on with it. It isn't as if the wedding is imminent. Enjoy your engagement. You're strong enough to cope with any woman, never mind the ex. Remember, she is history. He'd be back with her by now if he wanted her.'

'I'm sure you're right.' Lucinda agreed.

Kate assured her that everything would work out, but her private opinion was that Diego was too beautiful to make a good husband. She decided to keep her mouth shut. Lucinda could expect it to be a reasonable success, maybe not for ever and ever, but not many marriages lasted a lifetime, these days.

On Sunday Charlie was waiting in his car outside the house with Emily when Kate returned from a walk. 'Can I have a word?' he asked politely.

Emily tugged at her jacket. 'Daddy wants to take me on a special holiday.'

'While you're in Nice I wondered if I could take Emily to Trabolgin.'

'Yippee,' Emily said.

'She'll be missing school,' Kate said.

'That won't hurt her.'

'Please can I go, Mum?' Emily pleaded.

Not wanting to argue in front of the child, Kate said, 'I suppose so.'

'Great.' Charlie smiled his old roguish smile.

Kate turned away, instantly doubtful about her decision, but not wanting to backtrack for Emily's sake.

Emily put her arms round her and gave her a kiss. 'Thanks, Mum,' she said.

Back inside, Kate sat brooding about her response. She was floundering, exhausted, and wondered if she'd done the right thing.

'I can't win with Charlie. Emily adores him,' she said to Barbara, when she called round to explain to her why Emily would be missing school.

'He's an attentive father, you can't deny that,' Barbara said. 'Anyway, it's only for a few days and it'll do her good.'

Kate heaved a sigh of relief. Barbara was right. She'd be in Nice for five days and Emily would be enjoying herself too. Kate wouldn't have to worry about her, and she'd be back a couple of days after her return.

34

Mary, Kate and Jack flew to Nice for the big day, the airline tickets having been booked and paid for by Diego.

Diego, casual in jeans and sweatshirt, met them at Nice airport. He kissed Mary and Kate in turn, and slapped Jack on the back.

'Good of you to come, man,' he said, with a glowing smile.

'Glad to be here,' Jack responded.

Diego drove them to Nice, past the Promenade des Anglais, and turned left up a winding road to his home above the city. They passed through a stone archway into the elegant, shadowy courtyard of a beautiful rose-coloured villa bordered by a wonderland garden. Kate got out of the car, walked a few paces and stopped to admire the scene. The garden was divided by green box hedges and stone paths, lined with purple lavender and pink and white roses. Just below it there was a tiny square, part of a convent and chapel. Beyond the rooftops she could see the sea, a sliver of silver in the twilight.

Lucinda came running down the steps of the villa to greet them.

'Lovely to see you,' she said, as she stepped towards Mary and hugged her first, then Kate.

She kissed Jack on both cheeks. 'Delighted you could make it, Jack,' she said.

Jack shot her a mischievous grin. 'I wouldn't have missed it for the world.'

A tall, swarthy young man, a younger version of Diego, appeared.

'This has to be your brother,' Mary said.

'Yes, this is Antonio,' Diego said. He came forward shyly to be introduced, then Diego led them up the geranium-lined steps and into a wide, sparsely furnished hall with a highly polished wooden floor. Paintings lined the walls along a corridor that led to a terrace. 'What a place!' Jack said, looking over the twinkling lights of Nice to the horizon.

'How wonderful,' Mary breathed.

'Absolutely!' Kate agreed.

'Nice is not called the Jewel of the Riviera for nothing,' Diego said.

'How much of this land is yours?' Jack asked.

Diego waved an arm to encompass the garden and the barn. 'As far as the trees. I decided to convert the barn into an office. That way it didn't seem such an extravagance, and by now it's paid for itself.'

As they stood on the shaded terrace Diego dispensed drinks and welcomed them with a toast to an enjoyable stay. Mary and he sat together on the reclining chairs, Diego naming the various flowers for her.

'I'll show you to your rooms,' Lucinda said, looking at her watch. 'You have time to shower and change before dinner. The table at the restaurant is booked for eight o'clock.'

The luxurious bedrooms were all on the same corridor.

'This is like a hotel,' Mary said, sinking down into her big bed.

From Kate's window there was a magnificent view

of gardens and rooftops, the square and chapel below, miles of beach and blue sea fading into the horizon. She unpacked and showered, feeling excited as she changed into a printed silk chiffon dress – tonight she'd go for the sophisticated look. She even applied a touch of glitter to her cheeks. She was going to make the most of her time here, and enjoy herself.

There was a knock on her bedroom door.

'Ready?' Jack called.

It was a shock to see him dressed up in a suit with a crisp white shirt and dark blue tie. He looked immaculate.

'Yes,' Kate said, still ill at ease with him, struggling to switch back to friendship mode. Judging by Jack's awkwardness he was finding it difficult too.

Downstairs they waited with Mary and Antonio for Diego and Lucinda, Antonio replying dutifully to Mary's endless questions. Finally, the couple swept down the staircase, arm in arm, looking as if they'd come straight off a film set, Lucinda at ease in her surroundings, as if she'd lived there all her life.

Mary said, 'They're the perfect match,' and Jack smiled in agreement.

Diego drove them down to the glittering coastline, along the palm-lined Promenades des Anglais, with its breathtaking beach on the right and old-world villas and hotels on the left, to the legendary Cours Saleya restaurant. It was in the heart of the bustling old town, renowned for its seafood.

The restaurant was busy, the buzz breaking like waves around the full tables. Diego ordered lavishly, clinked glasses with everyone, toasted old friendships and new, everyone's health, wealth and happiness. During the meal everyone laughed and joked, enjoying the delicious food and drink.

When the meal was over Diego called for silence. 'Come on, let's party,' he announced, to a loud cheer of 'Yes!'

He put Mary into a taxi back to the villa, then led the way down the street to a nearby crowded night-club from where hip-hop music pulsated. As the evening unfolded, the drink flowed and Diego became the life and soul of the place, the drinks and music triggering his energy. Everyone jumped into life and danced crazily. The laughter grew louder and louder, the decibel level ascending into the stratosphere, everything forgotten except the sheer enjoyment of the night. Kate did her best to generate energy, but found it astonishingly hard work.

Lucinda shimmied up to her. 'This is a party, you're meant to be having a good time,' she said.

'I am,' Kate said.

'Let yourself go.'

After another drink Kate had relaxed and her spirits rose, adrenaline making her buzz. Her heels clacked sharply as she swivelled round to locate Jack. He was dancing straight and stiff, his movements gauche, so she wiggled around him in an effort to radiate infectious enthusiasm and promptly fell into the crook of his arm. Everyone else laughed and he gave her an embarrassed smile as she extricated herself.

When they got back to the house in the small hours Jack escorted her to her bedroom, his arm steadying her. He opened her door, snapped on the light and led her to the bed. The ceiling tilted as Kate flopped back on to the pillows. She giggled, and then, feeling the comfort of the cool white sheets, she gave a long sigh.

'You okay?' Jack asked.

'This is good,' she said, looking up at him, her eyes inviting, her arms thrown wide.

But he only waited long enough to make sure she was all right.

'Good night,' he said, and retreated to his own room next door.

At dawn Kate woke up. She got up, undressed, removed her makeup, and got into bed properly. She fell into a deep sleep and dreamed that Jack was finding his way in the dark to her room, in hot pursuit of her. She woke in a cold sweat, craving him, her body tingling with desire, knowing it wouldn't happen. They had spoilt whatever it was that had been between them on the night they had nearly made love. He'd never mentioned it since. It was forgotten and they were friends again, if reserved.

Although Kate found him devastatingly desirable still, she was determined not to become just another casualty on his list. The incident had obviously been on his mind when he'd left her bedroom in such haste. He would not make the same mistake again. She knew for certain now that he would never make another pass at her, or take a chance on a second rejection.

When she woke up again the sky was an astonishing blue. Sober now, she got out of bed and went to the window. Even from this distance she could see that the beach was lined with colourful umbrellas and palm trees, and dotted with deck-chairs. The sparkling azure sea receded into a golden haze.

When she got downstairs they were all eating breakfast on the terrace. Lucinda was talking languorously to Mary of unfamiliar far-flung places where the cruises would go. Jack was listening, while enjoying his croissants and strong coffee. Diego was standing nearby, going over his keynote speech.

'Hello, there,' Jack said casually. 'Coffee?' He raised an eyebrow and the coffee pot.

'Yes, please,' Kate said, and sat down.

'Did you sleep well? he asked formally.

'Very, thanks,' Kate said.

'We're going sailing this morning,' Diego announced, when he joined them. 'Are you on, Kate?'

'Wouldn't miss it,' she said.

'Neither would I,' Mary chimed in.

After breakfast Diego drove his convertible through winding roads to Villefranche and its beautiful natural harbour where his yacht was moored. The smell of the sea was in the air. As soon as he parked they got out and made their way along the lively waterfront, past bars and cafés to Chapelle St-Pierre on the quay where magnificent boats bobbed lazily.

As Diego's yacht moved gracefully forward Kate marvelled at the tightly packed buildings above the harbour, huddled together for protection, accessed by tunnels. The blue water rippled outwards in ever-increasing circles. Flashes of gold erupted on it as if a magical spell had been cast. This was more of the Riviera's enchantment and Kate was hooked. She sat back in a cocoon of total relaxation.

Several miles along the coast they dropped anchor near the sandy beach of Les Issambres, north of Sainte-Maxime. They went ashore and walked along a narrow footpath lined with magenta and deep pink bougainvillaea to a curving cove of smooth sand, passing fishermen on the way. The sun climbed high in the sky, and the day grew hotter and hotter. They plunged into the sea and swam, splashing one another. Later, they ate a picnic of onion tart, pizza and Brie, washed down by ice cold white Côtes du Rhône, and finished with fruit, watching the liners and other ships on the horizon.

While they basked in the sun Diego moved off to take an important business call on his mobile phone.

Gradually they returned to the yacht, protesting at having to leave the beach.

That evening Diego took Lucinda's arm as they swept into Le Negresco where the launch party was taking place. Lucinda was a vision in a simple pink chiffon dress, her hair caught up in a gold clip. Kate walked behind her, gorgeous in this season's Dolce and Gabbana white trouser suit, which Lucinda had bought for her, her hair coiffed, lips glossy. Mary, next to her, was lovely in powder blue.

The suite of rooms Diego had hired for the party were dazzling in the evening sunlight. Soft sofas and armchairs lined the reception area. Apart from Diego's brother, Antonio, the guests were mainly friends Diego had made through business whom he wanted to impress, and included the heads of large corporate-finance companies in Europe and America, accompanied by their glamorous, skinny wives.

Diego introduced everyone. Donny, one of his basketball friends from his team in the States and a business associate, was with his wife, Cheryl. Pierre, whose business Diego had taken over, was acting as if he owned the place. Throughout, Diego was attentive to Mary, translating conversations for her.

'Ours is one of the largest finance houses in the world,' boasted Donny, to anyone within earshot.

His wife gazed at him adoringly. 'Diego gets all his financial advice from Donny, when to buy stocks when to sell. Relies on him totally,' said Cheryl to Kate confidentially. 'They met in Dubai.'

'Really,' Kate said.

'That's where we were married,' Cheryl continued, 'as soon as Donny's divorce came through. We lived there for a couple of years. I loved it – the duty-free shops and the gold. Diego loved it there, too. He had started out in business there with his first wife. They were happy and I was sure they were married for life, but there you go. I suppose these things happen.' A sharp look from her husband cut her off in mid-flow.

'I've never been to Dubai,' Kate said.

'It's well worth a visit. Tell me, what do you do?'

'I'm a hotel receptionist,' Kate said.

'Nice.' Cheryl lost interest in her, fast. 'I love hotels, don't you? Especially ones like this,' she said.

'It's magnificent,' Kate agreed.

'Cheryl!' Donny called loudly.

'Excuse me, Donny'll be wanting to introduce me to some important people.' She disappeared. Kate glanced at Lucinda, and could tell that she was nervous. She only relaxed when they sat down for the meal.

The lights were dim; candles flickered and dipped merrily. Beautiful waitresses served mouthwatering dishes of seafood and salad. Smart men in smarter suits talked together. Jack, seated at the far end of the table, looked so attractive that Kate couldn't take her eyes off him.

Diego stood up and thanked everyone for coming. 'I'm glad we left the *hacienda* in Mexico,' he said. 'I've come a long way since I discovered I had a knack for making money, and an even bigger one for spending it.'

Everyone cheered.

'I love vacations, but when I grew tired of staying at ultra-expensive hotels I had to try something different so I hired a yacht. I loved the experience so much I bought the company.'

Everyone clapped.

'It's amazing, isn't it?' Kate said, to Lucinda.

'Everyone's getting on famously,' her sister replied.

Antonio was relishing the wine.

Diego's mother, brothers and sisters had sent a telegram of congratulations from New York.

'It's a shame your mother couldn't manage the journey,' Mary said to Diego. 'It would have been nice to have more of your family here.'

'You make up for it,' Diego said magnanimously.

'Oh, thank you,' Mary said. 'And I'll make sure to be here for the wedding, and christening,' she added, with a wink.

'Mum!' Lucinda gasped.

'Will you be all right when we've gone home?' Kate asked her. 'No more doubts?'

'No – I've got Diego to myself for a whole week, and he's promised to keep his mobile switched off.' Lucinda smiled.

'What'll his ex do?'

'Who cares?' Lucinda laughed.

Kate found Jack standing on the balcony, which overlooked the Promenade des Anglais, its myriad lights sparkling like jewels illuminating the sea, which stretched out to the star-studded horizon. The scent of exotic flowers wafted to them in the warm air. 'Can you believe this?' he asked, mesmerised by the view.

'No, I can't.'

'Savour it for the long lonely nights ahead,' he said.

Mellow from the champagne, Jack put his arm around her waist. 'I'd like to take you out to dinner tomorrow evening,' Jack said. 'Do you think we could sneak off somewhere?'

Kate looked up at him in surprise.

'If you'd prefer not to I'll understand—'

'Oh, no,' she interrupted. 'I'd like that very much.'

35

Next day Kate regretted her impulsive decision to dine out with Jack, and thought about cancelling it. Then she told herself to stop being cautious: it was only dinner, and she always enjoyed Jack's company. She wore her new black dress and put on her makeup, blending it in the way Sonia had done to get that clear, dewy look.

Jack took her by taxi to a waterfront restaurant in Cannes.

Kate was nervous, and the conversation during the drive was laboured. However, once they had had a couple of cocktails they relaxed, and Jack amused her with tales of great artists like Picasso giving sketches and paintings in exchange for their meals in the local restaurants.

'What I love most about the Riviera, apart from its beauty, is being able to sit in places like this half the night,' Kate said.

'I've spent a lot of my time in exotic locations in the States. I could pay the rent and eat from my day's work, but I squandered the nights in smoky bars when I should have been wandering around taking photographs. Why the hell I stayed there so long I'll never know.'

'You had a girlfriend who moved in with you.'

Jack paused.

'Nothing wrong with having a past, Jack. It would be weird if you didn't. Why *did* you abandon her and America?'

'That's another story, and with this wine going to my head I'd better keep the conversation simple.' He was thoughtful for a minute. 'I'm a cautious Irish Mick. I thought America was a great dream, and when it came down to it, the job offer from *National Geographic* gave me a security and professional prestige I craved yet couldn't seem to achieve. So, that's it, really.'

'Who knows what might have happened if you'd stayed on?'

'I'm glad I returned to Ireland. I wouldn't have met you if I hadn't. You look sexy tonight,' Jack said, changing the subject.

'Thanks,' Kate said, self-conscious.

While they ate they talked about Lucinda and Diego's new-found happiness.

'I'm thinking of doing something useful with my life too,' Kate said.

'What?' Jack was all ears.

'I'd like to do a business course with a view to having my own company one day.'

'You think you have a talent for it?' he asked.

'Maybe so.'

Fearful, she waited for his calm sarcasm. Instead, he let it go without comment, and said, 'How are you doing for money and everything?'

She pressed her hands together. They were clammy. She felt as if everyone was watching her. Stop it! Keep cool. Don't blow this.

Kate looked into his eyes. 'I'm going to look for another lodger.'

'I see.'

*　　*　　*

Jack walked her to her bedroom door, gave her a goodnight kiss on the cheek.

His reticence came from the fact that he thought she wasn't interested in a romance with him: Kate knew this was why he didn't make a move.

'I was thinking of hiring a car tomorrow,' he said. 'How about doing a bit of sightseeing with me?'

'I can't leave Mum on her own.'

But Mary had her own itinerary: Donny and Cheryl had invited her to Monte Carlo for a turn at the tables in the casino.

The car Jack hired was a bright blue Rav. Kate slid into the high seat and fastened her seat-belt. They shot off up steep angles and zoomed along the stunningly high edge of a ravine, beneath which craggy rocks jutted out. They drove on through narrow, crowded streets of picturesque towns lined with hotels, through the beautiful atmospheric towns of Mougins and Vence, and reached St Paul-de-Vence in time for lunch at the famous Colombe d'Or. Afterwards they drove back along the road that snaked its way down the peninsula to Cap Ferrat. They passed exclusive villas and beautiful gardens, and parked to look at the fabulous yachts in the Saint-Jean marina, where they sat sipping coffee and admiring the view of the lighthouse at the end of the cape. Then they walked round the Pointe St-Hospice to the old houses overlooking the harbour.

'This is heavenly,' Kate said.

Jack took her hand, 'I've been wanting to talk to you, Kate.'

She looked up at him. 'What about?' she asked, although she thought she knew.

'Do you remember the night we nearly made love?'

She felt herself blush. 'I was upset.'

'I felt terrible about it too, but I thought we'd be all right next time we tried. Then, when Charlie came back, I was devastated. It was a nightmare thinking about you with him. My own stupid fault for losing my heart to a woman with a husband. Mind you, he was one man I never thought would be coming home, I might add.'

'Taking Charlie back was the biggest mistake I ever made.'

'I went to phone you several times, and didn't. I wrote to you and never posted the damn letters. I hated the thought of him reading them.'

'I'm sorry,' Kate said lamely.

'Don't be. You did what you thought was right. It was my own fault for having this romantic dream of us getting together. There's no point going over it now. It happened. We had good times together and I shouldn't have been cross with you for doing what you thought was best.'

'Guilt is a terrible thing,' Kate said. 'It makes you do things you know aren't right.'

Jack nodded. 'When I saw you at Lucinda's party, looking so gorgeous, I wanted to be with you but you hadn't sorted your life out properly, and my career was in the balance.'

'We can be friends again, can't we?' Kate asked. 'No strings attached.'

''Course we can. But, Kate, do you want to hear something daft?' Jack asked.

She looked at him, the blood pounding in her ears, knowing what was coming next. 'I think I know what you're going to say.'

'I don't like being on my own any more. Not since I lived with you.'

'Excuse me,' she said indignantly. 'You never lived with me.'

'In your basement, I mean.'

'That's better.'

They both laughed, seeing the funny side of it.

'So, we're good friends again.'

'We are.'

Neither of them wanted to disturb the equilibrium by going any further than that, but afterwards Kate thought what a fool she'd been, what a great big fool. She should have told him there and then how she felt about him.

She was married, but when had that ever stopped anyone having an affair?

It had stopped her and Jack, and she would be foolish to think that he'd ever want anything more than friendship from now.

She'd done the right thing. She liked Jack, wanted him to be her friend, for the moment. The break-up of her marriage would have to be dealt with, and she would do that as cleanly and painlessly as she could. Until then she wouldn't get involved with another man. Especially not Jack! Even if her desire for him continued to haunt her, she wouldn't lead him on. It would only bring more heartbreak.

Next morning Diego and Lucinda waved them off. Mary cried, embarrassing Kate. 'She'll be home soon for the autumn fashion shoot, Mum. You'll be seeing plenty of her. She's got a lot of work lined up in Dublin.'

'I think she'd be better employed staying by Diego's side.'

'Why?'

'First off, they should get married as soon as possible, have a baby, and then she should have another. Otherwise she'll have an awful time keeping a good-looking man like that on the straight and narrow.'

'That would tie her down terribly and would certainly put paid to her career,' Kate said, glaring at her mother, who, as usual, was making plans for Lucinda's life as though it were her business to do so.

Then, for the first time, she noticed that her mother was getting old. She felt, too, that her own life was going nowhere, and that she'd achieved nothing of any significance in all the years of marriage to Charlie. The only good thing she'd done was produce Emily. For that alone it had been worth while, she decided, and was grateful.

36

There was a voicemail from Charlie to say that he and Emily were having a great time. Relieved to hear from him, Kate went to work. The first question Vivian asked was 'How did you get on with Jack? It was the perfect place for reconciliation, wasn't it?'

'We made our peace. In fact, we had some pleasant times on our own.'

'Come for a drink after work, and tell me all about it.'

'I can't. Emily's coming home tomorrow and I have to shop. Besides, there's nothing more to tell.'

'You're keeping secrets from me.'

'No, honestly, there's nothing going on between Jack and me. We're good friends, that's all.'

'Yeah! Right!' Vivian gave her a knowing wink.

On the way home Kate stopped at the supermarket to stock up for Emily's return. While she was buying the sausages and rashers she felt queasy so as soon as she got in she put her feet up, had a cup of tea and phoned Charlie's mobile to find out the exact time of their return. It was switched off. Later she felt tired again, and went to bed early. In the morning when she woke up she was still queasy.

'Is something wrong, Kate?' Vivian asked. 'You're very pale.'

'I feel a bit sick. Could be the food we ate in Nice, it was very rich. I'm not used to it.'

As the morning wore on Kate forgot all about it, but the next morning she was violently sick as soon as she woke up. A cold sweat broke out on her forehead.

'Something I ate from the supermarket deli,' she said to Vivian later.

She refused the coffee Tim offered her at break-time.

'You're deathly pale. Shouldn't you see your doctor?' Vivian said.

'It's just a tummy-bug.'

'Any chance that you could be pregnant?' Vivian asked.

Kate laughed. 'No way. I haven't been with a man, you know that.'

Vivian's eyes flickered. She hesitated, then said, 'Not even when you got back with Charlie?'

'Well, yes, but that was ages ago.'

'You've had your period since then?'

She hadn't been keeping tabs. She stopped, calculated the weeks on her fingers. Yes, she'd missed one. With the excitement of the trip to Nice she'd forgotten about it. The change might have delayed it. She bought a kit, and did a pregnancy test. To her horror the dreaded blue line appeared. 'It couldn't be right,' she said to Vivian. 'There's no way.'

Vivian raised her eyebrows. 'It must be Charlie's – or are you keeping secrets?'

'If I'd had sex with Jack I'd have told you, Viv. Anyway, these things can be wrong.'

'There's only one way to find out. See Dr Duggan, he'll soon tell you.'

Dr Duggan said, 'I'll take a urine sample, that's one way to find out.' He told her to call back.

She went home sick as a dog, scared Charlie would notice, but he and Emily didn't arrive that evening.

When she went back to see Dr Duggan he said, with a smile, 'The test is positive. You're pregnant, Mrs Conway. Congratulations!'

Thanks,' she said, weak with shock.

'I suggest you see an obstetrician without delay. It's a long time since you had Emily.'

Stunned, Kate looked at him.

'You're not happy about it, are you?' Dr Duggan said.

Kate burst into tears. 'Only because of the way things are between my husband and me.'

'I suggest you tell him all the same,' Dr Duggan said.

She left the surgery, and went to the hotel in a trance.

Vivian took one look at her. 'Bad news?'

'Yes.'

'I'm here for you any time you want to talk about it.'

Kate was reluctant to say any more in case she burst into tears.

By lunchtime, she could keep it to herself no longer, and finally confided in Vivian that, by her reckoning, she was about nine weeks pregnant.

'This must be terrible for you.'

Kate rested her head on Vivian's shoulder. 'I don't know what to do.'

'I wish to God I could help you, Kate.'

'Unfortunately, you can't.' Kate felt awful.

'I think you need to talk to Charlie,' Vivian said, pulling Kate towards her.

Kate flinched. 'No, I can't do that.'

'No more alcohol.' She told Tim why.

Shocked, he said, 'Was it the milkman again?'

'Worse. It was Charlie.'

'You don't have to go through with it,' Tim said. 'I know somebody who could help you if you don't want—'

Kate shook her head. 'I could never do it.'

'I was only suggesting it to give you an alternative, make you feel better.'

'I appreciate that, Tim. I don't know what to do – if I were to tell Charlie he'd want to patch things up. It'd be very hard to get out of it.'

'It's your call.'

'I don't know how I'll manage to raise two children on my own, though. One's difficult enough. And what will people say?'

'That should be the last of your worries.'

'Getting back with Charlie would seem to be the easiest solution.'

Kate felt trapped; there was no way out. She could never manage on her own so she would have to accept her fate. Much as she loathed the idea of resuming her life with her husband, to be the single mother of two children was inconceivable. To reject Charlie now would be reprehensible, and foolhardy. She would have liked to be one of those women who couldn't care less about convention, but fear of pregnancy outside marriage had been instilled in her by her mother.

Her mind was made up. As soon as Charlie returned with Emily she would tell him they were going to have a child. He would be overjoyed, and she would accept her fate for the sake of her family.

And Jack? Well, she'd just have to forget him. She thought about their last night in Nice, her inability to disguise her longing for him. She ran a bath and got undressed. Her sobs and the sound of the running water drowned the telephone.

Later Barbara called round to enquire about Emily's return to school.

'I'm expecting them back at any minute.' Then Kate burst into tears, and told her about her pregnancy.

Barbara looked at her with deep concern. 'I can't imagine the shock you must be feeling. I'm so sorry,' she said. 'What are you going to do?'

'Get back with Charlie. I don't have much choice in the matter. It's his child too, not that he deserves to know.' Kate sighed. 'I might patch things up but I'll never forgive him for what he did to me.'

'This doesn't mean you have to stick with him, Kate.'

'Quite honestly, I wouldn't mind an easier life, someone else shouldering the responsibility.'

'I don't blame you for thinking that way.'

Eyes full of tears, Kate said, 'I'd better accept the fact, and do what's best for the baby and Emily. She'll be over the moon.' Kate touched her stomach. 'I've made such a mess of things.'

'We all do it at some time or another.' Barbara put an arm round her.

'I've ruined my life,' Kate said.

'Stop being so dramatic! Of course you haven't. You'll have a lovely baby, a brother or sister for Emily. Congratulations, Kate. I'm on your side, I'll help you in any way I can.'

'You've been a great friend throughout.'

As soon as Barbara left, Kate was overtaken by sadness. The prospect of another baby didn't soften her feelings for Charlie. Nor did it give her any joy. She remembered the heartbreak when she'd discovered Charlie's affair and resolved not to tell him about her pregnancy yet: she'd wait until it became absolutely necessary. That decision helped her through the day and to cope with her desolation.

'You'll have to take it easy, put your feet up when you get home, all that sort of thing,' said Tim.

'I haven't planned on climbing Mount Everest.'

'You know what I mean. And you shouldn't be on your own in the house so much. I'll call round, spot check you in the evenings.'

Kate laughed. 'Listen to you, fussing like an old hen. Emily will be home tonight.'

When Charlie and Emily hadn't returned by dinnertime, Kate phoned Bramble Hill to find out if they were there. 'I haven't heard from him,' she told Frank.

'I spoke to him yesterday,' he said. 'He was fine. They met up with some friends and were having a really good time. He said he'd call on the way back. I said, "As long as you phone Kate and let her know," and he said he'd ring you *en route*.'

'Well, he didn't,' Kate said, annoyed. 'Did he say he was going anywhere else?'

'No, and I assumed he was coming straight here.'

'How was he?'

'In good spirits.'

He's always quiet when he's scheming something, Kate thought, and said, 'What time did he ring you?'

'Immediately after lunch, at about two.'

Kate glanced at her watch. 'He should be with you now,' she said, mystified.

'They might have stopped off for a bite to eat. I'm sure they'll show up soon.'

'Phone me as soon as they get there.'

Frank said he would, and rang off.

She took Tim's advice and rested, watching television.

On one level Kate was coming to terms with the idea of having Charlie back in her life. She would need his financial help to bring up this child. But every time she fell into a reverie about the future she lost her nerve and cried, only managing to calm herself with the thought that, one way or another, she'd find a way to cope.

Vivian rang.

'I thought you were Charlie,' Kate said. 'I'm expecting them home any time now.'

'How are you feeling?' Vivian asked.

'Shell-shocked. I dread getting big. Can you imagine the stares from people who know that Charlie and I are separated?'

'Your health is all that matters,' Vivian said.

37

During the evening Kate kept trying Charlie's mobile. It was switched off. He was probably driving. After a while she tried the number of the apartment he'd rented, in case he'd changed his plans and gone there. The phone rang out but there was no answer. What if Charlie had got back while she'd been at work? He would have left Emily at Mary's.

She phoned Mary, but she hadn't heard from Charlie either.

'I'm getting really worried now,' Kate said.

'I'm sure there's a perfectly reasonable explanation for the delay,' Mary said.

Kate drank coffee and read the newspaper she'd brought home from work. The evening sunlight streamed in at the window. Hot and restless, she stood up and opened the window as wide as it would go. She still hadn't heard if Mr Peterson had made an offer for the house. She switched on the radio and stood by the draining-board to empty the dishwasher while listening to the news, soothed when there was no report of an accident.

As the evening progressed, Kate paced up and down wondering what to do next. There was something peculiar about the wait, something wrong in the way they didn't ring. She tried to watch the telly but her eyes kept straying to Emily's toys, the Sugar Plum Fairy and the Nutcracker

Prince side by side in a corner of the shelf, her new Samantha Mumba and Harry Potter videos beside them, everything as she'd left it. The house was full of her, yet she wasn't there – as Kate said to Barbara when she phoned to ask if Emily would be going swimming the next day.

She phoned Bramble Hill again. Still no word from Charlie.

'I've tried his apartment. He's not there,' Kate said.

'Try it again,' Frank advised.

The phone rang out for a long time. Eventually someone answered, and said that Charlie had moved out. Kate's hand flew to her mouth. What was he up to? She phoned Bramble Hill back. 'Maybe they've had an accident,' she said.

'Nonsense, Kate,' Colette said, exasperated, 'you'd have heard if something had happened to them.'

'Could he have taken Emily away somewhere?' Kate asked tentatively. It was her worst nightmare.

'Don't be ridiculous, I'm sure there's a simple explanation. He won't have gone very far,' Colette said, reassuringly.

'I wonder if I should phone the police.'

Frank came back on the line. 'Wait until we've checked with Charlie's colleagues and friends. Someone out there must know where he is. We'll ring round and ask.'

Kate phoned Mr Hopkirk, Charlie's boss, at home. He said that Charlie had transferred to their New York branch, and was due to present himself for work there in a couple of weeks' time.

Kate's heart lurched. Rigid with fear, she sat on the stairs wondering what to do next. When she heard a car she hurried to the front door to give Charlie a piece of her mind for keeping Emily out so late.

It was Mary. 'I didn't like to think of you on your own,' she said.

'Something's wrong.' Kate's voice rose, 'I don't trust Charlie – he always does what he wants to do, and damn the consequences.'

'What about friends?' asked Mary.

Kate went to the phone and rang two of Charlie's hiking friends. 'Have you heard from Charlie?' she asked. They hadn't. Then she got the number from Colette and dialled Daniella's family home. An elderly woman answered, seeming befuddled, and had no idea what Kate was talking about.

'She hasn't seen him,' Kate told Mary.

'Let's think, is there anywhere else they could have gone?' Mary was pacing up and down, trying to think. 'He might have taken her to McDonald's for a Happy Meal?'

Kate shook her head. 'That wouldn't take so long.'

'Or to the cinema.'

'Not at this hour.' Kate burst into tears.

Mary put her arms round her. 'There, now, don't fret. I bet they've stopped off at the Cock and Rabbit for sausage and chips. You know Emily loves the basket meals they do there.'

'I didn't think of that,' Kate said. 'I'll phone Terry.'

She got through to Terry Daly, the landlord, straight away. 'Have you seen Charlie and Emily?' she asked. He told her he hadn't. 'Well, let me know if they do come in.' She hung up. 'I'm at my wit's end. I can't think what could have happened to them,' she said, her voice breaking. 'I'm going to ring Jack. He'll know what to do.'

Mary watched her with frightened eyes as she dialled.

He answered on the second ring.

'Jack, it's Kate. Charlie's disappeared and he's got Emily

with him. I know he wants to take care of her but . . .' she faltered.

'I'm coming round,' Jack said, and put down the phone.

Ten minutes later he was with her. 'Any word of them?' he asked.

Kate was convinced by now that Charlie had taken Emily. 'She's gone, Jack! They've gone missing.' She lost control.

He held her as she sobbed. 'Calm down, Kate. Of course they're not missing. They've not been gone that long. They have to be somewhere nearby.'

'We've tried everywhere we can think of,' she said. 'What if he takes her away, Jack?'

'Tell her that's not going to happen,' Mary said to Jack. 'He can't do that, sure he can't.'

'No – and if he tries anything like that we'll find them,' Jack said.

'You think he won't take her, don't you? But he will,' Kate burst out.

'He hasn't got the right to do that.'

'Then where is he? Where is Emily?' Kate wailed, hysterical now.

'I can't believe he'd just waltz off like that with Emily,' Jack said. 'I'm sure he'll be here any minute.' He gazed at Kate, who was hunched on the stairs, ashen-faced.

Kate wasn't so sure. 'This is my fault. I shouldn't have let her go with him. I had my reservations about it all the time.' She looked at Mary helplessly.

'Stop blaming yourself. That isn't going to find her,' Mary said. She produced a large bag from her pocket. 'Here, have a bullseye, give you something to chew while you're waiting.'

'No, thanks.'

'I'll get you something to eat,' Mary said, and disappeared into the kitchen. 'Ready,' she called, ten minutes later. 'Ham sandwiches, all I could find.'

Kate didn't eat a thing and Jack hadn't much appetite.

As the night wore on Jack persuaded Kate to try to get some sleep, assuring her that he would keep vigil by the phone, but Mary insisted on staying on so he went home.

In bed, Kate wondered how she'd get through the hot, oppressive night. Fear gnawed at her, making her limbs heavy, she had a headache and felt trapped. She thought about Charlie. A change had occurred in him recently. He had deteriorated, both physically and mentally, but she hadn't realised just how far. She remembered the look in his eyes when she told him Emily couldn't live with him and pictured the child in a different place – a place from which Kate was prohibited. What if she had gone for good, never to return? Never to walk through Dun Laoghaire again, never live in this house. It was an impossible notion: Emily would be home in no time, and Kate would feel foolish and apologetic.

Next morning Kate phoned the school to tell them Emily wouldn't be in. Miss Stern, Emily's teacher, said she was aware of that. Charlie had contacted her to let her know that Emily would not be returning for the present.

'What?' Mary couldn't take it in.

'Is he crazy?' Jack said, when Kate phoned him.

'Why is he doing this to me? To get his own back?' she asked, digging her fingernails into the palms of her hands.

'I don't know,' Jack said.

'Supposing he's gone crazy, and does something to her,' she said, in despair.

'He won't harm her,' Jack said.

'I think he's gone off the rails.'

'He's not a maniac, he's her father,' Mary said, but Kate wasn't comforted.

'I'm going to phone the police,' Jack said decisively. He got on to Dun Laoghaire Garda station and told a Garda there what had happened.

The Garda explained that as the child's father Charlie had rights to his daughter, and that he wasn't breaking the law.

'But he's taken her away without her mother's knowledge or consent,' Jack argued.

The Garda asked to speak to Kate. She explained in more detail her relationship with Charlie and his behaviour since their split. 'I'm scared he'll try to take her out of the country. He can't do that, can he?'

'You'll have to get on to your solicitor, check it out with him. He has certain rights as a parent, Mrs Conway.'

'If I could just talk to him, get some idea of what's on his mind, see what he's up to, we might be able to sort things out like a couple of grown-ups.'

The Garda said he'd take details, and try to find Charlie. Kate gave him a description of Charlie's car and its registration number, then added that she had no idea where they might be heading. The Garda said he'd do his best to track down the car but with the amount of traffic on the roads, and the number of Opal Vectras among it, it might be impossible. Soon the Guards would put out a request on the radio for Charlie Conway, travelling with his eight-year-old daughter, Emily, to check back home for an urgent message.

When she hung up Kate collapsed in tears, and Jack held her in his arms while she sobbed. 'It's all right,' he said. 'Everything's going to be all right. We'll get Emily back, I promise you.'

Early the next morning Kate made an urgent appointment with Mary's solicitor, Percy Fetherstone. Jack drove her to his office, and waited outside for her. She felt numb as she gazed at the office walls while she waited for him. Percy had been their family solicitor for as long as Kate could remember and she knew that he was fond of Mary. A large man, with a round, kindly face, he looked businesslike in his bespoke pinstripe suit, which gave his figure the illusion of slimness. 'You're in a spot of bother,' he said, his eyes kindly behind thick glasses.

'To put it mildly.' Kate elaborated, then concluded, 'Emily's on his passport. He can't take her out of the country, can he?'

'Strictly speaking, not without your consent. He'd be a very foolish man to try a stunt like that because it would be classed as abduction, and that's a serious crime. However, if he did manage to sneak her out, you might have a lot of trouble on your hands. Are you sure Charlie would want a fight like this?'

'I've no idea,' Kate told him truthfully. 'He bitterly resents being a part-time dad. I haven't been very sympathetic to him since our separation, only letting him take Emily out on Sundays. He hates that because he loves her, and loves being with her.'

'I'm sure,' Percy said thoughtfully.

'And the sad thing is that she's mad about him too.'

'Difficult.' Percy sighed. 'If he wants to take Emily permanently to America he will have to make a court application. At that point you can have him stopped by refusing your consent.'

'I'll do anything. I want Emily back with me where she belongs.'

Percy coughed. 'You have to be prepared for the consequences. You could be fighting Charlie through the courts for a long time to come. Once the lawyers move in they tend to take up residence.'

'He might have got her out of the country already.' Kate began to sob. 'Emily is at risk with Charlie. He's not capable of looking after her on his own. He'd never be able to bring her up properly and work at the same time. She'd miss her home, her friends, school. She's a happy child.' Kate stopped. 'But she wasn't too happy about our separation.'

'Take it easy. Let's assume that she's still in Ireland.' Percy proffered a box of tissues – at the ready for such occasions. 'There's no reason why Charlie would have to abduct her. Even if he goes abroad he can see plenty of Emily. He'll have visiting rights, and there are cheap flights back and forth. Mind you, if you do get a legal separation he'd have to fit in with the arrangements made in court.'

'That mightn't suit him,' Kate said.

'Take a word of advice from me. I've been a long time in this business and once it goes legal it becomes costly. Try to settle your differences, and come to some agreement between you. Otherwise you could be in for a long, drawn-out legal battle. That would be unpleasant, and could take every penny you've got.'

'I'll do whatever it takes, for as long as it takes,' Kate said resolutely.

'Meanwhile, I'm sure the Gardai will try their best to prevent him doing anything stupid. They get involved when there's concern that a child is at risk.' Percy got to his feet. 'I'll wait to hear from you. I hope you find them safe and well and not too far away, for Charlie's sake as much as anything.'

Jack drove her home, Kate relaying to him what Percy had said.

'You'll get her back,' Jack said. 'I know you will.' He went off to work, promising to phone her hourly. The house was quiet, everywhere too tidy. Kate went up to Emily's bedroom, the one room in the house where she could feel her child's presence. She sat on the bed, covered with the new Groovy Chick duvet Kate had bought in a sale. A poster of Westlife had recently replaced one of Harry Potter, and cheap gloss lipstick, eye-shadow and glittery nail polish glinted on the vanity unit beside the ballerina jewellery box. The pink crop top of which Kate disapproved was folded among Emily's clothes.

She picked up a photograph of Emily taken on holiday in Marbella two years previously. Her cherubic face glowed with happiness as she looked into the camera, Charlie's arms protectively around her. She'd grown up a lot since then, Kate reflected, and was continuing to do so. She needed Kate more than ever. Suddenly she noticed Emily's ballet shoes lying beside her bed where she'd dropped them. She knelt on the floor, picked them up and held them tight to her chest.

When Jack came that evening he found her prostrate on the couch. He sat beside her, stroked her hair.

'What if I never see her again?' Kate said.

'You can't think like that. You will see her,' he insisted. 'You know you will.'

She sat up. 'I haven't heard a word from them and it's frightening.'

'I know it is. Now, I bet you haven't eaten all day.'

He went into the kitchen and made a tortilla for them.

He served it with a tomato salad. Kate ate a small amount. It was delicious but she didn't have any appetite. 'I can't win with Charlie, I never could. Emily doesn't belong to him – he can't do this,' she said.

Jack said, 'Unfortunately she belongs to him as much as she does you. But you're going to put up the fight of your life, and there's no question of losing. There's no way the bastard's going to get away with this. He's a loser, Kate, always was.'

'I never thought he would become so bitter.'

'Things haven't worked out for him, and now he wants to dodge the fallout. But Emily doesn't have to be the victim – she's got rights too. Surely she can choose where she wants to be, even if she is a minor.'

'I want her back, that's all that matters to me.'

'The mother gets custody of the child in nine cases out of ten, no matter what the situation is,' Jack said encouragingly.

Fortified by his positive attitude Kate went to bed and managed to fall asleep while Jack slept on the couch in the living room. Late into the night the phone rang, waking Kate. She could hear Jack scrambling to get it. She ran downstairs. Please, God, let it be Charlie, she prayed.

It was the Guards.

'They've located Charlie,' Jack told Kate.

'Where is he? Make them tell us where he is.'

He nodded.

She held her breath as she heard him say, 'We'll come right away. It'll take us a few hours to get there.'

'Jesus!' Kate's hands flew to her mouth. She could hardly breathe, and her tongue felt as if it was stuck to the roof of her mouth as she said, 'Where are they?'

'They're in a bed-and-breakfast outside Cork City. The

owner recognised Charlie from the SOS on the radio, thought he was acting suspiciously and alerted the cops.'

'But why is he there?' Kate's stricken face was inches from his.

'The Guards think he was planning to take the ferry to Swansea, but Emily was ill, and he couldn't travel yesterday.'

'Oh, no! What's wrong with her?' She was shaking with fear.

'Nothing to worry about,' Jack said. 'It's certainly not serious.'

'I want her back.'

'We'll go and get her. Put a couple of things you might need in a bag.'

'I haven't time,' she said, looking at her watch.

'You have a couple of minutes.' Jack squeezed her hand. 'Run upstairs, get your things. It'll all work out, I promise you.'

As soon as she was out of earshot Jack rang Mary and told her what had happened. 'We'll have to hurry. The Guards think he's probably planning to take off soon,' he said.

'Drive carefully,' Mary said. 'Take as long as you like. Tell Kate I'll look after Oscar and the budgie.'

They set off, Jack driving as fast as he dared. When they were on the dual carriageway, he picked up speed as they drove through the midlands.

'I haven't got the bottle for this. I'm a coward,' Kate said.

'You've got more guts than any other woman I know. It's Charlie who's the coward. He's like all bullies.'

They drove on in silence, everything forgotten except their quest to find Emily and get her back safely. Once they were on the motorway the countryside spread out before them, and Jack tore through it. Kate kept finding that she was holding her breath, and her palms were sweaty.

In Cashel the early-morning traffic was heavy, and she lost count of the squares they crawled through with all the commuter traffic. Once they were on the motorway again they speeded up. In Fermoy, Jack drove through the streets as if he'd lived there all his life. Once in Mitchelstown, Kate gripped her seat. They were almost there.

Suppose Charlie had seen the police and taken off again. What would she do? Did he have any idea of the pain he was causing her? She felt her rights as a mother were being violated.

As they drew near to their destination she panicked. What if Charlie had already gone? Cold fear gripped her and her chest felt heavy, as if the walls of the car were pressing in on her, closing off her air supply. She was losing her nerve. Terrified, she gasped for breath, knowing she must keep calm for Emily's sake. 'I don't think I can cope if he isn't here,' she said.

'Think positive,' Jack said. 'You can't afford not to.'

They screeched to a halt outside a row of houses. A squad car was parked further down the road, a Garda in the driver's seat. Kate got out, her stomach churning, and stood against the wall, waiting while Jack spoke to him. Suddenly another Garda appeared from nowhere.

'That's the house,' the first man said to Kate. 'We've spoken to Mr Conway. He says he's on holiday with his daughter.'

Kate peered at it. There was a partial view of the sitting room through the window. The curtains were drawn across the upstairs windows. When she got the signal she went forward.

'I'll wait here,' Jack said. 'Chin up.'

Kate followed the Garda, who approached the door and knocked. Her knees wobbled and her fists were clenched. She wondered what madness had brought Charlie here. Eventually the door opened. A large woman stood before them.

'Charlie Conway?'

'I'll go and get him.'

Charlie appeared, shoulders hunched, hair tousled. He stared at the Garda. When his eyes met Kate's he swung away.

It was too late. The Garda had his foot in the doorway. 'We'd like a word, Mr Conway,' he said.

'Where's Emily?' Kate shouted.

Charlie stood motionless, staring from one to the other angrily. 'I spoke to you already,' he said to the officer.

'You have some explaining to do, Mr Conway. Why don't we go inside for a chat. You owe your wife some sort of explanation.'

'I owe her nothing. I told you, I'm here for a quiet holiday with my daughter.'

'She has reason to believe that you're planning to take the child out of the country.'

'I don't have to explain myself. I'm within my rights.'

The Garda said, 'You can't just take off without letting her know, if that's your intention. Look at her, she was at her wit's end.'

Charlie's lips curved into a twisted smile.

Emily appeared at the top of the stairs. Her face was pale, her shoes were muddy, her socks round her ankles. As soon as she saw Kate she tore down the stairs. 'Mummy! Mummy!' she shouted, and ran to Kate, throwing her arms round her.

Kate had the impression that Emily had been waiting for her. With a whoop of joy she lifted her into her arms and hugged her. 'Are you all right, love?' she asked anxiously.

'Yeah, but I was sick, and I wanted you.'

'I missed you too,' Kate said squeezing her tightly, as if she'd never let her go again. Then she squared up to Charlie. 'What were you thinking of, Charlie Conway, keeping my daughter away from me?'

Charlie said, 'She's my daughter too. I'm going to the States and I'm taking her with me.'

'Are you crazy?'

'No. I have it all planned and you're not going to stop me.'

'You can't do that.'

'Oh, yes, I can.'

'Your job is here.'

'I have a job over there now.'

'And you think you'll get away with this?' Kate was nearly hysterical. 'If I'd known you were planning on dragging her half-way round the world I wouldn't have let her out of my sight. You'll lose everything this way.'

'It's your fault. You haven't allowed me to spend enough time with her or settle down anywhere.'

'Can we conduct this conversation in a civilised manner?' the Garda asked, putting his hand on Charlie's shoulder and steering him inside the house.

'What it's got to do with you, anyway?' Charlie asked him. 'It's not as if it's a kidnap. The child is mine.' He turned to Kate. 'I'm within my rights. Emily's on my passport. You've had her all the time, and I only get to see her when it's convenient for you. Now I'm taking her and that's that.'

'No, you're not,' Kate said, gripping Emily tightly.

Emily started to cry. 'I don't want to go, Daddy. I want to go home with Mummy.' She clung to Kate.

'I think you'd better see a solicitor,' the Garda advised Charlie. 'Sort out your right of access.'

Kate tried to calm Emily, but there were tears in her eyes as she said, 'How could you do this, Charlie?' She was making a supreme effort to keep her temper under control in front of the child. Quietly she said, 'I've put up with a lot from you, Charlie Conway, and I'm not putting up with any more.' She put Emily down, took her hand and walked away. Emily's eyes widened with pleasure when she saw Jack standing in the garden.

'Hello, Emily,' he said.

She pushed back her hair and peered at him. 'Did you come to get me too?'

'I drove your mummy here.'

'I was worried about you,' Kate said.

'I don't like this part of the holiday,' Emily whispered to Kate. 'I told Daddy I didn't. Our bedroom was full of bees and spiders. I don't like the countryside, I like the seaside. We had a great time in Trabolgin – we played the slot machines. Mum, can we go home now?'

'Of course we can, darling,' Kate said.

'I miss Granny too, and Oscar, and everything.'

'You'll see them soon,' she said.

'Come on, Mum, let's go,' Emily said, and pulled Kate's hand.

Walking to Jack's car was like a dream. The Guards stood together on one side of the road, and other people had gathered opposite them, neighbours and friends talking about the disturbance in their usually quiet part of the city. It was strange for Kate to see lots of faces she didn't know smiling at her and Emily, affection in their faces. Charlie watched them go. 'You haven't heard the last of this,' he called to Kate. 'I'll be on to my solicitor today. We'll see who gets custody then.'

'You're perfectly within your rights to do that,' a Garda said, to calm him down.

They drove home, Kate thinking of all the changes that had taken place, and those still to come. Like them or not, she would find the courage to face them. She would have to see her solicitor too – and soon – to make life secure for Emily.

38

Luckily, Emily had come to no harm. As she told Kate later, she had tried to puzzle things out for herself. At first she'd accepted her father's explanation that Kate needed a break so they were going on a really splendid holiday to Disneyland. She'd asked Charlie why she couldn't see her mummy before they left. Charlie's explanation that Kate was ill baffled her.

While Emily had had the tummy-bug she'd been disconcerted by Charlie's constant patrolling of the garden, his watchfulness as he looked out of the window and over the fence. She couldn't understand it. Sometimes his tension had frightened her. Uncertain, she'd asked him if her mummy would be looking for her, and Charlie had assured her that Kate knew where she was. Without realising it, she hadn't trusted his answers, but there was no one else to tell her anything. The landlady, Mrs McEvoy, had noticed how unhappy she was and asked her what was the matter.

'I told her I wanted my mummy, and that I thought we were lost and you wouldn't be able to find us.'

'How could he have done that to her?' Kate asked Jack, when Emily was tucked up in bed.

'Beats me,' Jack said. 'He knew she was miserable. He's certainly botched up this time.'

'I wonder how he feels now he knows I was up the walls with worry.'

'Charlie has a real knack for self-forgiveness,' Jack said.

'He's sick,' Kate said bitterly.

'Worryingly so,' Jack agreed.

Over the coming week Kate kept a steady eye on Emily, watching for signs of disorientation and reassuring her every time she worried about anything. Emily made a quick recovery once she was home and reunited with her friends at school.

Kate, however, felt so ill that she went to see Dr Duggan again.

'Everything's fine, but I would advise you to rest as much as possible after your recent trauma,' he said, when he'd examined her.

'How did you know about that?'

'Dun Laoghaire is a small town when it comes to gossip.'

'I suppose so.'

'Have you told Charlie about your pregnancy?'

'Not yet.'

'He's bound to hear about it, and that'll make him feel like a complete eejit. Perhaps it would be better if you tell him soon. It would make life easier for you.'

'I'll tell him,' Kate conceded, 'but it won't make any difference to how I feel about him. I'm not having him back under any circumstances.'

Dr Duggan nodded. 'That's your decision.'

Kate didn't want Charlie to know about her pregnancy and sensed that there'd be trouble when he found out, but she resolved to tell him the following Sunday when he came to take Emily to Bramble Hill for the day, as arranged through their solicitors. The next morning she woke up with a pain in her stomach. She phoned the hotel and told Vivian. 'Did you call Dr Duggan?' her friend asked.

'It's nothing, probably a reaction to the events of last week.'

'Stay in bed. I'll come round at lunchtime.'

Kate let the phone drop and raced to the bathroom, her stomach heaving. She vomited before she had even reached the lavatory. Dizzy and chilled, she went down to the kitchen to get a glass of water only to have to rush back upstairs again to retch violently. She crouched over the lavatory holding on to it for support. She lost track of time, so ill she couldn't move. When the retching stopped she staggered back to her room and collapsed into her bed, exhausted. As the morning progressed she felt weaker and weaker as the pain worsened. Finally, she fell into an exhausted sleep.

The loud banging on the door and Vivian calling her name woke her. She made her way slowly downstairs, clutching the banisters, feeling so ill that she barely made it to the hall door. As soon as she opened it she fell into Vivian's arms in a dead faint. When she came to she was lying in a pool of blood, her nightdress soaked crimson and stuck to her skin. Vivian's arms were round her and her voice said comfortingly, 'The ambulance is on its way.'

A stab of pain left Kate too weak to answer. When she came round again two paramedics were hoisting her gently into an ambulance. 'Take it easy, Mrs Conway, we'll soon have you there,' a soothing voice said to her, as pain shot through her again.

The next thing, she was being wheeled into an operating theatre, surrounded by nurses and a doctor. When she woke up she was in a semi-dark room, hooked up to a drip. Her body was on fire, her head aching, the pain in her abdomen excruciating. She opened her mouth to cry out, but no sound came. A nurse appeared beside her.

'You're going to be all right, Kate,' she said. 'I'll give you something for the pain.'

Kate wanted to say something to her, but her vision blurred and her eyes closed. She drifted off in a cloud of forgetfulness.

The ferocious pain in her stomach woke her. The nurse was checking her pulse. 'Good morning, Kate,' she said softly. 'How's the pain now?'

'Awful,' she said, in a weak voice. 'I've lost my baby, haven't I?'

The nurse nodded. 'I'm so sorry,' she said gently. 'Here's something to ease the pain.'

She held out a tablet and a glass of water and helped Kate drink it.

As soon as she left Kate buried her face in her hands and wept, thinking of the life that had not survived. It was all her fault. Her insides turned to jelly and she shuddered at the thought of the horrendous drive across the country to find Emily.

Next time she woke, the doctor who'd been in the operating theatre was standing by her bed. 'Hello, Kate,' he said. 'I'm Paul Edmond, your consultant. How are you feeling now?'

'A little better.'

'I'm sorry about the baby. We did everything we could but I'm afraid it was too late to save it.'

'It's my own fault,' she said bleakly. 'I didn't take enough care.'

'Please don't blame yourself, Kate. Dr Duggan told me what happened, and it had nothing to do with your losing the baby.' He took her pulse. 'It's difficult to determine the reason for a miscarriage at this early stage. Could be a number of factors.'

'I didn't even want this baby. Now I do, and it's too late.'

'There's nothing unusual about that. I can assure you that nothing you could have done would have saved it. There's no reason or justification for a miscarriage like the one you have just suffered. You're a healthy woman with a healthy womb. You're perfectly capable of having more babies.'

Drained, Kate lay staring out of the window, thinking of the last time she'd been in hospital, when she'd given birth to Emily. How different she'd felt then. She had been in a state of euphoria for days. Charlie had been there with her, his arms round her, her baby's head at her breast. Life couldn't have been better. Then Daniella had come back into their lives and ruined everything.

'What a tragedy,' Mary said, when she arrived. 'And I never suspected a thing.'

'Neither did I for ages,' Kate said, swallowing tears.

'You must get plenty of rest and you'll be right as rain. Did they say when you could go home?'

Kate shook her head.

'Well, take your time and don't worry about Emily. I'll keep her until you're better.'

'Thanks, Mum.'

Mary put a bunch of grapes into a bowl and flowers into a vase, then fluffed up Kate's pillows. 'I believe Mr Edmond is very good. Does he know your circumstances?'

'You mean no husband, no lover, and no likelihood of there ever being one again?'

'Don't say that, love. Sure you never know what the future might hold. I suppose this puts paid to Charlie?'

'Who'd want to go through all that again, or the heartache of another relationship? Not me, I've had enough.'

'I've heard that one before,' Mary said, under her breath.

Kate slept on and off for the rest of the day, the pain reduced to a dull ache by the painkillers administered regularly by the nurse.

'May I go home?' she asked Mr Edmond, when she next saw him.

He studied her face. 'I think it's best if you stay for another twenty-four hours. You lost a lot of blood and you'll be very weak.'

That evening Charlie came to see her. Kate got a shock when she saw him standing sheepishly inside the door of her room, an enormous bouquet in his arms. She couldn't bear to look at him.

'How are you feeling?' he asked.

'I'm all right.' She couldn't look him in the eye.

'I'm sorry about the baby,' he said, shuffling awkwardly. 'I had no idea you were pregnant.'

Kate averted her eyes. 'I'd rather not talk about it.'

'We have to—'

She put up her hand. 'Please go.' She tried to sound authoritative but her voice was weak.

Charlie turned towards the door. 'I'll leave these here, and I'll phone you when you get home.'

'No, you won't.'

'You're tired.' He put the flowers at the end of the bed. 'We'll talk when you're feeling better.'

'We have nothing to say to each other.'

'We have to discuss the future, Kate. There's Emily, and the house, and I want to know if the baby was mine.'

Enraged, Kate raised herself up. 'Get out,' she said, pointing to the door, 'and take your flowers with you. I don't ever want to see you again.'

Charlie stood rigid with surprise. 'You can't mean that.'

'I do, I never want to lay eyes on you again – except in court.' She was shaking all over, perspiration breaking out on her forehead.

Evidently the nurse had heard the commotion for she rushed into the room. She went to Kate, eased her back on to her pillows. 'I think you'd better leave now, Mr Conway,' she said. 'Your wife needs to rest as much as she can before she goes home.'

Without another word Charlie took the flowers and left.

The following day Tim took her home. He walked her gently to his new car, and kept his arm round her, asking all the time if she was all right. Kate walked slowly, and assured him she was fine, with a bright smile, which was about all she had the energy for.

Mary wanted her to go to her house, but Kate refused. She was glad to be back home in her own bed, where she spent the rest of the week. The pain was easing but the depression was more difficult to deal with. Every time she found herself in a downward spiral she'd try to read a magazine, or phone Vivian or Barbara, but it didn't do any good. Life was too difficult to deal with. She cried endlessly. She couldn't sleep. Mary was minding Emily, but she came over regularly with food to 'keep you going'. Barbara ministered to her in whatever way she could too. But Kate felt a failure: she couldn't do anything right, not even something as natural as having a child. Isolated and strange she felt that she'd never be a normal human being again.

Vivian insisted on staying with her for a couple of nights.

Kate's sadness resurfaced every time she thought about her loss. She felt lonely, as if someone close to her had died. 'That's exactly what has happened, and you have every right to grieve,' Vivian told her. 'By the way Tim sends his love. He can't wait to pour you a double vodka.'

'Tell him I'll be back soon.' Kate couldn't imagine feeling fit enough for work.

'How did Jack take it?'

'He doesn't know, I haven't even told him about the pregnancy.'

'You're still in love with him?'

Kate looked at her sharply. 'Who said anything about love?'

Vivian smiled. 'It's written all over your face.'

Kate sighed sadly. 'It's over with Jack, Viv – over before it began. I've frightened him off.'

'Oh dear, I am sorry. I shouldn't have told him.'

'You did the right thing. He'd have heard about it sooner or later.'

'Don't let this get you down,' Vivian said. 'You're a young woman with your life to look forward to. You'll feel better as time goes by.'

Each morning Mary came round after she'd left Emily at school. She brought Kate delicious quiche, or a chicken sandwich, something tasty to tempt back her appetite.

'You shouldn't go to so much trouble,' Kate said, levering herself up in bed.

'Why not? You're my daughter, and I want to get you well. Emily sends her love – she's dying to come home.'

'You didn't tell her about the baby?'

'No, I thought it best to say nothing after what she's been through.'

'There's no need for her to know, is there?' Kate asked.

'No, it would only worry her little mind.'

'I can't stay in bed all day,' she said. 'I need to be doing something.'

'You're recovering. Make the most of it. You need to build your strength for when Emily comes home. She's a livewire.'

'I can't wait to have her back,' Kate said.

'That'll be soon enough. Take your time. I've brought you a bagel with cream cheese, and Brian in the bakery sent you this cake.'

'That's kind of him.'

'How about a nice cup of tea with it?'

'Lovely.'

Mary went off to make it. She was back five minutes later. 'Careful, it's hot,' she said, as she handed Kate the mug, treating her as she would Emily.

Kate ate a slice of cake, and enjoyed it.

'Can't stay too long,' Mary said. 'Emily's got dancing and I have to get her things ready. She's always dancing, rehearsing that ballet.'

'I know,' Kate said, with a smile.

'The *corps de ballet* isn't enough for her at all, she'd like to be the Sugar Plum Fairy,' Mary said. 'She was kicking her legs in the air, higher and higher, and I said to her, "You'll do yourself an injury," but she only laughed. She's growing so fast she'll need new ballet shoes soon. Her toes are squashed in the ones she has.'

'I'll get them as soon as I'm up and about.'

'She's clever too, only she's not concentrating. Miss Stern has her right up at the front of the class to keep an eye on her.'

'Poor little thing, I miss her. Bring her home,' Kate said.

'She'd be too much for you at the moment. She can come in a day or two.'

'Please, Mum!'

'All right. Now, don't cry, you'll spoil your eyes.'

Kate dried them, but there was a lump in her throat.

'I'll bring you a nice bowl of chicken broth tomorrow,' Mary said, when she was leaving.

Kate heard the door close and swallowed a last mouthful of tea. It hit the sore spot in her stomach. So much for making her feel better. Here she was, alone: her life had gone wrong. Maybe she'd expected too much. That was her problem: she had always believed that things would go well if she did her best, but life wasn't like that.

Next day was Vivian's day off and she called to see Kate. Tim had sent a box of Black Magic with a card saying, 'Get well soon, thinking of you.'

'That's very kind of him.'

'He's worried about you. Any word of Jack?'

'No, he's away as far as I know. I'm feeling so much better I'd love to go out for a bit. It's such a nice day.'

'Come on, get your shoes on and we'll go for a little walk.'

'I've been wanting to go out for days,' Kate said, as she put on her jacket.

'Take it slowly,' Vivian said, as they set off.

They walked as far as the corner then turned round and walked back slowly. Kate wondered if she'd ever get back to normal.

39

Jack called to see her unexpectedly. He looked awful: his eyes were sunken and he hadn't shaved. 'Hello, Kate, Vivian rang me,' he said, running his hands through his hair.

'Hello, Jack.' Kate felt awkward.

'I'm sorry about what happened. I had no idea you were . . .' He paused. 'Why didn't you tell me?' he asked.

'I wanted to. Then you were away and . . .' she shrugged '. . . was too late.' She didn't want to go into it all again, even if he felt she owed him an explanation. In the silence that followed, she hoped he'd go because of the awkwardness between them.

'Thanks for coming to see me,' she said.

'Can I ask you something?'

'Yes?'

'Did you know you were pregnant when Emily went missing?'

'Yes.'

'You should have said. I'd have been more careful with the driving and that.'

'It had nothing to do with the journey or the stress, according to my consultant. He said it was one of those inexplicable things, something not quite right with the foetus. It wouldn't have survived on its own. He says I'm healthy and that I'll have more . . .' she blurted out, then sucked in her breath as sorrow assailed her.

'I'm sure of it,' Jack murmured.

'I'm sorry, Jack,' she said her voice barely above a whisper, 'I've made a complete mess of everything.'

'Don't worry about it now, we'll talk another time,' he said, and went quickly down the steps.

But Kate knew that it wouldn't be all right, as sure as she knew that Jack couldn't wait to get away from her.

She went back over their conversation. If only she could have gone into his arms he could have held her tight, soothed her by saying he understood, and that together they would work it out. But that could never be the case. She'd blown it with Jack by getting pregnant with Charlie. Why was it that it was always the woman who paid the price? Not that she should be surprised. She wondered what would be the next catastrophe to befall her.

When Emily came home Kate was resting. Emily skipped around, her hair flying, stopping only to plant another kiss on Kate's cheek, delighted to be back. 'Are you better now, Mum?' she asked.

'Yes, sweetheart, I'm fine.'

'You're very pale. Are you still upset with Daddy?'

'No, of course not.'

'Nice hot cup of tea?' Mary asked. 'Go and put on your new Britney CD for Mummy.'

Emily dashed off.

'That'll keep her quiet for a while,' Mary said.

'You spoil her, Mum, spending your pension on her. I'll have to pay you back.'

'You'll do no such thing. Just get back on your feet, that's all I ask.'

Britney sang 'Where Are You Now', and Emily came to ask Kate, 'Would you like a doughnut? We bought the ones with jam in them especially for you.'

'No, thanks, sweetheart, not at the moment.'

'I'll make you a sandwich, then,' Emily said. 'Would you like Marmite?'

Kate smiled. 'That would be lovely.'

Emily went to the kitchen, and returned with the nicely made sandwich.

'Good girl,' Kate said, and took a bite.

Emily had brought a doughnut for herself. She bit into it, still hopping around.

'I've got a present for you,' Kate said.

'It's not my birthday yet.'

'This can't wait,' Kate said, handing her a gift-wrapped box.

With her mouth full, Emily tore it open and gasped with delight at the pink satin ballet shoes snuggled in tissue paper. 'Wow! They're fabulous. Can I do my dance for you?'

'Oh, yes, please,' Kate said.

Emily licked sugar off her fingers, took the box and went upstairs.

'Wash your hands before you put on your leotard,' Mary called to her. Then she changed the music to *The Nutcracker Suite* and they sat back, waiting while Emily changed. 'This could take a while,' she said to Kate.

'Did you notice that she loves dressing up and putting on makeup now?'

Mary nodded. 'She's growing up so fast.'

Emily reappeared at the door in her leotard and new ballet shoes, Kate's eye makeup smudged on to her eyelids, her own bright red lipstick plastered on her lips. As soon as the music flooded the room she picked her way daintily across the floor. She danced with confidence, her head gracefully erect as she pirouetted and preened, lost in the music. The constant practice at school had paid off: she was already an aspiring ballerina, poised and confident.

'You're wonderful,' Kate said, surprised, and hugged her when the music stopped. 'I'm so proud of you.'

'She's got the balance right, hasn't she?' Mary was as proud as if she'd taught her herself. 'She's going to be a real star, the next Margot Fonteyn.'

'I want to be like Britney,' Emily protested, and went to put her CD on again.

'Yes, if that's what you want,' said her indulgent grandmother. Then, to Kate, she said, 'I can't stay long. You're all right now, though, aren't you?'

'I've been having weird dreams, not very nice.' Kate shivered.

'You think too much. Get a hold of yourself.'

The first day Kate was back at work Jack phoned. His voice was clipped as he said, 'I'd like to see you.'

It was on the tip of Kate's tongue to put him off but the urgency in his voice made her relent.

'Can you make it to the pub tomorrow night?' he asked.

'Yes.' She kept her voice neutral.

She might as well hear whatever it was he wanted to say. It was probably that he didn't want to see her again.

She did her best to look smart, but she'd lost so much weight that she looked like a scarecrow. Her hair was dull and lifeless, no matter how hard she brushed it. Her jeans were a size too big, and her black leather jacket hung off her.

She was first to arrive, and saw him as soon as he entered the pub. He looked around nervously. She wanted to turn and run. Instead she resisted the temptation and, with a slurp of her drink to steady her, she forced herself to look at him. He'd gone to the trouble of putting on a dazzling white shirt, and his skin was smooth. But he'd lost weight too: his cheekbones were jutting out, and his jeans were hanging loose around his hips. When he saw her he made his way through the narrow space between the tables. 'Hello, Kate.'

'Hello, Jack.' Suddenly she felt shy, didn't know what to say next.

'How are you?'

'Much better, thanks. And you?'

'I'm okay, keeping busy.' He looked at her half-empty glass. 'Same again?'

'Yes, please.'

He got the drinks, and sat down next to her. He seemed edgy as he said, 'I wanted to see you to tell you face-to-face I'm moving to Southampton.'

'Southampton?'

'I've got a job there, photographer for a new yachting magazine called *Windcatcher*.'

Kate swallowed hard. 'It's a shame you have to uproot yourself so soon again. Just as you were getting established.'

'There's nothing here at the moment, with the sudden death of the Celtic Tiger, and I'm keen on this new assignment. It's interesting, something I'm keen to do, and there's travel involved. I'll be photographing the start of the America's Cup off Auckland.'

'Wow.'

'Prime hurricane months, too. Won't be long before

they encounter a storm. It'd be exciting if they sent me to cover it.'

'You take care,' Kate said, fearing for his safety.

'I'll be back when I get more experience of this kind under my belt. I'll be better equipped to set up properly on my own then.'

'When are you going?'

'I have to go over next week, meet everyone. With so many races – Vendée Globe, Route de Rhum – crossing the Atlantic I'll be kept busy.'

'What about your apartment?'

'I'll give it to Sherry Fitzgerald to let for a year.'

'This is all so sudden.'

'It's what I want to do – for now, anyway.'

'Good for you, congratulations. I'm really pleased for you,' she said, and meant it.

'Thanks . . . I couldn't leave without saying goodbye.'

He spoke casually but Kate could tell by the look on his face that he was upset. She wanted to reach out and take his hand but she stopped herself. 'This has nothing to do with me, has it?'

'No, it hasn't.'

'Jack, I'm sorry about the way things turned out.'

'I wasn't meant to find out about your pregnancy, was I?'

There was blame and sadness in his eyes, and her heart turned over. 'I had every intention of telling you.'

'When it had become too obvious to hide.'

'When I'd recovered from the shock.'

Jack wasn't having any of it. 'It all makes sense now, why you kept me at arm's length, why you wouldn't make love to me. When I lived at your place and you'd ask me up for a drink or a meal that was all right by me because I thought there was a chance for us. Who could blame me? You were living alone, about to be separated. But now I realise that Charlie was the one all along. You'd never got over him.'

Kate started to say something but the words wouldn't come out.

'Obviously you had your reasons for doing what you did.'

'It wasn't like that, and I never thought for a moment I'd fall for a baby.'

'You don't have to tell me. I don't need to know.'

Her nerves were so taut that another word about the whole sorry business would make her scream. She wanted to go home.

Jack caught her eye. 'I'm sorry, I didn't mean to upset you. Would you like another drink?

'No, thanks.' She felt numb and awkward, like when she was a child and she'd been sent to her room for being bold.

Jack was looking at her with pity in his eyes. She couldn't bear it. Her throat tightened. Tears threatened. If she cried now she'd disgrace herself, but it was all going wrong between them.

She stood up. 'I must go, I haven't much energy these days. I hope we can we still be friends?' she said, knowing that there wasn't the remotest possibility of it.

'Of course,' Jack said, dimples appearing as he smiled. 'I'll take you home.'

He drove in silence. Kate couldn't think of anything to say either. As he walked up the steps with her, her heart heaved – she wanted desperately to say something to make it right between them. 'I'm sorry I hurt you, Jack.'

'Don't worry about it. What's done is done. No looking

back. It can't have been easy for you either, being cooped up here all the time.'

'Not for much longer, I hope. Keep in touch.'

'Yes, I'll do that. Goodbye, Kate.'

'Goodbye.'

She watched him drive away, then went inside. She shouldn't have gone to meet him in the first place: it had been too much for her to deal with, the way she was still feeling. He'd shown little mercy either. In his own quiet way he'd laid the burden of guilt squarely at her feet and she hadn't been fit for an argument. Then, at her front door, he'd sort of exonerated her by telling her it couldn't be helped. He'd almost let her off the hook in going so far as advising her to forget about it, and she'd felt so grateful that she nearly asked him in for a drink. But she hadn't because she couldn't risk hurting him again. It was all about him and how he felt, nothing about her feelings at all. What about the baby she'd just lost? What about her hopes and dreams?

Jack had been the only man who'd come close to giving her another chance at happiness. Now Kate wondered if he was just another emotional cripple who couldn't take trouble. She should have defended herself. But the words wouldn't come when she'd needed them. What could she have said that hadn't been said already? Or done? He blamed her and that was that. She blamed herself for what had happened. She didn't know when she'd accepted Charlie back into her life that she was dragging out something that was long over, and that her accidental pregnancy would end her relationship with Jack.

The next day Lucinda arrived home. 'I wish I'd been here for you,' she said to Kate.

'I missed you.' Kate was too choked up to say more. Suddenly she was sobbing and Lucinda's arms were around her. Kate buried her head in her sister's shoulder.

'Have a good cry, that's what you need.'

Eventually, when she had no more tears left, Kate said, 'I suppose you know that Jack's gone to England.'

'I had a long chat with him. He was worried about you.'

'He hasn't forgiven me for the pregnancy.'

'Oh, Kate,' Lucinda gave her a sad smile, 'of course he has. It was a shock for him, but he'll get over it. He really fancied you.' She leaned towards Kate. 'Surely you realise he was in love with you. He told me so. He talked about you all the time. He only got friendly with me so he could keep in contact with you. Kate, you've gone very pale.'

'I put him right off,' Kate said.

'What are you going to do about it?' Lucinda asked.

'I haven't a clue. What would you do?'

'Nothing.'

'Really?' Kate was puzzled.

'Trust me. Do nothing for the present. What could you say that would change anything? Only time will help.'

'You're right. Anyway, he's gone now.'

'Not far. England is only a short flight away.'

'True.'

'Meanwhile, what about Charlie? There's no chance of you two ever—'

'None whatsoever,' Kate interrupted. 'He can go and chase Daniella to his heart's content or anyone else he fancies.'

'Good idea.'

'It's been so traumatic since we were in Nice I just can't deal with it. Still, it's great to have you back, Lu.

I missed you so much. It was so hard going through it all without you.'

'Ssh.' Lucinda stroked her hair. 'Don't think of it as a disaster. A learning curve, maybe, but you'll deal with it. You have to, for Emily's sake, now you've got her home. I'm here too, and we've got Mum, and it's a lovely day.'

Kate glanced at her. 'You're so right. Tell me all about Diego. How is he?'

'Wonderful, of course. He sends his love. He's coming over for the autumn league race in the yacht club, and the masked ball afterwards.'

'Great! I'm looking forward to it,' Kate said, and realised that it was true. It was the first time since the miscarriage that she had been able to look forward to something.

40

Dealing with Charlie turned out to be the nightmare Kate had suspected it would be. He came to talk to her one Sunday evening when he returned with Emily from her riding lesson at Bramble Hill. She wouldn't have entertained a conversation with him except that Emily asked him in to show him her new ballet shoes. Kate could tell by the haunted expression in his eyes that he hadn't been sleeping well.

As soon as Emily was out of earshot he said, 'I want us to give it another chance.'

Kate couldn't believe what she was hearing.

'I'm begging you, Kate. Let's not lose everything. I'll do anything I can to make it up to you. I'll support you in anything you want.'

'I'm afraid it's too late for that, Charlie.'

He reached for the bottle of whiskey in the cupboard and poured himself a drink. 'I've been going around dazed, thinking I can't let you go.'

'You need to see your solicitor,' she said quietly, not wanting to upset Emily who was preparing for bed after a pleasant day out. She'd be upset enough when the break came.

'I'm not having some prick of a lawyer telling me what to do about my family,' Charlie said, 'and end up fighting in court, paying out vast sums just for the pleasure of putting paid to a marriage I don't want to finish.'

'We did that ourselves a long time ago.' Kate was adamant. 'I want to go legal on this.'

Emily came downstairs in her pyjamas, with cardboard, glitter and paste. 'Can I stay up to make a card for Hannah's birthday tomorrow?' she asked Kate.

'No, it's late and you're tired. I'll get you up early in the morning to do it.'

'Ah, Mum! Please!'

'No, Emily, you must go to bed.'

'Go on, do as your mum says. I'll see you next Sunday, Princess, for another lesson, all right?' Charlie said. He lifted her up and twirled her round. 'She's coming on really well, aren't you, pet?'

'Yeah – I can canter now!' Emily said, her arms round his neck.

As soon as she'd left the room Charlie leaned his head against the door jamb and stared out of the window. 'I hate the law. Once you involve them they take every penny,' he said.

'You know it's the only way.'

He looked around sadly. 'I'll never have another home like this one,' he said. 'Don't you miss us being a family?'

She sighed. 'If you want the truth, no, I don't. I don't miss the past – trying to keep your dinner warm before we had the microwave, being treated like a housekeeper while you were pretending to be working late, building up your career, when all the time you were screwing around.'

Charlie winced. 'I wasn't "screwing around", as you put it. My job was always the most important thing to me.'

'What about *my* career? You never gave it a thought.'

'You were never a career woman.'

'So my job was just a hobby to be squeezed in while Emily was at school. Well, let me tell you that it's kept the wolf from the door since you left. It's paid the bills.'

'If you hadn't forced me out, the bills would have been paid as usual.'

'Let's leave it at that,' Kate said wearily. 'I'd rather talk to my solicitor about a separation and, eventually, divorce.'

He turned to her, eyes bright with tears. 'You can't let it go to that, Kate. I know I'm not perfect, but neither are you. Beside anything else, I'll be seen as a complete failure at work. It would have a drastic effect on my career.'

'We have to do it, we've no choice. One way or the other we've lost our marriage.'

'Then the best thing I can do is leave the country forever.'

'If that's what you want. I'm sure you'll find a comfortable place in New York and plenty of work too. And you'll get away from the legal stuff you hate so much. Not that it won't happen but you might handle it easier from a distance.' Kate couldn't help the sarcastic note in her voice.

'The trouble is that I can't bear to be parted from Emily.' He was almost sobbing. 'I'd hate to be away from her for a long time.'

'You don't have to. Take her out at the weekend and tell her you'll be back at Christmas.'

All his striving, all his ambition was nothing compared to his need for his daughter. 'How did I get into this mess? I know people spend their lives wishing for what I'd had.'

'Then see your solicitor as soon as possible. We'll resolve everything that way.'

'I doubt it – I have a lot of debts.' He went to the door. 'I tried, I really did, with you, Kate. I never wanted this.'

Kate almost said, 'Not hard enough,' but she let it go. It had all been said before.

Exhausted, she went to bed early and slept, but woke during the night thinking about Charlie, furious at how he had used Emily again as his excuse to get into the house and engage her in conversation. It would be a good thing if he did go away. His departure would give her the respite she badly needed from the pressure he was bringing to bear on her. But it would be hard on Emily, who would miss him terribly.

'You're marriage is over, then,' Percy said matter-of-factly, getting straight to the point.

'I'm afraid so,' Kate said. 'I want to settle things as amicably as possible.'

'You're entitled to alimony, and a good maintenance, which I'm sure I'll have no trouble getting for you.'

'I want the house, because I never want anything to do with him again.'

'Tall order when you share a child.'

'I want custody of Emily to make sure he can't take her out of the country, ever, without my permission. I'm willing to grant him visiting rights within reason.'

'Leave it with me. I'll call you when I have something to tell you. Meantime, take my advice and don't get involved in any kind of slanging match with him.'

Kate was happy to agree to that. She'd bide her time and resolve everything once Charlie was on the other side of the Atlantic Ocean. She'd pay off the mortgage with a lump sum from Charlie that she'd ask for instead of alimony. He could sell some of his shares to fund it. That way she'd make a clean break with him, and wouldn't have to see him again.

Or so she thought.

Miss Stern sent Kate a note asking her to come and see her.

Charlie was at the school gate, waiting for her. He was dressed in a business suit, looking more sombre than ever.

'What are you doing here?' she asked, puzzled.

'Miss Stern phoned me and said she'd like to see me before I go away.'

'Oh! She rang me too, but she didn't mention she was contacting you.'

Miss Stern was waiting for them in the corridor outside her classroom. Her face softened as she greeted them. 'Ah,' she said, extending her hand, 'I'm glad you could both come.'

She took them into the empty staff room. 'Do sit down.' She indicated two chairs opposite hers. 'Emily's missed quite a bit of school so far this term.'

'Unfortunately, yes,' Kate said.

'Couldn't be helped,' said Charlie.

Miss Stern gave him a pointed look, and he looked away sheepishly.

'Her schoolwork has suffered, and since her return her concentration is poor. She seems preoccupied.'

Silence.

Keeping her eyes on Charlie, Miss Stern said, 'She's obviously been through a lot of trauma recently.'

That's putting it mildly, Kate thought.

Charlie had the decency to blush.

Miss Stern, the soul of tact, chose her words carefully: 'She's finding it hard to adjust since you . . .' She looked from one to the other.

'Split up,' Kate supplied.

Miss Stern smiled at her. 'Yes. She tells me that you're going to live in New York, Mr Conway?'

'That's correct,' Charlie said.

'She's upset about it,' Miss Stern said bluntly. 'And I think in fact that that is affecting her schoolwork most of all. She misses the way things were before all this.'

'I have to go,' Charlie mumbled. 'But I'll be home . . . er . . . back for Christmas.'

Kate was doing her best to keep her temper.

'She's afraid of losing one or other of you, and she doesn't deserve that. She's a good child, and an excellent little student.'

'What can we do to get her back on track?' Kate asked.

'I suggest you get help for her. Take her to see a child psychologist. I can recommend an excellent one.'

Charlie's face went puce. 'Certainly not,' he spluttered. 'My daughter's perfectly normal. Why would she need to see a shrink? I can't stand all that mumbo-jumbo. She'll be all right when she gets the new pony I'm buying for her.'

'I don't think it's as simple as that, Mr Conway. Emily needs to feel loved, and secure in her home, and not to feel used as a weapon between the two of you in this whole sorry business.' Miss Stern was still treading carefully, feeling her way through the minefield, but determined to leave Kate and Charlie in no doubt as to the true nature of the situation.

Charlie didn't want to hear any more. He rubbed his hands together restlessly – a sure sign that he wanted the meeting to end. He stood up, ready for the off. 'We care deeply for Emily. We'll sort her out.'

'Do give me the name of the psychologist. I'll make an appointment,' Kate said.

'Certainly.' Miss Stern smiled.

Once out in the playground, Charlie said, 'What was the point in dragging up all that crap about what happened? I'll make it up to Emily.'

'When are you going?'

'Next week.'

'There's not much you can do in that time.'

'None of it matters as much as Emily does. She knows I love her, and she loves me.'

That was true. Emily *did* love him, and he adored her. That was the difficulty.

41

The gilt-edged invitation to the masked ball in the National Yacht Club arrived.

'He's seriously considering buying a stake in the new marina. Wouldn't it be great if he was living here for a while?' Kate said.

'He's going to buy a chunk of the marina?' Mary was thrilled. 'Wait till I tell the neighbours – they'll never believe it. And just imagine – he's soon to be a member of our family.' She lifted her shoulders proudly.

'The fact that he's going to tear himself away from the sunny Riviera to be here is amazing,' Kate said.

Lucinda laughed. 'I'll see him before then. We're meeting up in Paris for my birthday next week.'

'I'm telling you, Lucinda, don't take your eyes off him for a second. He's such a catch.'

'You won't be happy, Mum, until she has him locked up in a cage,' Kate said.

'And the key thrown away,' Mary agreed. 'Think of all those half-naked skinny models Lucinda works with all dying to get their hands on him.'

'Diego doesn't like most of them. He finds them too juvenile.' Lucinda giggled.

'Sounds like a dream come true,' Kate observed. 'And it wouldn't do Dun Laoghaire any harm to have a bit of his money invested in it.'

'This ball will be something special,' Lucinda said. Let's hire some really super costumes.'

Kate hadn't made up her mind about selling the house until Percy phoned early one morning to tell her that an offer from Mr Peterson was in. He tried to persuade her it was too good to turn down: getting a decent financial settlement from Charlie would be easier if he had cash from the property. At first Kate felt she was losing her grip on everything she held dear and giving in to Charlie's wishes, which didn't suit her. But a cash buyer was enticing so Kate decided to let it go.

Helen Horton delivered the next blow. It was the one that broke the proverbial camel's back. 'Management have decided to advertise your job,' she said casually one morning.

'My job?' Kate said, puzzled.

'They want somebody full-time.'

'But I've been doing so many extra hours that I might as well have been permanent.'

'Yes, but that was part-time housekeeper. As regards your job as receptionist, management have decided that there's to be no more part-time workers. Someone with whom the guests can become acquainted on an on-going basis is required. Someone who's available to work five or possibly six days a week, with overtime.'

'That's out of the question for me.'

'I know you have your child to consider so you can't give this job total commitment.' She shifted her gaze to the wall behind Kate's head.

Kate was fit to be tied. She thought about the extra she'd worked, and the lunch hours she'd put in just to get Helen out of a bind. She felt resentful, until Helen reminded her of the schedules that had to be arranged occasionally to accommodate her. The time she'd taken off when Emily was ill and Vivian had stepped in at a moment's notice to fill in for her. 'Rules are rules and management feel they can't continue making exceptions for you. You can either apply for the full-time position or look for one that suits you better,' Helen said, and took herself off.

'I'll have to leave,' Kate said to Vivian.

'You don't mean that?'

'I do.'

'Typical! You break your backside for them and that's all the thanks you get.'

'Emily's too young to leave all day long, and I feel guilty for the time she spends with Mum. Mum's getting the best of her growing-up years. Anyway, with losing my job and everything, I can start off again with a clean slate.'

'What'll you do?'

'I'm not sure yet. I'm toying with a few ideas.'

In her free time Kate leafed through a galaxy of brochures and checked out dilapidated old houses. One, described as a 'Victorian dream with sea views', was a derelict monstrosity; the sea view was at the top of four flights of rickety stairs. Another that seemed promising was a dark, nightmarish pile in Clarinda Park, too far from the town. The third was situated on a corner, next door to a chip shop.

One day she was taking a short-cut through Crofton Lane when a for-sale sign outside number twenty-three caught her eye. She gazed up at the three-storey Victorian red-brick house, with the beautiful, tranquil gardens of the Royal Marine Hotel next door to it. It was the most perfect house she'd ever seen, with long sash windows and a dark green front door, a stained-glass fanlight above it. The good-sized garden was full of carefully tended shrubs. This was a house that had been cherished and cared-for, and Kate fell in love with it.

'You've got to see it,' she enthused, to a surprised Mary.

The following day she secured the keys from the auctioneers and dragged her mother along to view it.

They gazed around the impressive high-ceilinged hallway, lit by a stained-glass arched window. The spacious reception rooms were in good decorative order, with cream-painted walls and pale wooden floors. Sunlight streamed into the large, airy kitchen from the long back garden, and glanced off the chrome on the black range, and the handles on the numerous white presses.

Kate led the way up the wide staircase, lit by an oval skylight, to the bedrooms and bathrooms. From the balcony off the master bedroom they gazed at the panoramic view of Dun Laoghaire harbour, stretching to Sandycove on the right and the West Pier to the left.

'What do you think?' Kate asked her.

Mary drew in her breath. 'Magnificent, but far too big for you to take on.'

'Why?' Kate protested. 'I'm young and fit, and I know the business inside out.'

Mary shook her head. 'Too much hassle for a woman on her own.'

'I wouldn't be on my own. I'd have you.'

Mary's jaw dropped. 'You mean you'd be expecting me to work here too?'

'Help out a bit. You're always saying you haven't enough to do – and I'd pay you.'

Mary squinted in the sun, and shielded her eyes with her hand. 'Too many rooms.'

'Ideally I could do with more to make it really work,' Kate said.

'You're a glutton for punishment.'

Back downstairs Mary opened the double doors from the kitchen and went out into the garden, taking in the expanse of lawn and perfectly tended borders. 'How can you afford to buy it? You're struggling to keep the other.'

'With the sale of the house and a loan from the bank that I'd pay off with the income it would generate.'

'I'm not convinced.'

'But, Mum, it's a fabulous house. It's the right location and it'll pay for itself. I need somewhere to live and a job. This would double up as both.'

Mary looked confused. 'Well, it's lovely, but not practical for you. The basement alone would house a large family.'

'You do like it, don't you, Mum?'

'It's challenging.'

'Certainly, and I like a challenge.' They went back downstairs.

As Kate pulled the hall door shut behind her, Mary's eyes narrowed. 'You'll be forever decorating and maintaining it,' she said.

'I'd like that. I want to do something for myself.'

'But where will you get the guests from?'

'The overflow from the Royal Marine next door, and Helen Horton is always looking for quality guest-houses to recommend to people in the high season when she's full.'

'I'm not convinced.'

Standing at the top of the wide steps, Kate said, 'Look around you, Mum. Dun Laoghaire is booming with new shopping centres and boutiques with the latest fashions.

There are coffee bars, wine bars, top restaurants, cinemas, a theatre, a health club, and London hairdressers. Everyone's making a fortune. Look at the millions' worth of boats in the marina, and the cars are bigger and faster than anything ever seen here before.'

Mary looked around her. 'We're choked with fast cars. We're all inhaling car fumes, there are too many car washes, and what about the drop-in centres? It's not the idyllic picture you're painting.'

'And you're painting a very gloomy one.'

'All I'm saying is that this town has its problems. What about the homeless, the down-and-outs and the failures, not to mention the young ones overdosing themselves on drugs? Did I tell you that Mr Cahill, my bank manager, is having a nervous breakdown? Poor devil can't take the stress. He's shivering in his house, won't even answer the door, never mind come out and face the world. There's plenty like him, too, who are feeling the pressure. You don't want that scenario, do you?'

She marched down the steps and opened the car door. 'Why do you want to strangle yourself with a pile of debts? Why don't you buy a small place in Myrtle Park, or somewhere like that, and have a nice long rest?'

Kate felt frustrated. 'I'm too young to vegetate. I want to be my own person, with my own business.'

Mary drove in silence, and Kate was in a world of her own, thinking about her dream home, how she'd furnish it with deep-pile rugs and pale sofas. When they got to Mary's house Lucinda was in the kitchen, waiting for them. Her face was gaunt, eyes hollow, hair stringy.

'Lu, what's up?' Mary asked, shocked by her appearance.

'It's Diego. He stood me up in Paris on my birthday.'

'He never showed up?' Kate asked.

'In the middle of Paris?' Mary said incredulously.

'He let me down in front of all my friends, totally betrayed me.'

'What was his excuse?' Kate asked.

'None!'

'That's disgraceful,' Kate said.

'I mean, there are things you expect from your fiancé, and being there is one of them.' Lucinda's smooth forehead crinkled like a sheet of corrugated iron.

Kate poured her a vodka and tonic. 'Here, take this.'

Lucinda's hand shook as she lifted the glass to her lips.

Mary plonked herself down on a chair in the kitchen. 'So, tell me, what did he say?'

'He's in the States', Lucinda said dismally, 'and I can't reach him on his mobile. It's switched off.'

'Men!' Kate cried.

'I thought he'd be different, but he's worse in a way, too much for me to handle.' She let out a long sad sigh.

'Maybe something very important came up that he had to go to,' Mary suggested.

'There's no excuse for bad behaviour, Mum. I'm thinking of calling the whole thing off.'

'Oh, don't do that – not until after the masked ball, at least.'

'Why not? I feel let down and cheated.'

'But he didn't cheat on you, pet. You're far too sensitive, that's your trouble. You know, you were always low on tolerance and you're going to have to toughen up if you're to break through to his world.'

'Tell me about it.' Lucinda sniffed. 'He's suffering

from this new terminal disease called wealth. He can't stop making money. It's on to the next deal or fix and to hell with everyone else. It'll kill him in the end, if I don't do it first.'

'I was reading all about it in the *Sunday Times*. People like him who've got everything get bored very quickly, all right. But it's not only that. He'll keep working because he'll always be insecure because of his background. But you know that underneath all that bravado and brashness there's a pussycat miaowing to get out.'

Kate almost choked on her biscuit, and Lucinda's newly plucked eyebrows shot up. 'You have him thoroughly sussed out, Mum.'

'I've studied Diego, and what he needs is someone just like you, Lucinda, to look after him properly.'

'I don't want to be his mammy, thank you very much.' Lucinda sat in a cocoon of self-pity, pensively chewing her lip. Mary and Kate clutched their drinks, huddled together, trying to work out the quickest way to get in contact with Diego.

There was a knock on the door. When Mary opened it he was standing outside with a bouquet of flowers the size of a small island. 'Diego!' she rushed him inside.

'What do you want?' Lucinda snapped.

He dropped the flowers to the floor. 'You, my darling!' He seized her.

Her arms dropped to her sides.

Diego's hair feathered his face. He only dared to look at her when she said, 'What?'

His face was a study in despair as he said, 'I'm really sorry I forgot your birthday.'

'Bollocks!' Lucinda stormed. 'What kind of a jerk are you to give me an excuse like that?'

The silence sent Mary into a spin of rinsing glasses. She handed Diego a vodka and tonic. 'Drink that,' she commanded him.

He gulped it down, but still looked drained. 'It's the truth. I hadn't written it in my diary and—'

'You bastard! You sleaze-bag! You—' Lost for words she smacked his jaw.

Kate leaped to her feet and started for the door.

'Lucinda!' Mary was appalled.

Diego, hand to his face, gave Lucinda a fierce look – and then they both burst out laughing. In the blink of an eye they were in each other's arms, Diego kissing her. They headed for the sitting room and flopped on to the couch.

'That's what I love about Diego,' Mary confided to Kate. 'He doesn't bear a grudge.'

Later, Kate went home and did calculations to work out roughly how much of an income she could expect to earn in a season, and how much the bank would ask in repayments if she was lucky enough to get a loan. A spasm of dread shot through her as she thought about it all, but at least she had a plan.

Next day she phoned the bank manager and made an appointment to see him.

When she went into his office, she acted as cool as a cucumber, although she was quaking inside. She answered lots of questions and listened to the boring technical details, but all she wanted to know was if there was any point in taking on the house. Mr Mitchell said that there was nothing that couldn't be taken care of in practical hands. Her instincts told her that this venture might be murder, but the urge to go for it was strong.

'If all else fails, after running it for a year as a guest-house you could sell it in a booming market. Or any time, in fact,' Mr Mitchell advised. 'House prices are going through the roof,' he added, and laughed at his wit.

42

The National Yacht Club was full of glamorous people, crammed in everywhere. Two burly bouncers guarded the entrance. Huge displays of flowers decorated the foyer. Lights flashed, transforming the whole place into a fun palace. The main reception room was afloat with streamers. Corks popped above the din, and the place was awash with glasses of pink champagne, bubbling at the brim. Important local dignitaries, squeezed into scuba-diving suits and diving costumes, rolled by. Gyrating gorgeous creatures in outrageously scanty costumes mixed with boating aficionados. Naughty vicars danced with Barbie dolls. Everyone present was connected with boats.

Diego arrived with his entourage. As Neptune, the god of the sea, he stood head and shoulders above the crowd, magnificent in golden robes, a garland of seaweed on his head, a trident in his hand, a golden bow and arrow slung over his shoulder. Lucinda, at his side, was his beautiful goddess in a low-cut iridescent dress, and a gold crown in her hair.

Kate, as Helen of Troy, wore a long white robe trimmed with gold, and a straight black wig.

'I'd let you sink my ship any time,' a male voice in a dolphin costume said.

She ignored him and looked around the star-studded throng from kohl-outlined eyes, at the beautiful models thinly disguised as film and rock stars, displaying plenty of bosom and bare, tanned backs, the men with their biceps and six-packs. Giddy with the glamour of it all, she moved forward.

'Well, what do you think?' asked Tim, who was serving champagne in a skin-tight seal suit. 'It's like Tracy Cox's hot sex, we all want it, we can all get it, and she's shown us how.'

Kate laughed and turned to see a tall man in a black cloak, and Napoleon hat swish in beside a tall, beautiful woman with a fabulous fake tan and lots of gold jewellery.

Nerves jangling, Kate stared at him.

He stood before her, dark eyes glittering, a crescent smile splitting his face. His face was so close to Kate's that she could smell his unmistakable sweet musk scent. 'Jack!'

'Captain Bligh!' the woman with him corrected her. 'Don't you think he's handsome?' she asked, in a lilting foreign tone.

'I'd know him anywhere,' Kate said. 'Hi, Jack.'

'Kate! It's you.'

'Well done.'

'How are you?'

'Fine. What are you doing here?' she asked him.

'I'm a guest of Diego.'

'And he's spoken for,' said the woman, slipping her arm through his proprietorially.

'Am I?' Jack asked her flirtatiously.

'You certainly are, my darling.' She tightened her grip on him. 'And you are?' the woman asked.

'Kate Conway.'

'I'm Monique, a friend of Jack.'

Jack smiled at her, squeezed her arm reassuringly.

Kate's head swam. She felt her face go red, and wished she could disappear there and then.

Trays of glasses were passed around by sea urchins. Kate took one. She sipped it and watched Monique work her way round the room, Jack in tow, breaking up tight groups of yacht crews who all knew each other, Monique laughing raucously. Kate was trying to decide whether they were in harmony with each other or whether it was all for show. She couldn't tell. All she was aware of was that Jack was the only man in the room who counted as far as she was concerned. She kept her eyes on him as she sipped her champagne. There was no law against that.

More people arrived, Lucinda and Diego's friends, Donny and Cheryl among them, Cheryl in a see-through sailor suit, whining about the cold weather. 'It's warmer at the North Pole,' she said. 'Tomorrow I'm packing my Louis Vuitton bags and going to the Gulf. Now, where's the team?' She went forward to introduce herself to the club luminaries.

Suddenly, Jack was beside Kate. He dropped his eyes to hers and held her in his gaze. His smile was wider and more dazzling than ever, electrifying the very air around them. Kate took in every detail of him, from his new haircut to his sun-tanned face, and turquoise eyes. He had never looked so well. Was it possible that she had forgotten just how attractive he was?

'I don't need to ask how you are. You look fabulous,' he said admiringly.

'So do you.'

'Thanks.' Jack raised his eyebrows. 'How are you really doing?' He spoke softly but looked hard at her.

'I'm doing fine, thanks.'

He seemed genuinely pleased. 'And how's Emily?'

'She's great, settling down again after everything.'

'Good.'

'So, how come you're here?' she asked, changing the subject quickly.

'Diego has a business friend he thought I should meet so I flew over this morning. A guy who owns an advertising company. One of his accounts is the magazine, *Windcatcher*, and he's looking for a freelance photographer to cover racing events, starting with the autumn league. He seems to like my stuff,' he added, with his usual modesty.

'That's great news. Does it mean you'd be moving back here?' she asked, trying to keep her voice even.

'Unfortunately no, but who knows? With a few more contracts like that I could be in business if word gets round. There's Arthur over there. Come and meet him.' He pointed to a giant of a man wrapped in a long blue sail, a small gold ship on his head. 'Let me introduce you to him.'

He moved gracefully through the crowd, Kate by his side, his hand on her arm sending shivers down her spine and curling her toes.

'Kate, this is Arthur Murphy. Arthur is the owner of Godson's Advertising.'

Kate was awestruck by the giant of a man who was squashing her hand in his huge paw. 'Jack was telling me about the magazine,' she said.

'I have several projects in the pipeline that Jack might eventually get involved in,' Arthur said, 'but first we have to get the magazine off the ground.'

'Jack's to take charge of all the photography,' Monique said, appearing from nowhere.

'I'm encouraged by him. He has some terrific ideas,' Arthur enthused. 'He's shrewd, you know, and as determined as I am to make this thing a success.'

'Thank you,' Jack said.

'The finance is organised, and we're pouring money into it,' Arthur went on.

'It'll work – there's a real need for it, with more Irish people sailing and buying boats,' said Monique.

'The races are as much about what goes on off the water as on it. It's the intrigue, the cash sloshing around, enough to wipe out a Third World debt,' Arthur confided, 'and we're going to cover it all.'

'You'll be bringing back stories that'll make your hair stand on end, and Jack's photographs will be the most sought-after,' said Monique.

Her dogged determination and boasting impressed Kate, but she couldn't help wondering what her relationship with Jack was.

'And you're a friend of Jack too?' Monique asked her.

'Yes, we've known each other quite a while.'

'And where is your partner?' Monique drawled.

'In New York. We're getting divorced.'

'Oh, I'm sorry.'

'Don't be. It's all the rage, the in-thing in Ireland, and Kate here has always been an intrepid trend follower.' Lucinda had come to the rescue.

'You must come to visit us some time,' Arthur said to Kate suddenly. 'We have a small place near Baltimore, in Cork, just ten bedrooms. We can have a cosy chat, get to know each other.'

'Jack's been down already, haven't you, darling?' Monique's teasing eyes were on him as she spoke.

Jack had the grace to blush.

'We have the contacts,' Monique said. 'Well, most of them, some rich and famous.'

'Plenty of money out there, plenty of work for Jack,' Arthur added.

Jack squared his shoulders, his eyes crinkling with pleasure.

How could Kate possibly go to Baltimore, especially if Jack was there with Monique? She couldn't survive this Monique, whoever she was, and Baltimore had connotations of another Baltimore – in the States: Daniella's old address.

Lucinda rescued her again, taking her off to meet some of her friends. Laughter and music mingled. Couples floated around like ships in full sail; others rotated to the beat. Kate dodged endless trays of food. Just as she was flagging she saw Jack leaning against a pillar, his turquoise blue eyes trained on her with such intensity that her heart flipped. He came over to her. 'Enjoying yourself?'

'It's great fun.'

He slipped his arm round her, and she turned to him, breathed slowly, concentrated on making herself relax.

'OK?' he asked.

'Just about, I think I've had enough. I'm going to phone for a taxi.'

'Don't do that. I'll get you one, if you could wait a few more minutes.'

'What about Monique?'

'She'll be fine, Arthur'll take care of her till I get back.'

'OK, then, if you're sure.'

A little later they waited on the street, which was shiny with rain and reflecting the promenade lights. A white line of pre-dawn sky stretched towards the sea. Kate glanced at Jack. Cold with perspiration and nerves, she shivered. 'How long are you in Ireland?' she asked.

'A week, but we're off down to Baltimore tomorrow for meetings and a spot of sailing.'

Kate was afraid to look at him again, wishing she could disappear rather than have to go through the trauma of saying goodbye.

'Sorry I couldn't leave the party sooner,' Jack said. 'I had to stay long enough to make an impression.'

'You've done that,' Kate said. 'It won't be long before you have the rest of the Arthurs in this city eating out of your hand – and the Moniques,' she said.

Jack laughed. 'It's not easy to put on a show, sparkle and be on your best behaviour while your head is on the block. It's hard not to feel foolish while you're being judged.'

'Sounds terrifying, but you put on a good performance. And you have an admirer in Monique.' She said it lightly.

Jack laughed. 'Only one?'

'One's enough,' Kate said.

The taxi swished to a halt beside them. She went to get in. To her surprise, Jack put his hand on her arm to detain her. 'Kate, I'm sorry I let you down. I wasn't very sympathetic when you—'

'It's water under the bridge,' she said brusquely, not wanting him to say words she couldn't bear to hear.

'Maybe we could have a drink before I leave?' He looked hopeful. 'Just for a chat.'

'If you want.'

The taxi driver revved up, and Kate started to get in.

'I'll call you.' With great gallantry, he kissed the palm of her hand.

She closed her fingers tight over it, and kept her eyes on the road.

43

Kate wasn't looking forward to her next encounter with Jack. She worried all week about it.

'Why don't you want to see him?' Lucinda asked. 'If you like him that much it shouldn't be a problem.'

'It's too late for us,' Kate explained. 'Now that he's with this Monique you met.'

'She may not be with him.'

'She was all over him. I'm telling you, she had him in a vice-grip. As soon as he spoke to me she barged in, getting him engrossed in their magazine stuff. And he was so coy with her it was sickening. I think he fancies her.'

Lucinda shrugged. 'If you're just friends with him, Kate, what's the harm in having a drink with him?'

'I've got enough problems without bringing him back into my life,' Kate muttered.

'If you're still in love with him, you should get in there fast before that French woman gets her claws into him.'

Kate looked away.

'It's not too late to do something about it – you *are* going to do something about it, aren't you?'

'What can I do?'

'He was in love with you not so very long ago. Sure didn't Charlie moving back in with you break his heart? He got stuck into his work to try to forget.'

'No, you're wrong. He couldn't take the fact that I'd got myself pregnant with Charlie's baby so he took himself off.'

'Be straight about this, Kate. He had to get work.'

Kate gave her a suspicious glance. 'Whose side are you on?'

Lucinda laughed. 'I'm only trying to be fair.'

'It's all different now. Monique might have changed his mind.' Kate closed her eyes, unable to bear the thought of anything sexual happening between Jack and Monique.

'She couldn't have, not in such a short time.'

'He mightn't be interested in me any more. After all, I did let him down, so to speak.'

Lucinda looked at Kate's miserable face. 'There's only one way to find out.'

'What's that?'

'Ask him straight out.'

'I couldn't do that,' Kate said, shocked.

'You'll have to, if you want answers.'

Jack didn't phone. Kate wasn't surprised. Asking if they could have a chat had been his way of easing himself out of her life, she reckoned, and in a way she understood that. He was off to seek pastures new, and she was beginning to accept that.

He knocked on her door just after she had put Oscar out for his night's prowl.

'Jack!' Automatically she smoothed down her hair, and stepped back from the harsh glare of the hall light so he wouldn't see the circles under her eyes. 'I didn't think you'd come.'

'I rang you several times.'

'You should have left a message. I thought you'd gone back to Southampton.'

'Not before I'd had a chat with you,' he said indignantly.

'Come in.'

He sank into the couch, like he'd always done. They sat in silence for a few moments.

'How was Baltimore?'

'Very enjoyable.'

Kate waited for him to say what he'd come to say.

He didn't.

'And Monique, you were with her?'

Expecting a deafening denial she was amazed to hear him say, 'Yes, I was.'

Jealousy caught her off-guard, almost knocking her sideways. She steeled herself against it, controlled it. If that was why he was here, to tell her about his new romance, she wouldn't make a fool of herself. She'd play her cards close to her chest.

'At least you're honest about it. I thought you were going to give me some spiel about being just good friends.'

He shifted uneasily, then said, 'Monique and I've been seeing quite a bit of each other through work. She's our PR and she's good at her job. She won the PR of the Year award last year,' he added.

Kate, overcome by jealousy now, flashed him a smile to try to hide it. 'I'm not surprised. I heard her in action. If that's what you came to tell me, then congratulations, I hope you'll be very happy together. Now, I really must say good night. It's getting late.'

'That's not why I came.'

'Oh?'

'I think I left my skis in your basement and didn't miss them until now.'

'You're going skiing?'

'Will be when we get a break.'

'With Monique?' she blurted out, furious with herself.

Jack nodded. 'And the rest of the group. It's work.'

Kate shifted away from him. 'You'd better go and get them. They might be in one of the boxes you left here.'

Jack got up. 'Thanks.'

Talk about feeling stupid. She'd win Fool of the Year award hands down for imagining there was any possibility of rekindling the romance that had been blossoming between them. They hadn't even touched on that, and he was on his way. She'd have to be grateful for small mercies that she hadn't said anything worse.

A few minutes later, he reappeared. 'They're not there.'

'I didn't think they were.'

He was on the doorstep now. 'Kate.'

'Goodbye, Jack.'

'No, listen. I want to say something.' His eyes were haunted as he said, 'I behaved badly, Kate, when you lost your baby, and I feel terrible about it.'

Quivering with emotion she stood stock-still.

'I was a jealous asshole. When I heard about your pregnancy I couldn't handle it. I let you down, just when you were barely hanging in there and needed someone. I really regret it and I'm sorry.'

Suddenly he leaned towards her, put his hands on her arms. She pulled back as if her skin had been scorched by his touch.

He looked intently into her face as if he were seeing raw pain in it. 'Can you forgive me?'

She couldn't speak.

'I can't leave until you say you can. You're the only person in Dublin – in Ireland, for God's sake – who matters to me. Last time I left here I was shattered. I can't leave again like that.' He was so close to her she could feel his breath on her face.

'There's nothing to forgive,' she said. Her throat was croaky. She wanted to say, 'Don't go,' but there was no point.

He cupped her face in his hands. 'Thank you.'

Her cheeks burned.

'You know, I really fancied you at the masked ball.' He smiled his mocking smile.

'Hold it right there.' Kate raised her hand as if she were stopping traffic. 'What about Monique?'

There wasn't a trace of mockery in his voice as he said, 'I'm not in a relationship with her, Kate. We're workmates. She's not my type at all.'

Relief swept over her and her hand itched to wallop him for the jealousy he'd caused her – on purpose, no doubt. In a tight voice she said, 'You'd better go before I do something I might regret.'

He started to laugh. 'But, Kate, there's still you and me to discuss.'

She looked at his candid eyes, his sexy mouth. 'No, there isn't. I'd never get anywhere with you because everyone seems to want bits of you, and I'm not prepared to make do. I wouldn't share . . .'

Slowly, he leaned towards her, tilted her face up with his forefinger. 'You don't have to. I'm happy to make do with you.' He laid his head on her shoulder. He smelt of fresh linen and shampoo. As her arms encircled him, shivers ran down her spine.

'Are you sure that this is what you want, Jack?' she said unsteadily. 'Because I don't want to be messed around any more.'

'Let's forget all about the Moniques of this world,' he

whispered, and pulled her tightly into his arms, moved her back into the house, kicked the door shut and kissed her hard.

She broke away from him. 'Are you *sure* you want this, Jack?'

'Never surer,' he said, and kissed her until they were both breathless.

He stroked her hair and kissed her again. She was burning up inside. She felt as though her lips were on fire. She wanted the kiss to go on and on.

'I want to make love to you,' he said, into her hair.

'I do too.'

She led him back into the living room turned off the lamp, lit a fat, scented candle and took a sip of the wine Jack had poured for them earlier. He put on a CD. Nina Simone, 'I Put A Spell On You', his CD, which Kate had found in the basement with some others.

She was shaking as he took her into his arms. They kissed again, losing track of time. He ran his finger down her throat, touched her breasts. She was as taut as wire when he lowered her on to the carpet and helped her out of her dress. This time she wasn't embarrassed to take off her clothes in front of him. She'd been too cautious in the past, keeping him at bay. Now it was different and her body arched towards him.

'It's been so long . . .' he said.

'Too long,' she whispered tenderly.

'You're beautiful,' he whispered, taking her in his arms, holding her tight.

'So are you.' He was naked too, the candlelight throwing shapes across his lean, tanned body.

She was twitching, suddenly nervous again, like the last time they'd started to make love, but she craved him so much there was no escaping it now. He kissed her while moving his hand across the expanse of her stomach, then her breasts, her thighs, his eyes worshipping her, driving her mad with longing, making her forget about her cellulite, her thickening waist, her roughening hands.

She felt the tension in his body as he leaned over her. They looked into each other's eyes.

'You OK?' he asked.

'Perfect,' she replied, and wrapped herself around him.

He pushed away her arms, then inched his way downwards, his tongue circling each breast, then moving on, each flick an exquisite sensation that went on and on until she could bear it no longer. 'Jack!' she cried out, her whole body tensing as a spasm of pleasure shot through her. Wave after wave of more pleasure washed over her, receding to a ripple.

Jack's skin glowed, and his face shone as she caressed him. He sighed, then jerked. 'Oh, Jesus, Kate!' he gasped.

Nina Simone's husky voice shifted to a sweeter texture as she sang 'Ne Me Quitte Pas'.

Jack pulled her to him. 'I love you,' he said softly.

She couldn't believe her ears. She knew it hadn't come easy to him to say it because he felt he was giving too much of himself away. He'd told her so. It was as if she'd waited her whole life for this. If this went wrong there would certainly be no replacement. Her whole past with Charlie came back suddenly. All the pain, all the hopelessness. If Jack ever did to her what Charlie had done she would never survive it – she knew it as she knew her name was Kate.

As if reading her thoughts he said, 'You're the only one I want. The only one I want to make love to right now this minute.'

'I'm glad to hear it.'

Later, curled up on the couch, she said, 'Do you really think this will last?'

'It's up to us to make it last,' he said.

'Do you ever think about your past in America, feel sorry that things went wrong?'

'No, it was a long time ago.' He looked at her. 'In the past I never thought about a future with anyone. It wasn't like this.' He took her face in his hands. 'You make me happier than I've ever been in my whole life. I told you, you're the one I want to spend the rest of my life with. I love you so much.'

'I love you too.' The words felt strange on her lips.

'I made a mistake, Kate, a very bad one. I thought Charlie was the one who mattered to you, and clearly he wasn't.'

'He was once,' Kate said softly, 'but that's so long ago now.'

'I missed you. I want you to give us another chance.'

She found it hard to believe that he wanted her as badly as she wanted him. When Charlie had left she was sure that there would never be anyone else, that she'd go through life alone. Now, here she was with Jack Marsden, and his way of making love was a whole new experience.

But she was scared too. What would happen next time there was a crisis? Would Jack leave her? This job in England had given him the perfect opportunity to put his own needs first and to hell with the consequences. Of course he'd been upset, so much so that he had refused to listen to her explanation of her pregnancy. And there was still Emily to think about. If she got involved with Jack, could she be sure that he'd be there for her too? Emily's needs would have to come first. She'd been through too much already, and Kate wasn't going to compromise her happiness any more.

'What are you scared of, Kate?'

'Everything. Making the wrong choice again. I've messed things up enough. I don't want to make any more mistakes.' The harshness in her voice melted as she said, 'I should have told you about the baby myself, not let you find out the way you did. That was a terrible mistake. It must have been such a shock.' Her voice trailed off. In trying to explain herself she was bringing it all back, making things worse. She flicked her hair out of her eyes, watched him as she tried to regain her composure.

'Kate, listen, we've had some good times. The best of times, in fact, when I first came to live here and there was no pressure, neither of us wanting anything more than a bit of company. You may find this hard to believe but in England, when I thought back, those memories were my happiest. That's what I want again.'

She nodded. He leaned forward and touched her lips with his. 'I really fancy you, Kate Conway,' he said, against her ear.

She fancied him madly too and he knew it.

He looked steadily at her. 'Let's put our cards on the table, shall we? I don't fancy being messed around either. Now, I'm a mature bloke. I own an apartment, I earn a decent living, although I don't have a permanent job yet, but I will have and I'm ready to settle down, and I can cook. I like a drink as much as the next fella, but I don't over-indulge. Now, your turn.' He waited.

'I'm unemployed, soon I'll be homeless.' She purposely didn't mention the house she had set her sights on in case her plans fell through. 'I've survived a marriage break-up and a miscarriage without having a nervous breakdown, and I'm helplessly in love with the biggest ride in Ireland.'

'*What?*' Shocked, Jack burst out laughing.

'And there's nothing I can do about it.' Kate was deadly serious.

'Come here.'

Gently he held her face as if it were the most delicate bone china, kissed her eyelids first, then her nose, her mouth and her chin.

'I'll never hurt you again, as long as I live, Kate Conway, I promise.'

44

When she returned from school the next morning, Jack was waiting for her. 'I can't get enough of you,' he said, taking her in his arms.

Afterwards they went for a walk in the park, alone, wandering along the paths, Jack taking photographs of the pale spires in the distance, waiting patiently for a cloud to shift, for light to fall upon a statue, or a house with a bay window. At the marina he photographed the boats, the sun shining on them, people walking around admiring them. 'Dun Laoghaire's getting very trendy,' he said.

'It'll be a millionaire's paradise if Diego gets a foothold.'

They paused to look at Arthur's new sloop, *Windcatcher*, christened after the magazine.

'Arthur's such a keen sailor he won't stop until he's circumnavigated the world.'

The morning sunshine had brought out other walkers. Jack focused his camera on Kate, smiling, as he said, 'I need something of you to take back with me, remind me that I must hurry back to you.'

She kissed him. 'Lest you forget.'

'There's no chance of that. Especially not after this weekend.' He was serious suddenly. 'I don't want to lose you again.'

The idea sent a shiver of fear down Kate's spine.

That evening Jack sketched, with Emily.

'Let me see it,' she said.

'When it's finished.'

Emily sighed impatiently. Jack laughed. 'There you are,' he said, passing it to her.

It was a drawing in ink of Oscar stretched out in the sun, his paws in front of his face, his eyes dreamy. 'Lazy Poser', was written underneath.

'It's terrific,' Emily said. 'Can I keep it?'

'The best one so far,' Kate said. 'We'll have to get it framed.'

'It's my birthday on the tenth of October, Jack. Will you come to my party?'

'I'll certainly try,' he said.

Early next morning he said goodbye, then stepped out of the house, his camera slung over his shoulder, as if he was going to do a day's work. 'No big deal, I'll be back soon. There's no way I'm going to lose you now.'

Kate smiled, although her feelings were mangled inside her. She couldn't explain it to herself but she was fearful as she watched the taxi drive away, waving until it was out of sight. She wondered when she would see him again, and if their love could survive a long separation. What if he realised there were too many obstacles in the way?

It was an Indian summer's day. The sun shone through the trees on the bouncy castle in the back garden, which was heaving with small girls in frilly party frocks bouncing up and down to the blare of Britney Spears singing 'Oops! I Did It Again'. The Lion, the Straw Man and Dorothy from *The Wizard of Oz*, painted on the sides, grimaced with each bounce.

When she saw Jack, Emily jumped higher. The letters 'POSH', emblazoned across the front of her pink top, sparkled. Josh, in combat gear, was the only boy present, a concession to him because he was Emily's cousin. Emily didn't take much notice of him: she was too involved in bouncing around.

'I see you're busy,' Jack said to a surprised Kate. 'I phoned but there was no answer so I took a cab. You didn't hear the doorbell with all the commotion.'

Flustered, she said, 'I'm sorry, Jack, I was up to my eyes getting this party ready.'

'That's understandable.' He laughed. 'And all this noise and excitement takes some getting used to.'

'You're telling me. I'll be glad to be back to normal tomorrow.' She went into the kitchen, Jack following, and handed him a packet of mini bars. 'Put that on the table, will you, please?'

She put crisps into a huge bowl, and bunged a huge bag of toffees into another. 'It's what they want,' she said. 'Get yourself a drink.'

Jack poured himself a beer and raised his glass. 'To the best mother in the world.'

'Jack! You've come specially?' Emily said, running in flushed and breathless.

'I sure did.'

'What have you brought me?' she asked, hands on her hips, watched by an entourage of little girls in party frocks, with sparkly bobbles holding back their hair.

'Nothing! Why? Is it a special occasion?' Jack teased.

'It's my birthday, silly,' Emily said indignantly.

He slapped his forehead. 'Oops, I forgot.'

''Course you didn't.' She laughed. 'Didn't Mum tell you what I wanted?'

'No, Emily, I didn't,' Kate said. 'That would have been rude.'

'What do you want?' Jack asked.

'A horse.'

'Pony,' Kate corrected. 'And your daddy's getting you one for Christmas.'

Jack put his hand into his pocket, slid it around and took out a tiny pink parcel covered in shiny red hearts. 'Happy birthday, Emily,' he said, and kissed her forehead.

'What is it?' she asked, ripping off the paper, and opening the box. 'It's a ticket – for Eurodisney!' she shrieked.

Kate took it from her. 'Eurodisney?' Kate gasped.

'Where is it?' Emily pranced up and down.

'France, outside Paris,' Jack said.

Emily snatched back the ticket, and waved it at her friends. 'I'm going to Eurodisney.'

'And she can't go on her own,' Jack said. 'You'll have to take her.' He produced another ticket from his wallet.

Kate stared at Jack in silence. 'This must have cost a fortune.'

'Worth it just to see Emily's face.'

'It won't be much fun on our own,' she said.

'Would you like someone to escort you? Someone charming and handsome whom you could have a bit of fun with?'

'Why not, if it's someone I fancy?' she said.

Later, when Emily and her friends disappeared upstairs to play on the computer, leaving S Club Seven doing their dance sequence on the video, Kate took Jack's hand. 'Thanks for making this a brilliant birthday.'

'You're welcome,' he said.

They kissed under a bunch of balloons and coloured streamers.

Later, relaxing in the living room after Emily had gone to bed, Jack said, 'How about making that trip to Eurodisney soon?'

'Half-term is the only time I can take Emily out of school,' Kate said wistfully.

'That's perfect for me. Did I tell you you looked fabulous today?' he said, taking her in his arms and kissing her amid the party debris.

The phone rang.

'Who could that be?' Kate said, surprised.

'Someone who thinks the party's still on,' Jack said.

'It's unusual for my friends to ring so late.'

'Don't move, I'll get it.'

Kate took a sip of her drink. Then she heard Jack's voice say, 'Hello, Charlie,' and, 'Yes, Kate is in.'

Oh, bugger! He'd freak out at the thought of Jack being here. There'd be a hell of a fight if Charlie lost his temper. No, not on Emily's birthday.

Jack handed her the receiver. 'Charlie! I wasn't expecting you,' she said.

'You didn't think I'd forget Emily's birthday? I told her I'd phone.'

'She's just gone to bed. Hold on, I'll see if she's still awake.' Kate went upstairs. 'Daddy's on the phone to wish you happy birthday, sweetheart.'

Emily ran downstairs. 'Daddy, guess what! We had a big party, and Jack and Mummy are taking me to Eurodisney for Hallowe'en.'

Oh, no! Kate felt weak at the knees. Charlie would have a fit at that news. 'I feel guilty,' she said to Jack. 'He may be a rotten husband but he's Emily's father, and he's bound to feel left out.'

'Calm down. Charlie's a big boy now. He knows that life has to go on. It's good for him to know you and Emily are managing.'

Kate sat down and took the refilled glass of wine Jack proffered.

When she came into the room Emily said, 'I told Daddy about Eurodisney.'

'What did he say?'

'That he's definitely coming home for Christmas, Mum, and he'll have my birthday present with him. I hope it's my horse.'

'Pony,' Kate corrected.

Emily was so tired that she let Jack carry her up to bed. He left Kate to tuck her in, and Emily was falling asleep as Kate closed her bedroom door.

As soon as she returned Jack took her in his arms. It was wonderful to feel them round her. His kisses were as passionate as ever, and they made love by the fire.

At dawn Jack left for the airport.

'No regrets?' she asked, as he kissed her.

'None.'

'Me neither.'

He left for England, promising to phone her as soon as he landed.

45

It was the Easter holidays, and Kate was upstairs, packing for Emily who was sitting on the side of her bed watching, solemn-faced. Kate had never seen her less excited about a holiday and she didn't blame her. 'You'll be all right with Auntie Colette, sweetheart?'

She nodded, then chewed her bottom lip.

'What is it?'

'I'm a bit worried. I don't want to live where Daddy lives,' she said. 'He won't make me, will he, Mum?'

'No, darling, it's only a holiday. Auntie Colette and Uncle Frank will bring you home with them. Daddy has agreed. You're happy with that, aren't you?'

'Yes, but I hate leaving Star and Oscar behind,' she said. She picked up Oscar to stroke him.

The cat purred loudly and Emily kissed the top of his head. 'Star is lovely, isn't he, Mum?'

'Yes, he is.'

Star was a quiet, patient pony, stabled at Bramble Hill, who let Emily boss him around mercilessly.

'He'll be waiting for you when you come back. So will I, and Granny.'

'But you won't be here any more.' Emily looked around wistfully. 'You'll be in the new house.'

'That won't change anything. I'll be waiting there for

you and you have your mobile phone now so you can ring me any time.'

'Even in the night.'

'Especially in the night if you need me.' Kate put her arm round her daughter reassuringly.

Emily perked up. 'Mum, can I take my ballet shoes? I'd like to do my dance routine for Daddy.'

'Of course you can, sweetheart.' Kate picked them up and pushed them down the side of Emily's over-stuffed bag.

Emily added the Nutcracker Prince.

'Do you have to take him?'

'Yes.'

'Wouldn't Sugar Plum do on her own?'

'No, she'd be miserable without him.' Emily squeezed them both into the bag.

It was only when she heard the sound of Frank's car that she got excited, and ran to the window to check that it was them. 'They're here,' she called out, and rushed downstairs to let them in.

Kate zipped up the bag and hauled it down after her.

Mary was helping Emily into her coat, while Emily gave her instructions about which bedroom was to be hers in the new house.

'Hey up, you should have let me bring it downstairs.' Frank took the bag from Kate and carried it out to the car.

'We're late as usual,' Colette said, and gave Kate a peck on the cheek. 'I couldn't get Frank going.'

'That's right, blame me,' Frank said.

Kate escorted Emily to the car, fussing over her, helping her in, giving her a last kiss and hug.

'The airport will be packed so we'd better get a move on,' Frank said, flustered.

'I'll phone you as soon as I get there, Mum,' Emily said, joyful at last to be going on her holidays.

'Don't forget to brush your teeth, night and morning, and wear your gloves – it'll be cold.'

Kate stood on the path waving. Regret and loneliness stabbed into her heart at the thought of her child going so far away without her. She walked slowly back into the house, past the packed tea-chests, into the living room where books, toys, CDs and glassware were all packed neatly in cardboard boxes.

'Drink that while it's hot,' Mary said, and handed her a cup of scalding tea.

Kate stared at the black sack of Emily's outgrown clothes, waiting to be delivered to Oxfam. 'I can't believe that my little daughter is on her way to New York – and to think I had to persuade her to go.'

'She's coming back, don't forget. It's a fun-packed adventure she's going on, Kate, not to the gallows. And it's only a fortnight.'

'I know, Mum, but we've messed her around, Charlie and I.'

'Hey, it wasn't your fault. He's the one who started it all.'

'But how will I cope when she goes away for longer stretches? Charlie will want her for whole summers and probably Christmases too. If he meets someone else it'll get messier still. He'll want her more. I don't know if I'll face that. I get scared and lonely just thinking about it.'

'Who knows what'll happen in the future? Charlie might come back here to live. Don't plan her whole life. Live for now, and enjoy her to the full.'

'I hadn't thought of that.'

Mary put her arms round Kate and held her. 'Listen,

you're a capable woman. You'll manage no matter what happens. I coped without you when you went travelling all over the world.'

'You had Dad.'

'That's true.' Mary reflected for a moment. 'He'd be so proud of you if he could see you now.'

'Would he?'

'Most certainly. Look at you, a beautiful independent young woman, with a lovely daughter whom you're rearing well, and a mother you're good to.'

'A mother who's good to me.' Kate smiled.

'And a magnificent home of your own.'

'With a huge mortgage.'

'And a young man who's crazy about you. You'll have Jack back soon.'

I hope so, Kate thought, still unsure.

'Now, let's get on with this packing. I'd prefer to get it done now rather than leave it until the last minute.'

As Mary busied herself with wrapping crockery in newspaper, Kate said, 'Thanks, Mum, you've been marvellous. I don't know what I'd do without you.'

'You won't have to, I'm in for the long haul.'

The next day was beautiful. The sun shone through the canopy of trees at the back of 23 Crofton Lane, dazzling the green of the newly unfurled leaves. The hedges on either side were shrouded in white lace, and early tulips were appearing. Everything about the garden was new and pretty as a bride on her way to the altar.

Lucinda had just returned from a visit to Diego's family, and was being shown around the recently purchased property. She was glowing with happiness.

'I've done the packing, decided what to take and what to send to Bramble Hill for Charlie,' Kate told her. 'And

I've picked out the colours for the hall and sitting room. The rest will have to wait for a while.' She handed Lucinda the colour chart. 'It's that Amber White.'

'Lovely. You're doing a great job,' Lucinda said, gazing up at the house approvingly. 'When are you moving in?'

'As soon as I get the keys, which will probably be at the end of the month.'

'What'll Jack say when he sees it?'

Kate smiled. 'I'm keeping it as a surprise. He thinks I'm buying an artisan cottage down by the coalyard.'

Lucinda laughed. 'He's in for a shock!'

'I know. How about you and Diego? Have you decided where the wedding is going to be?'

Lucinda leaned forward pensively. 'Rome has such wonderful traditions and atmosphere.'

'Rome! What does Diego think?'

'Oh, I haven't said anything to him yet. It's only a dream at the moment. But we could have such a party there, don't you think? All the glitterati. But, hey, listen to me going on about myself. Tell me all about Jack. Where is he at the moment?'

'He's just back from the Azores. He's so busy I don't know when I'll see him.'

They stayed in the garden chatting, making the most of the good weather.

Kate saw Jack again sooner than she had expected. When he scooped up first prize for his seascapes in the Photographer of the Year awards, he came over for the ceremony at the Four Seasons hotel.

Now it was the morning after. They sat up in bed so close together that their shoulders and arms were touching.

The warmth of Jack's body seeped through Kate like a small furnace.

'I never thought I'd win, thought I'd make it to the finals maybe. Out of all those entries!' Jack was smiling, his face fresh and handsome in the morning light despite the champagne celebration of the previous evening.

'It was a very special night, and to think I didn't even know you'd been entered.'

'Arthur didn't make much of it at the time.'

'He does now. Should be good for promotion.'

'Or job offers here,' Jack said.

'Are you tired of England yet?'

'No, but I miss you. We've hardly spent any time together since Eurodisney, just a couple of days at Christmas.'

'Your busy schedule.'

'When I come back, will you move in with me?'

'I've just bought a place.'

'Sell it, and we'll pool our resources.'

Kate looked into his eyes: the creases around them were deeper, as were the laughter lines around his mouth. Her first reaction was to jump at the chance, but a tiny voice in her head warned her against it.

'We'll get our own place together, no past to intrude. Somewhere the three of us can call home. We might even get married some day. Now, that's something I never tried before,' Jack said. 'Kate?'

The pressure of his hand in hers increased and his eyes were intense. Suddenly she was scared of commitment. 'But how do we know we can make a go of it?'

'We don't, until we've tried. I want to be with you, nobody else. We're good together, we make each other laugh.' He lowered his voice. 'We satisfy each other in bed – what more could we wish for?'

'You're a hopeless romantic, Jack Marsden.'

'What's the harm in that?'

Could she run the risk of failure a second time?

'I'm scared too, but I love you too much to let that stop me. I think we've got something, really I do,' he coaxed.

'We'd have to be mad – we don't know what we'd be letting ourselves in for.'

'I'm willing to take a chance on it, if you are. We don't know how it's going to be but it's worth taking the risk, isn't it?'

'Before we make any decisions I'd better show you my new house.'

'Good idea.'

Outside number twenty-three Jack looked up at the three storeys, surprised. 'This isn't your new house?'

'Yes, and it's ready to move into.'

'But I thought you were trading down,' he said.

'I never said that. You assumed it.'

'I never imagined anything like this!'

'I was keeping it as a surprise.'

'But how did you buy it?'

'With the help of a sympathetic bank manager, and I got a good settlement from Charlie after a bit of persuasion from Percy. Mum cashed in an endowment policy, said I might as well have it now.'

She felt like a teenager as she ran through the puddles up the steps, opened the door and led him inside. Jack couldn't believe his eyes as he followed Kate from room to room. 'This is gorgeous.'

'Wait until you see the view from the upstairs rooms,' she said, running ahead of him.

At the top floor Jack said, 'Amazing!' as he gazed

over the bay. 'Nice meets Dun Laoghaire. Easy to spot *Windcatcher* among the boats.'

They stood watching people walking past, everything tranquil in the late-October sunlight.

Kate turned to him. 'So, how would you like to be my lodger, Mr Marsden? It would be a great help towards the mortgage.'

Silence.

'It worked out fine before, didn't it?' She asked nervously. Her heart throbbed as she waited.

'Only if I can rent this floor,' he said, scratching his jaw. 'More fun up here, watching everyone go by, and the light is wonderful.'

'I think that's possible.'

He swung round. 'Are you serious? Do you really think it would be feasible?'

'It's a wonderful idea, Jack,' Kate said putting her arms round him, holding him tight.